中华经典故事精选

中华经典故事传播与留学生华文素养提升叙事研究成果

ZHONGHUA JINGDIAN GUSHI JINGXUAN TONGSU DUBEN

通俗读本

陈梦然　编著

江西人民出版社
Jiangxi People's Publishing House
全国百佳出版社

图书在版编目(ＣＩＰ)数据

中华经典故事精选通俗读本:汉英对照 / 陈梦然编著.
—南昌:江西人民出版社,2016.8
ISBN 978-7-210-08468-6

Ⅰ.①中… Ⅱ.①陈… Ⅲ.①故事—作品集—中国—汉、英 Ⅳ.①I247.8

中国版本图书馆 CIP 数据核字(2016)第 090654 号

中华经典故事精选通俗读本(汉英对照)   陈梦然◎编著

责任编辑	章华荣 蒲 浩
装帧设计	同异文化传媒
出版发行	江西人民出版社
社 址	南昌市三经路 47 号附 1 号（33006）
承 印	南昌市红星印刷有限公司
开 本	787 毫米×1092 毫米 1/16 印张 20.75
版 次	2016 年 8 月第 1 版第 1 次印刷
字 数	400 千字
书 号	ISBN 978-7-210-08468-6
定 价	49.80 元

赣版权登字—01—2016—319
版权所有,侵权必究

发 行 部 0791-86898815
编 辑 部 0791-86899010 E-mail taxue888@foxmail.com

赣人版图书凡属印刷、装订错误,请随时向承印厂调换

前　言

高校在推动公共外交和人文交流方面，既有得天独厚的优势，又担当着重大的社会责任。九江学院举办本科教育以来，主动传承创新优秀传统文化，发挥文化育人的作用，推进公共外交和人文交流，取得了明显的成效。

这种成效，主要表现在教育国际合作与交流领域：在柬埔寨首都金边市和美国佐治亚州萨凡纳市创建了孔子学院；面向海外华人开展华文教育，在柬埔寨主流社会推广汉语，并且将孔子学院办学与华文教育较好地结合起来。这不仅为促进学校开展公共外交与人文交流工作奠定了扎实的基础，也在国际社会上产生了良好的影响，提高了九江学院的办学声誉。

赵启正先生指出："推广公共外交是高等学校的社会责任。"九江学院立足高校留学生教育这个平台，传播中国优秀文化，弘扬中华文明。《国学经典故事传播与留学生华文素养提升的叙事研究》（简称"叙事研究"）课题组依托学校留学生教育，以拓展华文教育内涵、弘扬中华文化为己任，在跨文化交流的公共外交活动中，从学理角度探究中华经典故事在留学生华文素养教育中的必要性与可行性、目的性与效用性；从文献学角度探究留学生华文素质教育的基本内涵，即以中国国学精髓之孝、悌、仁、义、礼、智、信、忠、廉、耻为依据筛选中华经典故事，建构提升留学生华文素养品位所需的《中华经典故事精选通俗读本》（简称"故事读本"）的基本框架。

《故事读本》围绕国学精髓"孝、悌、仁、义、礼、智、忠、信、廉、耻"十个专题的历史人事或圣贤名流的嘉言善行，组成一百个经典故事；《故事读本》所选取的，虽然只是历史小故事，但却蕴含着人生的大道理。有利于引导学习者从中了解中国历史上不同时代的一些优秀人物及其高尚道德情操，感悟优秀的中国传统美德是怎样深入一个人的内心并支配其行动的，欣赏人生应具有的真、善、美的品质，进而激励、完善其道德和人格。

《故事读本》作为 2014 年九江学院公共外交科研招标项目《叙事研究》课题的重要成果形式,其主要读者对象是在华留学生。考虑到留学生的汉语文化基础和汉语言的运用能力,编写中注重通俗简明、体例科学,选取的故事主题鲜明、内容具体、情节生动,以此引导留学生进行拓展式阅读:了解中国经典故事、体验中华美德、熏陶人格品质、提升人文素养,同时帮助留学生学习汉语文字、了解中华文化、崇尚中华文明,逐步养成尊重并爱好中华传统文化的习惯。由于品味《故事读本》的本身就是一种跨文化交流的公共外交的心灵对话,所以,这是一种探讨国学经典故事传播与留学生华文素养教育有机结合的途径。

基于公共外交呈现出一些新的趋势和特点,新公共外交强调双向对话,将公众视为意义的共同创造者与信息的共同传递者,其主要表达形式是信息和语言。课题组采取汉语拼音和中英对照相结合的方式,编撰的这个贴近海内外读者对"华文教育"需求的《故事读本》,服务于热心中文和尊重中华文化的学习者,努力促进跨文化交流工作的普及和发展。因此,《故事读本》可作为传播中华软实力的文化思想库中的重要媒介,兼具华教资讯、华语读本、华文素质教育的性质和作用;同时作为文化素质教育的读物,还能够使读者在品读生动经典故事中咀嚼启人心智的圣贤之道,在感受博大精深的中华传统文化中品味沁人心脾的心灵鸡汤。就这个意义而言,这个读本,可以视同为一部了解中国文化、丰富历史知识的简明通俗读本,也是一本启人心智、生动活泼的素质教育参考书。

Preface

Colleges not only have unique advantages in promoting public diplomacy and humanistic exchanges, but also shoulder significantly social responsibility. Since Jiujiang University offered the Bachelor's programs, great progress has been made in inheriting and innovating traditionally brilliant culture, fully playing the role of educating people with culture, and promoting the public diplomacy.

Such progress is mainly shown in the filed of internationally educational cooperation and exchanges, i.e. establishing the Confucius Institute in both Phnom Penh of the Kingdom of Cambodia, as well as the Savannah City, the State of Georgia of U.S.; providing Chinese language and culture education for the Chinese overseas, promoting the Chinese language in the mainstream society of Cambodia, and properly combining the school-running of the Confucius Institute with the Chinese language and culture education. It has not only laid a solid foundation for the development of public diplomacy and humanistic exchanges, but also achieved a good result in international community and made Jiujiang University enjoy a good reputation in school-running.

Mr. Zhao Qizheng suggests that "colleges shall shoulder the social responsibility to promote public diplomacy." Based on the Education Platform for Overseas Students, Jiujiang University has exerted its greatest efforts to spread the Chinese traditionally brilliant culture, and carry forward the Chinese civilization. The research group of "Narrative Research on the Spreading of Chinese Classic Stories and the Promotion of Chinese Literacy Attainments for Overseas students" (hereafter referred to as "The Narrative Research"), relying on its education for international students, has fulfilled its own duty to explore, from the theoretical aspect, the necessity and the feasibility, and the finality as well as the utility of the promotion of overseas students' Chinese literacy attainments with the Chinese classic stories, aiming at broadening the contents of the Chinese culture and developing the Chinese culture in public diplomacy of intercultural communications. It has also discussed the basic contents of the overseas students' Chinese literacy attainments from the perspective of philology by selecting the Chinese classic stories from Chinese national cultural essences, i.e. filial piety, respect, benevolence, righteousness, propriety, wisdom, loyalty, integrity, honesty, and shame, so as to construct the fundamental framework of the book *Selective Readings of Chinese Classic Stories* (hereafter referred to as "The Stories") needed for improving the overseas students' Chinese literacy attainments.

"The Stories" includes one hundred classic tales about the figures and the events in the history, and the sages and the celebrities' good words and deeds, focused on the following ten topics of Chinese national cultural essences, i.e. filial piety, respect, benevolence, righteousness, propriety, wisdom, loyalty, integrity, honesty, and shame. Though the tales selected by "*The Stories*" are short ones happened in the history, yet they have contained a big truth of life. They can help the learners to understand the preeminent figures and their nobly morals in different times of the Chinese history, know how excellent Chinese traditional virtues are deepened in people's heart and dominate their behaviors, and appreciate such good qualities as truth, goodness and beauty needed for one's life, thus stimulating and improving the learners' morality and personality.

"The Stories", being an important achievement of "The Narrative Research", tendered for the Jiujiang University's Scientific Research Program of Public Diplomacy in 2014, the targeted readers of which are overseas students studying in China. Taking into consideration the overseas students' fundamentals of Chinese language and culture, and their capabilities in using Chinese language, this book has paid much attention to simplicity and conciseness, and scientific style. All the selected tales are distinct in themes, specific in contents, and vivid in plots, with a regard to leading the overseas students to expand their reading, and helping them to know Chinese classic tales, experience Chinese virtues, edifying their personality, and improving their literacy attainments. Meanwhile, the tales can facilitate the overseas students to learn Chinese characters, know Chinese culture, and uphold Chinese civilization, so as to cultivate the habit of respecting and loving the Chinese traditional culture. When the learners read "*The Stories*", it is a heart to heart dialogue of public diplomacy in the field of intercultural communications.

Based on the fact that public diplomacy shows new trends and characteristics, the new public diplomacy stresses on two-way dialogues, and regards the public as a co-creator of meaning as well as a co-transmitter of information, the main expressive form of which are information and language. By the means of pinyin and Chinese-English

Preface

bilingual versions, the research group compiles "*The Stories*" catering to the needs of readers both at home and overseas for Chinese literacy education, serves the learners who are keen on learning Chinese language and respect the Chinese culture, in order to popularize and develop the intercultural communications. Therefore, "*The Stories*", as an important medium to spread Chinese "soft power" of culture and thoughts, functions as the useful information of Chinese education, a Chinese language textbook, and as the education of Chinese literacy attainments. Meanwhile, "*The Stories*", being a textbook for improving the readers' Chinese culture, can help them to taste the instructions of the sages embodied in the vividly classic tales and refresh their minds by the extensive and profound Chinese traditional culture. In this sense, "*The Stories*" can be taken as a concise and popular textbook to come to understand the Chinese culture and enrich the knowledge of Chinese history. No doubt, it is also a vivid and vigorous reference book of quality-oriented education for broadening people's minds.

目录

壹 孝(Filial Piety)   1

闵损谏父(Mǐn Sǔn Jiàn Fù)   3
老莱娱亲(Lǎo Lái Yú Qīn)   6
鹿乳奉亲(Lù Rǔ Fèng Qīn)   8
汉文尝药(Hàn Wén Cháng Yào)   11
负母逃难(Fè Mǔ Táo Nàn)   14
姜诗出妇(Jiāng Shī Chū Fù)   17
董永卖身(Dǒng Yǒng Mài Shēn)   20
薛包侍亲(Xuē Bāo Shì Qīn)   23
庭坚涤秽(Tíng Jiān Dí Huì)   26
杨黼活佛(Yáng Fǔ Huó Fó)   28

贰 悌(Respect)   31

泰伯让位(Tài Bó Ràng Wèi)   33
缪肜自挝(Miào Tóng Zì Zhuā)   36
兄弟折箭(Xiōng Dì Zhé Jiàn)   40
牛弘不问(Niú Hóng Bù Wèn)   42
李绩焚须(Lǐ Jì Fén Xū)   45
张闰无私(Zhāng Rùn Wú Sī)   47
朱显焚券(Zhū Xiǎn Fén Xuàn)   50
章溢代戮(Zhāng Yì Dài Lù)   53
廷机教弟(Tíng Jī Jiào Dì)   56
严凤敬兄(Yán Fèng Jìng Xiōng)   58

中华经典故事精选通俗读本

叁 仁（Benevolence） 61

以德报怨（Yǐ Dé Bào Yuàn） 64
韩信报恩（Hán Xìn Bào Ēn） 67
与人为善（Yǔ Rén Wéi Shàn） 70
雪中送炭（Xuě Zhōng Sòng Tàn） 73
仁义胡同（Rén Yì Hú Tóng） 76
钱徽焚书（Qián Huī Fén Shū） 78
于义决讼（Yú Yì Jué Sòng） 81
思永拾钏（Sī Yǒng Shí Chuàn） 83
汉宾惠人（Hàn Bīn Huì Rén） 86
善有善报（Shàn Yǒu Shàn Bào） 88

肆 义（Righteousness） 90

栾布就烹（Luán Bù Jiù Pēng） 92
关公秉烛（Guān Gōng Bǐng Zhú） 95
宋弘念旧（Sòng Hóng Niàn Jiù） 98
王修哭谭（Wáng Xiū Kū Tán） 101
公义变俗（Gōng Yì Biàn Sú） 104
仲淹义田（Zhòng Yān Yì Tián） 107
苏轼还屋（Sū Shì Huán Wū） 110
孝基还财（Xiào Jī Huán Cái） 113
天祥衣带（Tiān Xiáng Yī Dài） 116
世期义行（Shì Qī Yì Xíng） 119

伍 礼（Propriety） 121

孔子尽礼（Kǒng Zǐ Jìn Lǐ） 123
宋桓罪己（Sòng Huán Zuì Jǐ） 126
伯禽趋跪（Bó Qín Qū Guì） 129
石奋恭谨（Shí Fèn Gōng Jǐn） 131
规妻礼宗（Guī Qī Lǐ Zōng） 134
杨刘责子（Yáng Liú Zé Zǐ） 137

2

目录

卢植楷模（Lú Zhí Kǎi Mó） 139

孔融让梨（Kǒng Róng Ràng Lí） 142

彦光易俗（Yàn Guāng Yì Sú） 145

程门立雪（Chéng Mén Lì Xuě） 149

陆 智（Wisdom） 152

虞舜躬行（Yú Shùn Gōng Xíng） 154

不耻下问（Bù Chǐ Xià Wèn） 156

晏子使楚（Yàn Zǐ Shǐ Chǔ） 159

田单破燕（Tián Dān Pò Yān） 163

韩信忍辱（Hán Xìn Rěn Rǔ） 167

英勇班超（Yīng Yǒng Bān Chāo） 170

孔融拜客（Kǒng Róng Bài Kè） 174

羲之教子（Xī Zhī Jiào Zǐ） 178

用人不疑（Yòng Rén Bù Yí） 182

画龙点睛（Huà Lóng Diǎn Jīng） 185

柒 忠（Loyalty） 188

比干死争（Bǐ Gān Sǐ Zhēng） 190

张良复仇（Zhāng Liáng Fù Chóu） 193

纪信代死（Jì Xìn Dài Sǐ） 196

朱云折槛（Zhū Yún Zhé Kǎn） 199

敬德瘢痍（Jìng Dé Bān Yí） 203

李绛善谏（Lǐ Jiàng Shàn Jiàn） 207

孟容制强（Mèng Róng Zhì Qiáng） 210

金藏剖心（Jīn Zàng Pōu Xīn） 213

洪皓就鼎（Hóng Hào Jiù Dǐng） 216

岳母刺字（Yuè Mǔ Cì Zì） 219

捌 信（Integrity） 222

以身作则（Yǐ Shēn Zuò Zé） 225

季札挂剑（Jì Zhá Guà Jiàn） 228

中华经典故事精选通俗读本

季布一诺(Jì Bù Yī Nuò)	231
孺子可教(Rú Zǐ Kě Jiào)	234
郭伋亭候(Guō Jí Tíng Hòu)	238
魏征妩媚(Wèi Zhēng Wǔ Mèi)	242
宋璟责说(Sòng Jǐng Zé Yuè)	246
曹彬激诚(Cáo Bīn Jī Chéng)	249
杨荣谏征(Yáng Róng Jiàn Zhēng)	252
宋濂借书(Sòng Lián Jiè Shū)	255

玖 廉(Honesty) 258

子罕却玉(Zǐ Hǎn Què Yù)	260
杨震拒金(Yáng Zhèn Jù Jīn)	263
刘宠钱清(Liú Chǒng Qián Qīng)	266
孔明洁身(Kǒng Míng Jié Shēn)	269
傅昭静廉(Fù Zhāo Jìng Lián)	271
甄彬赎苎(Zhēn Bīn Shú Zhù)	274
老虎引路(Lǎo Hǔ Yǐn Lù)	276
裴度还带(Péi Dù Huán Dài)	279
清官包拯(Qīng Guān Bāo Zhěng)	282
杨罗出俸(Yáng Luó Chū Fèng)	284

拾 耻(Shame) 286

卧薪尝胆(Wò Xīn Cháng Dǎn)	288
夷齐采薇(Yí Qí Cǎi Wēi)	291
节姑赴火(Jié Gū Fù Huǒ)	294
胡妻耻见(Hú Qī Chǐ Jiàn)	296
负荆请罪(Fù Jīng Qǐng Zuì)	299
管宁善化(Guǎn Níng Shàn Huà)	302
朱冲送牛(Zhū Chōng Sòng Niú)	305
崔卢仕训(Cuī Lú Shì Xùn)	308
唾面自干(Tuò Miàn Zì Gān)	311
弄巧成拙(Nòng Qiǎo Chéng Zhuō)	314

4

壹

Filial Piety

在中国传统文化中,"孝"是各种美德的根本。有这样一句话:百善孝为首。孔子认为:孝是天之经、地之义、民之行;孝悌是"仁的基础,人之行,莫大于孝"。孝,不只限于对父母的赡养,还包括对父母和长辈的尊重,如果缺乏孝敬的心意,那么,赡养父母也就与饲养家畜一样了,是大逆不道的。孔子还认为,父母可能有过失,做儿女的应该委婉地规劝,帮助他们改正,而不是对父母的绝对服从。这些思想,正是中国古代道德文明的体现。

"身体发之父母,受之父母,不敢毁伤"是孝的起点;"立身行道,扬名于后世"是孝的归属。对儒家把孝的作用过于绝对化的观点,道家不以为然。老子也承认"孝"是人的本性,但他认为"不必宣扬,过犹不及"。我们对儒、道关于"孝"的分歧不进行

— 1 —

深入讨论,仅从自然界中乌鸦反哺、羔羊跪乳的故事中,就知道"孝"本来是自然伦理,贯穿在生命的一切行为之中。对于儒家主张的"孝始于事亲、中于事君、终于立身"这种与封建社会的统治联系到一起的观点,鲁迅先生曾对它有过尖锐的批判。对此,我们应吸其精华,弃其糟粕。

做人的根本,是从一个"孝"字开始的。懂得了父母对我们的恩情,才会知道回馈、报答、感恩,但回馈报答父母的方式并不只是"对他们好"那么简单就可以了。当然,"孝"的观念,在不同历史时期的演变中,也有其合理因素,比如提倡子女对父母的尊敬、养老,将"孝亲"与"忠于民族大义"相结合,等等,都值得发扬光大。

    In traditional Chinese culture, filial piety is the root of different kinds of virtues, being ranked at the first position. Confucius believed that filial piety is the essence under the sun, and it's the base of being kind. It is not only meant to be the support towards parents, but also the action of being respectful to them. Confucius also thought that when the parents made mistakes, it is a better way to help them correct rather than being totally obedient, which is the reflection of Chinese ancient culture.

    "No change of your body, for it's from your parents" is the start of filial piety, and leaving your legacy is the result. But Taoism holds different views, and believes that it is not good to over stress this virtue. We can tell from some natural actions from animals that filial piety is the natural law. To the situation that filial piety got connected with politics, Mr. Lu Xun criticized.

    When we understand our parents, we know how to feed back. It's not simply the good actions. With the different times background, it shows different significance, like respect or patriotism.

壹 孝(Filial Piety)

闵损谏父
Mǐn Sǔn Jiàn Fù

【出处】《弟子规》:亲有过,谏使更;号泣随,挞无怨。

【释义】 父母亲如果有了过错,做子女的就要耐心地劝导他们改正;如果不能如愿,就要等待时机继续劝导,即使遭遇责骂或痛打,也无怨无悔。

【Definition】 If parents made mistakes, children have to persuade them patiently, and if that doesn't work, the persuasion needs to be continued when chances arrive. There must be no regrets under any circumstances.

【造句】 闵损谏父的故事,说的是闵损用孝道侍候、奉养父母,最终感化了顽固的心结,赢得了父母的爱心。

【Example】 Min Sun Jian Fu, treating parents well, moving stubborn minds, finally regained parents' love.

【故事】

　　zhōu cháo shí　yǒu gè xiào shùn fù mǔ de ér zǐ jiào mǐn sǔn　shì kǒng zǐ de xué shēng　tā yīn wèi dé
　　周 朝 时, 有个孝 顺 父 母 的 儿 子 叫 闵 损, 是 孔 子 的 学 生。他 因 为 德

háng hǎo　lǎo chéng chí zhòng　ér yǔ kǒng zǐ de lìng yī gè míng jiào yán yuān de xué shēng yī yàng yǒu hǎo
行 好、老 成 持 重, 而 与 孔 子 的 另 一 个 名 叫 颜 渊 的 学 生 一 样 有 好

míng shēng　mǐn sǔn zé yóu qí yīn wèi　xiào xíng　fāng miàn chāo qún ér wén míng yú shì
名 声, 闵 损 则 尤 其 因 为"孝 行"方 面 超 群 而 闻 名 于 世。

mǐn sǔn hěn xiǎo de shí hòu jiù sǐ liǎo mǔ qīn　tā fù qīn qǔ liǎo yī gè hòu qī　zuò tā de jì mǔ　jì mǔ
闵 损 很 小 的 时 候 就 死 了 母 亲。他 父 亲 娶 了 一 个 后 妻, 做 他 的 继 母。继 母

jīng cháng yòng cán rěn de shǒu duàn duì dài nián shǎo de mǐn sǔn　mǐn sǔn què cóng bù　duì bié rén jiǎng zhè xiē　hái
经 常 用 残 忍 的 手 段 对 待 年 少 的 闵 损。闵 损 却 从 不 对 别 人 讲 这 些, 还

xiàng xiào shùn qīn mā yī yàng de lái duì dài jì mǔ　bìng qiě zài guān jiàn de shí hòu hái bāng jì mǔ shuō huà　dàn
像 孝 顺 亲 妈 一 样 地 来 对 待 继 母, 并 且 在 关 键 的 时 候 还 帮 继 母 说 话, 但

jì mǔ què bù lǐng tā zhè gè qíng　yīn wèi hěn yàn è tā　dōng tiān de shí hòu zuò dōng yī　tā gěi zì jǐ qīn
继 母 却 不 领 他 这 个 情。因 为 很 厌 恶 他, 冬 天 的 时 候 做 冬 衣, 她 给 自 己 亲

shēng de liǎng gè ér zi yòng bǎo nuǎn de mián xù　ér gěi mǐn sǔn zuò de yī fú lǐ miàn què yòng bù bǎo nuǎn
生 的 两 个 儿 子 用 保 暖 的 棉 絮, 而 给 闵 损 做 的 衣 服 里 面 却 用 不 保 暖

de lú huā
的 芦 花。

— 3 —

很冷的一天,父亲叫闵损推车子出外办事。小闵损因为衣服不保暖,冻得嘴唇发紫,拉车时不小心,将驾马车用的皮带子失掉了。父亲认为是他太粗心,很生气,就用鞭子打他。抽了几鞭子,小闵损的衣服破了,露出的全是不保暖的芦花,随着漫天的风雪飞去……

回家后,闵损的父亲就有意地摸摸另外两个孩子的衣服,发现是丝绒布里包着暖和的棉花。他心里一下子明白了:原来是心肠不好的后妻,故意不关心闵损。于是,他父亲在很气愤的时候发了狠,要赶走这个"有两样心"的继母。

闵损立即跪下来,向父亲苦苦请求说:"母亲留在家里,没有别的,最多就我一人受些冷冻。如果母亲离开了这个家,我和可怜的弟弟们因为没有娘照顾,就都孤单了。父亲啊,就留下母亲吧!"父亲觉得闵损的话有道理,就答应了。

继母从这件事中,认真检讨了自己不对的地方,改正了错误,成了慈母,对待闵损像自己亲生的儿子一样了。

In Zhou Dynasty, Confucius had a student, named Min Sun, who had a same good reputation as the student Yan Yuan, and he was famous for his filial piety.

Min Sun lost his mother when he was young. His father married another woman, who tormented him a lot. But Min Sun did not tell anyone anything about that, and treated her like his own mother. However, that did not pay off at all. His stepmother made Min Sun a coat filled with reed catkins instead of cotton.

In a cold day, Min Sun's father asked him to drive a coach out. For the low quality of his coat, Min Sun was frozen, and accidentally lost the driving belt. His father

壹 孝 (Filial Piety)

thought it must be caused by Min Sun's carelessness, and whipped him for punishment, which made the coat broken, and reed catkins exposed.

When got back, father touched the coats of the other two children, and found those were made by cotton. And he realized that the stepmother deliberately ignore Min Sun. He was upset and decided to banish the stepmother.

Min Sun kneed down and begged: "If the mother is gone, every child will not be cared by mother. So let her stay." And his father thought it made sense and agreed.

The stepmother reflected and made corrections, and became an excellent mother.

【点评】

闵损孝敬父母的德行是先天性的。不管父亲、继母对他是憎恶还是疼爱，他始终都是用心尽孝的，因此安稳了一家人的心，让一家人分享了天伦之乐，保全了一个接近破碎的家庭。

No matter the father or stepmother hated him or loved him, Min Sun kept his filial piety, which made his family complete.

老莱娱亲
Lǎo Lái Yú Qīn

【出处】《太平御览·孝子传》：老莱七十，戏彩娱亲。作婴儿状，烂漫天真。

【释义】 老莱子年龄七十多岁了，在父母面前还像小孩一样，纯洁、天真地逗父母开心。

【Definition】 Lao lai, who was over 70 years old, acted like a child for entertaining his parents.

【造句】 老莱娱亲这个成语，形容子女想尽办法让年事已高的父母心情舒畅。

【Example】 The idiom "Lao Lai Yu Qin" means that children try their best to make their parents happy.

【故事】

春秋时，楚国有个名士叫老莱子。这个老莱子，非常孝顺父母，不仅生活上对父母关怀照顾得十分周到，凡是吃的喝的，总是给双亲喜欢的可口食品，还千方百计地让父母开心过日子。为了让父母过得快乐，他专门养了几只美丽、爱叫的鸟让父母玩耍、取乐。他自己也经常引逗鸟儿玩，让鸟儿发出动听的叫声。父亲听了很高兴，总是笑着说："这鸟叫的声音真好听！"老莱子见父母脸上有笑容，他也就非常高兴。

难得的是，老莱子自己年纪大了，虽然七十多岁了，但是他平常所说的话，总没有一句说出自己"老"的意思来，时刻都注意到《礼记》中"父母在，不称老"那句话的教导。

一天，父母看着花白头发的儿子，叹气说："连儿子都这么老了，我们在世的日子也不长了。"老莱子听了这话，为减轻父母的忧愁，就想法子让父母高兴高兴。就用多种花色布专门拼做了一套漂亮的衣服穿

壹 孝 (Filial Piety)

_{zhe zǒu lù yě zhuāng zhe tiào wǔ de yàng zi   fù mǔ kàn liǎo tā nà gè mó yàng   lè hē hē de}
着，走路也 装 着跳舞的样子。父母看了他那个模样，乐呵呵的。
　　_{yī cì tā wèi fù mǔ sòng dòu jiāng shàng tīng táng shí bù xiǎo xīn diē liǎo yī jiāo   tā pà fù mǔ nán guò shāng xīn   shùn}
一次，他为父母送豆浆，上厅堂时不小心跌了一跤。他怕父母难过伤心，顺
_{shì jiù zài dì shàng dǎ gǔn   hái gù yì zhuāng chū yīng ér tí kū de shēng yīn   tā de fù mǔ yǐ wéi ér zi shì gù}
势就在地上打滚，还故意 装 出婴儿啼哭的声音。他的父母以为儿子是故
_{yì zhè yàng de   nǎ lǐ rěn dé zhù   hā hā dà xiào qǐ lái   jiǎn zhí kuài huó jí liǎo   guò liǎo hǎo yī huì er   jiàn lǎo}
意这样的，哪里忍得住，哈哈大笑起来，简直快活极了。过了好一会儿，见老
_{lái zǐ yī zhí bù pá qǐ lái   jiù xiào zhe shuō   zhēn hǎo wán a   gòu liǎo   lái zǐ kuài qǐ lái ba}
莱子一直不爬起来，就笑着说："真好玩啊，够了。莱子，快起来吧。"

　　In Chun–qiu Dynasty, there was a celebrity named Lao Laizi, who treated his parents best. He provided best food and entertainments as well to his parents. He, especially fed a few beautiful birds to entertain his parents. Every time, when his parents had fun, he felt happy.

　　Lao Laizi was in his 70s at that time, but never showed his age. He always remembered a saying in *Liji*, i.e., "When parents are alive, never say you get old."

　　One day, his parents looked at him, and said: "Our son is old now, and we are not living long."Lao Laizi heard and was looking for the way to make them happy. He dressed in colorful clothes, and walked as dancing, which made his parents happy.

　　Once, he served his parents some soymilk, but fell down. For avoiding making his parents sad, Lao Laizi rolled on the ground, and acted crying like a baby. His parents thought he did it on purpose, and laughed for a long time.

【点评】

_{lǎo lái zǐ zài fù mǔ de miàn qián jìn xiào dào   wèi liǎo ràng fù mǔ néng gòu gāo xìng   jí shǐ tā zì jǐ lǎo}
老莱子在父母的面前尽孝道，为了让父母能够高兴，即使他自己老
_{liǎo   yě shí cháng bàn yǎn zhe lǎo wán tóng de jué sè   zuò chū yī xiē guài yàng de biǎo xiàn   zhuāng qīng chún}
了，也时常扮演着老顽童的角色，做出一些怪样的表现，装 清纯。
_{zhè shì tā xiào jìng fù mǔ   zūn jìng zhǎng bèi de dú tè fāng shì   tǐ xiàn liǎo zhè yī jiā rén zhǎng yòu zhī jiān zhēn}
这是他孝敬父母、尊敬长 辈的独特方式，体现了这一家人长幼之间真
_{zhì de ài}
挚的爱。

　　Lao Laizi made his parents happy, even when he was at his old age, by acting like a child with strange actions. That's his special way to show filial piety and true love among family members.

鹿乳奉亲

Lù Rǔ Fèng Qīn

【出处】《二十四孝》：周郯(tán)子，性至孝。父母年老，俱患双眼，思食鹿乳。

【释义】 郯子尽孝道非常用心，父母年老时患了眼病，需要喝鹿奶，他就设法办到了。

【Definition】 Tanzi, for his parents had eye disease, tried his best to find deer milk, and he succeeded.

【造句】 郯子鹿乳奉亲，为我们树立了孝顺父母长辈的光辉典范。

【Example】 Lu Ru Feng Qin has set a good example of well treating parents for us.

【故事】

郯子，是春秋时期的人。日子一天一天地度过，他逐渐长大成人。同时，父母也渐渐变老，头发都白了。不幸的是，两位老人都害了眼病，几乎快要失明了。内心的苦闷，令双亲陷入了对生活的绝望之中。

孝顺的郯子看在眼里，痛在心上。心想：不能让父母在黑暗中度过余生啊，能有什么办法，让父母的眼睛好起来呢？他平日一边安慰父母，一边加紧寻医问药，想尽一切办法来解除父母的痛苦，使双亲感受到欢乐、快活、满足的生活气息。

在郯子的精心的照顾下，双亲的心情恢复了不少，家里也出现了久违的欢笑声。一次，他听医生说，治这种病最好的办法是食用鹿奶。郯子记在心里，开始计划如何才能获得鹿乳。由于母鹿是不会轻易让别人采集奶汁的，郯子就乔装打扮，披上鹿皮，扮成一只鹿，钻进深山寻

壹 孝 (Filial Piety)

找机会。因为郯子的装扮非常逼真,还仿照鹿的姿势和动作,所以当他进入鹿群生活的地方后,并没有惊动鹿群,也没有引起母鹿的怀疑。终于,他小心翼翼地取到了鹿奶。

内心的喜悦,令郯子忘记脱去身上的装束,他一心想着父母能尽快吃到鹿乳,只顾快些回家。但在半路上正巧遇到打猎的人,郯子逼真的装扮迷惑了猎人的眼睛,猎人抽出箭来就要射击他了。郯子急忙中马上掀掉鹿皮,并大声说话,向猎人告诉详细的情形,这才免掉了一场危险。猎人听了,都被郯子的孝行所感动,称他是好孝子。

郯子回家,将鹿乳调剂好,喂父母喝下。就这样,过了一段时间,父母的眼睛果然复明了。

Tanzi was living in Chunqiu dynasty. As he had been growing to an adult, his parents had been getting old with serious eye disease, which might lead to being blind. That made them living in despair.

Tanzi thought it was not acceptable to make his parents living in dark, and tried his best to comfort them and look for good therapies. His actions made the family happy and alive.

Once, he heard from a doctor that the best way to cure the disease was to drink deer milk. However, mother deer never allowed men to collect their milk. Tanzi disguised as a deer, and went to the deep of mountain, looking for the chance. Finally, he successfully got some deer milk from a group of deer.

The excitement made Tanzi forget to take off the deer costume, and came across a hunter. For the appearance, the hunter almost shot him. At the very moment, he took off the disguise, and talked loudly to avoid being shot.

When Tanzi got back home, cooked the deer milk and fed his parents. For a certain period time, his parents recovered.

【点评】

奉养双亲,是每一个为人子的应尽职责。对父母的孝养,不仅在于养父母的身体,更要滋养父母的心志。做为子女,以反哺之道切身力行,才能成就自己的孝子之德,令父母心安。为了父母,郯子可以冒着生命危险进入深山获取鹿奶,这种孝行和胆识,的确令人佩服。

Being a son or daughter, taking care of parents is a must. It is not only on taking care of their health, but also on helping their mind. Those make parents comfortable. Tanzi took deer milk at the life-risk, which is an action to admire.

壹 孝 (Filial Piety)

汉文尝药
Hàn Wén Cháng Yào

【出处】《史记·孝文本纪》:汉孝文帝,母病在床,三载侍疾,汤药亲尝。

【释义】 汉文帝因为母亲生病,三年如一日,为母亲煎药、尝药,尽心伺候。

【Definition】 Emperor Han Wen Di kept making herb medicine soup and tasting before handing to his mother who were being sick for three years.

【造句】 汉文尝药说明:孝不分贫贱,不分富贵;言教不能令人折服,唯有身教才能摄于无形。

【Example】 The story "Han Wen Chang Yao" tells us that well-treating parents is nothing to do with your financial situation, social position; when words do not work, actions are the best approach to influence.

【故事】

汉文帝刘恒是历史上有名的施仁政、有孝行的皇帝。他照顾母亲的尝药故事,流传很广。

平时,文帝在家,坚持每天向母亲问安;如果公务不是很忙,他还特别抽出时间,陪伴在母亲身边尽孝。在他心中,始终把照顾好母亲当作自己生命中的大事。只要母亲身心平安、康泰,他就感到是最大的快乐。

日子一天一天地过去了,母亲开始变得衰老,身体也差了。文帝更担忧母亲的健康。有一天,母亲生病了,文帝请来最好的医生给母亲治病,大家为这事都忙得不可开交。

这时候,文帝的心里非常的着急,生怕母亲一病不起,甚至会离自己

— 11 —

中华经典故事精选通俗读本

而去。于是特别牵挂着母亲，已经放心不下宫女们对（太后）母亲的照顾。只要完成公务，他就马上来到母亲身边，守护在母亲床前。看到母亲憔悴的面容，文帝吃什么东西都觉得没有味道，夜晚不能安稳睡觉，他坚持亲自为母亲端水送药，一心希望母亲尽快好起来。只要母亲感觉好了一些，他心中就感到无限的喜悦。

母亲这一病，就是三年。在这三年里，身为一国之君的汉文帝，几乎没有睡过一个安稳觉。即使是晚上休息的时候，文帝也从不脱衣服，生怕在母亲呼唤的时候，由于自己一时的怠慢而有违母亲的心愿。为了更好地照顾母亲，文帝还向医师请教所用汤药的药效、剂量，并牢记在心里，对什么时候用药、如何熬制才能充分发挥药效等等，他都很好地掌握了。每次给母亲服药前，文帝定会亲自先尝尝，品一品熬煮的浓度是否适当、温度是否合适，然后进行调制，直到适合母亲服用的时候，才放心地端给母亲。就这样，在文帝全心全意的照料下，母亲的病终于好转了。

As a kind Emperor, Han Wen Di's story of tasting medicine for his mother was widely spread.

In normal days, Han Wen Di greeted to his mother everyday; if he had free time, he would stay by his mother. In his opinion, taking good care of mother was an important issue. He felt happy as long as his mother was well.

His mother was getting old and weak. Han Wen Di got more worried about her. One day, his mother was sick, and Han Wen Di asked the best doctor to diagnose.

For trusting no servants, Han Wen Di took care of his mother himself after finishing the court issues. He served food and medicine, and when his mother got a little bit

壹 孝 (Filial Piety)

better, he released a lot.

His mother had been sick for three years, and he had no good sleep. Even deep in the night, Han Wen Di never took off his clothes in case his mother needed him. For a better care, Han Wen Di asked the doctor about the usage of the medicine, and tasted the medicine before giving it to his mother. Under Han Wen Di's careful care, his mother cured.

【点评】

常言说：久病床前无孝子。对病人三年无微不至地照顾，这对一个普通的人来讲，本来就是一件不容易做到的事。可是，汉文帝作为一个日理万机的君王，他不仅做到了，而且做得很好，就因为他有一颗真诚、恳切的孝敬母亲的心。

It is said, there are no good children if the parents are continuously sick. To take care of a patient for three years is never an easy thing for ordinary people, let alone an Emperor. Han Wen Di successfully did it because of his sincere and devoting mind.

负母逃难
Fù Mǔ Táo Nàn

【出处】《二十四孝》：江革避难，负母保身，乱平贫苦，行佣供亲。

【释义】 为躲避战乱、盗贼，江革背着母亲逃难；虽然脱离了战乱，但生活贫穷困苦，他就靠做苦力、自己省吃俭用，优先保障供养母亲的需要。

【Definition】 To avoid wars, Jiang Ge carried his mother to escape. They ran away from wars, but became poor, Jiang Ge tried his best to make living and put his mother's needs first.

【造句】 江革负母，是《二十四孝》中的著名故事，讲述了东汉初年著名孝子江革背母逃难和侍奉母亲的动人事迹。

【Example】 Jiang Ge Fu Mu is one of the 24 filial piety stories, telling us the moving event of Jiang Ge carrying his mother to escape wars in Dong Han dynasty.

【故事】

东汉初年，王莽篡位建立的新朝，政治腐败，地方势力经常因为争地盘而打仗，天下大乱。当时，山东临淄有个人叫江革，他很小的时候就没有了父亲，和母亲相依为命。因为战乱，各地盗贼四起。盗贼不仅抢财物，还常常把家中的男人抓去，逼他们入伙做贼。为了躲避灾难，江革就带着母亲离家出走逃难。但是母亲年纪大了，腿脚走路不方便，江革就背着母亲赶路。

逃难的路上，江革多次遇到盗贼。盗贼不但洗劫了他身上的东西，还要逼他入伙做贼。遇到这种情况，江革就向盗贼苦苦地哀求说："我从小死了父亲，无依无靠的，是母亲饱受辛苦把我拉扯成人。如果没有母亲，就

壹 孝 (Filial Piety)

没有我的今天了。今天大王如果把我抓走了，留下我孤零零的老母亲，现在这兵荒马乱的，她老人家以后怎么活啊？恳请大王放过我吧！"盗贼被他的孝心所感动，不但放过他，还告诉他如何选择逃难路线，免得再遇到其他劫匪。

后来平息了动乱，江革带着母亲来到江苏境内居住。他找了一份苦力活，挣来钱供养母亲。即使挣的钱很少，但只要是母亲日常生活必需的用品，他都尽自己最大的努力，替母亲准备好。

这样过了一段日子。母亲去世了，江革非常难过，每天守在墓地伤心地哭。他悲伤到极点的哭诉超过了一般的常人，感动了村子和附近的人。整整三年，江革就在母亲的坟旁搭个草屋住着，因为深切思念母亲，连晚上睡觉的时候也不愿脱掉孝服。

他对母亲行孝的表现，不但感动邻里，还感动了地方的父母官，于是被推举为孝廉，后来又被推举为贤良方正，担任中郎将。告老还乡后，当朝皇帝因为很敬重他的为人，每年都派人去慰问，并且供给他吃、穿、用的一切，直到他去世。

Early in Dong Han Dynasty, Wang Mang started a coup, and set up a new court. Different areas fought for a larger territory. Jiang Ge, from Linzi, Shandong, had no father since he was little, living together with his mother. For the wars, burglars were everywhere. They did not only rob treasures, but also forced men to join them. For avoiding the disaster, Jiang Ge ran away with his mother. Due to the age, his mother could not walk easily, so Jiang Ge carried her on the way.

Jiang Ge came across burglars for many times. Every time when burglars forced him to join them, Jiang Ge begged and said to them: "My mother is the only parent who feed me up, and now, if I leave her, she would have no one. In this situation, how could she survive? Please let me go!" Burglars were moved by him, and released him, as well as telling him the best way to escape in order to avoid other burglars.

Afterwards, the country was much in peace. Jiang Ge and his mother lived in Jiangsu Province. He got a labor job, and earned money to support his mother. Though the income was very limited, he tried his best to prepare everything his mother needed.

After a few years, his mother passed away. Jiang Ge was so sad that stayed in cemetery to whip every day. His action moved people nearby. Jiang Ge built up a shelter and lived in near his mother's cemetery for 3 years, and he even refused to take off the mourning clothes.

His action made him famous among governors, and was selected as a representative, and even promoted to the position of Zhong Lang Jiang. For the Emperor admired him so much, after his retirement, the country provided all him living consuming till he died.

【点评】

乱世生活中，江革背着母亲逃难，受尽了磨难，并尽最大努力来保障母亲的安全和生活。即使在那样居无定所、食不果腹的日子里，他坚持对母亲要有最好的孝养。这才是真孝道。

Living with the suffering from escaping, Jiang Ge tired to guarantee his mother's safety and living. That's the true filial piety.

壹 孝(Filial Piety)

姜诗出妇
Jiāng Shī Chū Fù

【出处】《范书》：姜诗夫妻,孝奉甘旨,舍侧涌泉,日跃双鲤。

【释义】 姜诗和他的妻子对母亲行孝感动了天地,结果收获了治愈母亲眼病的美味食物。

【Definition】 The filial piety story of Jiang Shi and his wife moved all people, and they finally got the tasty food which cured his mother's eye illness.

【造句】 姜诗出妇故事中提倡对父母孝行固然天经地义、值得仿效,但同时也告诫我们:在处理夫妻矛盾关系的问题方面也务必慎重。

【Example】 The story "Jiang Shi Chu Fu" remind us that well treating parents is something we need to do, while dealing with the contradictories between husband and wife also need to be cautious.

【故事】

　　hàn cháo de jiāng shī　　běn lái jiù hěn xiào shùn mǔ qīn　　tā mǔ qīn yīn wèi yǎn jīng hài bìng　　shēng huó bù fāng
　　汉朝的姜诗,本来就很孝顺母亲。他母亲因为眼睛害病,生活不方
biàn　　jiāng shī fū fù duì mǔ qīn de zhào gù jiù gèng jiā xiǎo xīn zài yì liǎo
便,姜诗夫妇对母亲的照顾就更加小心在意了。
　　yī tiān wǎn shàng　　mǔ qīn zuò mèng dé zhī　　lí jiā liù qī lǐ de jiāng shuǐ kě yǐ zhì hǎo zì jǐ de yǎn bìng
　　一天晚上,母亲做梦得知:离家六七里的江水可以治好自己的眼病。
dì èr tiān jiù duì ér zi hé xí fù shuō qǐ zhè jiàn shì　　jiāng shī mǎ shàng zhǔ fù qī zi páng shì qù jiāng zhōng qǔ
第二天就对儿子和媳妇说起这件事。姜诗马上嘱咐妻子庞氏去江中取
shuǐ　　bù néng yǒu sī háo dài màn　　páng shì zì rán lǐ jiě zhàng fū de zhè piàn xiào xīn　　cóng cǐ　　měi tiān dū bù
水,不能有丝毫怠慢。庞氏自然理解丈夫的这片孝心,从此,每天都步
háng qù jiāng zhōng qǔ shuǐ huí lái gěi pó po yǐn yòng　　xī wàng zhēn néng zhì hǎo pó po de yǎn bìng　　jiù zhè yàng
行去江中取水回来给婆婆饮用,希望真能治好婆婆的眼病。就这样,
jǐ nián rú yī rì　　háo wú yuàn yán
几年如一日,毫无怨言。
　　qiū dōng de jì jié　　tiān qì hěn gān zào　　yī tiān　　jiāng mǔ yǎn tòng bìng yòu fàn liǎo　　xū yào nà jiāng shuǐ jiě
　　秋冬的季节,天气很干燥。一天,姜母眼痛病又犯了,需要那江水解
kě　　páng shì yī dà zǎo jiù qù jiāng zhōng qǔ shuǐ　　dàn shì lǎo tiān yé bù bāng máng　　guā qǐ liǎo dà fēng　　fēng shā
渴。庞氏一大早就去江中取水。但是老天爷不帮忙,刮起了大风,风沙
chuī dé páng shì de yǎn jīng méi yǒu bàn fǎ zhēng kāi　　yīn cǐ huí jiā de lù shàng zǒu de màn liǎo　　děng tā huí dào jiā
吹得庞氏的眼睛没有办法睁开,因此回家的路上走得慢了。等她回到家

— 17 —

里的时候，婆婆的眼病加重了。姜诗不问青红皂白就责备妻子，说她不孝，还把她赶出了家门。庞氏性格本就温顺，现在遇到这个变化，虽然心里感到很委屈，但丈夫的话还是要听的。离家路上，想起丈夫平日里的体贴关爱、儿子的调皮与可爱这些情景，就很舍不得离开，于是悄悄地在邻居大妈家住下，以便能够继续关心她的婆婆和丈夫、孩子。

庞氏借用大妈的织布机日夜纺纱织布，用卖出布匹得来的钱财，去街市买些好吃的，再麻烦邻居大妈送到家中给婆婆食用。这样过了一阵子，婆婆觉得奇怪，就问邻居大妈："近来你为什么常送好的东西给我吃，以前却没有？"邻居大妈是个实心人，就把一切告诉了她的婆婆。婆婆听了很感动，就要儿子接庞氏回家。

从这以后，姜诗夫妇孝顺母亲更加尽心。日子一天天过去，姜母年纪大了，常常想吃鱼。虽然家中贫寒，但姜诗夫妇更加勤劳，将所有积蓄用来买鱼孝敬母亲。

一天夜里，狂风大作，雷雨交加。第二天，庞氏起来经过院子，惊奇地发现：屋旁边空地上有一个桶大的窟窿，正汩汩地往外涌着泉水。在泉眼旁边，有两条活蹦乱跳的鲤鱼；再看泉井里面，还有好多尾鲤鱼在游动。庞氏看到这一切，心里特别高兴，又尝了尝泉水，同六七里外的江水一个味。从此，她每天就汲这口泉水给婆婆喝，捞鲤鱼做鱼脍给婆婆吃。不久后，姜母的眼病就治好了。

Jiang Shi, a man in Han Dynasty, carefully took good care of his mother whose eyes were ill.

Once, his mother dreamed that the river water 3 kilometer away was effective in

壹 孝(Filial Piety)

curing the disease, and told Jiang Shi and his wife when awake. Jiang Shi asked his wife to carry water from the river, and she followed for years and hoped this might help.

The weather got dry in winter. One day, the mother's eyes pained severely, and needed the river water. Pang Shi got up early to carry water. It was a windy day, and Pang Shi was not able to walk in a normal speed. Jiang Shi blamed his wife for getting back late, and drove him away from home. Pang Shi felt bitter, but could only obey her husband. Missing her family, she stayed in a neighbor's place.

Pangshi borrowed neighbor's loom to weave, and sold the cloth for good food, and then asked the neighbor to send the food to her mother in law. The mother felt weird, and asked the neighbor: "why do you regularly give me good food recently?" and the neighbor told her the truth, which moved her, and asked her son to take Pangshi back home.

From that moment on, Jiang Shi couple treated their mother even better. The mother wanted to have fish, they spent all they have buying fish for her.

After one stormy night, Pangshi found there was a big hole where a stream of spring came out besides their house. There were two fish near the hole, and many in the water. She tasted the water, and it was the same as the river water. Then she took the water and gave it to the mother everyday, and cooked the fish for her. Their mother cured in this way after a few days.

【点评】

姜诗尽心孝养母亲，首先是顺从母亲的心愿，让人明白"百善孝为先"的真谛。而姜诗的妻子对婆婆的孝更加可贵：她孝顺自己的婆婆无怨无悔，即使在被赶出家门、满心委屈的时候，心里还能想着婆婆，并默默地用辛勤劳动继续尽心奉养婆婆，不仅感动了婆婆和丈夫，也赢得了他人和社会的尊重。

Jiang Shi followed his mother's wish, and his wife did even better. Even when she was driven away, she still worried the mother and worked for her, which moved her family and gained respect from others.

董永卖身

Dǒng Yǒng Mài Shēn

【出处】《搜神记》:董永家贫,卖身葬亲,天遣(qiǎn)仙女,织缣(jiān)完缗(mín)。

【释义】 身无分文的董永,为安葬父亲而卖身到财主家做雇工,得到织女的帮助。

【Definition】 For burying his father, Dong Yong traded himself to work for a rich family, and luckily got the help of fairy Zhi Nü.

【造句】 董永卖身,体现的是一种淳朴的孝行情愫(sù),感人至深。

【Example】 Dong Yong Mai Shen is a genuine action of well-treating parents, which moves us a lot.

【故事】

传说汉朝时,山东省博兴这个地方有一个人叫董永。他很小的时候就失去了母亲,家境又十分贫寒,与父亲相依为命。董永小时候就非常孝顺父亲,又很勤快、懂事,从来不把自己当小孩子看,每天跟着父亲一起到田里耕地,尽力做事,为父亲分担辛劳。每次回家的路上,他总是让辛苦了一天的父亲坐在老牛车上,自己跟在后面走。

后来,他父亲过世了。一贫如洗的他没什么可以用来安葬父亲,董永就只好出卖自己的身子,来换取安葬父亲的费用。一位员外听说这个情况后,拿出钱来帮他办了丧事。董永承诺:为父亲守丧后,一定去员外家里做工,报恩偿还。

壹 孝 (Filial Piety)

三年守丧期满，董永就前往员外家里去做工。半路上，在一棵大槐树下，他意外地碰见一位年轻美貌的女子。那女子自称孤身一人无家可归，情愿与董永结为夫妻，凭她能够织布的手艺，可以一起去员外家里做工还钱。董永就和这个女子一同前往员外的家里去做工。

董永见了员外施礼说："承蒙您的恩惠，我父亲得以入土为安，现守丧期满。我虽然穷困又没有地位，但也想尽自己的全力来您家里做事，这样就可以报答您的恩德了。"员外明白董永报恩的用心，但看到他身边的女子时，不免又疑虑地问道："你来做事倒是可以，但这位女子又能做什么呢？"董永回答说："她能织布。"

员外就对他们说："那好，你们就为我织一百匹布吧。完工以后，就可以回家了。"于是，他俩就在员外家里织布。本来，织成一百匹布需要很长的时间，但在那女子的帮助下，他们只用了不到一个月就完成了，这使员外感到很惊奇，董永自己也感到莫名其妙。

于是，员外就送他们离开了。董永怀着对女子的无限感恩与喜悦，来到他们相遇的那棵槐树下。只见那个女子停下脚步，向董永行礼并告辞说："我是天上的织女。是你的至诚孝心感动了我，于是特意来帮助你。"说完话，她就凌空而起，一眨眼就不见了踪影。

Dong Yong, a man in Boxing, Shandong, in Han Dynasty, lost his mother when he was very young, and lived with his father in a very bad financial situation. He was very kind to his father, never considering himself as a little boy. He did the farm work with his father, sharing the pressure. On the way back home, he asked his father to sit on the cottage, and he walked behind.

Later, his father passed away, and for the poor condition, he had no money to bury his father. Dong Yong could only sell himself to earn the money. One rich man heard that, and paid enough money to him. Dong Yong promised to work in the rich man's place after the mourning years for his father.

After three year, Dong Yong went to work in the rich man's place. Accidentally, he came across a beautiful young lady who claimed being alone, and willing to marry to him. For her skills of weaving, they could make money together.

Dong Yong thanked the rich man, and said that he wanted to work for him for his kind actions. The rich man understood, but doubted the young lady, and asked what she could do. Dong Yong replied that she could weave.

The rich man said if they were able to finish 100 pi cloth, they could go back home. So Dong Yong and the lady stayed to weave. With the help of the lady, they finished it less than a month, which was way too shorter than it was supposed to be. They all felt surprised.

They were free to go, and walked under the tree where they first met. The lady stopped and waved goodbye to Dong Yong. She told him that she was a fairy lady, and she came to help because of his kind actions to parents.

【点评】

行孝，是立身处世的根本德行。孝顺父母历来是中华民族的传统美德。董永卖身葬父是一种极尽孝道的行为。这是每个中国家庭都知道的一个故事，并且代代相传。人们敬佩卖身葬父的董永，于是给董永的故事增加了仙女相助的美好传说，增强了故事的趣味性。

Filial piety is the basic morality, and it is a good Chinese tradition. Dong Yong's story is a well-known story in China. It is interesting to mix the fairy tale with the story of Dong Yong.

壹 孝 (Filial Piety)

薛包侍亲
Xuē Bāo Shì Qīn

【出处】《三字经》:亲爱我,孝何难?亲恶(wù)我,孝方贤。

【释义】 父母爱我、关心我的时候,我孝敬父母有什么困难呢?难得的是父母不喜欢我的时候,我还能一样的孝顺,这样才是真正的孝。

【Definition】 When parents treat you well, it is not different to treat them well back; it is precious that you can treat your parents well even though parents do not treat you well.

【造句】 薛包侍亲的故事,表现出一种仁爱、忠厚的悌孝美德,感人至深。

【Example】 The story "Xue Bao Shi Qin" shows the kindness and humbleness of being a child.

【故事】

东汉的薛包,在他很小的时候,妈妈生病在床,他就整日守在母亲身边伺候。妈妈去世后,父亲因为娶了后妻就憎恶薛包,还要他离家外出居住。薛包因为不愿离开家,结果被父亲驱赶、殴打。实在没有办法,薛包就在屋外搭了一间草屋,暂时住着,但每天早晨和以往一样,都去父母屋里打扫卫生、做家务,用心照顾他们。即使这样,他的父母还是很生气,还是要赶他出家门。薛包只好回到自己的草屋,心想反正习惯了,也没有怨气,仍然坚持每天早晨回家问安、夜晚为父母安铺床席,更加谨慎地孝敬他们,从不间断。这样过了一年多,父母终于被薛包的孝心感动了,就让薛包回家了。

这样一起生活了一段时间,父母去世以后,成年的弟弟们要求分配家里财产,各自生活。薛包劝阻不了,只好平分家产。用人方面,自己就留用年老的奴婢,对弟媳们说:"老奴婢和我共事年久,你们不能使唤。"他又把荒废的田园、庐舍留给自己,借口说:"这是我少年时代所经营整理的,心中留恋舍不得。"分衣服、家具,还是要破旧的,他解释说:"这些是我平素穿着、使用惯了的,用起来比较顺手。"

分了家产以后,到了下一代人的手上,有些侄儿不会经营,加上生活奢侈浪费,不久就将财产耗费、破败了。薛包关切地开导侄儿们,并经常把自己的财产、粮食和钱,拿去救济他们。

薛包这种孝亲、爱侄儿的德行,早已传遍远近,后来被荐举到朝廷去做官,但他不愿意做官,仍旧在家里务农,享年八十多岁,善终。

Xue Bao, a Dong Han man, served his ill mother when he was little. After his mother passed away, his father began to resent him because of his step-mother and ask him to leave home. Xue Bao built a straw shelter besides the house and lived in, but took care of the family as usual.

Even it was like that, his family were still mad at him, driving him away. Xue Bao could only return to his shelter, Xue Bao got used to that, having no complains, insisting on greeting to and taking care of his family every day. After one year, his family got moved and let him come back.

After his parents passing away, his step brothers asked to separate family legacy, and he could only equally split. He kept old servants and said to his sister in law that they were working with me for years, and others could not ask them to serve. He kept the deserted gardens and houses, and said that those were his memory of childhood. He kept all old clothes and furniture, and said he got used to those and like them.

Some of his nephews had no business brain, and had a luxurious life, so they spent all the property quickly. Xue Bao always supported them financially.

He got very famous for his good acts, and selected to be an official in court. But he was not willing to do so, still farming at home till he peacefully died at 80.

【点评】

薛包的母亲死后，对嫌弃他的父亲和继母，他没有怨言；尽管遭遇打骂，甚至被赶出家门，他还是一如既往地孝敬着父亲和继母，硬是用真诚的孝道感动了铁石心肠一样的父母。更难得的是，父母去世后，他又将这一份敬爱的心意转移到其他亲人的身上。这种"孝亲"的行为，是他立身行道、扬名于后世的根本所在。

Xu Bao had no complains to his father and step mother who resented him. Even when he was driven away, he still treated them kindly, which moved them finally. After the parents passed away, he treated other members of family as well as usual; those are why he got so famous.

庭坚涤秽

Tíng Jiān Dí Huì

【出处】《宋史·黄庭坚传》：宋黄庭坚，官居太史，亲涤溺(nì)器，不以为耻。

【释义】 官居太史之位的黄庭坚，经常为母亲清洗便盆，从没有羞耻的感觉。

【Definition】 As a high position officer, Huang Tingjian often cleaned toilet for his mother, without feeling embarrassed.

【造句】 庭坚涤秽的故事告诉我们：既为人子，孝行父母就应该至诚，而不是做样子给别人看的。

【Example】 The story "Ting Jian Di Hui" tells us that as children, people need to be sincere to treat parents well, rather than act to show.

【故事】

黄庭坚是宋朝有名的大诗人。他做太史官的时候，尽管公务很忙，家里也有仆人，由于从小养成孝顺父母的习惯，对照顾父母的事，无论大小，都会认真努力去做好，亲自照顾母亲的生活点滴，从不懈怠。他每天忙完公事回来，一定陪在母亲的身边，以便随时感受母亲各方面的身心需要，并且亲力亲为地精心奉养着母亲，使母亲满意。母亲有特别爱清洁卫生的习惯，但那时候的房间里没有卫生间，为了夜里方便上厕所，一般都会准备一个应急的便桶放在房里。黄庭坚为了保证让年迈的母亲身心安稳，避免因为仆人的卫生清洁程度不够而影响母亲的心情，他就坚持每天亲自为母亲刷洗便桶，几十年如一日，从来没有间断过。

壹 孝 (Filial Piety)

黄庭坚的做法，当时曾引起一些人的不理解。有人问他："您身为高贵的朝廷命官，家中还有那么多的仆人，为什么一定要自己做这些杂乱、细小的事，甚至还亲手刷洗你母亲的便桶这样卑贱的事情呢？"

黄庭坚回答说："孝顺父母是我的本分，怎么可以让仆人去代劳呢？再说孝敬父母的事情，是出自个人对父母真心实意的感恩的本性，同自己的身份地位没有任何关系，又怎么会有高贵与卑贱的区别呢？"

Huang Tingjian, a famous poet in Song Dynasty, was busy as an senior officer. He took care of his parents by himself no matter it was anything important or not. Every day, after he finished his work, he stayed by his mother and took care of her.

His mother loved clean environment, but there was no toilet in the room. For her convenience, a toilet bucket was placed in the room. For giving a good environment, Huang Tingjian cleaned the toilet bucket every day for several decades.

Many people did not understand his action, and asked: "As an officer, why are you willing to do things like that?"

Huang Tingjian replied: "That's what I should do, and it was not acceptable to ask servants to do that. This is from my heart, and has nothing to do with my position."

【点评】

自古以来，上至国家君王，下到平民百姓，都以孝敬父母为修身立德的根本。黄庭坚效法古圣先贤的德行，做到恪尽子道，以至诚的孝心、恳切的表达和敦厚的品行，影响着后人。

From the old time, no matter the emperor or common people are all morally rooted by filial piety. Huang Tingjian set a good example to show the offspring the good actions of filial piety.

杨黼活佛

Yáng Fǔ Huó Fó

【出处】《明史·杨黼传》：杨黼修心，无际良簪(zān)，母既活佛，倒屣(lǚ)披衿(jīn)。

【释义】 杨黼想拜无际大师为师来修养心性，大师劝他将自己母亲当作活佛供养，就是最高修行。

【Definition】 Yang Fu wanted to study from Master Wuji to promote his mental state, while the Master told him that it was better to treat his own parents as living Buddhas, which could be considered as the highest training.

【造句】 "杨黼活佛"使世人警醒：父母才是我们心中真正的活佛！

【Example】 The story "Yang Fu Huo Fo" reminds us that parents are living Buddhas on our mind.

【故事】

明朝时，有个人叫杨黼，一心想要修行。因为十分敬慕四川地方的一个名叫无际大师的人的道行，就起程专门去拜访他。走到半路，遇到一个老僧人。老僧竟然叫出了他的名字，还问他要到哪里去？杨黼说："我要去拜访无际大师。"老僧说："无际大师就是我的师傅。师傅叫我来传话：你不必去见他了，他让你去见另一个活佛。"杨黼问："这个活佛在哪里？"老僧道："你转回身，一直往东走，如果看到一个披散着衣襟、鞋子也倒穿了的人，那就是活佛了。"杨黼就回转身往来路走，走到半夜，却发现又转回到自己家门口了。他怀疑半路遇见的那个老僧不过是在戏弄他，不由得很沮丧，但也只好

壹 孝 (Filial Piety)

去敲自家的门。屋里的母亲一听到是杨黼的声音,高兴得一爬起来就去开门,敞着的衣领也来不及扣好,鞋子也倒穿了,就走了出来,出现在杨黼面前。

杨黼一见母亲的模样,顿时大悟,原来,母亲就是自己的活佛呀!当即就感悟修行应从何处下手了。从此以后,他尽力孝顺母亲,并且因为注释了一部几万字的《孝经》而闻名。

In Ming Dynasty, Yang Fu was in the mood for mental practice. He admired a master named Wuji in Sicuan area, and planned to visit him.

On the halfway, he came across an old monk, and surprisingly, the monk spoke his name out, and asked where he would go. Yang Fu said: "I want to visit Master Wuji." The monk told him that he was the student of Master Wuji, and said he should meet another Master instead of him.

Yang Fu asked: "Where is the living Buddha?" The monk answered: "You turn around, and go to the east. If you see a person with clothes untied, wearing wrong shoes, the person is the living Buddha."

Yang Fu followed the monk's words. In the midnight, he found he reached his home, and doubted that the monk teased him. He could only knock the door. His mother heard, feeling so happy to open the door with clothes untied, wearing wrong shoes.

Yang Fu suddenly realized that his mother was the living Buddha, and from that moment on, he tried his best to take care of his mother and wrote a book of *Xiao Jin*.

【点评】

人在深夜归宿,敲别人家的门是很少有回应的。只有慈母得知孩子远归回家时,因为心生欢喜,往往来不及穿衣系扣、把鞋穿好,就赶忙开门去。这样的慈悲心,与活佛有什么不同呢?其实每个家庭里都有一尊知寒问暖的活佛,但人们对这尊活佛往往很容易忽略,反而舍近求远,去拜远方的什么精神菩萨,确实值得人们沉思。

Just few people respond when the door is knocked in midnight. Only mothers feel so happy to open the door with clothes untied, wearing wrong shoes, which is similar to actions of living Buddha. People admire living Buddha in distance, and always forget one besides. Yang Fu realized that, which causes people's reflections.

贰 悌

Respect

悌，是儒家核心思想之一，意思是对兄长顺从、敬爱。孔子非常重视"悌"的品德，要求在家孝顺父母，在外尊敬兄长、师长。这样将"悌"和"孝"并称，当作"为仁之本"。

"悌"本作"弟"，即兄弟之间要有"长幼之节"，兄要像兄，弟要像弟。既要求幼从长，同时也要求长护幼。谁都承认人世间这样的一种感情：没有比骨肉之情更亲的亲情了，兄弟姐妹之间的手足情是心连心、长且久的。有道是：一回相见一回老，能得几时为弟兄？因此，趁兄弟姐妹都在的时候，倍加珍惜，相互鼓励，相互扶持，共建和睦、幸福、美好的家庭。

"孝悌"既是儒家的重要思想，也是中国人的传统美德。对孔子"孝悌"思想的理解，今人一般只注意其"孝"而很少提到

"悌",这实在是一个很大的失误。事实上,"悌"所起的社会作用,并不亚于"孝"。孔子说"出则悌",说明"悌"并不局限于家庭,在社会上同样需要讲究"悌",那就是尊重社会上所有比自己年长的人,爱护、谦让所有比自己年少的人,也就是现实生活中所谓的"尊老爱幼"的高度概括。由此,人们不但不能忽略"悌",而且必须高度重视,应大力提倡"悌",并使之继续发扬光大。

As the core of Confucianism, respect can be interpreted as obedience and esteem to older brothers and parents. Respect and filial piety are regarded to be the basis of benevolence.

Respect, brother indeed ("Di" in Chinese), means a mutual respect and love between brothers in the family. There is no doubt that the ties of blood and brotherhood are the best and longest to last. A happy and harmonious family involves the mutual respect and support between brothers and sisters in the family.

Both filial piety and respect are the core parts of Confucianism and Chinese traditional virtues as well. But it is a common misunderstanding that people often focus on "filial piety" other than "respect". In fact, the social influence of "respect" is no less than that of "filial piety". According to Confucius, "respect" requires people to show respect to all seniors and love all juniors in the society.

贰 悌 (Respect)

泰伯让位
Tài Bó Ràng Wèi

【出处】《史记·泰伯世家》：泰伯让国，曲顺其亲，之荆采药，披发文身。

【释义】 泰伯为实现父亲的心愿，借外出采药的机会，躲到偏远的地方隐居起来。

【Definition】 To realize his father's wish, Ji Taibo was hidden in a remote place by a chance of outgoing for collecting herbs.

【造句】 泰伯让位的积极意义在于：引导人们崇孝悌，薄名利，顾大局，明道义。

【Example】 The story "Tai Bo Rang Wei" leads us to understanding of the ignorance of fame, the importance of seeing big picture, and the reasons.

【故事】

姬泰伯是商朝末年的一个孝、悌两全的人。他是诸侯周太王的大儿子。他有两个弟弟，大弟叫仲雍，二弟叫季历。季历的儿子姬昌出生的时候，有一对赤色雀鸟嘴里衔了丹书，停在门户上。周太王认为这是圣人出世的祥瑞和迹象，后来又看到这个小孙子确实有不同于一般人的才能，就产生了将王位传给季历，之后再由季历传位给姬昌的想法。可是古代有长子继位的传统，周太王因此非常为难。泰伯知道父亲的心思，就和大弟仲雍商讨办法，应该如何顺从父亲的心愿。

一天，周太王生病了，于是泰伯就和仲雍以采药为名离开周国，来到南方偏远的一个地方（现在东南沿海一带）隐居起来。当时为了寻找泰伯回国管事，周太王派人寻到了泰伯他们的藏身之地，但泰伯为了不被别人认出来，就披发纹身，用这个办法表示自己不可以重用：一则逃避父王派人追查；二则表示自己愿意把周国的王位让给老三季历。就这样，在父亲去世的时候，季历的这两个哥哥都没有回去奔丧，季历顺理成章地继承了王位。好在季历也是一个非常仁慈、厚道、有能力的人，想到两个哥哥如此礼让他，就发愤图强，不负众望，把国家治理得很好，临终时把王位传给了姬昌。姬昌就是历史上很有名的周文王。

    Ji Tai Bo was a man of filial piety and fraternal respect. As the eldest son of Vassal King of Tai Zhou, he had two younger brothers, the elder one was called Zhong Yong, and another was called Ji Li. When Ji Li's son, Ji Chang was born, a pair of red birds held Dan Book in their mouths, and stopped on the door of Ji Li's house.

    King of Tai Zhou regarded it as the auspicious sign of saint's birth, and found that Ji Chang got an exceptional talent. He therefore had a thought of passing his power to Ji Li and then to Ji Chang. However, there was a tradition that the eldest son will be the successor of father's power in ancient China. In light of that, King of Tai Zhou was in a dilemma. Considering the worry of father, Tai Bo discussed with Zhong Yong on how to release father's worry.

    One day, King of Tai Zhou was sick, Tai Bo and Zhong Yong left the state of Zhou under the name of herb gathering. They came to a remote place in the south (now located in the southeast coastal area) and lived as hermits. At that time, King of Tai Zhou dispatched people to get Tai Bo back to govern the state. However, Tai Bo disheveled his hair and tattooed himself in case other people will recognize him. He also wanted to tell others that he is willing to abdicate the throne of Zhou and pass to Ji Li in this way.

    Even when King of Tai Zhou passed away, Tai Bo and Zhong Yong did not come

贰 悌(Respect)

back to attend funeral. Consequently, Ji Li became the King of Zhou logically. Ji Li is a lenient and honest man with good capability. Inspired by two brothers' care and thought, he governed the state well and lived up to the expectations. In the end of his life, he passed the power to Ji Chang who was the famous King Wen of Zhou in history.

【点评】

历史上,为争夺一国之主,曾经发生过很多悲惨的事件,有的人不惜杀父弑兄,发动战争,死伤无数。在王位、权欲面前,姬泰伯是个例外:作为长子,他首先想到的是设法满足自己父亲的愿望。他的弟弟季历不负众望,把周朝治理得井井有条,为八百年周朝盛世的出现奠定了良好的基础。

In the history of China, there were many tragedies had happened in scrambling for the throne. To be crowned, some killed their father or brothers, or even declared a war which caused massacres. In face of throne and power, Ji Tai bo is an exception. As the eldest son of King of Tai Zhou, the priority in his mind was trying to meet his father's demand. Fortunately, Ji Li lived up to people's expectations and governed Zhou Dynasty in an orderly way, which laid a solid foundation for the 800 years' prosperity of Zhou Dynasty.

缪彤自挝

Miào Tóng Zì Zhuā

【出处】《二十四悌》:缪彤化弟,闭户自挝,诸妇谢罪,得以齐家。

【释义】 为教化弟弟、妯娌的德行,缪彤闭门自挝、自责,唤醒了各位弟弟和弟媳们的知耻心、忏悔心,重建了和睦家族。

【Definition】 For educating young brothers and sisters-in-law, through self reflection, Miao Tong reminded them of the shames and regrets, and rebuilded a harmonious family.

【造句】 缪彤自挝提示我们:每一个人只有用一颗"行有不得,反求诸己"的心,立身行道,才能实现"修身、齐家、治国、平天下"的目标。

【Example】 Miao Tong Zi Zhua reminds us that everyone can only realize the aims of self perfection, family perfection and country perfection by the way of self reflection.

【故事】

汉朝的缪彤,在他小时候,父母就双双过世,留下他兄弟四人相依为命。他作为长兄,承担起了照顾、抚养弟弟们的重担。家庭的不幸,生活的磨炼,锻造了缪彤坚毅、正直的性格。他深感自己的责任重大,如果不把几个弟弟抚养成人,就无法告慰父母的在天之灵。兄弟几个虽然生活艰难,但是由于长兄无微不至的照顾,弟弟们得以健康成长,并深刻感念到哥哥的付出,因此对长兄非常尊敬,手足之情一天比一天加深。

兄弟们长大成人,相继成家了。但结婚只是承担另一种责任的

贰 悌 (Respect)

开始。喜庆的气氛在带给家庭短暂的欢愉之后,新的生活如何展开,成为大家必须面对的现实。由于家中增添了不少新人,生活已不再像以前那样方便,人际关系也不如以前那样融和,妯娌们各自心里有打算。因此,生活中的碰撞与冲突,有时也会伤及感情;偶尔的口角,常使大家闹得不欢而散。妯娌几个各自思量,打算分家单过。

缪肜对此不禁十分感慨:要是父母在世,面对孩子们的不和,该会多么失望啊。叹息之余,经常痛苦地自责。一日,又听到两个弟媳因为一点琐事争执不休,他感到羞愧难当,心想这都是因为自己没做好榜样。于是,他把自己反锁在房里,一边抽打自己,一边厉声谴责自己:"缪肜啊缪肜,你天天都说要修身谨行,学习古圣先贤的教诲,来齐整风俗、匡扶正气。可现在连自己的家庭都不能管好,看来你的理想都是妄想了,你辜负了祖宗的教诲了,实在是不孝子孙啊!"说完,就放声痛哭。

弟弟、弟媳们顺着哭声聚拢过来,守候在屋外,听到长兄的自责,惭愧地低下了头。想到长兄为了家庭和睦,日夜操劳;想到长兄平日那张和蔼的笑脸,这时在屋里却是泪流满面;想到长兄平时的殷殷教诲,而自己却一次次置之脑后……大家想起自己过去的种种错误,流下了忏悔的泪水,于是跪在门外对屋里说:"哥哥,都是我们的错。因为纷争而忘了手足之情,我们对不起祖宗,对不起父亲的教诲,对不起您对我们的期望,您责罚我们吧!"

真诚的忏悔,深深地感动了缪肜,于是开门出来。弟弟弟媳们赶紧上前一起说："哥哥，我们以后决不再提分家的事了，决不再做出让您伤心的事情了。我们都愿意和气地生活在一起。"从这以后，缪家又恢复了往日的和睦、快乐的气氛。

In Han Dynasty, there was a man called Miao Tong. His parents died when he was little. Therefore, he and his three younger brothers had to rely on each other so as to exist in this world. As the eldest brother, Miao Tong shouldered the responsibilities of raising and taking care of his younger brothers. The misfortune of family and hardship of life developed Miao Tong into a persistent and righteous man. He always knew that he was responsible for raising younger brothers, and only by doing this, can he comfort his parents in heaven. Even they lived a hard life, Miao Tong's younger brothers grew up healthily with his meticulous care. Therefore, they felt grateful and showed respect for Miao Tong.

As time goes by, they all got married. But marriage marked the beginning of another kind of responsibility. How to begin a new life was something they need to face with after the transient joy and pleasure brought by their weddings. As new people joined into their family, life and relations between family members were no longer as usual. Their wives all had their own plans, which led to the conflict and quarrel in family. And over time, their wives separately planned to divide up family property and lived apart.

Miao Tong felt so sad and guilty about the family conflict, and thought that if their parents were still alive, how disappointed they would be. One day, two of his sister-in-law quarreled with each other for some trivial things. Miao Tong felt so ashamed about it and blamed it to himself. Therefore, he locked himself in his room, beating and condemning himself. He said: "Miao Tong, you always say that you want to cultivate mind and correct behaviors, learning the instruction of sages in order to make contribution to the society. But now, you even cannot manage your family well. How could you realize your vision! You are an unfilial son." After saying these, he burst into tears.

贰 悌(Respect)

Younger brothers and their wives all gathered outside the door when they heard Miao Tong was crying. They all felt ashamed as they think about efforts eldest brother made and hardship suffered. They keened down outside the door with repent on their face, saying: "Brother, it is all ours faults. We set aside brotherhood for conflict raised by some trivial things. We cannot live up to your expectation and disappoint father and ancestors. Please punish us!"

Moved by their sincere confession, Miao Tong opened the door and came out. Younger brothers and their wives all gathered around him, saying: "Brother, we will never talk about dividing up family property and living apart. We will never do anything that makes you sad. We are willing to live together harmoniously." From then on, their family became harmonious and happy again.

【点评】

缪彤自挝的故事，生动地为现代家庭上了"修身"而后"齐家"的一课。面对家人种种不当做法，缪彤并没有直接批评指责别人，而是以自责的方式，直接承担过错，从而感化了各位弟弟和弟媳，唤醒了他们的忏悔心。其中的真情与"求诸己"的智慧，正是家中严父长兄亲睦家族、敦睦乡里、行教化于天下的大法则。

This story vividly teaches modern families a lesson. Faced with improper behaviors of family members, Miao Tong did not blame them but shouldered the responsibility, which evoked their repentance. The brotherhood and self-reflection taught in this story are what we need adopt to manage family and interpersonal relations.

兄弟折箭

Xiōng Dì Zhé Jiàn

【出处】《魏书·吐谷浑传》:"单者易折,众则难摧,戮力一心,然后社稷可固。"

【释义】 团队中的成员如果齐心协力,就能有所作为,否则百无一用。

【Definition】 Team members should be united to accomplish an aim, or they will lose.

【造句】"兄弟折箭"这个故事告诉我们:只有精诚团结、合作,才有强大的力量。

【Example】 The story "Xiong Di Zhe Jian" tells us that the great power force comes from the unity.

【故事】

从前,有个国王,他有十个儿子,但是这十个儿子互相争权夺势,一点都不团结。老国王担心自己死后,他们兄弟间因为争夺王位而互相残杀,这样下去,国家一定会四分五裂。

一天,他把这十个儿子叫到跟前,给他们每人一枝箭,让折断。结果,每个儿子轻轻一折,不费吹灰之力就把手中的箭折断了。之后,国王就给儿子每人十枝箭,这十枝箭是紧紧捆在一起的。这回,每个儿子不管怎么使劲,没有一人能折断成捆的箭枝。

这时,老国王说话了:"你们兄弟十个,就像这十枝箭。如果只凭一个人的力量,很容易被打败,如果大家团结在一起,就会像这捆紧的箭杆,力量才强大。你们兄弟之间,打断骨头连着筋,一定要相互团结,只有大家齐心协力,才能战无不胜啊!"

贰 悌（Respect）

<small>ér zi men yīn cǐ xǐng wù liǎo cóng cǐ yǐ hòu xiāng chù de fēi cháng hé mù zài yě bù nào máo dùn liǎo</small>
儿子们因此醒悟了。从此以后，相处得非常和睦，再也不闹矛盾了。

Once up a time, there was a king who had ten sons. But the ten sons were not friendly to each other. The old king worried about his sons would kill each other for the crown after he passes away. If this happen, the kingdom will be split up.

One day, he gathered all of his sons together, and gave them an arrow respectively. Then, he asked them to snap it. Consequently, the arrow was broken off easily. Later, he gave each son ten arrows in a bundle. This time, his son were all failed to snap the arrow bundle.

At this time, the old king said: "You guys are like the ten arrows. United, you stand; divided, you fall. You are brothers, and blood is thicker than water. Only united together can you guys be invincible."

His words awoke his sons. From then on, they were friendly to each other and united as one.

【点评】

<small>cháng yán dào tuán jié jiù shì lì liàng hé zuò gòng shì chéng gōng de bǎ wò gèng dà suǒ yǐ shuō yī</small>
常言道：团结就是力量。合作共事，成功的把握更大。所以说，一
<small>gè tuán duì bù lùn zuò shén me shì zuì hǎo bù yào dān dú xíng dòng yào yī kào dà jiā de lì liàng gòng tóng xié</small>
个团队，不论做什么事，最好不要单独行动，要依靠大家的力量共同协
<small>zuò cái néng gèng yǒu zuò wéi xiōng dì zhī jiān yīn wèi xuè mài xiāng tōng jiù xiàng yī kē shù yī yàng lián zhī tóng</small>
作，才能更有作为。兄弟之间，因为血脉相通，就像一棵树一样连枝同
<small>gēn gèng yào xiāng hù guān ài rú guǒ xiōng dì jiě mèi zhī jiān shàng qiě bù néng hé mù xiāng chǔ nà me yǔ qí</small>
根，更要相互关爱。如果兄弟姐妹之间尚且不能和睦相处，那么，与其
<small>tā rén jiù gèng nán xiāng chǔ liǎo</small>
他人就更难相处了。

An old saying goes: "One finger cannot lift a stone." Cooperation makes things easy. Therefore, team members had better not work alone but cooperate with others. Brothers are branches in a tree. They need care about each other. If brother and sisters cannot get on well on each other, it will be a worse case for others who have no genetic connection.

牛弘不问

Niú Hóng Bù Wèn

【出处】《隋书·牛弘传》：牛弘之弟，酗(xù)酒杀牛，其妻往诉，不问不尤。

【释义】 牛弘对妻子状告弟弟喝醉酒射杀他驾车的马一事，并不过问。

【Definition】 Niu Hong ignored the issue that his wife accused his younger brother killed his horse when his brother got drunk.

【造句】 牛弘不问的故事，为我们处理兄弟之间日常的感情关系问题提供了很好的借鉴。

【Example】 The story "Niu Hong Bu Wen" provides us with a good demonstration of dealing with the relationship between brothers.

【故事】

隋朝牛弘，本来姓寮，他的父亲叫寮允，是南北朝时北魏的侍中，因为做事非常勤恳踏实、别无他求，皇上就赐他姓牛。牛弘非常喜欢读书，见闻广博，为人厚道。

在牛弘还是婴儿的时候。一次，有个会看相的人经过他家，看到了牛弘相貌，就告诉他的父亲说："这个儿子将来一定富贵，应当好好地培养他。"果然，通过努力，牛弘后来官至吏部尚书。

他有个弟弟叫牛弼，经常无节制地喝酒，而且不醉不归。有一天，弟弟牛弼又喝醉了，回家就把牛弘驾车的一头牛用箭射死了。牛弘的妻子看到这情景很惊讶，认为这是很大的事情，急忙就去告诉牛弘："不知道为什么，你弟弟今天把你驾车的那头牛射死了。"

贰 悌（Respect）

牛弘听了，只回答说："牛死了，做成肉干、肉松之类的好了。"妻子误认为丈夫在读书没听清，就走到他面前又说了一遍，但牛弘只说了一句："我知道了。"他的妻子还是以为丈夫读书太用心，可能没有在意，又重复了一遍。牛弘还是说："我已经知道了。"他的脸色很自然，仍然读着书，丝毫没受影响，更没有责怪弟弟的意思。他的妻子这才不好意思地离开。

In Sui Dynasty, there was a man called Niu Hong. His original name was Liao Hong. Emperor at that time gave him the name for his diligence, integrity and contentment. Interested in reading, he is a man of wide knowledge and experience.

When Niu Hong was still in his infancy, a fortune-teller passed by his house and saw him, saying to his father: "You son is destined to be someone in future, you should cultivate him well." As expected, Niu Hong later became a senior official who was charge of personnel through his efforts.

Niu Hong had a younger brother called Niu Bi who was an alcoholic. One day, Niu Bi was drunk and shot one of his brother's oxen for cart driving dead with an arrow. Niu Hong's wife was so shocked and thought it a big deal. She hurried to tell his husband: "Your brother somehow shot your ox for cart driving dead!"

Niu Hong responded: "A dead ox can be made into beef jerky and floss, that's not bad." His wife thought Niu Hong was concentrated in reading and did not hear it clearly. Therefore, she told him again. Niu Hong then only said: "I see."

His wife still thought he was too focusing on reading to hear it clearly, so she repeated it again. However, Niu Hong still responded: "I already knew it." He looked so natural and centered on reading. He didn't show any reproach to his brother. Therefore, his wife was left embarrassedly.

【点评】

历史的教训值得注意：兄弟间为什么不能和睦相处？很多情况下可能是由

于妯娌姑嫂不善于处理一些麻纱关系、棘手问题才引起的。但对于真正友爱、情笃的兄弟骨肉,即使是再能挑拨是非的人,又怎能奈何之?牛弘的妻子将叔叔射杀牛弘驾车的一头牛的事告诉牛弘,而且是一而再、再而三,但牛弘以宽宏大量的心态作出冷静而理智的处理,实在高妙。

History has taught us a lesson: Why brothers cannot support each other and maintain an amicable relationship? In many case, it might because sisters-in-law are not good at tackling with some sensitive and problematical issues. However, for those brothers with unbroken family ties and affection, no one can undermine their brotherhood. In this story, Niu Hong's wife told him that Niu Bi shot his ox for cart driving dead again and again, but Niu Hong handled it quite wisely with great generosity. It is really a brilliant move!

贰 悌 (Respect)

李绩焚须
Lǐ Jì Fén Xū

【出处】《旧唐书·李绩传》：李绩在官,为姐煮粥(zhōu),火焚其须,不用妾仆。

【释义】李绩探望姐姐的时候,以宰相身份亲自为姐姐煮粥吃,烧了胡须也无所谓。

【Definition】When visiting his sister, as the prime minister, Li Ji cooked porridge for her without minding his beard burnt.

【造句】李绩焚须的故事表明,在李绩心中,时时不忘的,是身后的姐弟情谊。

【Example】The story of "Li Ji Fen Xu" shows that the deep affections between sisters and brothers.

【故事】

唐朝有位大臣叫李绩,因为功劳卓着,深得唐太宗的垂爱。有一次李绩生病了,御医说：给李绩治病的药方中要用胡须做药引。唐太宗听后,二话不说,提刀就把自己的胡子割下来拿给御医。李绩知道这个消息后非常感动,就到皇上面前谢恩。

以李绩这样一个朝中重臣的身份,他对自己的姐姐也非常恭敬。他平时去看望姐姐时,还亲自帮姐姐煮粥。李绩有一次煮粥,因为火势太强,把他的胡须烧了。他姐姐一看,就对李绩说："家里的仆人很多,让他们去做就好了,你又何苦亲自来做这些事？"

李绩回答说："我不是因为没有人的缘故啊。姐姐,你从小对我关怀备至,我时时都想要回报你。我是因为现在姐姐的年纪大了,我也老了,虽然希望能够经常为姐姐煮粥,但我是皇帝身边的人。我们姐弟相处在一起的机会本来就不多，今后，我为姐姐煮粥的机会越来越少了啊。"李绩的姐姐听了这话，内心非常感动。

Li Ji, a senior official in Tang Dynasty, was highly esteemed by Emperor Taizong of Tang for his outstanding contribution to country. One day, Li ji was sick. In order to cure his disease, beard should be added to the prescription as efficacy-enhancer, the imperial physician said. Upon hearing this, Emperor Taizong of Tang cut off his beard to the imperial physician. Li Ji was deeply touched, and then expressed his great gratitude to the Emperor..

Even Li Ji was a senior official, he respected his elder sister very much. He often cooks porridge for his sister in person when he paid visits. His beard was burnt by strong fire when he was cooking porridge once. His sister noticed and said: "There are many servants in house. You do not need to do this by yourself, just let them do."

Li Ji responded: "Sister, you have always been the one who takes care of me. Now I want to look after you in return. I serve the Emperor, so we may not have much time getting together. I cherish each opportunity of cooking porridge for you." His sister was deeply moved by Li Ji's sincere words.

【点评】

李绩事亲极孝。他不仅用心照顾父亲，对姐姐的照顾也一样用心。他以当时的宰相身份为姐姐煮粥，胡须被火烧了也无所谓。我们读这个故事，读到他回答姐姐所说的几句话时，那种和乐、恻隐之思，溢于言外，令人难免顿生凄然之感和敬佩之情。

Li Ji is a very filial person. He not only takes care of his parents attentively, but also his elder sister. As a prime minister, he cooked porridge for his sister, and even did not care that his beard was burnt. When reading those words he responded with, we can feel his great love for sister and pitiful thoughts, which arouse our compassion and respect.

贰 悌 (Respect)

张闰无私
Zhāng Rùn Wú Sī

【出处】《元史·张闰传》:张闰无私,八世同居,共织互乳,缙绅不如。

【释义】 张闰治家有方,八代同堂,和睦相处,快乐生活,令人非常羡慕。

【Definition】 Through effective managing methods, Zhang Run owned a big, harmonious and happy family of eight generations, which was admired by others.

【造句】 张闰无私,讲述的是元朝张闰家中八代不分炊、却过得和乐融融的故事。

【Example】 Zhang Run Wu Si describes a big happy family of eight generations living together.

【故事】

元朝的张闰,他家里有八代人共同生活,吃一锅饭。最难能可贵的是,一家上下有一百多口人,都非常和睦,从没有是非,没有闲话。张闰的哥哥过世后,张闰就以长辈的名义,把家族的理事权交给他哥哥的儿子、自己的侄儿张聚。张聚婉言拜辞说:"叔叔,父亲已经离开我们了,现在您是长辈,您管理家族理所应当。"张闰却说:"侄儿,你是家族下一代的嫡长子,由你主管家族的事更合适。"这样相互推让很久,最终还是由侄儿张聚来主持家政,但张聚恳请叔叔"多多顾问"。

张闰每天就领着家里一大班侄女、媳妇们,在一个工作坊里,做着裁缝或织布之类的活儿。工作结束后,所有织好的布、做好的衣服,统一收归在仓库之中,由专人支配,没有人占为己有。

每逢有小孩啼哭的时候,家里那些妇女们无论哪一个看见了,就抱起来给他吃奶,不管是不是自己亲生的,都当作自己的孩子一样来对待和爱护。而这些孩子也一样不分是不是自己的母亲,只要是有人喂他吃的,就会停止啼哭。因此,如果有哪个媳妇需要回娘家探亲,就常常很放心地把亲生的小孩留在家里,妯娌们一定会好好照看的。

同村的一些当官的或大户人家看在眼里,都自愧不如张闰一家相处得和睦、融洽,羡慕不已。这事传到朝廷,朝廷里就派了钦差前来表彰他家,把他家作为大家学习的榜样。

In Yuan Dynasty, there was a man called Zhang Run who owned a big family of eight generations. With more than 100 family members, they still lived in a harmonious and happy life.

After his elder brother's death, Zhang Run appointed Zhang Ju to take charge the whole family in the name of family elder. Zhang Ju, the son of his elder brother, graciously declined: "Uncle, you are the elder of our family after father's death. You are more suitable to manage family affairs." Zhang Run responded: "As the eldest son of next generation, you are destined to take charge our family." After a long talk, Zhang Ju finally decided to shoulder the responsibility with his uncle's assistance.

Zhang Run gathers a group of nieces and daughter-in-law doing needlework in a workshop everyday. After a whole day's work, they designated a special person to be in charge of the clothes in the family warehouse. No one will make them their own.

All the women in family whoever saw a baby crying will hug and feed him or her, and the baby will stop crying. They regarded all the babies as their own children. Hence all the daughter-in-law in family will be at ease about leaving their children at home when they need to visit their side of family.

Some wealthy and influential families in the same village felt humbled by and envied the harmonious family Zhang Run owns. Having heard this, the Emperor rewarded Zhang Run's family and set it as an example for others.

贰 悌(Respect)

【点评】

家庭成员之间是否和睦,是否闹纠纷、有意见,关键在于这个家族是什么样的家风,在于这个家族的长辈秉持着什么样的治家观念。张闰作为一个大家族的长辈,用"无私友爱"的价值标准齐家处事,做到公正公平,一心为大家,让所有的家人受益。

A harmonious family must have a good manager or elder. As the elder of a big family, Zhang Run handled family affairs with the values of selflessness and care. By practicing fairness and equality in family, he benefited all the family members.

朱显焚券

Zhū Xiǎn Fén Quàn

【出处】《新元史》：朱显兄弟，祖产已分。不敢异处，取券尽焚。

【释义】尽管祖父已经将家产分割到个人手中，但到了朱显这一代，为了生活困难的侄儿们有依有靠，他召集各家一起焚烧了自有的家产清单，重新组建起一个大家庭。

【Definition】 Though fathers had divide the big family into individuals, for helping relatives, Zhu Xian called on all family members to burn the procession lists, and rebuilded the big family.

【造句】朱显焚券，不但是尽了兄弟应有的手足情义，也是对父母尽最大的孝心。

【Example】 Zhu Xian Fen Quan does not only reflect the affections of brotherhood, but also is the best respond to parents.

【故事】

元朝时，有个人叫朱显。某一年，朱显的祖父生了大病，想到自己不久于人世，他在弥留之际，将家产按等份分好，还立下了字据，把后事交代得非常妥当。

又过了一段时间，朱显的哥哥也因病过世了，留下几个嗷嗷待哺的孩子，家里的日子一天比一天难过。朱显看到侄子们孤苦无依，心里很不好受，就在日常生活中，对侄儿们给予特别的照顾，把他们看作自己的亲生孩子一样，无微不至地关怀着。

由于侄子们太小，不能自立，加上嫂嫂身体又不好，照顾子女生活本来就困难，教育、引导孩子们成长就更加力不从心了，何况成长

贰 悌(Respect)

中还有其他想象不到的种种问题和困难。如果没有人帮助他们的话,往后的情形将会怎样?但如果对他们不管的话,于心又何忍?

于是,朱显就与弟弟朱耀商议说:"父子兄弟,本来就同气连枝,不可分离。现在,哥哥已经离开我们了,他的孩子们都那么小,无论情理还是道义上,我们都要代替哥哥来承担长辈应有的责任,让侄子今后的生活没有后顾之忧,培养他们的厚道、善良。所以,我建议把分了的再家聚拢起来,让家族所有人共同生活,互相好有个照应。"

弟弟听哥哥这么一说,想起平日里哥哥对大家的好处,感到由衷的佩服与敬爱,很爽快地表态了。于是,他们一同来到祖父的墓前,把祖父留下来的分家产的文契全部焚毁。从此以后,这一家继续快乐地共同生活在一起,互相关怀照顾,日子过得很温和、舒坦。

In Yuan Dynasty, there was a man called Zhu Xian. His grandfather was seriously sick in a year and knew he was going to die soon. In his final days, he divided the property equally and made a written will to make sure everything settled after his death.

Sometime afterward, Zhu's brother died from disease, leaving serval little kids. Seeing the hardship they suffered, Zhu felt so sorry. Hence he treated nephews as his own sons and took good care of them in daily life.

It is never an easy job for parents to raise children. What's worse, kids are too young and the sister-in-law is out of condition. They cannot live a good life without help. "How can I stand by? I have the responsibility to take care of them," Zhu said to himself.

Therefore, Zhu discussed with his younger brother: "Family members should take care of each other. Brother passed away, leaving those poor little kids in the world. As their uncles, we have to shoulder the responsibilities of elders to ensure they can live a happy and comfortable life and become honest and kind people. Hence I suggest persuade all the family members to live together and look out for each other."

Hearing that and recalling the good deeds Zhu did to the whole family, the younger brother admired and agreed with him. Later, they burned the written will which wrote the way of dividing property behind the tomb of grandfather. Living together and taking care of each other, they led a happy and cozy life ever after.

【点评】

年少就失去父亲,这是人间的至痛。如果没有亲情的力量来维持家庭的温暖,那么,孩子们如何心智健全地成长呢?如何培养他们热切关怀周围一切、经营积极向上的人生?在侄子们最艰难的时候,朱显带领大家将祖父留下的田产文契全部烧毁,一家大小继续生活在一起。这份良苦用心,体现了朱显对长辈的一片孝心、对晚辈的真诚关爱。

The most painful thing is losing father in one's childhood. A child cannot grow up healthily without a warm family atmosphere and the power of family love. But how to help children lead an enthusiastic and positive life? Zhu Xian united the whole family to take care of his sister-in-law and nephew in their hardest time. This demonstrated his filial piety to elders and care to the younger generation.

章溢代戮

Zhāng Yì Dài Lù

【出处】《明史·章溢传》：章溢之侄，为寇（kòu）所擒（qín），愿以身代，贼亦心钦（qīn）。

【释义】章溢宁愿用自己的性命换取自己侄儿性命的做法，让盗贼深受感动。

【Definition】 Zhang Yi would rather sacrifice himself to trade his nephew, which moved the killer.

【造句】章溢代戮，弘扬孝悌之道，在中国千百年的历史中，历来为名家所赞颂。

【Example】 Zhang Yi Dai Lu was highlighted by celebrities in thousands of years.

【故事】

元顺帝年间（公元1352年），有一伙盗贼从福建那边过来，危害浙江龙泉赞、善等一带地方。当时那地方有个非常友爱兄弟的人叫章溢，同他的侄子章存仁，一起逃到山里避乱。不料，章存仁被盗贼捉住了，章溢赶紧向盗贼求情说："这是我的侄儿，他的年纪还小。我哥哥只有这一个儿子，不可以叫我哥哥没有后代，我情愿自己替我侄儿去死，千万不要杀害我侄儿。"贼人因此深受感动，不但不杀他，反而想招降章溢。

但是章溢不愿做盗贼，就被绑在柱子上，盗贼要他好好想想。到了夜间，他通过哄骗值班的看守，得到脱身回家的机会，当即召集同乡百姓组成义兵，上山打败贼寇，救出了侄儿章存仁。地方府官闻信随即率军而来，要杀尽有牵连的贼人。章溢就劝说府官领头人说："这些贼人好多都是贫苦百姓，这之前是迫于饥寒才做盗贼的,就放他们一条活路吧。"领队官员觉得他的话有理,接受了他的意见,并将他留在自己的身边做帮手。

回官府论功封赏的时候,章溢被授为浙东都元帅府佥事。章溢却说:"我所率领的都是故乡子弟,他们奋勇向前没有得到任何好处,而只有我获得功名,这使我于心不忍。"因此,坚决推辞不受封赏。

元朝灭亡后,章溢成为明太祖朱元璋的得力助手。明太祖登基做皇帝时,询问章溢说:"像现在这样,应该如何治理天下?"章溢说:"天道无常,唯德是福。只有以德治国,才能长治久安;不轻易杀人,实行仁政,就能治理天下。"由此可见,他是多么厚道、多么有爱心的人。

During Emperor Shun's reign of Yuan Dynasty (1325A.D.), a group of bandits from Fu Jian province came to Long Quan city, Zhe Jiang province and did evils there. At that time, there was a man of fraternity called Zhang Ji who ran away to mountainous areas with his nephew in order to escape from bandit disaster. Unfortunately, they were got caught. Zhang begged those bandits and said: "Please don't kill my nephew, he is young and the only child of my elder brother. Kill me and let him go, PLEASE!" Those bandits were deeply touched by him and decided to absorb him into group instead of killing.

However, Zhang refused to be a bandit. They tied him to a post and asked him to reconsider it. At night, he fooled the watchman and escaped. He then organized country fellows to fight against bandits. They won the fight and rescued out Zhang's nephew. Hearing the bandit disaster, local officials immediately dispatched troops to eliminate all the bandits. Nevertheless, Zhang persuaded the troop leader: "Most of bandits were poor civilians who became bandits out of survival. Please don't kill them." The leader accepted his reasonable suggestion and recruited him as assistant.

贰 悌(Respect)

Zhang was offered a position in the local government for award. But Zhang refused and said: "I just an organizer for this fight, but all my country fellows who bravely fought with bandits regardless of death got nothing awarded, I cannot accept the appointment alone."

After the demise of Yuan Dynasty, Zhang became the right-handed man to the funding father of Ming Dynasty, Emperor Zhu Yuanzhang. When Emperor Zhu Yuanzhang ascended to the throne, he asked Zhang: "How should I govern the whole country now?" Zhang responded: "God helps virtuous people. Only by practicing the policy of benevolent and the rule of virtue, can a country achieve lasting stability and prosperity." We can see from his words and deeds that how merciful and virtuous he is!

【点评】

处变危急之时,最是充分检验人的真情的关键时刻。章溢和侄儿在生活困苦、到处流浪的境遇中,侄儿不幸被杀人不眨眼的强盗抓获。这时,章溢首先想到的是要设法保住哥哥独生子的性命,甘愿用自己的性命换取侄儿的生命,可见笃志深情。同时,谨慎地和强盗周旋,用计破贼后,又为他们向官府求情,保住了他们的性命,体现了"为仁之本"。

A man in need is a good man indeed. Zhang put his nephew life ahead of his, asking bandits to kill him and release his nephew. Besides, he interceded for bandits with local government officials after they won the battle. He saved their lives. He is such a merciful person!

廷机教弟

Tíng Jī Jiāo Dì

【出处】 廷机教弟,仍易旧冠,奉命维谨,可谓二难。

【释义】 李廷机教导弟弟为人处事要低调、不张扬,弟弟顺从并高兴地照办了。

【Definition】 Li Tingji taught his younger brother to keep low profile, and his brother happily followed.

【造句】 廷机教弟的故事说明:李廷机和他的弟弟,真是一对有修养、有德行的好兄弟。

【Example】 The story "Ting Ji Jiao Di" tells us Tingji and his brother were in good relationship and with descent qualities.

【故事】

明朝李廷机,他官居大学士,负责太子培养、奏折和宫庭教学。他的学问、道德、涵养、自律,都很好。可是他弟弟没有考上功名,只是个平民。有一天,他弟弟从家乡来到京城,探望哥哥李廷机。只见他头上戴着新的方巾(软帽),身上穿着新的衣服。廷机看见弟弟从家乡来,非常高兴,问了家里的事情,寒暄慰劳后,看着弟弟的这副打扮,非常惊讶,于是就问弟弟说:

"你是不是已经进学堂读书了,中了秀才?"弟弟回答:"没有。"他又问弟弟:"有没有考上功名?"(编者注:古代中国,考上功名后,国家就给一定的俸禄。)弟弟又回答:"没有。""那你原来的帽子到哪里去了?"弟弟说:"放在袖子里了。"李廷机说:"是这样啊。但我认为,你应该还戴原来的帽子,不应该跟着习俗戴方巾。"

于是弟弟就把方巾拿下,戴上原来的帽子。最难得的是,弟弟一点没有

贰 悌 (Respect)

bù yú kuài de yàng zi　yě sī háo méi yǒu wèi nán de shén qíng　gāo gāo xìng xìng de jiē shòu liǎo
不愉快的样子，也丝毫没有为难的神情，高高兴兴地接受了。

Li Yanji, officer of the university, was responsible for tutoring the son of the emperor, filing reports for the future Emperor to read as well as teaching the staff of the royal court. He had great knowledge, morality, discipline and self-restraint. However, his brother failed the test and is nothing but a normal folk.

One day, his brother came from home to the city, wearing kerchief and brand-new outfit, to visit him. Li was very glad to see his brother and asked him about how things are going at home. He was surprised by the look of his brother, so he asked,

"Have you succeeded in the test?" His brother replied, "No." The he asked, "Have you gotten the scholarly honor on official rank?" (In ancient China, if one gets scholarly honor on official rank, they will receive some subsidy from the government) Again his brother said, "No." "Then what happened to your hold hat?" "Under my sleeves." Then Li said to his brother, "I see, but I think you should wear the old one instead of kerchief."

Hearing that, his brother took the kerchief down and put on the old hat. To his astonishment, his brother was not bothered by this at all. Instead, his brother was quite happy about that.

【点评】

zài yī bān rén kàn lái　zuò wèi méi yǒu gōng míng de dì di dào jīng chéng kàn wàng zuò dà guān de gē ge　kè
在一般人看来，作为没有功名的弟弟到京城看望做大官的哥哥，刻
yì zhuāng bàn yī fān　zhè zài rén qián kě yǐ xiǎn dé tǐ miàn yī xiē　yǐ miǎn gěi gē ge zào chéng bù hǎo de yǐng
意装扮一番，这在人前可以显得体面一些，以免给哥哥造成不好的影
xiǎng　zhè běn lái shì wú kě hòu fēi de　dàn lǐ tíng jī cóng ài hù dì di de běn yì chū fā　bù rěn dì di luò xià
响。这本来是无可厚非的。但李廷机从爱护弟弟的本意出发，不忍弟弟落下
ràng shì rén xiào huà de míng shēng　duì dì di jìn xíng liǎo yī fān xún xún shàn yòu de quàn dǎo　dì di tīng liǎo
让世人笑话的名声，对弟弟进行了一番循循善诱的劝导。弟弟听了，
chéng kěn bìng yú kuài de jiē shòu liǎo gē ge de yì jiàn　huàn huí liǎo zhuāng shù　zhè zhǒng　zhǎng yòu zhī jié
诚恳并愉快地接受了哥哥的意见，换回了装束。这种"长幼之节"，
kān chèng kǎi mó
堪称楷模。

In our eyes, there is nothing wrong for a brother that has nothing dresses up to see his brother holding a great position in the royal court so that his brother won't be the laughing stock because he has a loser brother. However, Li Yanji is not ashamed of his brother at all and encourages him to be who he is. After the exhortation, his brother gladly changed his look back. We should always set examples for the younger generation to follow suit.

严凤敬兄
Yán Fèng Jìng Xiōng

【出处】《太上感应篇》：严凤宴客，进箸(zhù)稍迟，兄批其颊(jiá)，欣然受之。

【释义】 族兄在严凤宴请客人的场面上打他的脸，严凤还是一如既往地敬爱族兄。

【Definition】 Yan Feng's cousin slammed him in front of guests, but Yan Feng respected him as usual.

【造句】 严凤敬兄的故事，是人们一生修身、养性、处事、为人的好教材。

【Example】 The story "Yan Feng Jin Xiong" is collected in textbook, and it's one of the famous 24 Respect stories.

【故事】

明朝严凤，天性非常的孝、悌，照顾他的兄长如同对待父亲一般。后来，在朝廷做官的严凤，当他年纪大时告老还乡，看到族兄已经年老了，而且家里很穷苦，他就把族兄请到自己家里奉养着。每逢家中宴请客人，严凤就请族兄走在前头，由哥哥拿着酒杯来敬客人的酒，他自己就像个仆人一样，跟在族兄后面手拿筷子，以便哥哥敬酒后吃菜用。

一天，严凤又宴请客人。严凤的族兄和客人碰杯后，想夹菜吃，回转身来拿筷子。可严凤当时还没把筷子准备好，族兄大怒，立即朝严凤一巴掌扇过去。当时，谁都以为严凤肯定受不了这个，但严凤仍旧谨慎谦和，接受族兄的怒气，一点也没有不愉快的样子，仍然在酒席上谈笑自如，直到宴请结束，宾客尽欢。

贰 悌 (Respect)

这次请客,严凤的族兄喝得大醉,严凤就亲自将他扶回了卧室。第二天,天还没亮,严凤因为记挂着年岁已高、还躺在床上的族兄,就早早地来到了他的床前,问候道:"哥哥感觉还好吗?昨天喝得还愉快吗?一夜睡得可好?"根本没把昨天被打的事放在心上。

就这样,严凤尽心尽意地关心、照顾着族兄,侍奉族兄到终老天年。严凤因族兄去世,感到很痛苦,哭得非常悲伤,并遵照礼节,为族兄操办了隆重的葬礼。

Yan Feng, officer at royal court in Ming Dynasty, was a filial kid who respects his brothers very much. When he retired from the royal court and went back home, all his brothers were old and poor. Then he decided to take all his brothers in and served them with his heart and soul. He put himself in the position as a servant. He is often the one that holds his brothers chopsticks when they need them.

One day, Yan set up banquets to welcome the guests. One of his brothers turned around waiting for Yan to give him the chopsticks, only to find he was not there. He was very angry and slapped Yan on the face. Everyone there thought Yan would grow so angry but he didn't say or do anything. Instead, he acted as he is any other day, talking and having fun with guests.

The brother got very drunk after this banquet and Yan carried him all the way back to bed. The next day, Yan woke up early to check up on his brother. He asked, "How are you feeling? Did you have fun last night? How did you sleep? " Like he had never slapped him last night.

He kept serving his brothers like this till they all passed away. He wept sadly when his brothers passed away and held huge funerals for each of them.

【点评】

严凤对待族兄的态度，是无可挑剔的。即使哥哥当着客人的面打了他耳光，他也不计较；尽管他族兄的言行是错误的，但严凤对这个根本不在意，一如既往地敬爱和顺从族兄。他的修养就是这么高，所以令人敬佩。

The way Yan treated his brothers is very admirable. Even one of them slapped him in front of all the guests, he let it go. Wrong as his brother's doing was, he didn't hold a grudge to him. Instead, he chose to serve his brothers with love and obedience. That's what makes admirable.

叁 仁

Benevolence

仁，是儒家道德的基础与核心，它的本质是仁爱与正义，具体的外在表现为合乎"天理"。古代中国的"礼"，是合乎天理的节文；人只要守礼，便可顺"天理"，达到"仁"的境地。当今社会尽管鼓励多元发展，但依然不能忽略对别人的尊重这个"礼"，同时注重约束自我，使言行合乎道德观念和风俗习惯，就是做"仁义之事"。

就这个意义而言，"仁"就是对自己有节制、言行合乎礼法。对仁的理解，孔子要求"克己复礼"。一个人如果能克制私欲合乎礼法，就会得到别人的赞扬，但达成"仁德"是全靠自己的，而不能靠别人。有道德修养的人，无论何时何地、环境好坏、匆忙与否，都不会背离仁道，否则就不是君子了。有大志和有仁德的人，在关键的时候，不因为保全性命而损害仁道,而只会牺牲性命来成就仁道。

"仁"以"爱"为基本内涵,构建一个充满"仁爱"的和谐社会,一直是中华民族的不懈追求。中国传统的仁爱精神,追求人与人、人与社会、人与自然的协调与和谐,为现代社会文明提供了丰富的可资扬弃的道德文化资源。弘扬中华民族的仁爱精神,有助于走出现实社会生活中的某些困境,化解人际、文化、价值观念方面的种种冲突和社会道德危机等问题。

仁的具体内涵十分丰富,表现在人的行为的各个方面,诸如率先垂范、为仁由己、内省、慎独、力行,等等。本篇选取的这些故事,对"仁"的丰富内涵给予了生动的剖析,在引导人们挖掘其对当代仁爱精神的领会与培育等方面,具有现实的指导意义。

Benevolence is the basic and core of Confucian ethics. Its essence is kindness and justice. It is outwardly in accord with "heavenly principles". In ancient China, "propriety" is the abridged edition of heavenly principles. As long as people abide by the ritual, then people could comply with heavenly principles and finally achieve benevolence. Although diversified development is encouraged in today's society, "the ritual" ——respect others still can't be ignored. At the same time, we should pay attention to self-discipline in order to make our words and deeds conform to ethical ideas and customs. That is doing something kindheartedness and justice.

In this sense, "benevolence" means being self-restraint as well as words and deeds being conformed to the law and discipline rites. As for the understanding of "benevolence", Confucius asked for self-restraint and returning to the proprieties. If a person could restrain desires to conform to the law and discipline rites, he will be praised by others. But if he wants to be "kindhearted", he should do all by himself rather than relying on others. People with moral cultivation will not deviate from benevolence, no matter when and where, the environment is good or bad or whether he is in a hurry or not, otherwise, he is not a gentleman. People with ambitious and kindheartedness will not damage benevolence to save his life at crucial moment, but sacrifice himself to achievement benevolence.

"Love" is the basic connotation of "benevolence". Building a harmonious society full of "benevolence" has been an unremitting pursuit of Chinese nation. Chinese traditional spirit of benevolence is coordination and harmony between human beings, man and society and man and nature in order to provide rich and the possibility of the sublation of moral culture resources for modern social civilization. Promoting the spirit of "benevolence" is to help out some problems in real social life and to resolve conflicts between interpersonal, culture and values and solve social moral crisis and other issues.

Benevolence with rich connotations is manifested in all aspects of human behaviors, such as leading by examples, "benevolence depending on oneself", self-examination, inner concentration, practicing diligently and so on. The stories selected in Reader·Benevolence giving a vivid analysis of the rich connotation of "benevolence", which is of great realistic significance for guiding people to find the contemporary understanding of benevolence and cultivation.

以德报怨

Yǐ Dé Bào Yuàn

【出处】《论语·宪问》：以德报怨，何如？子曰：何以报德？以直报怨，以德报德。

【释义】 不记别人的仇，对于怨恨，以正直的心态对待，用恩惠的方式报答。

【Definition】 Do not show grudge while treat grudge with integrity and kindness.

【造句】 在这个关键的时候，我们应当以德报德，就有助于修好双方关系。

【Example】 At this critical moment, we should return good for evil so as to restore the good relationship between both sides.

【故事】

战国时，梁国与楚国交界的边境县的县令这个职务，由梁国的大夫宋就担任。当时，梁、楚两国都设有边亭。住在两国边亭的人员，各自开垦了一些瓜田。

梁国边亭的百姓十分勤劳，经常给瓜田浇水灌溉，他们种的瓜长势很好。可是，楚国人因为懒惰，给瓜田浇水灌溉的次数少，他们种的瓜长势不好。出于妒忌，楚国人趁天黑偷偷去糟蹋梁人的瓜苗。偏不凑巧，这事被梁亭的人员发觉了，立即向宋就报告并请求：允许他们也去糟蹋楚人的瓜苗。宋就说："仇怨是灾祸的根由。因为别人嫉妒你，你就去报复别人，这是偏激的做法，要不得。"

随后，他就安排人每晚悄悄地去为楚人浇瓜。这样，在梁人的帮助下，楚亭的瓜田长势一天比一天好起来。楚人感到奇怪，便暗中察访，发现是梁人干的。楚国人因此很受震撼，就把这件事报告到楚国朝廷。

叁 仁 (Benevolence)

楚王听到这件事,感到很惭愧,知道自己的百姓糊涂,做了错事。同时,楚王对梁国人能暗中忍让感到非常佩服,就派人带着丰厚的礼品向梁国边亭人员道歉,并请求与梁王交往。

原来,楚国与梁国的关系最初融洽,是从宋就妥善处理边亭瓜田事件开始的。《老子》说:"用恩惠来回报别人的仇怨",说的就是这一类事情。

In the Warring States Period, the county magistrate of the State of Liang, Song Jiu (a senior official in feudal China) took charge of the border county between Liang State and Chu State. At that time, there was a border area in the territorial boundary. People lived in that area reclaimed some melon patch.

In that area, Liang people were industrious. They watered the melon patch, and the melons paid back by growing well. However, Chu people were lazy. They seldom watered the melon, and got no harvest. Because of jealousy, Chu people spoiled the melons in Liang secretly at night, which was witnessed by Liang people. Liang people reported to Song Jiu, and asked him to allow them to fight back. Song Jiu replied:"Hatred is the cause of disaster. It is extreme and unacceptable to revenge."

After that, Song Jiu assigned people to water for Chu people every night secretly, which helped Liang people's melons growing much better. Chu People felt surprised, and found it was from the help of Liang People. So they reported it to the imperial court of Chu.

After hearing that, the Emperor Chu felt ashamed for what his people did, and admired Liang people for their tolerance. He gave generous gifts and apologized to Liang people, and asked for the diplomacy to Emperor Liang.

That's the start of the harmonious relationship between Chu and Liang. The saying "treat grudge with integrity and kindness" from Laozi, talks about this sort of acts.

【点评】

以德报怨,与人和睦相处,是一种修行。修行要从自己做起,能吃亏。俗语说"吃亏是福"。但是,虽然吃亏,却不糊涂;肯放弃自私自利,不怕吃亏,甘于忍受,这是一种仁德;别人不尊敬、不帮助他,他却能尊敬并且乐意帮助别人(包括伤害过他的人),这需要有仁义的品质:真正的慈悲为怀、希望众生得福、尽心舍己为人的人,说的是宋就这种人。

Returning good for the evil is a practice. One should start from his own practice and learn to suffer losses. As the old saying goes, "a loss is a blessing." Though he suffers losses, he is not stupid; instead, he is willing to give up his own interests; he is endure and never afraid of suffering losses. This is a kind of humanity. Though others don't respect and help him, he still can respect and be willing to help others (including person who once hurt him). Someone needs a quality of humanity and justice: really being filled with benevolence; hoping all to be blessed and sacrificing his own interests for the sake of others. Song jiu is that kind of person.

叁 仁 (Benevolence)

韩信报恩
Hán Xìn Bào Ēn

【出处】《史记·淮阴侯列传》:汉韩信少贫,在淮阴城钓鱼,有漂(piǎo)母见其饥,饭之。后信为楚王,召所从食漂母,赐千金。

【释义】 韩信一直感念家乡老婆婆对自己的帮助,发迹后报答了她对自己的恩情。

【Definition】 Taking account of the help from an old lady in his hometown, Han Xin pays a debt of gratitude to her after his success.

【造句】 韩信报恩的故事告诉我们:守信,是做人的根本。

【Example】 The story about Han Xin's gratitude to the old lady implies that faith-fulness is the fundamental philosophy in life.

【故事】

韩信是西汉的开国功臣。小时候,家里很贫穷,常常衣食没有依靠,虽然跟着哥哥嫂嫂住在一起,他只能吃些剩饭剩菜过日子。小韩信白天帮哥哥干活,晚上刻苦读书,也勤奋练武,但一向挑剔、无情的嫂嫂非常讨厌他读书,认为读书耗费了灯油,又没有用处。在家得不到温暖,韩信只好流落街头乞讨,更加经常吃不饱,过着非常贫困的生活,受尽了别人的冷眼。有个贫苦的老婆婆,她靠帮别人洗衣服来谋生,见韩信可怜,很同情他,就把自己的饭菜分给韩信吃,天天都是这样,还鼓励他读书。对老婆婆的一片心意,韩信很感激,动情地对老人说:"以后我一定要好好地报答您!"老婆婆听了,笑着说:"我是看你小,可怜你,才给饭吃你,难道还稀罕你的报答吗?"

但是,韩信一直记着这个婆婆的恩情。后来,他学业有成,为刘邦打天下立了大功,被封为楚王,在费尽周折之后,终于找到了这个老婆婆,就专门给她老人家送去千两黄金,还将老人接到自己的王府里吃、住,像对待自己的母亲一样。

Han Xin was the founder of the Western Han dynasty. In his childhood, his family was very poor. Though he lived with his brother and sister-in-law, he got along on leftovers. Little Han Xin helped his brother work during the day. At night, he studied very hard and practiced Wushu diligently. However, his sister-in-law was fastidious and ruthless, and always hated him reading a book, and thought that reading a book not only waste the lamp-oil but also was of no use.

He didn't feel ease at home, so he had to beg for food on the streets. He lived a very poor life often not having enough to eat and suffering cold-slighted. There was a poor old lady. She made a living by helping others to wash clothes. She saw poor Han xin and sympathized with him, so she shared her meal with Han xin every day. She also encouraged him studying. Han xin was very thankful to the old lady. He said to her, "I will pay a debt of gratitude for you in the future." The old lady smiled and said, "I help you because you are a little poor boy, I sympathize with you and share my meal with you. I couldn't care less about your rewards."

However, Han xin always remembered the old lady's kindness. Later, he achieved success. He was appointed as the King of Chu because he made great contributions when fighting a battle for Liu bang. After great efforts, he found the old lady and sent one thousand golds for her specially. He also received the old lady to his own palace, treating like his own mother.?

叁 仁(Benevolence)

【点评】

济困、报恩，都是中华民族的传统美德。韩信在困顿时，因为受过洗衣老大娘的好处，所以表示将来要报答她老人家的恩情，这很正常。别人对自己有帮助，不管多么微小，都应当时刻牢记在心；在有能力时，就给予回报，用一颗感恩的心去待人接物：这也是人之常情。虽然，"滴水之恩涌泉相报""一饭千金"也许一般人很难做到，但在条件允许的基础上真诚地回报他人，是值得提倡的。

Helping the poor and paying gratitude are the traditional virtues of Chinese nation. When Han xin was in trouble, he gained kindness from the old lady, which means he should repay her kindness in the future. This is very normal. If other people once helped ourselves, no matter how tiny the help was, we should always keep in mind. When we have the ability, we should pay gratitude and treat others with a thankful heart. This is very natural. Though it is hard for us to do just like the old sayings goes, "little help brings much return." and "pay back a debt of gratitude with rich reward." It is worth to advocate returning to others when it is allowed.

与人为善
Yǔ Rén Wéi Shàn

【出处】《孟子·公孙丑上》：取诸人以为善，是与人为善者也。

【释义】 善意地给予别人帮助。

【Definition】 Kindly help other people.

【造句】 他的心地很好，经常与人为善。

【Example】 It is very kind of him to often help others.

【故事】

宋代的王旦与寇准，同朝为官。王旦做宰相主管中书省，寇准做宰相副职负责枢密院。但这两个人性格截然不同，常有摩擦。在皇上面前，寇准屡次说王旦的短处，而王旦却极力称赞寇准的长处。

有一天，真宗笑着对王旦实话实说："在我面前，你常常称赞寇准的长处，但是他却专说你的短处呢。"王旦回答说："我在相位参与国家大事的时间久了，难免有许多缺点和失误的地方。寇准在您眼皮子下做事、说话，没有隐瞒，由此更见他的忠直，我所以才一次又一次地推荐他。"从这以后，真宗皇帝就更赏识王旦了。

一次，中书省有文件送到枢密院，但不符合诏书的格式。寇准就向真宗报告了这件事，王旦因此受到了责备，中书省的官吏也受到了处分。不久后，枢密院也有文件送中书省，同样不符合诏书格式，中书省的官吏很高兴地呈送王旦，认为报复的机会来了。可是王旦并不上奏，而是送回枢密院请更正。寇准十分惭愧，就去拜见王旦说："您真是有天大的度量啊。"

叁 仁 (Benevolence)

寇准被免去枢密院的职位后,曾私下求王旦提拔他为相,王旦惊异地回答说:"国家任命将相这样重要的官员,怎么可以走后门呢?"寇准心中觉得很不愉快。可是过后不久,朝庭宣布授予寇准任节度使同平章事。寇准入朝拜谢说:"如果不是承蒙陛下的知遇提拔之恩,我哪有今日的地位?"皇上这才告诉他说:"这是王旦又一次推荐的结果。"寇准听了,内心非常惭愧地感叹,觉得自己的品德、度量远远比不上王旦。

王旦这样的与人为善,宽容地对待同僚之间的摩擦,不仅消除了彼此之间的隔阂,确保了政坛稳定,还用自己的高尚情操,"善"出了政绩卓著的一代名相寇准。

Wang Dan and Kou Zhun were both officials in Song Dynasty, Wang the prime minister heading Central Secretariat and Kou a deputy prime minister in charge of Privy Council, but they had totally different characters, which sometimes caused conflicts between them. Kou spoke evil of Wang in front of the emperor for many times while Wang always tried to praise Kou's virtues.

One day, Emperor Zhenzong said to Wang, "it's quite funny that you've always tried to tell me how good Kou Zhun is, but in fact he only told me your mistakes." Wang said to the emperor: "I've been in the position of prime minister and dealing with the state affairs for so many years that it is inevitable that I may have made some mistakes. Kou reported every detail to you manifests that he is loyal and straightforward. And this is one of the reasons why I recommend him to you form time to time." After this conversation, Emperor Zhenzong appreciated Wang even more.

Once, some official files of Central Secretariat that did not meet the requirements of imperial edict was delivered to Privy Council. Kou report this to Emperor Zhenzong and then he blamed Wang and punished the other officials of Central Secretariat. Before long, some official files of Privy Council was sent to Central Secretariat and they did not meet the requirements of imperial edict, either. The officials of Central Secretariat was happy that they could finally get some revenge. However, after Wang get these files, he did not send them to the emperor but return them to Privy Council for them to correct. When Kou knew about this, he felt very ashamed for what he did and so he paid a visit to Wang and said to him, "you are so forgiving and broadminded".

Later, when Kou was dismissed from his position in Privy Council, he asked Wang in private to help him to be a prime minister. Wang said out of surprise, "generals and ministers is so important to our country. How can you pull the string to get the position?" Kou felt displeased about his answer. But before long, Kou was promoted as a prime minister. He said to the emperor, "thank you, Your Majesty. I can never reach this position without your promotion." The emperor told him that it was because Wang recommend him once again. Kou thus felt so embarrassed and realized that he could not compare with Wang in morality nor tolerance.

Wang always kindly help others with good intentions and dealt with the conflicts with his colleagues with tolerance, which not only dissolved the misunderstandings between them but also contributed to the stability of the political status. With his lofty morality and kindness, Wang brought the state an outstanding and distinguished prime minister.

【点评】

王旦与寇准同为北宋真宗皇帝时期的宰相，都得到器重。但是他们的性格、才能、表现、贡献却并不相同。这个故事告诉我们：人力资源管理理论所倡导的"要素有用"原理和"人才互补"效应，并非强调完美要素之间的整合或互补，而是要重视扬长避短式的人才开发与配置策略，从而达到最后的整体效益大于所有个体相加之和的效用。

Wang Dan and Kou Zhun have different characteristics, talents, performance and distributions, but the two prime ministers were both highly regarded by Emperor Zhenzong of Northern Song Dynasty. This story tells us that Elements Useful Theory and Complementary Talents Effect advocated by Human Resource Management Theory does not mean that every element should be perfect but that we should exploit the advantages and avoid the disadvantages when we search and use talents so that the overall efficiency can surpass the sum of individual utilities.

叁 仁 (Benevolence)

雪中送炭

Xuě Zhōng Sòng Tàn

【出处】《大雪送炭与芥隐》:不是雪中须送炭,聊(liáo)装风景要诗来。

【释义】 下雪天给人送炭取暖,即在别人急需时给予物质或精神的帮助、鼓励。

【Definition】 Offering fuel in snowy weather is indeed a timely help, support and encouragement to someone.

【造句】 今天气温忽然下降,妈妈给我送来了衣服,真是雪中送炭啊!

【Example】 Today, the temperature dropped sharply and my mother sent me warm clothes. What a timely help!

【故事】

这是发生在宋朝皇帝宋太宗身上的故事。

宋太宗继位后,生活十分节俭,但对百姓却毫不小气,也很同情、照顾老百姓。有一年,冬天很冷,天降大雪,太宗在皇宫中,穿着狐狸皮外套还觉得冷,就命人送来火盆、美酒。他一边喝酒,一边观赏着宫外大雪飘飘,心想:这么冷的天,那些缺粮少炭的人家更加难过吧?

于是,他把负责开封政务的最高长官召进宫来,当即说:"现在这么冷,我们这些吃穿不愁的人都觉得冷,那些缺衣少食、没有木炭的百姓肯定更加难过日子。你现在就带人拿了衣食和木炭去城里走走,去帮助帮助那些无衣、无柴、缺吃的百姓。"

开封府长官接受命令后,立刻带人拿着衣服、粮食和木炭,去问候那些贫困的百姓。受到救助的人都很感激。因此,历史上便留下了"雪中送炭"的千古佳话。

This is a story about Emperor Taizong of Song Dynasty.

After Emperor Taizong of Song Dynasty ascended the throne, he practiced thrift in his private life but treated civilians with generosity, sympathy and consideration. One cold and snowy winter, the emperor felt cold even in his fox-skin coat, so he ordered the servants to bring fire and wine for him to get warmer. As he drank the wine for warming and looked at the heavy snow in the sky outside the imperial palace, he thought, "in such cold days, civilians without enough charcoal must feel even colder and bitterer than I do."

So he summoned to the palace the top official in charge of the prefecture of Kaifeng, and said to him, "in these cold days, even we with good supplies feel so cold, our civilians who lack of clothes, food and charcoal must suffer more. You shall send some people to take some food, clothes and charcoal around the city to help those civilians in need."

The official took the imperial edict and then called up some servants and brought some clothes, food and charcoals to help those poor civilians. Those who benefited from the relief supplies felt so grateful. Thus, the story of "offering charcoal in snowy weather" is told for generations.

【点评】

"天下为公"是中华民族传统美德的重要规范、社会公德的最高原则。这既是领导者必须具备的品质，也是个人修养之要。它所要求的是关心他人、扶危济困，追求平等、公正，视公共利益高于一切。它的最高境界是在义利相矛盾、冲突的情况下，以"义"为重，"先义后利"乃至"公而忘私""大公无私"的自我牺牲。

叁 仁 (Benevolence)

"The world belongs to all" is an indispensible part of Chinese traditional virtues and a top principle of Chinese social morality. It is not only an quality that a leader should have, but also a must for every people to conduct himself. It means that people should care about others, help those in need, chase for equality and regard public interests as supreme. The highest state of it is that when faced with interest conflicts, people put "righteousness" in front of "interests", or people selflessly sacrifice their interests for the public.

仁义胡同

Rén Yì Hú Tóng

【出处】 《董笃行家书》:是亲不是亲,非亲却是亲。远水难救近火,远亲不如近邻。

【释义】 在山东省聊(liáo)城、山东济阳、河北迁安等地,"仁义胡同"的传说一直延续至今,教化意义深远。

【Definition】 The tale about alleyway of benevolence and righteousness comes down to people in Liaocheng and Jiyang of Shandong Province and Qian'an of Hebei Province, with significance in educating people.

【造句】 仁义胡同的故事,让我们在得与失之间淡泊名利,受益无穷。

【Example】 The story about Ren Yi Hu Tong helps us learn to be sensible to fame and fortune.

【故事】

明末清初时期,山东济阳有个叫董笃行的人,在京城做官。一天,他接到家里母亲的来信。信中说家里打算盖房子,但因为一堵墙和邻居起了冲突,要他出面说话,想借他的权势来解决这个问题。董笃行看完家书,立刻回信说:"是亲不是亲,非亲却是亲。远水难救近火,远亲不如近邻。彼此相让,才能结成好邻居。我们家修筑围墙,就让出几尺给邻居吧,这样不就解决问题了!"据传,信中还附了这样一首通俗的诗:"千里捎书只为墙,不禁使我笑断肠。你仁我义结近邻,让墙三尺又何妨?"

董母读了以后,觉得儿子说得很对,在盖房子的时候,就依儿子的话主动让出了几尺。邻居见董家这样的做法深受教育,也很感动,于是也退让出三尺宽的空地段。就这样,两家的房子中间空出了一条六尺宽的胡同。这就是有名的"仁义胡同"。

叁 仁 (Benevolence)

During the time of the late Ming Dynasty and the early Qing Dynasty, there was a famous person named Dong Duxing whose hometown is Ji yang, Shandong Province, and he worked as an governmental official in Beijing.

One day, Dong Duxing got a letter from his mother (who lived in Ji yang, Shandong Province) which said that his family had a conflict with his neighbor on the property territory when they were engaged in building house. His neighbor intended to occupied their territory by force, so his mother hoped Dong Duxing can negotiate with his neighbor on his behalf or solve the problem by his government relationship.

Dong Duxing replied his mother quickly, he said that distant water can't put out a fire close at hand, the neighbor would be helpful than the family from far away. So the neighbor would be helpful than the son. Keep benevolent and justice and got along with their neighbor would be better. Make a concession, let their neighbor do it and than the problem would be solved. "Mon, A three-inch wall means nothing, and it is not good to solve problems through my political relationship."Dong Duxing said in his letter.

After received Dong Duxing's letter, his mother changed's her mind stoping quarrel and made a concession initiatively. Seeing that, the neighbor moved and also make a same concession on it. So a broad alleyway came out between the new two houses. This is the tale about the famous alleyway of benevolence and righteousness.

【点评】

有时候，有些人是亲戚却不像亲戚，有些人虽不是亲戚却比亲戚还亲近。所谓"远水救不了近火，远亲不如近邻"就是这个意思。这个故事提醒我们：要重视和邻居的关系；与邻居交往，应学会多谦让，相互尊重，友好交流，才能和睦相处。

Distant water can't put out a fire close at hand, the neighbor would be helpful than the family from far away. The affection between blood relations might not works when the family members are far away from home but the neighbors works if he is friendly. This tale teaches us that we should attach great important to the neighbor relationship, modestly decline, respect, and get on well with our neighbors.

钱徽焚书

Qián Huī Fén Shū

【出处】《后唐书·钱徽传》:钱徽得书,取士无私,受诬(wū)不辨,出书焚之。

【释义】 负责科举考试的钱徽,对权贵来信的无理要求置之不理,因此受到诬陷被贬(biǎn),而他却不为自己辩护,并烧毁了对自己有利的证据(权贵营私舞弊的书信)。

【Definition】 Qian Hui, in charge of imperial examination of Tang Dynasty, was defamed and demoted for his indifference to unreasonable demands of dignitaries. But he did not defend himself and even burned all the letters that proved the corruption of those officials, instead.

【造句】 钱徽焚书的所作所为,是一个大丈夫应有的气度与修养。

【Example】 Qian Hui's action in burning letters shows grace and self-cultivation that a man should possess.

【故事】

唐朝时,有一个叫钱徽的人,官拜礼部侍郎。而刑部侍郎杨凭喜欢书画古董,家里收藏了很多古董。他的儿子杨浑之正准备考进士,为保考试成功,杨凭就到处托人找门路说情,不得已将一批非常珍贵的字画送给同样酷爱古玩的宰相段文昌。段文昌受了这个大贿赂,就多次写信推荐杨浑之,还亲自跑到钱徽家中说情,可是正直、公道的钱徽只表态说公事公办。翰林学士李绅也去找钱徽求情,希望能够让与自己有老交情的周汉宾考中进士。结果,钱徽坚持按照国家的制度规定来选拔人才,对权贵的不法请求都没理睬。

录取名单发布了,杨浑之和周汉宾都榜上无名。宰相段文昌因

叁 仁 (Benevolence)

为这事非常愤怒,反而用"取士以私"的罪名来弹劾钱徽,向皇帝告状说钱徽选取的进士都是一些学识浅薄的官宦子弟,皇帝就把钱徽贬到江西九江去做刺史。当时,有人为他打抱不平,知情的人都建议他:将段文昌和李绅写给他的书信呈给皇上看,认为皇上看后就明白了真相,这样他就可以洗清冤屈了。

但钱徽却说:"不能这样。我只求无愧于心,得和失都是无所谓的。做人,要修身养性,谨慎行事,怎么可以拿私人书信去为自己作证呢?"随即让亲信将这些书信都烧了。后来,因为钱徽在地方治理很有成效,再次被召回到中央任职,一直做到吏部尚书。

Qian Hui was the Ceremonial Master of Tang Dynasty, an official in charge of the Imperial Competitive Examination.

Yang Ping, the former minister of the Board of Punishments was keen on old calligraphies and paintings, and he collected a lot antiques at home. When his son Yang Hunzhi was to attend the Examination, Yang Ping walked around and looked for the related officials' help in order to make sure his son can success in the examination. For this intention, he gave away a series of very precious calligraphies and paintings to the prime minister Duan Wenchang, who was also fond of this kind of antiques. After Prime Minster Duan took Yang Ping's bribe, he wrote to recommend Yang Ping's son Yang Hunzhi for several times and he even came to Qian Hui's place to talk him into enrolling Yang Hunzhi. However, Qian Hui was an honest and fairy man, and he said that he would do it according to the official principals. Hanlin Academician Li Shen also went to Qian Hui intending to help his old acquaintance Zhou Hanbin. But in the end, Qian Hui enrolled the talents according to the official system regardless of all the illegal requests of the influential officials.

Neither Yang Hunzhi nor Zhou Hanbin was in the admission list. The prime Duan Wenchang felt so angry about that and impeached Qian Hui in official public that he enrolled the talents for his private interests. And he said to the emperor that Qian Hui enrolled people from official families but with little talents, for which he was degraded to govern Jiujiang in Jiangxi province. Some people who know about the facts advised him that he should show the emperor the letters from Duan Wenchang and Li Shen to prove that he is innocent.

However, Qian Hui replied, "I can't do this. All I need is that I have a clear conscience. Gains and losses are not that important. To conduct myself, I should be cultivated in mind and prudent in behavior. So how can I use these private letters from others to justify myself?" Then he burned all these letters. Latter, because of his merits in local governance, he was recalled to the central government and was promoted to Ministry of Personnel.

【点评】

社会生活中，暗中行贿托请、受贿徇私枉法之风盛行，无非是拉关系、结帮派，互相利用，各取所得。这种风气从古到今，无一例外，越是达官显贵，更是肆无忌惮，像故事中的宰相段文昌、制诰翰林李绅，谁敢违抗他们？但是，刚正的钱徽偏偏就不给他们面子，已是难能可贵了；更难得的是，在他受诬、被贬的时候，本来可以申辩、洗冤却不为自己辩白，还毁掉对自己有利的证据。这种心胸、度量和作为，是一般人根本做不到的。

In social life, there has always been some people who commit bribery and people who take bribery and bend the law for their interests. They practice partisan and take advantages of each others. This bad practice lasts from the ancient times to nowadays. Some high-brows are unscrupulous. Just like the prime minister Duan Wenchang and Hanlin Academician Li Shen, who dared say no to them? However, impartial Qian Hui did not buy it, which is good enough; even more valuable of him is that when he was framed and degraded, he destroyed the evidences that is beneficial to him. Ordinary people can hardly do it nor match his breadth in mind, tolerance and conduct.

叁 仁 (Benevolence)

于义决讼
Yú Yì Jué Sòng

【出处】《隋书·于义列传》：于义决讼，分与家财，安等愧耻，风化大开。

【释义】 于义对张、王二人钱财争夺案的判决，对安武当地的子民教育深刻，并使那里的人们相互友爱、互助、同情的崇仁尚德的风气盛行。

【Definition】 Yu Yi passed judgment on money dispute between Mr.Zhang and Wang, which educated the local citizens of Anwu so that the trend spread that people learned to love, support and sympathize each other.

【造句】 当今诉讼，讲究以事实为依据、以法律为准绳，公平公正断案，不再适用"于义决讼"的方式了。

【Example】 The present judgment of lawsuit is based on fact and evidence rather than the method of Yu Yi's judgment in court that time.

【故事】

南北朝时，北周于谨的儿子于义，因为父亲的功劳，被封为广都县的公爵，并担任安武地方的太守。他为官执政，崇尚教化，不主张用严厉的刑罚。

安武郡里有两个人，一个叫张善安，一个叫王叔儿，为了争夺钱财把官司打到了太守府。于义接案后，说："这是我做太守的道德浅薄的缘故啊。"就把自己的家产分给来打官司的两个人，好好地劝解了一番后，叫他们离开了太守府。

于义审判这个案件的消息，很快就传遍了安武郡。张善安和王叔儿两个人一想起这件事，就都觉得很惭愧，觉得在这个地方生存没有什

me miàn zi liǎo   yú shì jiù bān jiā dào bié de dì fāng qù liǎo   cóng cǐ yǐ hòu   ān wǔ zhè gè dì fāng de fēng huà
么面子了,于是就搬家到别的地方去了。从此以后,安武这个地方的风化

rì yì hé mù 、róng qià
日益和睦、融洽。

In the year of 420 A.D to 589 A.D, there was a very famous officer named Yu Yi who advocated to improve the social environment by educating people to be love, support and sympathize each other.

One day, there were two person (Zhang Shan an and Wang Shuer)who got conflict on the money and went to Yu Yi's office hoping to give a right judgment. Instead of criticism and punishment, however, in order to set a good example for them and teach them to be kindly to each other, Yu Yi ended with it by generously sharing his own private property with them and educating them to be friendly each other.

A couple of month later, this story was spread in every the conner of the prefecture. The two persons were feel so guilty and they even moved out to other prefecture furtively. At the same time, the people there were learned a lot from it and the relationship among people were getting better.

【点评】

rén zhě wú dí   zhè jiù shì dé xìng de lì liàng   zhōng guó wén huà zì gǔ yǐ lái jiù jiǎng jiū   yǐ dé fú
仁者无敌,这就是德性的力量。中国文化自古以来就讲究"以德服

rén   zhè zài hěn dà chéng dù shàng yǐng xiǎng bìng zào jiù liǎo zhōng huá mín zú de wén huà xìng gé   zhè yě zhèng
人",这在很大程度上影响并造就了中华民族的文化性格。这也正

shì rú jiā zhī suǒ yǐ zhǔ zhāng   dé zhì rén zhèng   de chóng yào yuán yīn   yú yì jué sòng   jiù zhāng xiǎn chū zhè
是儒家之所以主张"德治仁政"的重要原因。"于义决讼"就彰显出这

zhǒng shén qí de mèi lì hé xiào guǒ
种神奇的魅力和效果。

Confucianist advocated the government to be benevolent?to the people in ancient China , so "win people by virtue" becomes a very important rule in that time. And it also influenced the character of Chinese people from one generation to another generation. What's more worth mentioning is that this kind of rule still plays an important role till today.

叁 仁 (Benevolence)

思永拾钏
Sī Yǒng Shí Chuàn

【出处】《宋史·彭思永传》:思永年幼,拾金候还;失物不索,钏坠(zhuì)袖间。

【释义】 彭思永很小的时候就能够拾金不昧;长大后明知自己的财物被人窃取却不索还。

【Definition】 Peng Siyong learned to return the lost money or bracelet to others since his childhood and he did not claim what was stolen by others.

【造句】 无论思永拾钏还是失物不索,美好的品德总是令人感动并钦佩的。

【Example】 In both the stories of Si Yong's picking up bracelet and not claiming his lost belongings, his virtue deserves our admiration.

【故事】

宋朝有个彭思永。他很小的时候,一天早起,一个人去上学,在路上捡到了一只金钏。因为不知道是谁遗失的,他就坐在那个地方,等着失主回来认领。过了一会,那个遗失金钏的人,果然一路找来了。小思永对他仔细盘问了一番,确定那只金钏是他的,于是就把金钏还给他。失主觉得这个小朋友心地很好,就想给些钱来酬谢他。彭思永笑着拒绝说:"假使我心里喜欢钱,那就会把捡到的金钏藏起来,不还给你了。"

后来,彭思永长大了,完成了学业,准备赶考。因为家庭贫困没有现钱,他赶考的时候,随身只拿了几个手镯,准备典当后用作路费。一同参加科举考试的,还有其他好几个人,晚上住在一个旅店里,因为彭思永人缘好,大家都去拜访他。由于没有什么招待客人,他就拿出自己的手镯给大家赏玩。客人中有一个人起了贪心,将一个镯子悄悄地藏在自己的衣袖里。大家尽兴后,在收回去点数的时候,发现少了一只,大家就到处寻找。彭思永这时却说:"我的镯子没有少呵,本来就只有现在这个数。"于是,客人们依次拱手离去,轮到衣袖里藏了镯子的客人抬手作揖时,一个不小心,藏在他衣袖里的那个镯子就滑落掉在地上了。彭思永当作什么都没有发生,只顾满脸笑容地回礼,恭送大家离开。

彭思永就是这样一个人。凡是认识他的人,都佩服他的善良与宽宏大度。

In Song Dynasty, there was a man, named Peng Siyong. In his childhood, one day, he went to school alone in the morning, and he picked up a gold bracelet by accident. Since he didn't know who lost it, he sat in that place waiting for the loser. After a while, the loser came back. Little Siyong gave the bracelet back to him after careful inquire. The loser thought the little boy was kind, so he gave some money as the reward. Peng Siyong refused with smile and said, "If I love money in my mind, I would not return it."

Later on, Peng Siyong grew up and finished his school work. He prepared to take the imperial examinations. Because his poor family, he just carried several bracelets as the travelling expanses on his ways. Along with him, there were several other people. During the night, they lived in an inn. Peng Siyong was kind and popular, and everyone went to visit him. Since there was nothing to entertain guests, Peng Siyong took his bracelets for everyone to enjoy. Among the guests, there was a man in greedy and took a bracelet quietly hid in his sleeve. When they returning back the bracelets, they found that there was one missing, so everyone looked for it. At that time, Peng Siyong said, "I

叁 仁(Benevolence)

didn't lose anyone of them. It has the number as it was."

Then, guests bowed and left successively. The bracelet dropped down to the ground from the guest who hided the bracelet in the sleeve by accident. However, Peng Siyong regarded as nothing happened and smiled to say goodbye to everyone.

Peng Siyong was such a person. All admired his kindness and generosity.

【点评】

对彭思永的待人接物的表现,有人这样评价:在无人知道真相的前提下,见到值钱的东西却不据为己有,难得,尤其是未成年的人,能做到这一点,更是不容易;明知自己的财物被人窃取却不索还,反而为对方遮羞、打圆场,避免当事人当面出丑,要做到这一点,本来就难得了,何况当时彭思永的家穷得在他赶考时只能用几只手镯典当着用,在这样的困顿中,他却"失物不索",更是难得中的难得。由此看来,彭思永是个确实有雅量、有仁德、讲仁义的人。

Someone comments on Peng Siyong's behaviors like this: it is hard not to take the valuable things as one's own, which no one knows the truth, especially for the child. Knowing that other people steal his possessions, he won't claim to return back but to cover the truth for others, in order to avoid losing the stealer's face, which is hard to do this, let alone the poor family of Peng Siyong. On this occasion, he even does not claiming his lost belongings, which is rather rare. From this, Peng Siyong is indeed a person with generosity, kindhearted, justice and humanity.

汉宾惠人

Hàn Bīn Huì Rén

【出处】 《旧五代史·唐书·列传》：汉宾善政，感物降神，丧葬婚嫁，博济惠人。

【释义】 朱汉宾为官善于处理政务，与人交往乐善好施，他的业绩感动天地，一生的所作所为，惠及贫苦大众。

【Definition】 Zhu Hanbin was good at handling governmental affairs and very kind to people, so he had affected the poor people with his amazing achievements.

【造句】 汉宾惠人的故事，对当今的地方官员来说，是一面生动的镜子。

【Example】 To current officials in local government, Han Bin's story sets a good example.

【故事】

五代时，后梁国有一个勤政为民、声誉很好的人，叫朱汉宾。他做地方官，走到哪里，那里的老百姓就受益。因此，被称为"仁德"之人，是老百姓的"福星"和"救星"。

当时，后梁国的潞州（今山西长治）、晋州（今山西临汾）都闹蝗虫灾害，没有办法治理，地方官换了一拨又一拨。那时候，朱汉宾先做了潞州节度使，后来又调到晋州做地方官。奇怪的是，他每到一个地方任职，当地稻田里的蝗虫就都飞出他所治理的地界。

再后来，他被派到平阳这个地方任职。这里本来已经干旱很久了，田地都开裂了。可是，他来上任后不久，凑巧得很，天老爷竟然下了一场很大的雨，田地里的庄稼不但得救了，而且获得个丰收年。

86

叁 仁 (Benevolence)

朱汉宾告老还乡后，对那些家里穷苦的人，如有办不起丧葬的，就给他们棺木具殓；有办不起婚嫁的，就资助他们钱财。受着他恩惠的总共有好几百家，大家都很称赞他的仁德。

Zhu Han bin, an assiduous government officer who provided good service for people, was well known in the year of 202 AD. It was said that no matter where he stay, the people there would be get benefit from him. So he was also called "the god of the local people."

One day, there was a village got locust infestation and many officers were came together to take measures to solve it but no good results. While after Zhu Han bin was assigned to there, the locust all fly away in a night suddenly.

After that he was assigned to another village where there had no raining for a long time and the field were deeply cracked, fortunately, a big rain falls down as he arrived the village, and all the people there were got a good harvest in that year.

Years later, Zhu Han bin got old, retired and returned to his hometown. He was also very kind to people there and loved to do charitable things. Once the people got problems he would help them as possible as he could.

【点评】

本来，"为官一任，造福一方"是理所当然的。朱汉宾不仅恪守职责，而且树立起榜样。他一生勤于政事、体恤百姓、一心为民的德行，在老百姓心中打下深刻的烙印。做官做到这个地步，并在老百姓心目中获得很好的口碑，不愧为"父母官"的称号。

As an officer, he must good at handling governmental affairs and bring benefit to the people. Zhu Han bin did it. He took the responsibility to do it and also set a good example of it. He was really a good officer.

善有善报

Shàn Yǒu Shàn Bào

【出处】《新酒肉文》：行十恶者，受于恶报；行十善者，受于善报。

【释义】"善有善报"常与"恶有恶报"连用，意思是：做好事就会得到好的报应。

【Definition】 Virtue is its own reward, in contrast with that evil is rewarded with evil, means that good deeds may redound the doer.

【造句】 罗伦基创作的《善有善报》这部歌剧，堪与莫扎特的歌剧相匹敌。

【Example】 La Fedelta Premiata composed by G.B.Lorenzi can be compared to the operas of Mozart.

【故事】

古时候，有个姓刘的妇女，因为丈夫早死，她独自抚养孩子。白天在田里劳动，晚上就点着蜡烛在织布机上织布，日子倒也过得比较平和、舒服。平时，她依靠自己辛勤劳动所得，经常助人为乐，村里邻居有贫困的人家，她就拿些粮食去接济他们，或者把自己的衣服送给邻居。邻居们都说她太善良了，可她的儿子却不理解母亲为什么这样做。她就教育儿子说："对别人好是做人的本分，谁没有一些不顺心的事呢？在别人不顺心的时候，要对别人好，能帮助的就尽量帮助。"

后来，刘氏去世了。在她死后三年的某一天，刘家着了火，衣服、房屋都被烧毁了。邻居们都主动给刘家孩子送来衣物，并为刘家砍树建房子。到这时，刘氏的儿子才明白母亲为什么做善事。

叁 仁 (Benevolence)

Liu was a widow but very hardworking and friendly to people. She raised her son and lived a good life own with no helping from others. At the daytime, Liu worked in the field while in the night she weaved on the machine.

Once she got a good harvest, she would distribute some to the poor nearby. All the neighbors were moved and kept extolling of her kind. When her little son asked her "Mom, why don't you keep your private property in your own, and you are always so tired?" She said to her son: "there is not always rose in one's life, and it is not easy for people to live better." And she also educated her son that everyone might get in trouble in life, but if they help, support each other, all the problems can be solved easier, so we'd better help them as much as possible.

Three years later, her house got fire suddenly and all the things were broken. Hearing the fire diaster, all the neighbors had get helped from Liu before were came and gave a hand to her family. Some of them brought food and clothes to her, others brought some wooden to her, and some even helped her build a new house.

【点评】

人生中，每一件事情，都有转向的可能，关键在于怎么"转"。就在这"一转念"之间，生命可能从此不同。正如《爱的奉献》歌词所写："只要人人都献出一点爱，世界将变成美好的人间。"爱，无处不在，不但温暖别人，也温暖自己。人人需要爱，世界更需要爱。让世界充满爱，是每一个有仁义道德的人应尽的责任。

Just as the Chinese song goes, "if everyone can contribute a piece of love, the world will become a paradise." And virtue is its own reward. We need to remember this kind of rule. keep friendly to each other, help each other and make our world better.

肆 義

Righteousness

诗云:"大江东去,浪涛尽,千古风流人物。"在众多的文臣武将、诗人骚客中,有成功者,有失败者;有重义者,有忘义者。那么,什么是义?一指公正合宜的道理,一指亲情。但"义"之二解有时是矛盾的,比如,有人可能为了自己的亲情而有伤公道,这就不是义。

义有大、小之分。什么是大义?孟子对此早有论断:"生亦我所欲也,义亦我所欲也,二者不可得兼,舍生而取义者也。"如此之义,可舍生,不惧死,即是大义。现实生活中,有人不知义,只为自己,不为家;为自家,不为民;为自民,不为国;为自"国",不为人类之大义。其实,每个人都有守护一种民族大义、做一个真正"喻于义"的义士的责任。

那么,义的价值何在?正如北宋名相吕蒙正指出的那样:"五伦八德,非义莫能成。父子无义,则渎伦之事兴。君臣无义,则僭窃之乱作。兄弟无义,则萧墙之祸起。夫妇无义,则离异之端兆。朋友无义,则倾陷之机伏。故义者,至刚至正,有严有法,无偏无党。义之所在,懔若春雷,肃若秋

肆 义 (Righteousness)

霜,而不可犯。"我们的前人,在这方面有过杰出的表率。本篇所选的这些故事,可以给我们深刻的体念。

As the poem goes, "The endless river eastward flows; with its huge waves are gone all those gallant heroes of bygone years." Among those officials and Generals or poets and men of letter, there are winners and losers as well as men with righteousness and men of ingratitude. Then, what is Yi? Some think it refers to the principle of righteousness while the others regard it as the familial affection, but the two answers contradict each other. For example, people who damage the righteousness out of familial affection have nothing to do with Yi.

Yi varies in its significance. Then, what is Yi with great significance? Mencius the famous sage has already defined it, "Life is what I desire, and so is righteousness. If I cannot have them both, I would choose the latter and forsake the former." Such Yi is embodied in whoever disregards his own safety for righteousness. In reality, however, there are people who possess no awareness of Yi. He thinks only of himself rather than his family, or his family than the masses, or the masses than the country, or the country than the mankind. In fact, everybody have a share of responsibility of guarding the ethnic righteousness and to be a true righteous man with the awareness of Yi.

So what's the value of Yi Just as Lü Meng zheng, a famous chancellor of the Northern Song Dynasty, put it, "The five moral principles and eight virtues are based on Yi. The absence of Yi between father and son would trigger the violation of the ethical morality of respect for seniority; the absence of Yi between the monarch and his subjects would result in insubordination; the absence of Yi between brothers would cause internal strife; the absence of Yi between couples would end up in divorce; the absence of Yi between friends would destroy the friendship. Therefore, people who possess Yi are men of integrity, discipline and impartiality. Where there is Yi, there is principle formidable like spring thunder or autumn forest that cannot be violated." The predecessors have set good examples for us, which can be found in the following stories that will leave a deep impression on readers.

栾布就烹

Luán Bù Jiù Pēng

【出处】《史记·季布栾布列传》：梁臣栾布，痛哭彭王；舍生取义，就烹何妨。

【释义】 栾布为伸张正义，不顾自己的性命也要祭祀被处决的彭王，结果因祸得福。

【Definition】 Regardless his own life, Luan Bu insisted on the rituals to King Peng for justice, which turned out to be a blessing to Luan instead.

【造句】 "栾布就烹"的故事，再次说明了祸与福互相依存、互相转化的辩证关系。

【Example】 The story of "Luan Bu Jiu Peng" once again illustrates the dialectical relationships between curse and blessing interdependent and that of mutual transformation.

【故事】

西汉的栾布，是梁地人，有武艺，讲义气。当初，梁王彭越还是平民的时候，和栾布就有交往，并建立了深厚的感情。在梁王的帮助下，栾布担任汉朝梁国封地的大夫。

一次，栾布出使到齐国封地去，还没返回到梁地的时候，汉高祖召见彭越，以谋反的罪名，诛杀了他的三族，同时把彭越的头悬挂在洛阳城门下示众，还下命令说："有敢来收殓或探视彭越尸体的人，就立即逮捕。"栾布从齐国返回，得知彭越被杀，就在悬挂的彭越脑袋下面汇报自己出使的情况，边祭祀边哭泣。官吏就逮捕了他，并将这事报告了汉高祖。汉高祖责骂栾布说："你要和彭越一同谋反吗？我禁令任何人不得收尸、祭奠，你偏偏要祭他哭他，那你们一起造反就很清楚了！"于是下令架锅烧开水烹杀他。皇帝左右的人抬起栾布走向开水锅的时候，栾布回头

肆 义 (Righteousness)

说:"希望能让我说一句话再死。"

皇上同意了。栾布说:"皇上您当初在彭城被困,在荥阳、成皋打了败仗的时候,可是项王仍然不能顺利西进的原因,就是因为彭越据守着梁地,是他跟汉军联合、共同抵抗楚国军队的缘故啊。在那个关键时刻,只要彭越跟谁联合,他的对手那边就肯定惨败。再说垓下之战,没有彭越,项羽就不会灭亡。现在您的天下已经安定,彭越受了您的封号,也想把这个封爵世世代代地传下去。但陛下仅仅为了到梁国征兵,彭王因病不能够前来迎接,根本就没有任何谋反的形迹,陛下却怀疑他要谋反,随便找个借口就灭了他的家族。我担心今后每个有功之臣都会感到自己有生命危险了。现在彭越已经死了,我活着倒不如死去的好,您就烹了我吧。"

皇上听了,觉得有理,也很佩服栾布的勇气和义气,就赦免了他的罪,还任命他做都尉。到了汉文帝的时候,栾布担任燕国国相,还做了将军。

Luan Bu, a native of Liang State of the Western Han Dynasty (206 B.C.–A.D. 24), was famous for his gallantry and righteousness. Before Peng Yue, king of Liang, ascended to the throne, he had already had associations with Luan Bu and established deep friendship. With the assistance of Peng Yue, Luan Bu served as a senior officer in Liang State of the Han Dynasty.

One day, he was sent on a diplomatic mission to the Qi State, but before he returned Emperor Gaozu summoned Peng Yue and killed him together with all his kinsmen in the crime of treason, and humiliated him publicly by hanging his head on the gate of Luoyang, warning that whoever dared collect his body or mourned his death shall be arrested immediately.

When Luan Bu came back from Qi, he was informed that King Peng was executed. So he reported on his mission right under the head of King Peng, mourning and crying, which naturally attracted the guardian to arrest him and report it to the emperor.

Emperor Gaozu scolded him, "Are you engage in Peng Yue's revolt? I prohibited that nobody could collect his body or mourn for his death while you still violate it, so it is quite obvious that you are plotting a rebellion!" And he ordered to put on a pot with water and tried to boiled Luan Bu alive. As the imperial bodyguards dragged him to the boiling pot, Luan Bu turned around and said, "Shall I say a word before I die?"

The emperors agreed. "When Your Majesty trapped at Pengcheng and lost the battle in Xingyang and Chenggao, the reason why Xiang Yu cannot advanced west easily is that Peng Yue united the Han army to resist Chu. At that very moment, had Peng Yue combined with others, his opponent was doomed to fail. Without his help in Gaixia, you could not defeat Xiang Yu. After the country was secure, you conferred the title of nobility upon Peng Yue, hoping that he would hand down to his heirs for countless generations. However, Your Majesty came to the Liang State for recruitment and suspected that Peng Yue has rebelled, just because he failed to welcome you. Without any real evidence, you killed all his kinsmen. I am afraid that other officials who made contributions would feel their life is in danger. Now that Peng Yue was dead, I'd rather die with him than live. Just boil me to death!"

When the emperor heard his words, he thought it makes sense and admired his courage and loyalty, so he pardoned him and appointed him as a commander. During the reign of Emperor Hanwen, Luan Bu served as prime minster of Yan State and later as a general.

【点评】

栾布，出身社会下层，讲义气，重信用，爱打抱不平，具有侠客的个性。他知恩报恩，舍生取义，视死如归。在他身上，体现了我国古代劳动人民的许多优秀品质。他对刘邦说的一番话，理由充分，剖析深刻，很有说服力，结果因祸得福。

Luan Bu, born in the rabble, was loyal and trustworthy, and he had a character of chivalry with a sense of justice. He never took anything for granted and would die for righteousness. He epitomized the good qualities of our ancient working people. And the words he talked to Liu Bang were reasonable, persuasive and deeply analyzed, which got him good out of misfortune.

肆 义（Righteousness）

关公秉烛
Guān Gōng Bǐng Zhú

【出处】《三国演义》:关公大义,二嫂同居;秉烛达旦,终夜观书。

【释义】 作为正义的化身,关羽为了保障嫂嫂夜宿曹操兵营的安全,手持蜡烛整夜守卫在嫂嫂住宿帐篷的门口。

【Definition】 As the incarnation of justice, Guan Yu camp overnight in order to protect the safety of his brother's wife, holding candles in the night guard at the barrack of Cao.

【造句】 人们因为"关公秉烛",把赤胆忠心、义薄云天的关羽奉为"武圣人"。

【Example】 Because of the story "Guan Gong holding candle", people regard the utter devotion and the righteous spirit of Guan Yu as "Saint Wu".

【故事】

东汉末年,有个好汉叫关云长。蜀汉的先主刘备对待他像亲兄弟一样,吃饭同桌,睡觉同床。尽管如此,关公当着许多人的面,总是在刘备的旁边整日地立着。平时,他为刘备去周旋一切,无论遇到什么样的艰难危险,都毫不退避。

一次,曹操带了精兵强将,攻破了刘备驻军所在的下邳的地方城池,把刘备的妻子甘夫人和糜夫人都捉住了,同时把关公孤立在一座山上。因为关公是一个很有名的大将军,曹操很想收服他,就派了一个与关公有很好私交的叫张辽的人去劝他投降。考虑到当时的处境和自己对义兄刘备的责任,关公与张辽约定了三个条件:降汉不降曹;像原来一样照顾刘备家人；如果有刘备的消息，关羽就要回到刘备身边。曹操答应了关公的条件。当天晚上，曹操故意安排关公和二位夫人在一个房间里同住。关公把嫂嫂安排好后，自己点燃了蜡烛，就手拿烛火，站立在门外，为嫂嫂站岗警卫，直到天明，没有一丝睡意。曹操得到这个情况报告，更加敬重关羽。

In the late Eastern Han Dynasty, there was a hero named Guan Yuanchang. Liu Bei, the founding emperor of Kingdom Shu of the Han Dynasty, treated him like his own brother, sharing meals and bed with him. However, Guan Gong would always stand next to Liu Bei in presence of other. At other times he usually arranged everything for Liu Bei, and never shrank back even in face of immense difficulties.

One day, Cao Cao, with his well-trained troops, overwhelmed the garrison of Liu Bei at Xiapi and captured Lady Gan and Lady Mi. Besides, he also isolated Guan Yu in a mountain.

Because Guan Gong was a well-known general, Cao Cao attempted to subdue him so he sent Zhang Liao, who had deep friendship with Guan Gong, to persuade him to surrender. In consideration of the current situation and his responsibility to Liu Bei, he made conventions with Zhang Liao as long as his three requirements were fulfilled: first, he shall surrender to the Emperor of Han rather than Cao Cao; second, he must look after the Ladies as usual; third, he will return to Liu Bei as soon as he get the news of him.

Cao Cao agreed. But at that night, He deliberately arranged Guan Gong to share a room with the two Ladies. While Guan Gong just lit a candle and stood guard at the front door all night right after he got his sister-in-law settled and he never felt sleepy. When Cao Cao knew that, he payed more respect to him.

肆 义(Righteousness)

【点评】

关羽的一生,是扶助汉朝、安定刘家天下、尽忠竭义的一生,为刘备在魏、蜀、吴"三分天下"的角逐中立下了汗马功劳。即使在下邳之战中受困投靠曹操时,都不忘与曹操"约法三章"。为确保二位嫂嫂夜宿曹营的安全,他手持蜡烛,整夜守卫在寝室门口。这种罕见的参天大义之举,使人感到一股至大、至刚的浩然之气,充塞在天地之间。

In his whole life, Guan Yu supported Liu Bei to secure the state and made marvelous contributions in the competition among Wei, Shu and Wu, the three kingdoms of China at that time. Even when he was trapped in the battle of Xiapi and had to surrender, he still did not forget to set conditions with Cao Cao. He camped overnight in order to protect the safety of his brother's wives, holding candles in the night guard at the barrack of Cao. This kind of rare righteous deed was filled with noble spirit.

宋弘念旧

Sòng Hóng Niàn Jiù

【出处】《后汉书·宋弘传》：宋弘既贵，念及糟糠，不尚公主，大振纲常。

【释义】 宋弘做了高官后，一直不忘与自己共过患难的妻子，不因湖阳公主对他有好感而攀龙附凤，使夫妻伦理的规范得到发扬光大。

【Definition】 After Song Hong became an important official, he never forgot his wife through adversity; he did not turn snobbish although Princess Hu Yang adored him, which made the marital ethical norms to be carried forward.

【造句】 宋弘念旧，与为人所不齿的"陈世美"的行为相比，确实有天壤之别。

【Example】 Song Hong Nian Jiu, compared with the contemptible conduct of Chen Shimei; makes a big difference.

【故事】

东汉初年，光武帝刘秀起用西汉时期的侍中宋弘，任命他为太中大夫。当时，刘秀的姐姐湖阳公主刚好守着寡又正值年轻，光武帝就和湖阳公主谈论朝廷中的大臣们，以此来试探姐姐的心思。湖阳公主说："宋公有很威严的容貌，加上他的道德品质和见识都很好，在一班臣子里没有一个能赶上他的。"

光武帝听出了姐姐对宋弘的好感和心仪，就对姐姐说："我愿意撮合这件事。"于是就召见宋弘，问他对"贵易交，富易妻"的看法："常言道，做了官，就把贫贱时候的朋友换过了；有了钱，就把穷苦时候的妻子换过了，人情上不都是这个样子吗？"

肆 义 (Righteousness)

宋弘回答说:"所谓'贫贱之交不可忘,糟糠之妻不下堂'的意思是:贫贱时交的朋友,是不可以遗忘的;同过甘苦一起吃过糟糠的妻子,是不可以离异的。这才是君子所为。"光武帝听后,很赞赏他,就回湖阳公主的话说:"我们讨论的那事情,就算了吧。"

In the early Eastern Han Dynasty, Liu Xiu, Emperor Guangwu, promoted Song Hong from the former Privy Counselor to a Senate of the loyal court. Once Liu Xiu talked with his elder sister who was a young widow about the court ministers to see if she had feelings for somebody. "Song Hong, sedately dignified in appearance, possesses good morality and insight that no one in the court can be comparable to him," Princess Hu Yang replied.

Emperor Guangwu perceived the sense of her sister's answer, so he told her that he would like to make a match. And then he called Song Hong in and asked,

"As the saying goes, people gets rid of old friends when he becomes a government official; people dumps his wife when he gets rich. Such is human nature, and what's your opinion?"

Song Hong replied, "There is also an saying that friends of hard-up days shall not be forgotten and the wife you shared hardships with shall not be abandoned. I believe that a man of virtue should act like this." Emperor Guangwu appreciated his loyalty, so he sent back word to Princess Hu Yang: "the match I discussed with you, just forget about it."

【点评】

"贫贱之交不可忘,糟糠之妻不下堂"这句中国古训,是我们做人的准则之一,也是基本底线。它揭示了朋友之间感情的难能可贵和夫妻之间爱情的忠贞不渝。在这个故事里,我们看到的是宋弘的高尚人格,他与妻子同甘共苦、不离不弃,他不慕富贵、不贪荣华,即便在至高无上的皇帝面前也是如此。这在"利欲熏心心渐黑"的现实社会中,是有着深远的教育意义的。

As the Chinese old saying goes, friends of hard-up days shall not be forgotten and the wife you shared hardships with shall not be abandoned. It is one of the basic principles in life as well as the bottom line of a man. And it also indicates the valuable friendship among friends and the faithful love between husband and wife. In this story, Song Hong shared weal and woe with his wife and never yielded to wealth or fame even in front of the supremacy of the emperor. It has far-reaching educational significance in real society where people tend to put profit over conscience.

肆 义 (Righteousness)

王修哭谭
Wáng Xiū Kū Tán

【出处】 《三国志·魏志·王修传》：王修高义，痛哭袁谭：若得收葬，全戮(lù)亦甘。

【释义】 王修是一个品德高尚、富有正义感的人，在主人袁谭被曹操杀掉后，他甘愿用全家人的性命做赌注，冒险为袁谭哭丧、收尸、安葬。

【Definition】 Wang Xiu was a person of a moral character and a sense of justice. After his master Yuan Tan was killed by Cao Cao, Wang Xiu was willing to use the family's lives at stake and took the risk of attending the funeral for Yuan Tan.

【造句】 王修哭谭，表现了他尽忠尽义的品质，同时也"哀其不幸、恨其不争"，以至自取灭亡。

【Example】 Wang Xiu Ku Tan, demonstrated his loyalty and pursuit of justice, as well as his misfortune, unwillingness to fight and his suicide.

【故事】

袁绍死后，他儿子袁谭、袁尚相互之间有矛盾，动不动就刀兵相见。袁谭手下有个人叫王修，任职别驾（汉代州刺史的副官），劝袁谭对兄弟袁尚要和睦相处，并说："兄弟之间互相攻击，这是自取灭亡的道路。"袁谭不高兴，事后又来问王修："有什么计策对付吗？"

王修继续劝说他："兄弟，就如左右手。譬如一个人将要搏斗，却砍断自己的右手，反而说'我一定胜利'，像这样可以得胜吗？背弃兄弟而不亲近，天下还有谁亲近这种人呢！现在，下属有说坏话陷害别人的人，在你们兄弟之间挑起争斗，以求得一时的私利，希望您这样明智的人塞住耳朵不要去听。如果杀掉几个这种巧言献媚的属下,兄弟之间又亲密和睦,共同抵御四方敌人,就可以称霸天下了。"

很可惜,袁谭不肯听从王修的劝导,于是和袁尚相互攻打,结果袁谭的军队战败,向曹操请求救援。曹操帮他出兵攻占冀州以后,袁谭却背叛了曹操。曹操一怒之下,便带领军队攻打袁谭。王修当时在外地运送军粮,听说袁谭处境危急,立即带着所统领的兵马和几十个贴身随从人员赶赴袁谭那里。

王修到达时,袁谭已经被曹操杀死了。王修下马大声哭诉说:"没有您我该归附谁呢?"于是去见曹操,请求收殓埋葬袁谭的尸体。曹操知道王修的能耐,想观察他的心意,故意默不作声。王修就说:"我蒙受袁氏的深厚恩情,如果能收殓袁谭的尸体,然后被杀,我没有什么遗憾。"曹操称赞他的义气,就同意了他的请求,还任命王修做督运军粮的官员。

When Yuan Shao died, his two sons Yuan Tan and Yuan Shang were always in conflict, and they easily resorted to force. Wang Xiu, a subordinate of Yuan Tan, served as Biejia (an assistant of Cishi in the Han Dynasty), persuaded him to reconcile with his brother, saying, "It would be suicidal for you two to attack each other." Yuan Tan was unhappy, but he still inquired Wang Xiu that if he has any plans to deal with.

Wang Xiu continued, "Brothers are like the arms of a man. For instance, a man is about to fight, yet he cut off his arm, so how could he succeed? No one else would come to help those who isolate or betray his brothers. If there are subordinates, who speak evil of others or deliberately provoke contradictions between you and your brother for personal gains,I hope that you could turn a deaf ear to these words. And if you kill some of those glib‐tongued men, get well along with your brother and jointly resist invading enemies, you can win the country."

肆 义 (Righteousness)

Pathetically, Yuan Tan refused to follow the advice and still attacked his brother. When he lost the battle, he turned to Cao Cao for help and captured Jizhou with the assistance of Cao Cao. However, Yuan Tan then betrayed him, causing Cao Cao to lead an army to attack him. At this moment Wang Xiu was delivering military provisions far away. Hearing that Yuan Tan was in a critical situation, he immediately headed to Yuan Tan with his troops and decades of attendants.

When Wang Xiu got there, Yuan Tan had already been killed. He got down from horse and cried, "Who else can I work for except you?" Then he came to Cao Cao to ask for collecting the body and burying it. Knowing the capability of Wang Xiu, Cao Cao kept silent to test his loyalty. Then he stated, "I own a great debt of gratitude to Yuan Tan, and if I could bury his body to repay his kindness before I die, I would have no regret." Cao Cao praised him for his loyalty and agreed his request. Besides, he still appointed him as the official who supervised the transportation of military supplies.

【点评】

王修为袁谭哭丧,是出于对袁谭最真实的感激之情和忠厚之义。这种对人的忠贞、义气,人所共仰。曹操对王修为袁谭哭丧就有很高的评价,在《与王修书》中称之为"君澡身浴德,流声本州,忠能成绩,为世美谈,名实相符,过人甚远。"可见,王修是一个义薄云天的人,受到人们敬重。

Wang Xiu lamented the death of Yuan Tan out of his gratitude and loyalty, which is quiet admirable. Even Cao Cao thought highly of him. In his article the Story of Wang Xiu, he wrote, "He is a man of morality and nobility, whose fame is spread far and wide. His deeds of loyalty is a story passed on with approval, and he lives up to his fame." It indicates that Wang Xiu is truly a man with high morality and is respected by others.

公义变俗
Gōng Yì Biàn Sú

【出处】 《隋书·循吏传》：慈母公义，欲变岷俗。与病置厅，抚摩（抚摸）情笃。

【释义】 辛公义用慈母一样的情怀哺育、感化着岷州地区的百姓，使当地陋习得以废除。

【Definition】 By nurturing and moving the people of Minzhou region like a mother, Xin Gongyi helped to abandon the bad habits of people there.

【造句】 公义变俗的故事，使人很受启发，相信科学才是硬道理。

【Example】 The story of Gong Yi Bian Su inspires people very much, which assures people that truth only comes from science.

【故事】

隋朝开皇九年，辛公义被任命为岷州刺史。在去岷州上任的途中，他暗中体察民情，目睹了一位老母亲因为得了一种怪病，被两个亲生儿子狠心地抛弃在荒郊野外。他就把这位老母亲接到了衙门中，为她请医师治病，尽心照料。

从老人口中得知，岷州有这样一个荒谬的习俗：只要家中有人不幸得了这种怪病，夫妻儿女都会狠心地将自己的亲人抛弃，亲朋好友也会远远地躲开他们家，病人只有等死。辛公义听后心里非常忧愤，决心要改掉这种恶劣风俗。

于是，他就在岷州发布这样一份公告：家中如有患这种病的人，请亲属赶快把患者送到衙门里来医治。可是公告一出，不但没有亲属送来病人，反倒有好多人在说风凉话。辛公义感到百姓还是不信任衙门，就派人去患者家中将这种病人接到衙门。并且请来当地最好的大夫，努

肆 义 (Righteousness)

力研究治疗办法，终于找到了攻克这种疫病的良方。经过他日日夜夜的悉心照料，患病的人一个个渐渐地康复了，又被送回家去。每当这个时候，辛公义就对病人的家属说："人的死生是由命运决定的，和患病人接触没有关系。以前你们抛弃患病亲人，那病人就只能等死了，这是伤天害理的，要不得。现在我把患病的人都聚集在一起，还坐卧在病人之间，如果说疾病会传染的话，我怎么就可以不死，而病人如何又能康复呢？所以说，你们再也不要相信、恐惧病人的陋俗了。以后，遇到这样的情况，要想办法医治，并照顾好病人。"患者亲属们看到自己的亲人健康地回到了自己身边，对辛大人的救命之恩无比感激，并受到很大的教育。因此，全州的百姓都称呼辛公义叫"慈母"。岷州地方的这个坏风俗因此得以废除。

In the ninth year of Kaihuang of the Sui Dynasty, Xin Yigong was appointed as prefectural governor of Minzhou. On his way to take office, he observed secretly living conditions of the people, and once witnessed an old lady abandoned by her two sons cruelly in the wild because of the weird disease she had suffered. So he took the old mother to Yamen, the place where the government performed its duty, sent for a doctor to treat her disease and looked after her attentively.

From the old lady, he knew that there was a corrupt custom in Minzhou: as long as someone unfortunately caught this disease, his families would finally abandon the patient and his relatives would stay away from this family, and the patient could do nothing but wait for the last day to come. He felt both worried and angry after hearing this and resolved to abolish this abominable custom.

So he announced an official notice in Minzhou: anyone who suffered such a disease could be sent to Yamen for treatment. However, this notice didn't work at all, but only received many sarcastic remarks. Knowing that the public didn't trust the government, he sent officers to take the patient from home to Yamen. Then he invited the best local doctor and, after arduous work, finally found the way to cure the disease. As a result, the patient, through attentive care day and night, gradually recovered one after another and was sent back home.

At this moment, Xin Gongyi would tell the family of the patient: "it is harmless to contact with the patient because life and death are decided by fate. It is unwise to abandon your sick relative to his or her own fate, for it violates the principle of humanity and mortality. Now I gathered all patients here and sat between them. If the disease is contagious, why could I remain uninfected and why the disease could be cured? So you should never follow that bad custom any more. From now on, if the same things happen, you should take care of the patient and cure the disease."

When people saw their sick relatives came back home healthily, they all expressed sincere gratitude to him. After that, people of Minzhou honored Xin Gongyi as "loving mother" and the abominable custom was thus abolished.

【点评】

现实生活中,有些疫病是会传染的。但如果因为怕被传染,连家里的亲人也弃之不顾,这无论怎么说也是没有道义的。辛公义为官,正义凛然,魄力十足,深入实际,调查研究,不遗余力地改变陋俗民风。他遵循先贤的教诲,正己化人,不怕疾病传染,排除一切困难,不仅改变了地方遗留的陋俗,而且身体力行地推行孝义,被当地百姓称为"慈母"一样的官。

In real life, it is true that some epidemic diseases are contagious. But if we abandon our sick relative just because we are afraid of being infected, it is by all means against morality and righteousness. When Xin Gongyi served as the prefectural governor of Minzhou, he worked with righteousness and tremendous courage. He made in-depth investigation through going deep into the realty and spared no efforts to help the local to get rid of corrupt custom. He followed teachings of wise men and instructed others by correcting himself first to overcome all difficulties regardless of his own safety, not afraid of being infected. Moreover, he not only helped abolish local bad custom, but earnestly practiced the principles of filial piety and righteousness, thus earning the reverent title "loving mother" by the local people.

肆 义 (Righteousness)

仲淹义田
Zhòng Yān Yì Tián

【出处】《宋人佚事汇编》：宋范仲淹,千亩义田,以济群族,衣食赖焉。

【释义】 范仲淹当宰相,用自己的俸禄买了千亩田地,分给家乡那些穷困的人耕作,用这种方式让那些族人、穷人们得以生存。

【Definition】 When Fan Zhongyan became the prime minister, he used his own salary to buy thousands of acres of farmland and donated them to those poor people for their survival.

【造句】 世人若要为子孙谋福利的话,仲淹义田的善行是值得我们效法的。

【Example】 If people want to benefit future generations, the good deeds done by Zhong Yan Yi Tian will be worth emulating.

【故事】

范仲淹是宋朝的名臣。他幼年丧父,受尽了苦难。因此,他从小读书就十分刻苦,并在青年时就立志要做一个济世安民、有益于天下的人。他到朝廷任职后,除了革故鼎新、恪尽职守、任劳任怨工作外,他一生最喜欢做的事,就是救济穷苦人家。平时,他经常救济那些邻近的穷人家;即使是一些疏远的人,如果家里很贫穷,但凡有可造之才的,他都会不遗余力地来提携他们。

他当宰相时,为赡养族人和贫困人,用自己的俸禄买了老家附近的一千亩田地,分给那些贫穷的无田地的人耕作,称为"义田"。这些人因此有事做,有衣服穿,日子过得照样和乐。如果其中有嫁女儿、娶媳妇的,或是有亡故、需要安葬的种种事情，每家每户都可以利用义田所收入的钱财得到贴补。

对"义田"的管理，范仲淹聘请族里比较贤能、做事能力比较强的人来打理，一切财物的付出和收入，都管得有条有理的。就这样，实现了他年轻时念念不忘众生利益的愿望。

Fan Zhongyan was a famous official of the Song Dynasty. He lost his father when he was young and suffered countless hardships. Therefore, he worked hard at his studies even in early childhood and determined to be a man who will benefit the people and contribute to the country.

While holding a post in court, he vigorously promoted reform and innovation in all respects and devoted to his duties diligently without any complaint. Besides, he always liked to help poor families in his whole life, such as giving a hand to those neighboring poor families. For some needy families with members of talents while kept on bad terms with, he would also spare no efforts to support them.

When served as the prime minister, in order to support his clansmen and other poor people, he bought thousand acres of land near his hometown with his own salary and distributed the land to those poor people without land to make a living, which was called as "Yi Tian". Therefore, those poor people had land to plough and clothes to wear, thus could lead a happy life. When it came to some special occasions, like marriage or funeral, every family could receive the money earned from "Yi Tian" as a subsidy.

At the same time, he appointed some virtuous and capable clansmen to manage "Yi Tian". Hence all costs and gains about "Yi Tian" were well organized and clearly listed. By doing this, he realized his dream of benefiting the common people.

肆 义(Righteousness)

【点评】

范仲淹一生存心仁厚,乐善好施。他所置的田,所有的收入并不是为自己,而是让那些贫困的人共同分享。他的仁慈之心、布施之行,不只局限在义田而已,还顾及边疆地区的人民,真正地以天下为己任。他的"先天下之忧而忧,后天下之乐而乐"名言,就是范仲淹一生为人的真实写照,被历代仁人志士奉为经典,直到今天仍然闪烁着催人奋进的思想光辉。

Fan Zhongyan was kind-hearted for whole life and always ready to help others. The land he purchased was not used for personal gains, but to share with those poor people. The kindness and charity were not only reflected in "Yi Tian", but could also find expression in his care of people living in the border area, which showed his principle of taking the destiny of the country as one's own responsibility. His saying, "To be the first in the country to worry about the affairs of the state and the last in the country to enjoy oneself", which quiet truly mirrored his whole life, has long been regarded as code of conduct by people with lofty ideals of the successive dynasties. Till today, it is still shining in the history inspiring people move forward.

苏轼还屋

Sū Shì Huán Wū

【出处】《梁溪漫志》：苏轼夜行，闻妪(yù)悲声；焚券还屋，义重缗(mín)轻。

【释义】 苏轼从设身处地的角度，为那个悲伤的老婆婆一家解除了无家可归的痛苦。

【Definition】 Su Shi put himself into the sad old lady's shoe and offered her shelter from being homeless.

【造句】 我们从苏轼还屋的行为中看到，苏轼不仅重情重义、视钱财如粪土，而且是一个善于换位思考、毫不利己的人。

【Example】 We can learn form the story of Su Shi Huan Wu that Shu Shi is a loyal person who thinks money is nothing, in addition, he is a man of good empathy and unselfishness.

【故事】

苏轼是宋朝大文学家。他从海南儋州回来，打算定居在江苏宜兴这个地方。他的一个朋友邵民瞻为他在阳羡买了一座房子，花了五百串铜钱。苏东坡掏光所有积蓄，总算勉强应付过来了。

离乔迁之日只有几天了。一个夜晚，东坡和邵民瞻在月下散步，偶然到了一处村落，听到有一位老妇人哭得很悲伤的声音。东坡靠近倾听，说："奇怪了，这妇人为什么哭得这样悲伤呢？难道有什么非常难以割舍的事使她这么伤心吗？去问问她。"

于是，循声而去，他们看见一位老太太。老太太还在哭。东坡就问她为何这么哀伤？老太太说："我本来有一栋房子，是家传祖屋，已相传百

肆 义 (Righteousness)

年，一直保存到现在。可是我的儿子不成器，将它卖给他人了。我有打算搬到这里来住，到这里才知道这老房子已经失去了，怎能不心痛呢？

苏东坡听了，也替她感到非常难过，就问她的老房子在哪里？一问得知，原来就是自己买到的那栋房子。于是安慰老太太，并对她说："老太太，您的房子是我买了。您不必难过，我将这房子还给您老人家就好了。"就拿来屋契，当着老太太的面烧了。同时告诉她儿子第二天就接送母亲回老屋住，也没向她讨回买房的钱。

Su Shi, alas Dongpo, was a great litterateur of the Song Dynasty. He came back from Danzhou of Hainan province and was going to settle in Yixing of Jiangsu province. A friend of him named Shao Minzhan took 500 strings of copper coins and bought a house for him in Yangxian. Poor as he was, Su Shi took out all savings and merely managed to meet the expending.

It was only several days left before he moved to the new house. One night, he was walking with his friend Shao Minzhan under the moonlight. When coming to a village, they happened to hear a sad crying of an old lady. So he walked close and listened, said: "it is strange. Why this old lady crying so sadly? Have she encountered something that was too hard for her? Let's ask her."

So they walked following the cries and saw an old lady. She kept crying when they walked to her. Su Shi asked for the reason. The old lady replied, "I had an ancestral house which was handed down from the older generations and has lasted for hundred years. But now my good-for-nothing son, however, sold the house where I was about to move in. And it was not until I came here did I know that this century-old house had already been sold. This is the reason why I cried so bitterly."

Su Shi also felt sad after hearing this and asked where her old house was. It turned out that it was just the house he had bought. So he comforted the old lady and said:

"Don't worry. It is me who bought the house. There is no need to grieve. I will return it to you." Then he took out the title deed of the house and burned it down on the spot. Meanwhile, he told the son to take his mother back to the old house the next day without claiming back the money.

【点评】

一般说来,买主要一件东西,肯定是看中了的;既然看中了,就必然会想法子弄到手,并倍加爱护的,而不顾及其它。对苏轼来说,一个刚从海南那个荒蛮之地流放回到江苏这样富庶之地的人,花光了所有积蓄买下一座房子,为的是一家人有个安乐窝。但在他询问、听说那老妇人的一番痛苦遭遇之后,果断地将自己已经买下的房屋退还给她,并当面焚烧了购房契约,还不索回分文。这种行为,只有重情重义、淡泊名利的人才做得到。

Generally speaking, a buyer must desire for it when he buys it; since he desires for it, he will definitely try all ways available to get it and cherish it with care regardless of the difficulties may encounter. What Su Shi wanted after being exiled from Hainan province, a land of wildness and backwardness, to Jiangsu province, a land of civilization and abundance, was to have a cozy house for his family, especially when he spent all his savings on the house. However, he resolutely returned the house and burned the title deed on the spot without claiming back anything after knowing the painful experience of the old lady. Only a loyal and righteous man who is indifferent to fame or wealth can behave like this.

肆 义（Righteousness）

孝基还财
Xiào Jī Huán Cái

【出处】《厚德录》：宋张孝基，受岳家赀(zī)，屡试其子，悉以归之。

【释义】 宋朝的张孝基，入赘(zhuì)到过家，接收岳父所有家产后，设法对被赶出家门的大舅子进行教育转化工作，最终归还全部家产给过公子。

【Definition】 After his marriage into a rich family at Song Dynasty, Zhang Xiaoji received all the property from his father-in-law. However, he tried to educate the brother-in-law who was driven out from home and returned all property to him.

【造句】 孝基还财，体现了"君子爱财，取之有道"的中华传统美德。

【Example】 Xiao Ji Huan Cai, reflects the Chinese traditional virtues of "gentle-man's love of money, in a proper way".

【故事】

宋朝的张孝基，娶了同村的富人家过善的女儿做妻子。那过员外还有一个儿子叫过迁，因为品行很不好，富翁就把他的独生儿子赶出了家门。到富翁死的时候，就把全部家产都托付给了张孝基。张孝基果然不负众望，继承了岳父的德行及家风，家业蒸蒸日上。这期间，张孝基一直对过迁的行踪明察暗访，想要找回这位大舅哥。

原来，过迁被赶出家门后，衣食无靠，流落街头，成了叫化子。他因此一次次地悔恨落泪，却没有脸面回家。张孝基有一回外出，碰巧遇见了过迁，可这时的过迁已经认不出自己的妹夫了。为了让他能够重新做人，张孝基就隐瞒了自己的身份，并打算把他带回家去种田，给他一个改过自新的机会，就问他："我家中正好有些田地需要人耕种，不知你意下如何？"过迁感激地说："我愿意，只要有饭吃、有地方睡觉，再苦再累的活我都能做。"

于是，张孝基就叫他去耕种田地。果然，他做农活很卖劲，每天起早贪黑，从无怨言。张孝基就再问他："你还能不能够管理库房呢？"他又回答说："能的，只要您信得过我。"张孝基又让他管了库房。从此以后，他更加敦厚、谨慎、勤俭。过了一段时间，张孝基觉得大舅哥已经改造好了，可以管理家业了，就把岳父所给的全部家产，统统还给了他。

Zhang Xiaoji of the Song Dynasty married the daughter of a fellow rich man named Guo Shan, who gave all the property on his deathbed to Zhang Xiaoji, for his only son named Guo Qian behaved badly and thus was driven out of home by his father. As expected, Zhang Xiaoji, carrying forward the virtues of his father-in-law and fine family traditions, managed to run the whole family more thriving and prosperous. During this time, Zhang Xiaoji also tried in many ways to find tracks of his brother-in-law in hope of bringing him back.

In fact, after being driven out of home, Shi Qian, with nowhere to go and seek refuge, was reduced to a beggar tramping on the street. Although he felt extremely regretful for the past, he was reluctant to come back home due to his self-respect. Once Zhang Xiaoji went out and came across Shi Qian who then could not recognize him. In order to help Shi Qian to make a fresh start, Zhang Xiaoji concealed his name and intended to give Shi Qian a chance by taking him home to farming, so he asked, "My family just has some land and need someone to plough. Would you like to come?" "Yes, as long as I can have food and a shelter, I would like to do no matter how hard the work is." Shi Qian answered gratefully.

Hence, Zhang Xiaoji let Shi Qian to do the farming, and it turned out that Shi Qian did his work to the best of his ability. He worked from dawn to night without any complaints. So Zhang Xiaoji asked again, "Are you still capable of managing the storehouse?" Shi Qian replied, "Yes, if you trust me." Zhang Xiaojiao agreed. Since then, Shi Qian became even more honest, cautious and thrift. Finally, Zhang Xiaoji believed that his elder sister-in-law had changed completely and was capable of managing the family, so he returned voluntarily all the property succeeded from his father-in-law to Shi Qian.

【点评】

姓过的富人因儿子不肖，把全部家产交给女婿张孝基打理，本来只指望女婿能够在他百年之后料理好自己的后事，每年能按时祭祀，管好遗产，就很满足了。但张孝基不但不贪岳父家的财产，还时刻惦记着被赶出家门的大舅哥，找到了他后，还用心培养大舅哥持家理财的能力和品质。到大舅哥确实能够继承父业的时候，就归还他全部家产，让他当家作主，因此为后人所称道。

The rich man was compelled to deliver all the property to Zhang Xiaoji, his son-in-law, for his only son was unworthy and incapable. He should be quite satisfied if Zhang Xiaoji could make well arrangement for his funeral, offer sacrifice to him annually and take care of the property. Who could ever think Zhang Xiaoji, instead of making all the property his own, always concerned about his elder brother-in-law who was driven out of home and, after finding him, trained him attentively in aspects of conduct and capability to manage family and financial affairs. When it came that his elder brother-in-law was qualified to take over the family business, he returned voluntarily all the property and relinquished the master of the family. Such a fine virtue reflecting in these righteous behaviors has always been praised by the later generations.

天祥衣带

Tiān Xiáng Yī Dài

【出处】《宋史·文天祥传》：宋文天祥，涕泣勤王，惟义是尽，衣带名扬。

【释义】 文天祥手捧朝廷号令天下起兵勤王的诏书，忍不住泪如雨下。后来兵败被俘，慷慨就义，在衣带上留下一首名传千古的赞文。

【Definition】 Wen Tianxiang, holding court order to lead the revolt against king Qin, could not help but burst into tears. Later defeated and captured, he died, leaving a name to praise the text through the ages.

【造句】 天祥衣带的赞文，展现了他是个舍生取义伟丈夫的情怀。

【Example】 Tian Xiang yi dai's praises show the performance of his sacrifice justice in a great people's feelings.

【故事】

南宋末年，国破家亡，朝廷号令天下起兵勤王，护卫大宋国土。文天祥组建了一支义兵，来救大宋王朝。但毕竟是兵少，将也少，最后打了败仗，文天祥被元兵俘获。

文天祥是宋朝的一个大忠臣，很有名气。元世祖忽必烈惜爱人才，对文天祥非常敬重。他深知在马上打出来的天下，只有任贤举才，才能够保有永固的江山，于是决定招降文天祥。

面对高官厚禄，文天祥没有动心，态度坚决地回答道："国家灭亡，做臣子的就是以死相报，都不足以报答朝廷。我怎么能够苟且求安呢！现在我心里所想的，只求速死，就心满意足了。"在不得已的情况下，元世祖

肆 义 (Righteousness)

下令处死他。

文天祥英勇就义了。有人在他的衣带中发现了一首《赞文》，内容是："孔曰成仁，孟曰取义，惟其义尽，所以仁至。读圣贤书，所学何事？而今而后，庶几无愧。"意思是说，孔子说的杀身成仁、孟子说的舍生取义，因为这个"大义"能够尽到极点，那么，这个"仁心"也就到极点了；读了圣贤人的书，究竟明白了些什么？我今天才勉强可以说没有惭愧了。

In the late Southern Song Dynasty, the whole country was in a critical moment and the court ordered officials around the country to safeguard the country. So Wen Tianxiang organized a voluntary army to resist the enemy, but end up being defeated on account of limited number of both soldiers and generals, and he was also captured by the Yuan army.

Wen Tianxiang was a famous loyal official of the Song Dynasty. Emperor Shizu of the Yuan Dynasty knew that only by appointing those talented and capable men can a country built through force lasted forever, so he treated Wen Tianxiang with much respect, hoping that he would surrender and work for the Yuan Dynasty.

Wen Tianxiang, however, rejected to surrender despite of the high post with matched salary offered by the Yuan Dynasty, and said resolutely, "When the country perished, an official should die for it, how could I seek personal temporary ease and peace! Now a quick death is only what I have in mind." With no other choices, Emperor Shizu had to give the order to kill him.

At last, Wen Tianxiang was executed heroically. After his death, someone found in his pocket an eulogy, its content being "Confucius said that man should die for benevolence, while Mencius said that man should die for righteousness. When one has done a righteous cause, benevolence also comes. What I have learned from books of sages? From now on, I will not feel regretful at what I have done."

【点评】

自古至今的志士豪杰，无论身处怎样的风云变幻的环境中，没有任何力量能摧折、动摇那不屈的仁义、志节。文天祥视死如归，他躬身力行所体现的道德、节义，已经超过了生命本身。在他离世后的几百年间，每到民族危亡的时候，他的名字、他的诗句，总是为人传唱；他的事迹、品行和道义，成为华夏民族忠勇不屈、大义凛然、永生不息的精神象征。

Since the ancient times, man of ideal and integrity will never change their unyielding righteousness and integrity despite of the turbulent and harsh environment they were in. Wen Tianxiang, facing death unflinchingly, embodied high morality and righteousness, which has exceeded life itself. Several centuries after his death, his name and poems were always sung by the people when the nation was in a critical moment; his deed, morality and justice have symbolized the spirit of the Chinese nation of loyalty, unyieldingness, righteousness and unceasingness.

肆 义 (Righteousness)

世期义行
Shì Qī Yì Xíng

【出处】《宋书·列传第五十一》：世期义行，饥岁解推，露骸(hái)悉殡，复育其孩。

【释义】 严世期的仗义行为，有多种多样的表现形式。

【Definition】 There is a wide variety of forms of Yan Shiqi's justice behavior.

【造句】 世期义行的基本内涵在于：乐善好施，帮人解困，助人为乐。

【Example】 The basic meaning of "Shi Qi yi xing" is that a man should be of a good charity, and help people get out the trouble and care about others.

【故事】

南宋的严世期，他好行善事，经常拿自己的钱财、实物，送穷困人家。与他同村的张迈等三个人，都生了儿子，可是因为年成不好，家里又贫穷，打算丢弃孩子不养。严世期就帮他们把这些孩子都救了：将自己吃的东西分给小孩们吃，将自己衣服改装给小孩穿。这样去救济他们家的缺乏，直到这三个孩子长大成人。

再有就是，他族里的人严宏、同乡人潘伯等十五人，因为荒年饿死了，尸首抛露在野外，没有人收殓。严世期就为他们买了棺木，给安葬好了，并抚养他们遗下的小孩。

他的这种仗义行为，传到朝廷。当朝皇帝得知后，就御赐一块匾额挂在他家的门上。匾额有六个字，叫作"义行严氏之闾（大门）"，并且免了他家的工役和十年的赋税。

Yan Shiqi of the Southern Song Dynasty, quiet charitable in nature, often donated money and other materials to those poor families.

Once three fellow villagers including Zhang Mai each had a son, yet they decided to abandon the child due to bad harvest and poor family. When Yan Shiqi heard this, he offered to help these three families: he shared his own food with the children and altered his own clothes in child's size for them. Yan Shiqi continued to support these three families until the children grew up.

There was another story. Fifteen people including his clansman named Yan Hong and his fellow countryman Pan Bo were dead of famine, leaving their bodies exposed in the wildness. When Yan Shiqi learned of this, he bought coffins and buries them at his own expense. After that he also took voluntarily the responsibility of raising their children.

Later, his conducts of righteousness were spread to the court and heard by the emperor. The emperor presented a plaque to Yan Shiqi and hanged it on his front gate. The plaque had six Chinese Characters inscribed on it, "The door of Yan family who are righteous." Besides, the emperor also exempted his family from labor service and taxes for ten years.

【点评】

孔子说：君子看重的是道义，小人看重的是利益。严世期的一举一动，惟义是取；义之所在，无往不利。他对人的仁、义、恩、情，遍布人间，无论老少、活着的还是离开了人世的人，都感念得到，使他赢得了社会的高度认可。

The Confucius once said, "The gentleman seeks righteousness while the mean man seeks profit." Every act of Yan Shiqi conforms to righteousness; everything runs smoothly where the righteousness exists. The benevolence, righteousness, kindness and affection he showed to others, old or young, dead or alive, can be found everywhere, which enabled him to earn highly recognition of the society.

伍 禮

Propriety

礼，是由一定社会的道德观念和风俗习惯形成的大家共同遵守的仪节。仪节作为礼仪，是一种律己、敬人的行为规范，是表现对他人尊重和理解的过程和手段。礼使社会上每个人在贵贱、长幼、贫富各等级制中都有恰当的地位。在长期的历史发展中，礼作为中国社会的道德规范和生活准则，对中华民族精神素质的修养起了重要作用；同时，随着社会的变革和发展，礼不断被赋予新的内容，不断地发生着改变和调整。

礼在中国古代，是社会的典章制度和道德规范。作为伦理道德的"礼"的具体内容，包括孝、慈、恭、顺、敬、和、仁、义等，是孔子"道之以德，齐之以礼"的德治思想体系的重要部分，故《论语》有"不学礼，无以立"之说。文明礼仪不仅是个人素质、教养的体现，也是个人道德和社会公德的体现。所以，我们每个人在日常生活和工作中，都应学会礼仪，以礼待人。惟其如此，才能"洁身自爱，知节用和，克己制欲，不涉奸乱，端正心思，以德治事"。

礼仪，作为中华传统美德宝库中的一颗璀璨明珠，是中国古代文化的精髓。身处礼仪之邦，应为礼仪之民。知书达礼，待人以礼，应是现实生活中的人的一种基本素养。本篇所选取的故事，作为对当代大学生社交礼仪教育的题材，既是素质教育的必需，也是社会文明进步的基本要求。对包括在华留学生在内的大学生进行社交礼仪教育，具有跨时代、跨国界区域的特殊意义，有利于养成大学生知礼、守礼的文明行为，提升大学生的礼仪修养，浓郁大学校园精神文明建设氛围。

Propriety is a rite coming from social moral concept and custom to regulate human behaviors. The rite, a norm to discipline oneself and respect others, is reflected in the way of respecting and understanding people. Propriety endows human's status in hierarchy.

In the long history of China propriety has played a critical role in Chinese spirits, and surely it has been changing and adjusting for new understanding in the tie of social innovation.

In ancient China propriety was a part of laws and regulations and moral norms. From ethical aspect, propriety consists of filial piety, kindness, politeness, obedience, respect, harmony and righteousness. In The Analects, Confucius wrote "No propriety, no self-support." Not only propriety is shown through individual's quality but reflected by individual's morality and social ethics. It is requested that we follow the rules of propriety and show kindness and courtesy to other people.

As a shining pearl of Chinese traditional virtues, propriety has enriched our traditional culture and enhanced our quality. The stories about propriety selected below will help Chinese students and international students in the education of social propriety on campus.

伍 礼(Propriety)

孔子尽礼

Kǒng Zǐ Jìn Lǐ

【出处】 《论语·八佾(yì)》：至圣孔子,老聃(dān)是师,事君尽礼,温恭威仪。

【释义】 圣人孔子曾经拜老聃为师学习礼仪,他一生用礼的规范来约束自己的言行,态度温和,行为恭敬,仪容庄重。

【Definition】 Confucius once took Lao Ran as a teacher to learn propiety and bound his whole life with propiety norms, so as to have mild mannered, respectful behavior, grooming solemn.

【造句】 孔子尽礼,凡事以礼为先,奠定了中华礼仪、文明之邦的基础。

【Example】 Confucius's commitment to taking priority to propiety has laid the foundation for China's propiety and civilization.

【故事】

zhōu cháo shí hòu, zhū hóu fēng dì de lǔ guó yǒu gè dà shèng rén, tā jiù shì rén rén zuì zūn jìng de kǒng zǐ。
周朝时候,诸侯封地的鲁国有个大圣人,他就是人人最尊敬的孔子。

kǒng zǐ xiǎo shí hòu jiù shí fēn chóng shàng lǐ zhì, tā cōng míng hǎo xué, fù yú mó fǎng, wǔ suì shí jiù néng zǔ zhī
孔子小时候就十分崇尚礼制,他聪明好学,富于模仿,五岁时就能组织

ér tóng mó fǎng jì sì lǐ yí。 zhè dōu hé kǒng mǔ duì tā de zǎo qī jiào yù fēn bù kāi de。 tā tīng liǎo hěn duō guān
儿童模仿祭祀礼仪。这都和孔母对他的早期教育分不开的。他听了很多关

yú lǐ de gù shì。
于礼的故事。

luò yáng céng shì zhōu cháo de tǒng zhì zhōng xīn, yǒu dà liàng jiǎn cè tú jí、 wén shū dàng àn, shì zhōu cháo
洛阳曾是周朝的统治中心,有大量简册图籍、文书档案,是周朝

de wén huà huì cuì zhī dì。 dāng shí, lǎo zǐ zài zhè lǐ dān rèn guó jiā shǒu cáng shǐ。 kǒng zǐ wèi liǎo tōng lǐ lè zhī
的文化荟萃之地。当时,老子在这里担任国家守藏史。孔子为了通礼乐之

yuán、 míng dào dé zhī guī, jiù qián wǎng luò yáng xiàng lǎo zǐ qǐng jiào。
源、明道德之归,就前往洛阳向老子请教。

dào dá luò yáng hòu, kǒng zǐ jiù qián wǎng bài fǎng lǎo zǐ。 jiàn dào lǎo zǐ hòu, kǒng zǐ gōng gōng jìng jìng de
到达洛阳后,孔子就前往拜访老子。见到老子后,孔子恭恭敬敬地

xiàng lǎo zǐ xíng dì zǐ lǐ, zì qiān dào: wǒ xué shí qiǎn bó, duì gǔ dài de lǐ zhì yī wú suǒ zhī, tè lái xiàng
向老子行弟子礼,自谦道:"我学识浅薄,对古代的礼制一无所知,特来向

老师请教。"老子见孔子这样诚恳,就详细地阐述了自己对"礼"的见解。

后来,孔子在鲁国做司寇,出任代理相国,服事鲁国君王,非常尽礼。

上朝时,和上大夫交谈,他态度中正自然;和下大夫交谈,他态度和乐轻松。进入国君的宫门时,他低头弯腰,态度恭敬;快到国君面前时,他小步快行,态度端谨。走进周公的庙里,每一种事情的礼仪,他都要向人询问。

孔子在没有事的平时,他的容貌很舒畅,神色很愉快,外表恭谨,而心里平和。有时外表虽然温和,却仍旧带着严肃;有时外表虽然威严,却不流于刚猛。他遇到放得不正当的座位,就不肯坐下;在有丧事的人旁边吃饭,从来不吃饱;在这一天里哭过,就不再唱歌。孔圣人就是这样的人:对于小小的事情,从来都是不肯苟且的。

In Zhou Dynasty, there was a sage in Lu (a feudatory nation). He is the respected Confucius.

He adored rites since he was little. The clever little Confucius can organize children to imitate memorial rites. All these were contributed to the education he received from his mother. He was told many stories about rites.

As the political and cultural center at that time, Luo Yang stored a great many of books, documents and files. In order to understand rites and music well and know how to apply moral in daily life, he came to Luo Yang and consult Lao Tzu who was in charge of the national library.

After arrival, he paid a visit to Lao Tzu. Seeing Lao Tzu, Confucius treated him as a master and behaved humbly. Confucius said: "I am a man with little learning and know little about the ancient norms of propriety. Master, I want to have your advice on it." Touched by his sincere attitude, Lao Tzu shared his understanding on etiquette in

伍 礼(Propriety)

detail with Confucius.

Later, Confucius served King of Lu as Xiang Guo(Prime Minister at that time). He disciplined himself with norms of propriety and treated all the official, no matter what level they were in, politely. He applied the norms of propriety to all his behaviors.

When he was off duty, he often wears a respectful and cautious but joyful and peaceful expression. He is a gentle but serious man, a mixture of two characteristics. If the seat was appropriately placed, he won't sit down; if someone who was suffering family member's death ate beside him, he often eats little; if he cried, he won't sing at the same day. Sage Confucius always cares about details.

【点评】

中国古代社会被称为礼治社会。礼治,是中国古代政治的重要特点。礼治在西周时期确立,到春秋时已遭到极大的破坏。孔子为三代完人,他以弘扬西周的礼治为己任,不但继承了西周的礼治思想,还提出"仁"的思想,并且把两者很好地结合起来,形成了自己的礼治思想,体现了"礼制"精神,即现代意义上的秩序和制度,对后来的中国古代社会产生了深远影响,在今天依然具有积极的借鉴意义。

The ancient China is practicing the rule of rite which is a major feature of its political system. The rule of rite was established in the Western Zhou Dynasty and almost destroyed in the Spring and Autumn period. Acclaimed as the only perfect man during the three dynasties (Xia, Shang and Zhou), Confucius strove to develop and spread the rule of rite. He not only inherited norms of propriety of the Western Zhou Dynasty, but also put forward the thought of benevolence. He then combined the two together and formed his own thought of rite which is today's order and system. His own thought of rite exerted profound influence on ancient China, which can still provide positive guidance for in today's world.

宋桓罪己

Sòng Huán Zuì Jǐ

【出处】《史记·宋微子世家》：宋桓未立，深明大体；遇水恤(xù)民，言惧名礼。

【释义】 宋桓公还没有即位的时候就深明大义，敢于担当，得到境内外的一致称颂。

【Definition】 Before his accession to the throne, Duke Song Huan was principled, brave, and responsible and won consistent praise both inside and outside.

【造句】 在过错面前，我们要有宋桓罪己一样的胸怀，勇于担当。

【Example】 In front of the fault, we should have the courage to act like Duke Song Huan.

【故事】

春秋时，宋国遭遇了重大的水灾。鲁国国君派人去慰问。宋庄公就派他的儿子公子御说接待。公子御说对鲁国使者说："因为我的不敬，所以上天降下了灾祸，又使得贵国的君侯担心我国，这是我们觉得很抱歉的。"同时，恭敬地拜受了鲁国国君的慰问。

鲁国的大夫臧文仲听了这一番话，认为宋公子具有国君的情怀和器量，有恤民之心。事后，他对使者说："宋国将要兴起了。从前夏朝的禹王、商朝的汤王，都是经常把过错归结自己的人，所以他们治理的诸侯国都迅速地强大、兴起了。亡国的君主，比如夏朝的桀、商朝的纣，总是把自己做错的事都扣在别人的头上，所以他们都亡国了。按照惯例，在诸侯国面前，有了凶灾的事情，国君就自己称孤，这是最合乎礼的。

伍 礼(Propriety)

现在,宋国的公子说话既心怀恐惧,称呼又很合礼,这样说来,宋国的兴起是无疑的了。"

若干年后,御说果然成为一代明君,人称宋桓公,成为当时诸侯国的霸主。

During the Spring and Autumn period, a severe flood happened in Song State. The emperor of Lu State appointed someone to extend his regards. Then the emperor of Song State, Song Zhuanggong let his son Yuyue to receive the guest. Yuyue said to the guest from the Lu: "due to my irreverence, the God of the Heaven has made some disasters, which also cause great worries for your emperor. I feel so sorry for that." Meanwhile he accepted the regards from Lu's emperor.

Zang Wenzhong, a senior official of Lu States, heard about that. He thought that Song Zhuangzong's son had an emperor's heart and tolerance for he cared his people very much. After that, he said to the delegation: "Song State is going to rise. Both Emperor Yu of the Xia Dynasty and Emperor Tang of the Shang Dynasty often attributed their faults to themselves, so their states rose strongly and rapidly. On the other hand, emperors from the perished nations like Emperor Jie in the Xia Dynasty and Emperor Zhou in the Shang Dynasty always ascribed their faults to others, as a result, their states were extinct. Usually, when there are some unfortunate things happened among the states, the emperor would realize his mistake, which is in accordance with rites. Now the representative from the Song State was full of fear but behaved politely. So undoubtedly their state will rise up."

Many year later, Yuyue became a sage empreor called Song Huangong, a powerful chief in the Spring and Autumn Period.

【点评】

古人曾说:君子有了过错,就老老实实向人家认错道歉;小人有了过错,在向人家解释的时候,就极力掩饰自己的错误。宋桓公恤民、罪己,遇事能以君子的方式坦然地处理,所以能成为一代明主。事实上,虚心使人进步,骄傲使人落后。多反省自己,善于自我反省,看到自己的不足,并且过而能改,才有进步的可能和空间。

As the old saying goes, a gentleman often apologizes to others when he makes mistakes. While a base person often tries to hide his fault when he makes mistakes and explains to others. Song Huangong cares his people and is also aware of his mistakes. When in trouble, he would often deal with in a gentle manner. Thus he became a wise emperor. In fact, modesty makes people make progress while arrogance lags people behind. Therefore only when people often reflect themselves, are willing to do the self-questioning and admit their mistakes then improve themselves, will they possibly make progress.

伯禽趋跪

Bó Qín Qū Guì

【出处】《史记·鲁周公世家》:周鲁伯禽,观于桥梓(zǐ);入门而趋,登堂而跪。

【释义】 西周姬伯禽通过观察山上的桥梓之木的长势,明白了做人的道理。

【Definition】 Ji Boqin in Western Zhou Dynasty understood the truth in life by observing the growing of the mountain trees.

【造句】 伯禽趋跪的故事告诉我们:长幼有别,做晚辈的应当尊重长辈。

【Example】 The story tells us that younger people should respect the elders for their difference.

【故事】

西周初年,有一位大圣人叫周公旦。周公崇尚礼教,特别重视对人以礼相待。同时,他希望自己的孩子们都能成为懂礼、守礼的人。周公有个儿子名叫姬伯禽,跟了周公的弟弟康叔去见周公三次。结果被父亲痛打了三次。伯禽实在不理解,就去问商子:这是什么缘故?商子说:"南山的阳面有一种树,叫作桥木;北山的阴面有一种树,叫作梓木,你去看看就知道了!"伯禽听后,就去看了,只见桥木很高大,直立并且向上仰着;而梓木长得很低矮,而且有点下俯的样子。伯禽回来后,就把看到的情形告诉了商子。商子对伯禽说:"桥木高高在上,仰起生长,就是做父亲的道理。梓木低矮在下,屈膝俯身,就是做儿子的道理。"伯禽一下子明白了。到了第二天,伯禽去见父亲周公。一进大门,伯禽就赶快走上前去,一进厅堂就跪下去,向周公问安。这次,父亲赞许伯禽接受了贤人君子的指点。

In the early Western Zhou Dynasty, there was a sage named Zhou Gongdan. Zhougong upheld rites very much, therefore he often treated others with due respect. Meanwhile he wished that his children would grow up with courtesy and comity.

Zhougong had a son named Ji Boqin. Once he escorted Kangshu (Zhougong's brother) to visit Zhougong three times. However he was severely trounced by his father three times. Feeling confused, Ji Boqin went to ask Shangzi for the reasons.

Shangzi replied: "On Nanshan Mountain's sunny side grows one kind tree called Qiaomu while on its dark side grows another kind tree named Zimu. Go and see the trees and you will understand it." Taking Shangzi's advice, Boqin went there. He saw that Qiamu was very tall, standing uprightly to the sky. But Zimu is short, growing a bit downward. Then Boqin went back and told Shangzi what he saw.

Shangzi told Boqin: "Qiaomu is tall and grows upward, which is like a father. Zimu is short and grows downward, which is like son." Suddenly, Boqin understood that. Next day, Boqin went to visit his father. Entering the hall, Boqin kneeled and showed his respects to his father. This time Zhougong praised Boqin had accepted the wise man's advice.

【点评】

伯禽经过高人指点，终于明白：心中对父亲的尊敬，要靠言语、行为表达出来。如果言语、行动方面没做到，这只能说明他心中的诚意还不够。这也是周公见到伯禽没有跪下而抽打他的原因。商子用山中的桥木和梓木作比喻，让伯禽明白了自己错在哪里，因为作为晚辈，对长辈的恭敬心意是不可忽视的。

After accepting the wise man's suggestion, Boqin finally understood that he should respect for his father with words or actions. If he didn't do enough on the both, then it meant he was not sincere. That explains why Zhougong beat him when sawing him didn't kneel down. Shangzi used the two kinds of trees as examples to help Boqin understand his misbehaviors: As juniors, people should always remember to show their respect for their seniors.

伍 礼(Propriety)

石奋恭谨
Shí Fèn Gōng Jǐn

【出处】 《史记·万石张叔列传》:石奋父子,敬谨持躬,忠孝慈悌,万石(dàn)家风。

【释义】 石奋待人谦和恭谨、忠于君国、孝于长辈,并影响到他儿子,成为家风。

【Definition】 Shi Fen was modest, loyal to the monarch country, and respectful to the elderly, which had affected his son very much.

【造句】 石奋恭谨是出了名的,但他的大儿子石建比他做得还要好,真是后继有人。

【Example】 Shi Fen is well known for his modesty and his eldest son, Shi Jian, even did better than he did. What a good tradition!

【故事】

石奋生活在西汉初期,十五岁时开始做小官吏,侍侯汉高祖。高祖喜欢他的恭敬。有一次和他说话,问石奋说:"你家里还有什么人?"他回答说:"我只有母亲,不幸失明,还有一个姐姐。"高祖说:"你能跟随我身边吗?"他说:"愿意尽力效劳。"于是高祖召他姐姐来封为妃子,安排让石奋担任中涓的官职,把他的家也迁到长安城中。之后,他靠积累功劳,做官一直做到太中大夫。

虽然他没有文才学问,但他的恭敬、谨严却无人能比,并且做事干脆利落。他的四个儿子都因为品行善良、孝敬父母、办事谨严,在汉孝景帝即位后,都做了二千石的官。于是,景帝说:"石君和四个儿子都是二千石的官员,作为臣子的尊贵、光荣,都集中在他一家了。"因此,称呼石奋为"万石君"。

景帝末年，万石君告老还乡，享受上大夫的俸禄。在朝廷举行盛大典礼、朝令时，他都作为大臣被邀请来参加。他经过皇室宫门楼时，一定要下车走步，表示恭敬；见到皇帝的车驾，一定要手扶在车轼上表示致意。皇帝有时赏赐食物送到他家，全家人必定叩头跪拜之后，才弯腰、低头去吃，如同在皇帝面前一样。平时，他在外地做官的子孙辈回家看望他，万石君也一定要穿上朝服才接见他们，从不直呼他们的名字。子孙中如果有人犯了过错，他就坐到侧旁的座位上，对着餐桌不肯吃饭，这样以后其他的子孙们就纷纷责备那个有错误的人，再通过族中长辈求情，过错人裸露上身表示认错，并保证坚决改正，才答允他们的请求。已成年的子孙在身边时，即使是闲居在家，也一定要穿戴整齐，显示出严肃整齐的样子。他的仆人受他的影响，也都非常恭敬，特别谨慎。

由于言传身教到位，石奋的儿孙们都很孝顺，而其中最突出、最是继承了他谨严恭敬作风的，是长子石建。石建待人处事接物的恭谨，甚至超过了他父亲。

Shi Fen lived in the early stage of the western Han dynasty, who had been appointed to be a minor official, serving the Han emperor, Gaozu. His humbleness had always been appreciated by Gaozu. There was a time when he was asked by Gaozu: "Who else do you have in your family？" He replied: "Only my mother, blinded by the crucial fate, and a sister." Gaozu asked again: "Would you like to serve me by my side？" He answered: "I will give it my all." Then his sister had been given the sealing for concubine, and he had been promoted to Zhongjuan, as well as his family had been moved to Chang'an city. With his credits accumulated, he had been promoted to the doctor's in abnormality later on.

伍 礼(Propriety)

He had no literary talent but impressing humbleness, prudence and neatness. His four sons had all been appointed to satrap after the succession of the Han emperor, Xiaojing. The emperor said: "Since Mr. Shi and his four sons are in the position of satrap, all the respect and honor as courtiers have been centered on his family." Then the emperor calls him Mr. Master.

At the end of the ruling of the Emperor Xiaojing, Shi fen retired himself with the benefice of dignitary. Anytime when holding the ceremony or the court, he will be invited as a minister. Whenever he passes the palace he will get off the sedan and walk, for showing his respect to the royals. When he saw the emperor's carriage, he must bow with his hand on the handlebar. Sometimes the emperor reward foods to his house, the whole family would only kneel down to take it after kowtow, just like in front of the emperor. When the descendant with official position came back to visiting him, he will always in the court dress and never call them by name. If anyone one of them made mistake, he will sit in the side seat and refuse to eat while the culprit be criticized by the others. He will not be moved until the culprit bare his top, beg to the elders, ask for forgiveness and promise to correct. When the grown offspring around, he will suit up with the serious appearance even at home. His servants were also reverent and cautious, affected by him.

Due to his words and deeds, the decedents were obedient. The most outstanding one is his eldest son, Shi Jian, who has inherited all of his serious attitudes, in some aspects, even better than him.

【点评】

石家父子，一生谦虚谨慎，在朝为官，则忠诚于汉家皇室；赋闲在家，则孝敬父母、爱护幼小，教育晚辈，不用暴力，宽严有度。因此，养成敬谨持躬、忠孝慈悌的良好家风有口皆碑，成为别人家学习的榜样。

The Shi family has been humble and cautious for whole life. Loyal to the royals at politics, respect the old and cherish the young at home, using proper way but violence to educate children. That is how they cultivated the family traits of humbleness and benevolence, and became a well-known example for others.

规妻礼宗
Guī Qī Lǐ Zōng

【出处】《后汉书·列女传》：皇甫规妻，骂卓不从，速尽为惠，无愧礼宗。

【释义】 皇甫规妻子面对董卓的淫(yín)威，坚贞不屈，宁为玉碎，无愧于"礼宗"称号。

【Definition】 Huangfu Gui's wife was unyielding and showed the spirit of better to die rather than surrender while facing Dong Zhuo's abusive, which deserved the honor of Lizong.

【造句】 规妻礼宗的故事主人公，是古代列女中的巾帼英雄。

【Example】 The heroine in the story of Huangfu Gui's wife is really an ancient paragons of heroine.

【故事】

东汉时期的名将皇甫规，他的第一个妻子死后，又娶了第二房妻子。这个妻子不仅容貌姣好，还会写文章、写草书，经常替皇甫规当书记，众人惊讶她的才能。可惜人到中年，不幸丧夫。

当时的相国董卓爱慕皇甫规妻子的美貌和名声，就用一百辆彩车、二十匹马，以及许多奴婢、钱财作聘礼娶她。皇甫规妻子穿着便衣到董卓那里，恭敬地陈述自己的苦衷，明确表示从一而终的坚定意志，言语十分恳切，态度不卑不亢。

董卓见软的不行就来硬的，命令奴仆拔出钢刀把她包围起来，并训斥说："我的威教，将使天下人降服，难道在你一个妇人身上就行不通吗?"皇甫规妻子知道这次在劫难逃,最终不能免于一死,于是义正词严地大骂董卓:"你本来就是一个野杂种!你害了天下不少人,还不够吗?!我先辈的清德,全社会的人都知道!我丈夫皇甫规文武全才,是汉代忠臣,你过去还是他的部下呢!现在竟敢在你前任领导的夫人面前,干出非礼的勾当!"

董卓恼羞成怒,叫人把车子推到庭中,将皇甫规妻子的头悬在车辕上面,让奴仆们用鞭子、棍棒使劲地打。皇甫规的妻子对拿棒棍的人说:"怎么不下重手呢?快点打死我,就是对我的恩惠。"结果,被残酷地打死了。后来有人把她的形像画了起来,题了"礼宗"二字,认为她是贞洁、守礼而值得学习的妇女代表。

During the Eastern Han dynasty, a famous general named Huangfu Gui married his second wife after the death of the first one. His second wife was incredibly pretty and literary, able to write cursive. Unfortunately he died in the middle-age.

The Premier Dong Zhuo admired the beauty and fame of Huangfu Gui's wife, planning to marry her with a hundred floats, twenty horses, incomputable maidservants and fortune. Huangfu Gui's wife came to Dong Zhuo in plain clothes, declaring her loyalty to her husband, sincere but determined.

Then Dong Zhuo started to using force, ordered his servants to besiege her by steel blades. He said: "My stateliness could subdue the whole world, let alone a common woman." Having a fat chance to survive this, she rightly abused him: "You evil bustard haven't harmed enough innocents? My ancestors were known for their goodness, and my husband was endowed with civil and martial virtues, a loyal courtier, your superior! How dare you to do this to me?"

Dong Zhuo went mad, let his men pushed a vehicle into the yard and hung her head on the yoke, whipping and clubbing her hard. She shouted to the armed men: "why don't you beat me harder. Come and take my life!" Then she died in violence. Thereafter, people drew her image, inscribed with "Lizong", regarding her as a model of loyalty and commitment.

【点评】

皇甫规的妻子,有姿色,有文才,有妇德。不幸的是,却中年丧夫,但她娴静贞节,谨守节操。更加难得的是,在董卓丰厚的聘礼面前,她不为所动;在董卓的强权面前,她从容不迫,不卑不亢,义正词严;在董卓的淫威面前,她大义凛然,坚贞不屈,志不可夺。这种视富贵如粪土、不惧权贵、以死保节的气概,确实有巾帼不让须眉的风范。

Huangfu Gui's wife was pretty and literary, with noble virtues. Unfortunately she lost her husband in the middle-age. But her loyalty against Dong Zhuo's abundant bride-price has made her even rarer. She was unyielding and showed the spirit of better to die rather than surrender while facing Dong Zhuo's abuse, which deserved the honor of heroine.

伍 礼(Propriety)

杨刘责子
Yáng Liú Zé Zǐ

【出处】 《八德篇·女德》:刘氏达礼,其子醉归,不见十日,痛责其非。

【释义】 杨元琮的母亲对儿子的酗(xù)酒行为进行严厉批评教育,责令他改正。

【Definition】 Yang Yuancong's mother severely criticized him for drinking and ordered him to correct his behavior.

【造句】 杨刘责子给人的启示在于:教育孩子一定要注意方式方法,讲究效果。

【Example】 Yang Liu Ze Zi reveals that there should be proper ways to educate children.

【故事】

汉朝时候,杨元琮的母亲刘泰瑛,为人贞节、和顺,并且通达礼仪,教子有方。她的丈夫很早就死了,留下四个儿子,偏偏大儿子杨元琮不争气,常到外面喝酒,而且每次都大醉而归。

她对大儿子的这种表现很不满,就连续十天不允许他见娘的面。杨元琮这才知道自己真的错了,让母亲生了大气,就领了三个弟弟,到母亲面前去谢罪。

刘氏严厉地责备他说:"你难道不知道饮食是需要有节制的吗?不好酒贪杯,这是一个正常人的生活好习惯。现在你经常喝酒醉得不成样子,是不是荒唐到极点、太没有体统了啊?俗话说'有样学样',你作为大哥,不做好榜样,自己先第一个坏了礼法,怎么可能带好你几个弟弟呢?"

听了母亲的教导,杨元琮决心改掉不良习惯,给弟弟们做出一个好样子来。

During the Han dynasty, Yang Yuancong's mother Liu Taiying was a woman of chastity and amiableness. She was versed in etiquette and educating children. Her husband died early, left her four sons, which the eldest one Yang Yuancong was an alcoholic.

She was discontented with Yang Yuancong's behaviors and refused to meet him for ten days as the punishment. Later Yang Yuancong realized his wrongdoing had driven his mother mad, so he offered his apology together with his three brothers.

Mrs. Liu scolded Yang Yuancong: "Don't you know that human needs temperance diet? A normal man never addicted to alcohol, but you always drunk recently. Isn't it ridiculous? People follow examples, and now even the eldest one broke the rules, how can you lead your brothers?"

After the instruction of his mother, Yang Yuancong had made up his mind to change his ways in order to make an good example for his brothers.

【点评】

现实生活中,没有不犯错误的孩子;孩子犯了错误应该教育,包括适当的惩罚。但教育孩子的目的,是为了让孩子改正错误,脱离错误的行为,不能为教育而教育、为惩罚而惩罚。现在家庭大多是独生子女,在教育孩子方面,大部分家长都忽略了。怎样对待孩子的过错,让孩子少犯或不犯错误?这是一个值得严重关注的问题,刘氏的教子方式,值得借鉴。

There is no such a child could avoid making mistake in the real life; there should be indoctrination and proper punishment for the mistakes. But the purpose for educating children is to correct them from wrong rather than the aimless teaching or punishing. For the reason that most of the families nowadays only have one child, parents had been blurred from the correct awareness of education. How to deal with the mistakes that children have made? How to eliminate or lessen it? That's a matter for concern, which means we should learn from Liu's way to educate children.

伍 礼(Propriety)

卢植楷模
Lú Zhí Kǎi Mó

【出处】 《后汉书》:卢植侍师,左右美姬(jī),未尝一盼,数载如斯。

【释义】 卢植拜马融为师,专心求学,心无旁骛(wù),目不斜视,几年如一日,得到真传。

【Definition】 Lu Zhi worshiped Ma Rong as his teacher to learn how to concentrate on study, how to become less distracted and how to look straight ahead. As a result, he obtained the recipe of Ma's education.

【造句】 卢植楷模的故事展现了卢植非凡的优秀品质和传统美德,他的人格魅力光耀千古。

【Example】 The story of Lu Zhi here shows his excellent quality and traditional virtues, with his charisma shining through the ages.

【故事】

卢植是汉朝末年的政治家、军事家、经学家,他为人刚毅,很有气节。他年轻时不远千里,到都城洛阳求学,师从当时大儒马融。马融相貌堂堂,风流倜傥,博古通今,又是皇亲国戚,家中富裕。马融讲课的方法也特别,在用绛纱帐装饰的课堂里,他高坐讲堂上,前面是众多听课的学生,而在他的身后则有众多美女在舞台上轻歌曼舞。这样一来,听课的学生往往分心,不能专心致志。

卢植却始终专心听讲,几年如一日,从不斜视一眼。卢植学习儒家经典,不固守一家一派,不拘泥古人的解释,而是广泛学习,独立思考,深入钻研,有自己的理解和发挥,精通今文经和古文经。马融发现卢植的言谈

— 139 —

举止、音容笑貌，都给他留下了很好印象。因为这个缘故，马融也很敬重卢植，不久后就将"侍讲"的位子送给了他。

后来，大奸臣董卓造反，聚合了朝廷的臣子开会，讨论废立皇帝的事情。许多人都畏惧董卓的权威，大家唯唯诺诺，只有卢植说着反对的论调。

作为一个敢做敢为、有政治操守的学者，卢植的门下学生成群，其中就有后来做了蜀汉皇帝的刘备。刘备在十五岁时曾拜卢植为师，并深受卢植的影响。

Lu Zhi, a resolute man as a statesman, strategist, economist living in the last reign of Han dynasty. He came from far away to Luoyang city to worship Ma Rong as his teacher when he was young. Ma Rong had good looking and broad knowledge, with an eminent status as royal relative which ensured his massive fortune. Ma Rong had a different way to lecture, sitting high up in front of his students, with beauties singing and dancing behind. So that it distracted the students.

But Lu Zhi could always be concentrated on the class. For years he didn't even have a tiny bit of distraction. When he was learning the Confucian classics, he read wide, think deep rather than limit himself to one genre or existing explanation. He was good at Guwen Classics-Learning and Jinwen Classics-Learning, meanwhile his behaviors had left a good impression on Ma Rong Because of that Ma Rong very respect him and titled him as teaching assistant soon after.

Later treacherous courtier Dong Zhuo planned to rebel, gathered courtiers discussing about making or unmaking emperors. Many of them surrendered due to Dong Zhuo's power, only Lu Zhi against him.

As an aggressive scholar with political integrity, he had numerous students and Liu Bei who had later became the emperor of Shu-Han kingdom was one of them. Liu Bei had heavily affected by Lu Zhi since he worshipped Lu Zhi as his teacher when he was fifteen.

【点评】

儒家经典规定"男女授受不亲"是贵族的家礼,强调男女隔离与疏远,严防非夫妇关系的两性有接触的机会。本来,男人的心志,最易为美女所迁移。马融给学生讲学,却在厅堂上专门安排美女歌舞,目的在于测试每个学生的心灵品质,只是年少无知的学生不明白而已。这样的排场不但对学生的定力形成考量,也影响到他们的听课质量。但卢植求学数年,心无旁骛,听得认真,听得真切,听得明白。这在遵守礼教、奉行礼制方面,成为榜样。

Confucian classics had stipulated the etiquette that "men and women are forbidden to have intimate contact" as noble education, which emphasize the proper distance between the opposite sex in order to eradicate the intimate contact of the genders who were not couples. Naturally, males are easy to be distracted by beauties. The reason why Ma Rong arranges the performance of attracting ladies on his class is to test the quality of each student while they have no awareness of that. This arrangement had not only challenged their composure but also affected their performance. But Lu Zhi had always been concentrated on the study for years, and this had made an example on complying with the ethic code.

孔融让梨

Kǒng Róng Ràng Lí

【出处】《后汉书·孔融传》:年四岁时,与诸兄共食梨,融辄引小者。大人问其故,答曰:"我小儿,法当取小者。"

【释义】 孔融幼小的时候就懂得谦让,尊老爱幼,他四岁分梨就是典型的案例。

【Definition】 Kong Rong learned to be modest, care for the young, and respect the elder when he was a little boy. That he shared his pears with other kids when he was four is a typical case.

【造句】 妈妈买了两个书包,小红把漂亮的书包给了妹妹,她具有孔融让梨的品质。

【Example】 When Mom bought two bags, Xiao Hong gave the beautiful red bag to her younger sister, which shows her good quality like Kong Rong.

【故事】

孔融,是孔子的第二十世孙。孔融有五个哥哥、一个弟弟,他排行第六,大家都叫他小六儿。因为他性情活泼、随和,大家都喜欢他。

虽然家里兄弟多,但爸爸妈妈对他们每个人的要求都很严格:要勤奋读书;对人要懂礼貌;说话要和气;无论什么事,兄弟们都要互相谦让,不要光想着自己;别人有困难要给予帮助。孔融年纪虽小,对爸爸和妈妈的话,都记得清清楚楚。他自幼聪明好学,才思敏捷,巧言妙答,大家都夸他是神童;并且懂得礼节,又喜欢做家务,非常讨人喜欢。

在孔融四岁那年,有一天,他爸爸的一个学生来看老师和师母,并带来

伍 礼 (Propriety)

了一大框梨子。客人让孔融把梨分给大家吃,在爸爸点头同意后,小孔融就给大家分梨。他先拿最大个的给客人,然后挑两个大的送给爸爸、妈妈;再把剩下的大梨一个一个分给了哥哥和弟弟;最后,他在一堆梨中,拿了一个最小的自己吃。

客人看在眼里,心里想这孩子真懂事,就问小孔融:"你自己怎么拿最小的呢?我与你换一换吧。"于是就将自己的那个大梨给孔融。孔融摇头表示不要,并从容答道:"树有高有低,人有老有少。我年纪小,当然应该吃小的。再说,尊敬客人和长辈,是应该的。"客人听后十分惊喜,又问:"那弟弟也比你小啊,你为什么要给他大个梨子呢?"孔融说:"因为弟弟比我小,我应该让着他。"

客人听了孔融的回答,直夸他。后来,这个客人把孔融分梨、让梨的事写成了文章。于是,这事很快传遍了曲阜,并一直流传下来,成了许多父母教育子女的例子。

Kong Rong is Confucius' 20th grandchild. He had five older brothers and one younger brother and he was placed sixth so that everyone called him Xiao Liuer. He was popular due to his easygoing personality.

Though there were many siblings, their parents had very strict rules for each of them such as: must be hard-working, easy with people, mutual accommodation and give a hand when people needs help. Kong Rong had clear mind about what his parents told even he was young. He had showed his talents since he was a child, so people called him child prodigy. He was adored by everyone because he was aware of etiquette and willing to help with the housework.

When he was four, one day a student of his father came to visit his parents, carried a basket of pears. The guest asked Kong Rong to allocate the pears and he did it after the approval of his father. He picked the biggest one for the guest and two big pears for his parents. He had given each one of his brothers a big pear and left himself the smallest one.

The guest was impressed by his awareness and asked him: "why you pick the smallest one? Let me exchange with you." Kong Rong refused it and said: "The trees have difference of height, and people have that of age. I'm young so I deserve a small one. Besides, I should respect the elders and the guests." The guest was surprised and asked again: "Then why you give your younger brother a big pear?" Kong Rong replied: "It's my duty to take care of my younger brother."

The guest praised him for his answer and wrote down the story. Soon it spread across the Qufu city and came down to an example for parents to educate their children.

【点评】

孔融让梨的故事，教育意义深远。它告诉人们：无论做人做事，都应该谦让，而不是斤斤计较，自私自利。一个人如果懂得谦让，就会觉得生活是多么的欢乐。我们要学习孔融尊老爱幼的美德，并养成一种好习惯，用一颗善良的心去关心、爱护身边的每一个人，做一个懂得谦让、有爱心的人。

This story, Kong Rong Rang Li, has profound meanings. It tells us that a person should be modest and generous instead of selfish and miserly. A person would get a happy life if he or she knows give-and-take. We should learn the spirit that care for the younger and respect the elder from Kong Rong, to develop a good habit, to maintain a warm heart, to care for the others, to be a modest person.

彦光易俗
Yàn Guāng Yì Sú

【出处】《隋书·循吏传》：彦光立学，招致大儒；焦通礼阙(quē)，令其观图。

【释义】 对焦通这样不讲道德、不懂礼节的人，梁彦光通过办教育，引导他们养成好习惯。

【Definition】 To the people like Jiao Tong who are immoral and bad behaved, Liang Yanguang guided him through education and helped him to develop good habits.

【造句】 彦光易俗，真是用心良苦，更是深得民心。

【Example】 The story "Yan Guang Yi Su" is really well intentioned and popular among people.

【故事】

隋朝时，梁彦光在岐州为官。那里民风纯朴，他用"清静无为"的策略治理，全境大受感化，上交的赋税连年最多，为全国第一。后来调他到相州做刺史，他还按照在岐州的办法来管理。但是，相州人口杂居，民风不纯，人很狡诈，老百姓不服管教，还说他没有本事不能治理这个地方。隋文帝听说这事后责备彦光，并因此免了他的职。

一年多以后，朝廷任命他做赵州刺史。彦光对皇上说："我以前在相州获罪。罢职后，我不再抱做官的希望，没想到皇上又起用我。既然这样，请求让我重新去相州做刺史，希望能改变那里的民风，来报答陛下厚恩。"皇上同意了。相州的豪强地痞听说彦光是自己请求来做官的，大家都嗤笑他。可是，彦光一上任，就公布一些人的罪状，像有神灵指引一样，一抓一个准，相州全境大为震惊。于是，豪强地痞都老老实实了。

原来当初，齐亡以后，有身份的人都迁入关内，只有玩杂耍的、小商贩和说唱艺人住在关外的相州，这里人情险恶，经常谣言四起、诉告官员，变化无常。彦光打算革除这些弊端，就用官俸从殽山之东请来一批学问家，在每个乡都设立学堂，传授圣人先哲的道理，并且经常在一季的末月召集当地人，亲自组织考试、考核。如果有勤奋学习、成绩优异、聪明出众的，就升堂设宴招待，其余的都坐在廊下；有喜欢诉讼、懒惰而学业无成的，就让他们坐在堂中，给以粗茶淡饭；对学业有成的，就举行贡士的礼仪，送他们到外地求学，还在郊外饯行，并资助他们财物，使他们得到更好发展。于是，人人都刻苦自励，当地的风气大为改观。

滏阳有个人叫焦通，喜欢酗酒，又不好好对待父母，被他堂兄弟告到公堂。彦光没有对他问罪，而是把他带到州学，让他到孔子庙去参观。当时庙里有这样一幅画像：有个叫韩伯瑜的，因母亲打他觉得不痛，他为母亲没有力气而感到悲伤，于是对着母亲悲泣的情形。焦通看后很受触动，感到既悲伤又惭愧，无地自容；彦光借机教育了他一番，就让他回家了。后来焦通改正了过错，成为一个善待父母、品行善良的人。

就这样，彦光用道德教化当地百姓，大家都很乐意接受，不再有吵架、

伍 礼(Propriety)

gào zhuàng de
告 状 的。

During the Sui dynasty, Liang Yanguang was a government office at Qizhou, where the people are simple and honest. He topped the county on the list of national tax paying by using the inactive strategy to civilize the whole place. Later he had been promoted to be prefectural governor of Xiangzhou, using the same way to govern. But the people at Xiangzhou were sophisticated and unruled, blaming him for futility. Emperor Wen of Sui blamed him for the breach of duty and dismissed him.

After one year, he was again appointed to be the prefectural governor of Zhaozhou. But Yanguang said to the emperor: "I was dismissed from Xiangzhou. Later I never imagine that I could be back. Since now your majesty are willing to use me again, I hope I could back to Xiangzhou and change the folk customs there, to repay the trust that your majesty have laid on me." The emperor approved. The bullies were all laughing at him when they heard that he was asking for back here. But after Yanguang take over, he sentenced a bunch of guilty guys, precisely, like it was guide by god, shocked the whole prefecture. Then all the bullies were behaved.

After the downfall of the Qi Dynasty, people who were of high-level positions were all returned inland, left the entertainers and the peddlers at Xiangzhou which outside the pass, caused huge turbulence. Intended to clear it, Yanguang invited a group of scholars from Mountain Yao to set schools and teach maxim, by using his own salary. He also gathered the locals and organized examination for them at the last month of every season. Then he will treat the outstanding and diligent one a feast, rest of them would sit in the porch. Sit the one who were lazy and had no academic achievement at the hall, treating with simple diet. For the one who had big academic achievement, he will treat with the great manner and sponsor them for further education. So everyone was working hard and the atmosphere was much beter.

There was a man named Jiao Tong at Fuyang. As an alcoholic and unfilial son, he was accused by his cousin. Without any condemning, Yanguang took him to school and let him visit Confucius Shrine. There was a painting hung on the wall shows that a person named Han Boyu couldn't felt anything when his mother was beating him and cried out of sadness for her weakness. Jiao Tong was moved, feeling sad and guilty.

Yanguang took the chance and educated him then sent him back. Later Jiao Tong changed into a filial son with good personality. In this way, Yanguang educated the locals and it was widely accepted.

【点评】

梁彦光性情执着,不因挫折而屈服。相州民风不淳,有些人诽谤他任刺史不善为政,使得他获罪免官。但他后来重被起用时,却不惧失败,主动请求再回相州任职。用惩恶与教化兼施的策略果然凑效。他的政绩,不仅深为治所的百姓民众认可,也得到皇帝赏识。

Liang Yanguang was persistent and dauntless. He was dismissed from Xiangzhou where the customs were bad due to the slanders. Later when he was appointed again, without any fears, asked to go back to Xiangzhou. While the strategy of the stick and the carrot worked well, his political achievements were approved by the folks and the emperor.

程门立雪
Chéng Mén Lì Xuě

【出处】《宋史·道学传二·杨时》：(杨时)一日见颐(yí)，颐偶瞑(míng)坐，时与游酢(zuò)侍立不去。颐既觉，则门外雪深一尺矣。

【释义】 宋代学者杨时和游酢在隆冬大雪中等候老师午睡醒来，以便求教、精进课业。

【Definition】 Yang Shi and You Zuo, scholars at Song Dynasty, wondered in midwinter snow to wait for their teacher to wake up so that they could ask for advice on what they've learned.

【造句】 程门立雪的故事，是尊师重道的千古美谈。

【Example】 The story of "Cheng Men Li Xue" is a good example of respecting teachers for many years.

【故事】

杨时是南宋时期的人。他从小就聪明伶俐，四岁入村学，七岁能写诗，八岁能作赋，人称神童。他十五岁时攻读经史，二十三岁登进士第。他一生立志著书立说，曾在许多地方讲学，很受人欢迎。居住在家时，他潜心攻读、写作、教学。

尽管他已经很有学问了，但从来不骄傲自满。有一年，杨时赴任浏阳县令途中，不辞劳苦，绕道洛阳，拜师程颐，以求学问上进一步深造。再一次，杨时与他的学友游酢，因为对一个问题有不同看法，为了求得一个正确答案，他俩就一起去老师家请教。

正是隆冬时节，天寒地冻，浓云密布。走到半路上，朔风凛凛，瑞雪霏霏，冷飕飕的寒风肆无忌惮地灌进他们的衣领口。他们把衣服裹得紧紧的，匆匆赶路。来到程颐家时，适逢先生坐在炉旁打坐养神。杨时二人不敢惊动打扰老师，就恭恭敬敬站在门外，等候先生醒来。只见远山如玉簇，树林如银妆，房屋也披上了洁白的素装。杨时他们的脚都冻僵了，冷得发抖，但还是坚持恭敬侍立。过了很久，先生醒了，从窗口发现有人站立在风雪中，只见他们全身披雪，脚下的积雪有一尺多厚，赶忙起身迎他俩进屋。

程颐被他们诚心求学的精神所感动，更加尽心尽力地教授。从此以后，杨时一有机会就登门求学，并不负重望，终于学得程门理学的真谛；学成后回到南方，继续潜心研究和传播程氏理学。东南学者推杨时为"程学正宗"，世称"龟山先生"。

Yang Shi lived in Song dynasty. He was called child prodigy due to his cleverness since his childhood, went to school at four, able to write poets at seven and prose at eight. Fifteen, read hundreds schools of thought; twenty three, Tang Scholars section. He had devoted his while life to formulate his grand scheme of ideas, went to a lot of places to lecture, well-know by people. When he was in home, he sunk in reading, writing and teaching.

Although he had profound knowledge, he never lost in complacency. One year, he was on the journey to Liuyang County, specifically turn to Luoyang to worship Cheng Yi as teacher, looking for further education. Again, he and his friend You Zou went to visit the teacher, looking for a answer for their disagreement on an academic problem.

It was mid-winter, cold and cloudy. The road was covered by frozen snow, and the freezing wind poured into their clothes. They tightened the clothes and speeded up.

伍 礼（Propriety）

They reached Cheng Yi's house when he was taking a nap by the fire. They were too much respecting him so they just stood outside waiting deferentially.

The distant mountains, trees and roofs were all covered by heavy snow. They were frozen but still stood deferentially. After a long time, the teacher woke up, saw them through the window and invited them in immediately while they were covered by snow, left a foot of snow under their feet.

Cheng Yi was moved by their spirit of perusing knowledge, done his best to teach them. Ever since that day, Yang Shi will pay a visit for learning whenever he had time and finally he had learnt all the essence from Cheng Yi. After that, he went back to the south, keep on studying and spreading the theory. The scholars of the southeast regarded him as the authentic heres of the Cheng's theory, entitled him "Mr. Guishan".

【点评】

杨时因为尊师重教，且勤奋好学，深得老师程颐的器重，得到真传。《吕氏春秋》说"疾学在于尊师"，意思是要想很快学到知识，重要的是尊敬老师。程门立雪的故事，在宋代读书人中就流传很广。后来形容尊敬老师、诚恳求教时，人们就往往引用这个典故和这句成语来说事。

Yang Shi was regarded highly by his teacher Cheng Yi due to his respect and hard-working. It was wrote in *Lü's Commentaries of History (LüShiChunQiu)* that the secret of learning fast is to respect your teacher, which means if you want to learn things more quickly, the most important thing to do is to respect your teacher. The story of "Cheng Men Li Xue" was already well-known among the scholars at Song dynasty. Later when it comes to respect teacher, people quote this story.

陆 智

Wisdom

"智"同"知",是孔子的认识论和伦理学的基本范畴,与"慧"联合使用。"智"强调的是知识、见识与胆识,凭此,能够作出正确的判断、估量、选择与决策。"慧"主要是一种悟性,是对于是非、正误、成败、得失的迅速感受、理解与掌控。

综上,智慧是关于人的一种高级的、主要是知性方面的精神能力,即人对自身思想束缚的解放程度。智慧要求有远见、有眼光,尤其要求对于对象的整体性把握,不仅经得住一时一地一事的考验,而且经得住较为长期与全面的检验。智慧要求举一反三、融会贯通,要求有所不为、有所作为,要求学有新意、事有新意、言有新意。

在中国古人的意识中,不常用"智慧"这个词,而习惯用

"知"。但在儒家,讲得更多的是"学",强调人要重视学习,重视切磋、琢磨,求得学问,增长学识。由此可见,"智"的内涵主要涉及"知"的性质、来源、内容、效果等方面。

智慧的依据是生活,是世界,是实践,而不仅仅是书本知识。那么,怎样才能获得智慧?当然要汲取人类的一切智慧成果,弘扬民族文化的益智精华,倾听时代高端与科学前沿的信息与呼唤。更重要的是,面对现实的生活实践,有所发现,有所思索,有所实验,有所尝试,有所撷取,有所见解,有所创新,就能集智慧之大成,这是本篇的要旨所在。

The character "Zhi", meaning wisdom, toghter with "Hui", is used in epistemology and ethics, is mainly referred as knowledge or insight to help make correct judgment, assessment and right choice and decision. "Hui", meaning wisdom, is mainly referred as a comprehension to understand and control which is right or wrong, true or false, success or failure, gain or loss

As a higher intellectuality, wisdom requires us to be far-sighted and have deep insight into targeted things. wisdom requires us to stand up with the long-term social test, requires us to learn to be and learn not to be.

In ancient China, people often used the word "knowledge" instead of "wisdom". However, "learning" was more often used in Confucianism to emphasize the process of studying, learning from each other and building up knowledge. So wisdom involves every aspect of "learning".

Wisdom can be obtained more through life and social practice than text books. How to get wisdom can be learned from human's intellectual legacy, improvements in modern science and technology, more importantly, intelligence can be obtained through discoveries, experiments, attempts and innovations in social life.

虞舜躬行
Yú Shùn Gōng Xíng

【出处】《虞舜耕田》：昔舜在雷泽。见渔者，皆取深潭厚泽，而老弱则渔于急流浅滩之中。恻(cè)然哀之，往而渔焉。见争者，皆匿其过而不谈。见有让者，则揄扬而取法之。期年，皆以深潭厚泽相让矣。

【释义】舜懂得用自己的德行去影响人、感化人，使当地老百姓的价值观念得到了升华。

【Definition】Shun knows how to use his morality to influence people and probate people to make the values of local people sublimated.

【造句】虞舜躬行，靠的是待人以诚、以真，使人能感受到他善良的品性、淳厚的德行。

【Example】 "Yu Shun Gong Xing" refers to treating others with sincerity and integrity so that people can feel his good, pure and honest virtues.

【故事】

舜年轻的时候，在山东看捕鱼人抓鱼。他发现鱼藏丰富的静水、深潭之处，都被年轻力壮的人争相占取。而那些老弱的捕鱼人没有办法跟他们争，就被排斥在鱼少的急流、浅滩的水域，因此，不容易抓到鱼。

看到这个情景，舜感到非常伤感。于是，他就想办法来教化这些年轻人，让他们能够尊敬他人、关爱老人。舜用的方法很巧妙，他也下水一起抓鱼。见到有人相争，他就好言相劝，从中调解；如果当中有一两个相让的，他就表示很赞赏；如果碰到了别人过来抢他正在抓的鱼，他就有意地让那些来抢捕的人，没有抱怨；如果有人把鱼让给他抓捕，他就先道谢、再谦让。

陆 智 (Wisdom)

他用这个方法，与大家相处了一段时间。那些抢捕鱼的人，都被他感化了，不再你争我夺。就这样，渐渐在当地形成了一种相互礼让的风气。

Yu Shun was watching fishermen catching the fish at Shandong when he was young. He found that the fish usually hidden in the quiet deep pool where were taken by the young people. For the old and week one, they couldn't compete with them so that they were forced to catch the fish in the turbulence and shallows, which is not easy to do.

Yu Shun was sad by seeing this. Then he tried to figure a way to moralize the young, so that they will respect and care for the elder. He had a clever way to do this by going into the water and catching fish with them. When people argued, he mediated it; when one or two of them compromised he praised it; when someone grab away the fish that he was catching he left it without any complaints; when people gave the fish to him, he thanked them first with modesty.

Gradually in this way, people who were scrambled for catching fish were all moved by him. So the atmosphere of humbleness was rose.

【点评】

做一个对社会有益的人，很不容易。像舜那样，言传身教，潜移默化地改变着社会不良风气、人心状态，真是用心良苦。他念念不忘为大众着想，维护真理，坚持原则，既是一种礼节，一种与人为善，更是智慧人生价值的体现。舜是道德文化的鼻祖，舜文化是道德文化，是由野蛮走向文明的历史转折时期的中华文化。

It's never easy to be a person who benefit the society. It was precious for Yu Shun to change the bad customs by doing the good way himself, represented the value of wisdom. Shun was the originator of the moral tradition, part of the Chinese culture, which civilized us from savage。

不耻下问

Bù Chǐ Xià Wèn

【出处】《论语·公冶长》:敏而好学,不耻下问,是以谓之"文"也。

【释义】天资聪明而又爱好学习的人,认为如果有必要,即使是很低端的问题也会主动向人请教,并不因此感到羞耻。

【Definition】 A man, gifted and keen to learn, should take the initiative to ask some simple questions and do not therefore feel ashamed.

【造句】"不耻下问"这个成语,就是从孔子回答子贡的提问中概括出来的。

【Example】 "Bu Chi Xia Wen" is an idiom summarized in the Confucius's answers to Zi Gong's questions.

【故事】

孔子是我国春秋时期有名的思想家、政治家、教育家,儒家学派的创始人。他非常好学,对各种知识都很感兴趣,所以学识非常渊博,很有名望,人们都尊称他为圣人。但是他自己却不这么认为,他说:"谁都不是生下来就有学问的,我只是对学习不感到厌烦,对请教不感到可耻而已。"

一次,孔子到鲁国国君的祖庙参加典礼。他一进太庙,就向人问这问那,几乎每一件事都问到了。当时有人就在背后取笑孔子说:"他什么礼仪都不懂,见什么都问。"孔子听后坦然地说:"我遇见不懂的事情,就问个明白,这才是求知明礼的表现嘛。"

卫国大夫孔圉也聪明好学,更难得的是,他还是一个非常谦虚的人,但却英年早逝。卫国国君为了让后代的人都能学习和发扬孔圉的好学精神,就特地赐他一个"文公"的称号。后人就尊称孔圉为"孔文子"。

孔子的学生子贡也是卫国人,但他认为孔圉不配有那样高的评价,就问孔子说:"孔圉的学问及才华虽然很高,但是比他更杰出的人还有很多,凭什么赐给他'文公'的称号啊?"

孔子听了,和蔼地笑着说:"孔圉非常勤奋好学,脑子灵活,人又聪明,而且,如果他有任何不懂的事情,即使问题很简单,以他的地位或学问是应该理解、但可能理解的不全面,他都会很大方而谦虚地向人请教,并且不因此感到羞耻,这就是他难得的品质。所以说,赐给他'文公'的称号并不会不恰当。"经过孔子这样的解释,子贡终于信服了。

    Confucius, a Chinese ideologist, statesman, educator, originator of the Confucian school during the Spring and Autumn period. Entitled "Saint", he was eager to learn, curious about every kinds of knowledge which ensured his profound knowledge and fame. But he never thought like this, he said: "no one was born with knowledge, I am just never bored by learning, never shamed by asking."

    Once, he went to the ancestor temple of the emperor of Chu for attending the ceremony. Since he got in there, he wasn't stop asking questions. Someone was laughing behind him, said: "he has no awareness about etiquette so that he is asking about everything." When Confucius heard this, he replied calmly: "Ask the things you don't know is what we called the awareness of etiquette."

    An official of Empire Wei named Kong Yu was also eager to learn, preciously, he was a humble person who unfortunately died young. In order to promote the spirit, the emperor of Wei entitled him "Wen Gong". Later he was called "Kong Wenzi" by futurity.

Zi Gong, a student of Confucius, from Empire Wei, thought that Kong Yu didn't deserve the title and asked Confucius: "Although Kong Yu was knowledgeable and brilliant, there were numerous people better than him, why only him had been entitled "Wen Gong"?

Confucius smiled and replied: "Kong Yu was diligent and clever, besides, whenever he had confusion even it was a simple one which he supposed to know in his knowledge, he will ask people and not feel any shame on that; so this is his precious personality which fully deserve the title of 'Wen Gong'." Zi Gong was convinced by the explanation.

【点评】

"学问"就是不会就学，不懂就问。一个谦虚、好学的人，更应该真诚地向别人请问求教。在生活和学习中，如果有不明白的地方，就及时并虚心地向别人请教，不但可以学到新知识，还可以领悟其中的道理。善于学习的人，不会把向人求教当作耻辱的事，像万世师表的孔圣人和他的弟子孔圉那样：虚心求问，勤于求问，善于求问，不断积累知识、更新知识，不断地丰富和提高自己，才能适应社会的发展需要。

"Xue wen" means to learn or to ask when you don't know about a thing. A person who is modest and eager to learn should ask others for the answer sincerely. No matter it is in your life or study, if have any doubt, ask people, then you can learn the new knowledge and the truth. A person who knows how to study will never shame on asking for an answer, just like Confucius and his student Kong Yu. Only you ask modestly, diligently, properly; keep accumulating and updating your knowledge can you fit the demand of the social development.

晏子使楚
Yàn Zǐ Shǐ Chǔ

【出处】《晏子春秋》：楚王闻晏子将使楚，谓左右曰："晏婴，齐之习辞者也。今方来，吾欲辱之，何以也？"

【释义】 楚王得知齐国能言善辩的晏子出使到楚国，就召集手下人商量对付他的办法。

【Definition】 When Emperor Chu knew that Empery Qi would send Yan Zi, an eloquent delegate, to Chu, he summoned his men to discuss how to deal with Yan Zi.

【造句】 晏子使楚的故事，赞扬了晏子身上的凛然正气、爱国情怀和他高超的语言技巧。

【Example】 The story of Yan Zi here praised the awe-inspiring righteousness, patriotism and superb language skills of Yan Zi.

【故事】

晏子将出使到楚国。楚王听到这个消息，对手下说："晏婴是齐国善于言辞的人。他这次来，我想要羞辱他，用什么办法呢？"手下回答说："他见大王时，请允许我们绑着一个人从您面前走过。大王就问他是干什么的？我们回答说他是齐国人。大王再问他犯了什么罪？我们就说他犯了偷窃罪。"

晏子来到楚国。楚国人因为他身材矮小，就在城门旁边特意开了个小门请他进宫。晏子不同意，并说："只有出使狗国的人，才从狗洞中进去。现在我出使的是楚国，不应该从这小门进吧。"迎接他的人只好请晏子从正大门进去。

在宫殿里,晏子拜见楚王。楚王说:"齐国没有人了吗?"晏子回答说:"齐国首都临淄人口众多,张开衣袖连在一起可以遮天蔽日,挥洒汗水就像天下雨一样,肩挨着肩、脚跟着脚的,怎么能说齐国没有人呢?"楚王说:"既然这样,那为什么派你这样一个人来我们大楚国呢?"晏子回答说:"齐国派遣使臣有个规矩:贤明的人被派遣到贤明君主国,不贤或没有德才的人就派他到无能的君主国。我最无能,就派到楚国来了。"

接见仪式结束。楚王请晏子喝酒,喝到高潮时候,两个士兵绑着一个人走到楚王面前。楚王问:"绑着的人是做什么的?"士兵回答说:"他是齐国人,犯了偷窃罪。"楚王看着晏子问道:"齐国人本来就爱偷东西吗?"晏子起身,严肃地回答说:"我听说:橘生长在淮河以南就是橘子,生长在淮河以北就变成枳子,只是叶子的形状相似,可是它们的果实味道不同。这是什么原因呢?原来是水土条件不相同。同样的道理,齐国人在齐国能安居乐业,勤劳而诚恳,怎么一到楚国就成了盗贼了,也许是两国的水土不同吧。"

楚王听了,向晏子赔笑说:"我原来想和大夫您开个玩笑,没想到反被您开了我的玩笑了。"

Yan Zi was sent to Empire Chu. When Emperor Chu heard that, he said to his heeler:" Yan Zi is an eloquent delegate. In what way I can humiliate him?" Some said: "When he appeared himself, please allow us to tie up a man and walk through, then your majesty can ask who is he, we will reply he is a man of Qi. Your majesty can keep asking what has he done, we will say he is guilty of theft."

陆 智 (Wisdom)

When Yan Zi reached Empire Chu, they open a small door next to the main gate to let him in, for mocking his short figure. Yan Zi was discontent, said: "Only the person who was sent to a dog empire would walk through a dog hole. Since I was sent to Empire Chu, it shouldn't be like this kind of a small door." They can only let him walk inside through the main gate.

In the palace, Yan Zi paid a formal visit to Emperor Chu. Emperor Chu said: "No one else in Empire Qi could be sent?" Yan Zi replied: "In the capital of Empire Qi, Lin Zi, there has a huge population. They could cover the sky when they raise their sleeves, water the ground when they wipe their sweat. So much crowded and how can you say that we have no one in our country?" Emperor Chu argued: "Then why they sent you?" Yan Zi answered: "We have a rule like this: wise people will be sent to visit wise emperor, and vice versa. I am the most useless one, so that I was sent to Empire Chu."

After the meeting, Emperor Chu invited Yn Zi for drinking. At the climax, there were two solders holding a man to Emperor Chu. He asked: "Who is he?" The solder replied: "This man is a man of Qi, guilty of theft." The Emperor asked Yanzi, "Do you the people from the state of Qi like stealing?"

Yan zi stood up, left his seat, and said very respectfully: "I have heard that orange trees south of the Kuai River produce very good oranges, while those north of the river produce a kind of fruit that is very small and tastes sour. The trees south and north of the river have the same foliage, but the fruit of the latter is so different that it can hardly be called oranges. What causes this difference? It is the difference in their natural environment, including water and soil .Now, people born and brought up in Qi do not steal, but after they come to Chu, they become thieves. Does Chu have an environment that turns good people in to thieves?"

The duke laughed. "I should have known that a virtuous and learned man like you is not to be made fun of. I have only embarrassed myself." he said.

【点评】

yàn zǐ shì chūn qiū hòu qī yī wèi zhòng yào de zhèng zhì jiā sī xiǎng jiā wài jiāo jiā yīn wèi yǒu zhèng zhì
晏子是春秋后期一位 重 要 的 政 治家、思 想 家、外交家，因为有 政 治远见和卓越的外交才能而闻名于诸侯。楚国人本来想借晏子出使楚国的机会羞辱他,反而处处被动。晏子不辱使命,不仅维护了个人的尊严,更捍卫了齐的国格。之所以能赢得这场外交的胜利,就在于他不卑不亢,既针锋相对又有礼有节,思维敏捷,方式巧妙,说话得体,无懈可击。

Yan Zi was an important statesman, ideologist ,diplomat during the late Spring and Autumn Period,well-known for his political vision and diplomatic skills. Man of Chu wanted to humiliate him by the chance of his visit, but embarrassed themselves. Yan Zi completed his mission perfectly——defended not only his own dignity, but also the honor of Qi. The reason why he won is his attitude neither overbearing nor servile, also the quick-thinking, skillful debating and proper manner.

陆 智(Wisdom)

田单破燕
Tián Dān Pò Yān

【出处】《史记·田单列传》：田单知士卒之可用，乃身操版插，与士卒分功。妻妾编于行伍之间，尽散饮食飨(xiǎng)士。

【释义】 田单激起了士兵对敌作战的斗志，继续加强工事防御(yù)，扩充兵力，与士兵同甘共苦，出其不意攻敌不备，大获全胜。

【Definition】 Tian Dan motivated the soldiers' spirit to fight against the enemy, to strengthen the defense fortifications, to expand troops, and to attack the enemy until the victory.

【造句】 田单破燕这一仗，确实打得非常漂亮，历史学家司马迁对此给予了高度评价。

【Example】 The battle initiated by Tian Dan to defeat Empery Yan was a big victory and won the high praise of the historian Si Maqian.

【故事】

战国后期，周赧王三十一年，燕国将军乐毅率兵攻破齐国，连夺七十多座城池，接着又集中兵力围攻仅存的莒（今山东莒县）和即墨，齐国危在旦夕。当时，齐王被杀，他的儿子法章在莒被立为齐王，号召全民同心协力抗燕。乐毅率兵攻城一年没有拿下来，就命令燕军撤至距离两城九里以外的地方扎营，打算用攻心的方法取胜，于是形成双方相持的局面。

莒的邻地即墨，是齐国较大的一个城邑，物资充裕，人口较多，具有一定防御条件。即墨被围不久，保卫战中，守将战死，军民共推田单做将领。田单利用两军相持的时机，集结七千余士兵，加以整顿、扩充，增修城垒，巩固防务，和军民同甘共苦，不打仗的时候就编织草席，或者拿起农具搞劳动生产；要么就亲自巡视城防，还把家里的亲族不论男女老少都编入军队之中，因此深得军民信任。

田单在稳定内部的同时，为除掉最难对付的对手乐毅，就派人到燕国行使反间计，谎称：乐毅名义上在攻打齐国，其实想在齐国称王，故意缓攻即墨，拖延战机。如果燕国另派主将，即墨就会很快被拿下。燕惠王果然中计，就派了一个平庸的将领名叫骑劫的人，取代了乐毅。乐毅无路可走，就投奔赵国去了。

骑劫不用乐毅的战法，改用强攻，仍然不能拿下即墨，就用恐怖的手段慑服齐军。田单将计就计，诱使燕军对齐人采用割鼻、掘祖坟等暴行，即墨军民都痛恨到极点，发誓要与燕军决一死战。田单进一步地麻痹燕军，把精壮的甲士隐伏在城内，故意派老弱士兵、妇女登城守望。同时派遣使者献投降书；又让即墨富豪带上重金去贿赂燕国将领，假装投靠，只希望保全自家妻小。围城已超过三年的燕军，急欲停战回乡，见大功将成，只等受降，更加懈怠。

田单见反攻时机成熟，就集中一千多头牛，角缚利刃，尾扎浸油芦苇，身披五彩龙纹外衣，在一个夜间，下令点燃牛尾上的芦苇，牛被烧得负痛从城脚预先挖的几十个通道狂奔到燕营，五千精壮勇士紧随在后，城内军民擂鼓击器、呐喊助威。燕军见火光中无数角上有刀、身后冒火的怪物直冲而来，惊惶失措。齐军勇士乘势冲杀，城内军民紧跟助战，燕军夺路逃命，互相践踏，燕将骑劫在混乱中被杀。田单率

陆 智（Wisdom）

jūn chéng shèng zhuī jī　　qí guó mín zhòng yě chí xiè zhù zhàn　　hěn kuài jiāng yān jūn zhú chū guó jìng　　jìn fù shī dì
军乘胜追击，齐国民众也持械助战，很快将燕军逐出国境，尽复失地
qī shí yú chéng
七十余城。

  In the late period of the Warring States, the thirty-first year of the ruling of Emperor Zhou Nan, a general of empire Yan named Yue Yi conquered the Qi, took down over seventy cities, and then besieged the Ju and Jimo, put Qi in the crisis of perish. At that time, emperor Qi was murdered and his son, Fazhang succeeded at Ju, pulling together all the efforts to fight against Yan. After the attack lasted for one year, Yue Yi haven't took it down, so he let the army encamped nine miles away from the two cities, intended to crack it down from inside by using psychological strategy. So the situation was in a sort of glued state.

  Jimo, next to Ju, was a quite big city of Qi, which had abundant materials, huge population and defending ability. Soon after the besiegement, in the defending, the general of Jimo was sacrificed, so the armies and folks were all encouraged Tian Dan to be the leader. Tian Dan gathered seven thousands more solder by the chance of the glued state, trained the army, and built the fort. When fire ceased, he waved grass mat or worked in the field, together with the plebe. Otherwise he would check the defense of the city by himself. He also enrolled all of his relatives in the army, regardless of the gender or age, so people had faith on him.

  While he was trying to steady the internal, he sent people to Yan to spread the rumor that the real intention of Yue Yi is to make himself a king at Qi, that's why he delayed the attack. If Yan sent some other generals, soon Jimo will be taken. Emperor Hui fell into the trap as expected, sent a third-class general named Qi Jie to take over. Yue Yi was no way out then went to Zhao.

  Qi Jie used force to conquer Qi, but still failed, and then he threatened the army of Qi by means of terror. Tian Dan played along, tricked them to use the terror like slash the nose or grub the ancestral grave to infuriate the men of Jimo. Then he took a further step to make them flip and hided the force inside the wall; let the old, week solders and women guarded on the wall. Meanwhile, he sent messenger to surrender and asked the rich to bribe them with huge amount of fortune for surrender, in order to keep their families safe. The men of Yan have been on the war over three years, can't wait to go back home. Situation like this gave them an illusion of wining and made them more sluggish.

When Tian Dan thought it was the time to fight back, he gathered over a thousand oxen, in colorful dragon-embroidered coats, with sharp blades on horns, oily reeds on tails. One night, he ordered to fire the reeds, the oxen was burned with pain so that rushed towards the Yan's camps. With the tums and cheers from inside of the wall, five thousands warrior followed the oxen. Men of Yan were full of panics when they saw the monsters with blades and fire rushed towards them. They ran away in the fight with the warriors of Qi, and Qi Jie was killed in the chaos. Tian Dan followed up the victory, excluded all the enemies, and retrieved all of the lost territories.

【点评】

田单在极端不利的态势下，坚守孤城，积极创造反攻条件，巧妙运用反间计消耗劲敌、弱化对手；善于麻痹敌人，凝聚军心，激发斗志，坚定必胜信心；发明火牛阵实施夜间奇袭，最后反败为胜，成为中国古代战史上一个以弱胜强的很有创意的出色战例。故事给人的启发是：用兵打仗是一种诡诈的行为，具体战争中如何进行欺骗是不能预先进行规定的，讲究的是运筹帷幄，随机应变，出奇制胜。

Under the lose situation, Tian Dan refused to give up and took initiative steps to create the opportunity for fighting back, by sowing discord among the enemy to weaken the enemy. He inspired the spirit of the army and invented the fire bulls strategy that had became the turning point of the battle, which regarded as a creative example for triumphing over superior forces in our ancient war history. What the story tells is that using military forces is a crafty thing which is unpredictable, and it is all about outsmarting your enemy, adapting to the situation and ace in the hole.

陆 智 (Wisdom)

韩信忍辱
Hán Xìn Rěn Rǔ

【出处】《史记·淮阴侯列传》:得忍且忍,得耐且耐。不忍不耐,小事成大。

【释义】 小不忍则乱大谋;大丈夫能屈能伸,才可能在得志的时候大干一番。

【Definition】 A little impatience spoils great plans; a great man should learn to yield at right times and then can achieve his own ambitions eventually.

【造句】 像韩信忍辱那样,为了事业能屈能伸、能忍能让,才是最坚强的人。

【Example】 People like Han Xin who can tolerate and yield are the strongest ones at last.

【故事】

西汉的韩信,在他很小的时候,父母就去世了。作为一个普通人,他过着贫困的生活,有时候甚至连饭都吃不上。成年后,他一个大男人,整天挎把剑,啥也干不了,到处混饭吃,当地的人都很讨厌他。

因为他不讨人喜欢,大家就瞧不起他,当地的一些地痞无赖总欺负他。一天,一群无赖拦住韩信,其中一个带头人对他说:"你这个家伙,虽然长得又高又大,还佩带刀剑,其实你的胆子很小。如果你有胆子,就用你的佩剑来刺我;没胆子的话,就从我裤裆下钻过去吧!"

他这么一说,一大群泼皮无赖"呼啦"都围上来看热闹。韩信仔细地打量了他一番,单挑肯定没问题。但韩信知道,这个痞子是他们的老大,如果把他打趴后,众泼皮一哄而上,自己肯定吃亏。于是忍住一时之气,从那人的裤裆下钻了过去。满街的人都笑话韩信,认为他胆小。

这就是有名的胯下之辱。韩信把这次受辱当成前进的动力,来激励自己一定要有所作为,以便日后一展才华。后来他投军当兵,作为有名的军事家、战略战术家,不但英勇善战,而且足智多谋,帮助刘邦建立了西汉,成为集"王侯将相"于一身的人。

Han Xin, who lived in the Western Han Dynasty, had lost both his parents when he was young. As a civilian he lived a poor life, sometimes couldn't feed himself. After he grown up, he did nothing but hung around with a sword, which was despised by the others.

So he got bullied a lot. One day, a bunch of bullies got in his way and the leader said: "You idiot, though you have a strong body and a sword, still have no guts. Come stab me with your sword, or crawl through my crotch."

Then the other bullies came around to watch. Han Xin looked him and believed he can beat him down in a single combat. But he knew that there were loads of them who will definitely rush at him after he beat their leader and it will end with his defeat. So he took a deep breath and crawled through the crotch. People filled the street were all laugh at his cowardice.

This is the famous story of "Kua Xia Zhi Rui." Han Xin regarded this shame as an impetus to stimulate himself. Later he joined the army, became a famous militarist and strategist. Not only brave but also resourceful, he helped Liu Bang built the Empire of Western Han and became a powerful man.

【点评】

现实生活中,与人相处难免会有摩擦,有时候是没有必要生气的,能忍耐就尽量忍耐。一个能够沉得住气的人,才更能成就大的事业,比如韩信。他一直在寻找机会,来到刘邦军营里当兵,凭自己过硬的本领,

陆 智(Wisdom)

很快就当上了大将军,成就了一番辉煌的事业。如果韩信当初一气之下呈匹夫之勇,打败那个地痞头子、死杀几个小混混,但依照"杀人偿命"的法令,韩信就没有当上大将军的命了,更不可能成就一番轰轰烈烈的事业。

    In real life, there is always some friction between people, which is no need to be angry about. A man could tolerate can achieve a greater career, just like Han Xin. He kept looking for a chance then joined the army of Liu Bang, became a general on his own, glorified his life. Suppose he had beaten or killed several of the bullies in his anger, according to the law, he will be sentenced to death ,which means he couldn't even have his life to be a great general, let alone a glorious life.

英勇班超

Yīng Yǒng Bān Chāo

【出处】《后汉书·班超传》：不入虎穴，不得虎子。当今之计，独有因夜以火攻虏(lǔ)使，彼不知我多少，必大震怖，可殄(tiǎn)尽也。灭此虏则鄯(shàn)善破胆，功成事立矣。

【释义】 在非常时期，要取得意想不到的辉煌成果，就要担风险。

【Definition】 In critical times, we have to take risks to get unexpected brilliant achievements.

【造句】 英勇班超，集勇武、智慧、远见卓识于一身，是不可多得的优秀外交官。

【Example】 The hero Ban Chao is an excellent diplomat of valor, wisdom and visiont.

【故事】

为了抵抗匈奴，汉朝派都尉窦固出兵。窦固实施汉武帝的国防策略：派人联络西域各国，共同对付匈奴。窦固因为很赏识班超的才干，就任命班超为代司马，派他出使西域。西域有个鄯善国（今新疆境内），是丝绸之路的起点国，更是汉、匈两军争夺西域控制权的战略要地。而鄯善王在汉与匈的斗争中求生存，一向奉行"谁胜就倒向谁"的外交政策。

班超带着三十六个人到了鄯善。鄯善原来是归附匈奴的，由于匈奴逼他们纳税进贡，勒索财物，鄯善王对此很不满意，就想依附大汉朝。但最近几十年来，汉朝顾不到西域的事务，鄯善王只好勉强听命于匈奴；这次汉朝派了使者来，就很殷勤地招待着他们。

陆 智 (Wisdom)

过了几天,班超发现鄯善王对待他们的态度忽然冷淡了,就疑心起来,他跟随从人员说:"你们看出来吗?鄯善王对待我们的态度和前几天不一样了,我猜想一定有匈奴的使者来了。"正好这时,鄯善王派了仆人送酒食来。班超装着早就知道的样子,说:"匈奴的使者已经来了几天了,他们住在什么地方?"

鄯善王和匈奴使者打交道,本来就瞒着班超。那个仆人被班超这突然一问,以为班超已知道这件事,只好老实回答:"来了三天,他们住的地方离这三十里。"班超就把那个仆人扣留起来,立刻召集所有随从人员说:"我们来到西域,无非是想立功报国。现在匈奴使者才到几天,鄯善王的态度就变了。他要是把我们抓起来送给匈奴人,我们就连尸骨都不能送回老家了。大家看怎么办?"

随从都说:"现在情况危急,我们全听你的!"班超见大家士气高涨,趁机鼓舞说:"不入虎穴,焉得虎子?现在只有一个办法,趁着黑夜,到匈奴的帐篷周围,一面放火,一面进攻。他们不知道咱们人马多少,一定慌乱。只要杀了匈奴的使者,事情就好办了。"大家齐声说:"我们听司马的,一定和他们拼命!"

到了半夜,班超领三十六个壮士偷袭匈奴的帐篷。恰好赶上刮大风。班超吩咐十个人拿着战鼓躲在匈奴的帐篷后面,二十个人埋伏在帐篷前面,自己和其余的人顺风放火。安排妥当后,大家分头行事,火一烧起来,鼓声、呐喊声震天,埋伏在帐篷外面的人大喊大叫地杀进帐篷。匈奴人从梦里惊醒，到处乱窜，结果匈奴使者和几十个随从全部被杀死。

班超回到自己的营房里，天刚蒙蒙亮，立即派人请来鄯善王。鄯善王一听情况汇报，得知匈奴的使者已经全部被杀死，立刻表示，愿意臣服汉朝。

In order to fight against Huns, Han authority sent Dou Gu to lead the troops. Doug Gu used the defending strategy of Emperor Wudi, pulling together the countries of west region. Doug Gu appreciated Ban Chao's talent so he sent him to the west region. There was a country named Shanshan in the west region, which is the beginning of the Silk Road, and a strategic area that Han and Huns fought for. In this battle, the king of Shanshan declared that he will only take the winner's side.

Ban Chao reached Shanshan with 36 people. Shanshan used to be a dependency of Huns, but the heavy tax and extortion discontented the king so he wanted to attach to Han. Unfortunately Han didn't help them for decades, so that they were forced to compromise to Huns. They were extremely hospitable for the Han's delegators this time.

Few days later, Ban Chao found their hospitality has been declined, so he asked the attendants: "Can you feel that? The king has a different attitude than before; I think the delegator of Huns must come." Meanwhile, the king sent the servant for delivering the food. Ban Chao asked as if he already knew: "So the delegators of Huns have been here for days, where do they live?"

The king never told Ban Chao that he was meeting the delegator of Huns. As he asked in this way, the servants thought he already knew so confessed: "It's been three days; they have lived thirty miles away from here." Ban Chao detained the servant and gathered all the people: "We came here for serving our country. But the king's attitude has been changed since the delegator of our enemy came. If he catches us to be a present for Huns, we wouldn't leave a piece. What do you all think we should do?"

All the attendants said: "It's an emergency now, we follow you!" Ban Chao inspired them: "Nothing ventured, nothing gained. The only way out is to fire their camps and attack them at night. They must be flurried since they have no idea how many of us are attacking. Everything will be fine after we killed them." All said: "we will fight for your order with our lives."

In the midnight, Ban Chao led the 36 warriors attacked Huns' delegators. It happened to be a windy night. Ban Chao ordered ten warriors hide behind the camps with war drums, twenty ambushed in front of it, while he and the rest set the fire. When everybody on their position, the fire burned, the drums boomed, the men shouted and burst into the camps. The Huns woke up with a start and rushed around, all killed.

It was dawn when Ban Chao back to the barracks then he invited the king. As soon as the king was reported that all of the delegators of Huns were killed, he surrendered.

【点评】

班超在鄯善国,察知有变,便智诱鄯善国的仆人,并果断地采取相应措施,控制了形势;接着用激将法,发动官兵,鼓起同胞同仇敌忾的斗志,带领全部随从,深入虎穴,出敌不意,火攻匈奴,斩杀了匈奴的使者及随从,一举获胜,争取了鄯善国的绝对信任。在当时深入敌后、形势随时可能逆转的环境条件下,显示了班超的机智、果断、英勇和远见卓识。

The moment when Ban Chao felt the change at Shanshan, he tricked the servant and took the measures, handled the situation. Then he stimulates the fighting will and attacked the enemies, won the trust from Shanshan. In the dangerous and changeable situation, Ban Chao showed his wisdom, determination, brave and vision.

孔融拜客
Kǒng Róng Bài Kè

【出处】 《世说新语·言语》:孔文举年十岁,随父到洛。……小时了了,大未必佳。

【释义】 人不可貌相,因此,人不能因少年时聪明而断定他日后就一定有作为。

【Definition】 Never judge a man by appearance; therefore, though very smart at young age, a man cannot surely ensure success.

【造句】 孔融拜客的描述,让年龄虽小但机智异常的孔融形象体现得淋漓尽致。

【Example】 The description of Kong Rong presents a small boy but with witty personality.

【故事】

孔融是东汉文学家,位居"建安七子"之首。他小时候,不仅学习勤奋,而且善于思考。平时,父亲外出拜客,总是带着他去。十岁那年,父亲带他来到洛阳。洛阳城有个名气很大的人叫李膺,当时正担任纠察朝廷百官的司隶校尉之职,去他家登门拜访的人,都是些才智出众的或有很高声誉的人以及他的亲戚,一般的人都无缘登门拜访。

孔融来到洛阳,当然要想办法去拜访这个达官显贵。他独自来到李府官邸,大模大样地直接往李家府内走。守门人急忙拉住问他:"你是哪家小孩,到一边玩去!"孔融严肃地回答说:"请你进去通报,就说山东孔融来访。"守门人见他一本正经,不知是什么来头,就笑着问:"小公子,可有红帖?"孔融说:"我家和你家主人世代交往,又有师生之谊,无需红帖,请只管通报。"

陆 智 (Wisdom)

守门人怕慢待了贵客,赶紧去通报。这时李膺正和许多文人雅士在交谈,听了通报,一时想不起这孔融和自己有什么关系,打着哈哈说:"有请!有请!"守门人回身邀请,小孔融大大方方地走进大厅,一边向主人问候,一边拱手招呼各位来宾,态度不亢不卑。李膺一边让座,一边打量着这位俊才少年,心里好生奇怪:这小孩从未见过面,而他为何自称"世家"?于是问道:"小公子,你说我们两家世代交情,我怎么从未见过你啊?"

孔融微笑着说:"五百年前,孔子曾经问礼于老子。孔子姓孔,老子姓李,说明孔、李两家早就有师生之谊。今你姓李,我姓孔,也是师生关系,我们两家不是累世通家嘛。"

孔融语出惊人,在座客人无不暗暗称奇。太守李膺不禁哈哈大笑起来:"小公子真神童也。"其中有个太中大夫陈韪不以为然,冷冷地说:"小时候聪明的人,长大后未必有作为。"孔融听了,笑着对他说:"这样说来,想必先生小时候一定很聪明。"这一巧妙对答,弄得陈韪面红耳赤无言回对,只好坐在一旁生闷气。孔融则目不斜视,装着大人模样,一本正经地喝着茶,引得大家更是捧腹大笑。

Kong Rong, a litterateur, the first of Jian'an Qizi during the Eastern Han dynasty. He was diligent and thoughtful when he was young. His father always takes him when visiting others. He went to Luoyang with his father when he was ten. There was a famous man named Li Ying at Luoyang, serving as Sili Xiowei, whom only outstanding people or relatives are able to visit.

When Kong Rong reached Luoyang, he tried to visit him. He came to the Li Mansion and went straight into it. The porter pulled him and asks: "who are you little child? Step aside! " Kong Rong replied seriously: "Please inform your master that Kong Rong from Shandong came to visit." The porter confused by his serious looking, then smiled to him: "Little chided you have invitation letter? " Kong Rong said: "My family has friendship with your master for many generations, also the deep relationship between teacher and student, so there is no need for invitation. You just need to inform."

The porter was afraid he slighted the respected guest, hurried to inform. Li Ying was talking with many celebrities that time, couldn't remember what kind of relationship he might have between Kong Rong for a short while, so he told the porter to invite him inside. Kong Rong came in the hall calmly and greeted everyone, neither haughty nor humble. Li Ying was offering him a seat and observing him, wondering who is he and why he said they has family friendship. Then he asked: "Little childe, you said that we have family friendship, but it seems like I never saw you before."

Kong Rong smiled: "Five hundreds years ago, Confucius worshiped Laocius as teacher. The family name of Confucius is Kong, that of Laocius is Li, means Kong family and Li family had relationship of teacher and student since five hundreds years ago. Now you are from Li family and I'm from Kong family, so you are my teacher means we have family relationship for generations."

The guests were all surprised by his words. Li Ying laughed: "Little childe you are such a child prodigy." One man served as the doctor's in abnormality named Chen Wei frowned at him and said coldly: " Smart at childhood may not capable of outstanding achievements when grown up."Kong Rong siled and replied: " Then you must be very smart when you are a child." The answer embarrassed Chen Wei a lot. But Kong Rong looked steadily forward and drank the tea as if he was an adult, which made everyone roll in the aisles.

陆 智(Wisdom)

【点评】

一个十岁的小孩，竟然单独去拜访大名鼎鼎的李膺，能产生这样的念头，本身就是一种超常智慧的表现。无名之辈的小孔融，凭他的聪明才智顺利地弄到了"门票"，成为李膺的座上宾。在回答李膺的问话中，巧妙运用"亲戚关系"这个概念，将老子与孔子二者之间的师生关系延伸到李膺与自己的关系上，人们因其思维敏捷而称奇。在应对陈韪的奚落时，更加显示了小孔融的敏捷和机智。

A ten-year-old child dare to visit Li Ying the famous and have these wonderful words, it is a super intelligence itself. Anonymous child as Kong Rong is, used his smartness got the ticket to be the guest of Li Ying. He was too clever to use the concept of relative relationship in the communication between Li Ying, extended the relationship between Confucius and Laocius to himself and Li Ying, surprised people. Besides, he showed his impressive wit when facing the taunt from Chen Wei.

羲之教子

Xī Zhī Jiào Zǐ

【出处】《东观馀论》：王氏凝、操、徽、涣之四子书，与子敬书俱传，皆得家范，而体各不同。凝之得其韵，操之得其体，徽之得其势，涣之得其貌，献之得其源。

【释义】 东晋著名书法家王羲之的几个儿子，在书法涵养方面颇得其父家传，各有成就。

【Definition】 Wang Xizhi, a famous calligrapher in Dongjin Dynasty, had several sons who were affected by him in calligraphy and made great achievements.

【造句】 羲之教子，主要法子有：先是激发学习兴趣，再辅之以科学方法，果然有效。

【Example】 Ways taken by Wang Xizhi to teach his sons are: stimulating interest in learning and then effective scientific method.

【故事】

王羲之是东晋大书法家，他的书法艺术造诣很高，被公认为"书圣"。王献之是王羲之的第七个儿子，自幼聪明好学，七八岁时开始跟父亲学书法。书法上专工草书隶书，也擅长作画。一次，王羲之看献之正聚精会神地练习书法，便悄悄走到背后，突然伸手去抽献之手中的毛笔。献之握笔很牢，没被抽掉。父亲很高兴，夸赞道："此儿后当复有大名。"小献之听后，心中沾沾自喜。还有一次，羲之的一位朋友让献之在扇子上写字，献之挥笔便写，突然笔落扇上，把字污染了，小献之灵机一动，一头小牛栩栩如生地出现在扇面上。再加上众人对献之书法绘画赞不绝口，小献之滋长了骄傲情绪。他父母见此情景，若有所思。一天，小献之问妈妈："我练书法，只要再写

陆 智（Wisdom）

上三年就行了吧？"妈妈摇摇头。"五年总行了吧？"妈妈又摇摇头。献之急了，问妈妈说："那您说究竟要多长时间？""你要记住：写完院里这十八缸水，你的字才会有筋有骨、有血有肉，才会站得直、立得稳。"

献之闻言回头一看，原来父亲已经站在了他的背后。王献之心中不服，但什么都没说，一咬牙又练了五年，把一大堆写好的字送给父亲看，希望听到几句表扬的话。谁知，王羲之一张张掀过，一个劲地摇头。掀到一个"大"字，现出了较满意的表情，随手在"大"字下填了一个点，然后把字稿全部退还给献之。

小献之心中仍然不服，又将全部习字稿抱给母亲看，并说："我又练了五年，并且是完全按照父亲的字样练的。您仔细看看，我和父亲的字还有什么不同？"母亲果然认真地看了几天，最后指着王羲之在"大"字下加的那个点儿，叹了口气说："吾儿磨尽三缸水，惟有一点似羲之。"献之听后泄气了，有气无力地说："难啊！这样下去，啥时候才能有好结果呢？"母亲见他的骄气已经消尽了，就鼓励他说："孩子，只要功夫深，就没有翻不过的山。你只要像这几年一样坚持练下去，就一定会达到目的的！"献之听完后，深受感动，又锲而不舍地练下去。果然，功夫不负有心人。献之练字用尽了十八大缸水，书法艺术突飞猛进，功力也到了力透纸背、炉火纯青的程度。后来，他的字和王羲之的字并列，被称为"二王"。

Wang Xizhi was a famous calligrapher in Dongjin Dynasty. He is called as "saint calligraphist" due to his great attainment on calligraphy.Wang Xianzhi is the 7th son of Wang Xizhi. He was born clever and studious. Wang Xianzhi started to learn calligraphy from his father since 7 years old. He specialized in official script and cursive script.

Meanwhile, he was also good at painting.

One day, Wang Xizhi saw his son concentrating his attention on practicing calligraphy. Then he walked to the behind of Xianzhi and suddenly tried to take out his writing brush. But he failed due to the tight hold of Xianzhi. The father was pleased and praised that "This son will have great achievements in the future." It made Xianzhi complacent. Another day, one of Xizhi's friends wanted Xianzhi to write on a fan. He took the brush and started to write immediately. All of a sudden, the brush fell on the fan and polluted the writing. A bright idea occurred to Xianzhi's brain; he turned the stain into a little cow as vivid as alive. This event added with the surrounding compliments to the calligraphy and painting skill of Xianzhi made him real arrogant.

His parents started to worried about this child. Once little Xianzhi asked to mom "Three more years of calligraphy practice is enough for me, isn't it?" Mom shook her head. "Five years then?" Mom shook again. Xianzhi became anxious and asked: "How long does it need on earth?" "Remember, your writings will be stable and vivid only if you use up all the 18 vats of water in practicing calligraphy."

After hearing this, Xianzhi looked back and saw his father has stood behind him. Wang Xianzhi didn't say anything, but he was not going to give up. Instead, he continued his tough practice for another five years. Xianzhi took a pile of his work to father hoping for a few words of praise. However, Wang Xizhi kept shaking his head while looking the writings. He only showed a satisfactory expression when he saw the word "big" that the son wrote. Xizhi filled a dot under the word "big" and then returned all the works to Xianzhi.

Little Xianzhi still refused to accept this result. He held all the writing draft to see his mother and said: "I have practiced for five more years, and I did it completely in accordance with the father's writings. Take a look carefully, what's the difference between my writings and my father's?" His mother looked over it seriously for a few days, finally she pointed to the dot that Wang Xizhi added under the word "big", sighed and said: "my son used up all three vats of water, but only a dot looks like his father's work." Xianzhi felt discouraged and said in low spirit: "It's so difficult! When can I have good results?"

Heard this, mother knew that his arrogance has disappeared then encouraged him and said: "my child, as long as you insist in one thing, there are no mountains that you can't climb over. All you need to do is keep practicing like you did these years and then you will achieve your goal!"

陆 智（Wisdom）

Xianzhi was touched by those words and starting practicing again. Sure enough, hard work pays off. Xianzhi used up 18 vats of water and had a big improvement in calligraphy. His skill of calligraphy nearly reached the level of perfection. Later, his works are as good as his father and people call them "the two Wang".

【点评】

王羲之共有七个儿子。他曾费尽心思培养前六个儿子，但效果都不理想。于是吸取教训，改变教法，对第七子王献之来了个"欲擒故纵"：他写字的时候，故意不让献之进书房。献之好奇，就在书房楼上的地板中挖了个洞，往下偷看，见父亲笔走龙蛇、出神入化，顿生羡慕，在暗暗记着父亲的笔法之后，再来模仿。久而久之，他对书法产生了浓厚兴趣。羲之见献之有了学习的内动力，觉得时机已到，便开始教他。但不再用以前教儿子的那种方法，而是采用启发的方式，只是在紧要关头给予必要的点拨，很多道理让献之自己去观察、去琢磨、去思考。王献之如饥似渴地自主学习，书法与日俱进，终于和父亲并称"二王"，齐名天下。

Wang Xizhi has seven sons. He tried hard to cultivate the first six sons, but the effect is not ideal. So he took the lessons and changed the ways of teaching Xianzhi. He used a method called "at large the better to apprehend him". Wang Xizhi deliberately wouldn't let his little son enter his study room when he was writing. Being curious, Wang Xianzhi dug a hole on the floor of the upstairs to peek and he saw his father writing, reaching the acme of perfection. Little Xianzhi envied it. He secretly memorized father's brushwork and then imitated. In the course of time, he had a strong interest in calligraphy. Xizhi found that his son already had the inner motivation to learn, so he thought it's the time to teach him. He changed a way of teaching again, using elicitation method this time. Xizhi only gave him the necessary coaching at the crucial moment. Most things were waited for the son himself to observe and think. Wang Xianzhi autonomously learned as he was hunger and thirst. Finally he got a huge progress in calligraphy and became as famous as his father.

用人不疑

Yòng Rén Bù Yí

【出处】《三国志·魏书·郭嘉传》裴松之注引《傅子》：用人无疑，唯才所宜。

【释义】 任用一个人，就不要怀疑他，而要看他的能力合适做什么，就安排什么岗位。

【Definition】 By appointing a person, do not doubt him, but assign tasks according to his ability.

【造句】"用人不疑"与"疑人不用"并用，是领导者的用人哲学。

【Example】 Combination of "Yong Ren Bu Yi" and "Yi Ren Bu Yong" is a leader's employment philosophy.

【故事】

先前，齐桓公刚做中原盟主的时候，因宋国不辞而别，就打算收服宋。在任用高级管理人员的时候，遇到管仲推荐的宁戚，但在重用之前有个大臣建议先打听了解一下宁戚的情况。齐桓公说：既然仲父推荐就不要打听了，免得知道一些小毛病而影响对他的任用。这就是"用人不疑"的最初渊源。后来，宁戚果然在劝说宋国与齐国订立盟约方面做出了很大贡献。

无独有偶。宋太祖时，郭进的官职是西山巡检，有人密报说他暗地里与河东刘继元有交往，将来有可能造反。太祖听后大怒，认为这是诬害忠良之人，下令将告密的人绑起来交给郭进，让郭进自己处置。郭进并没有对告密人怎么样，只对他说："如果你能帮我攻占河东刘继元的一城

陆 智（Wisdom）

一寨，我不但赦免你的死罪，还能赏你一个官职。"过了一段时间，到了年终，这个告密的人前来向郭进交差说，已经将刘继元控制的一个城的人马诱降过来了。

郭进就把他做的这件事上报给朝廷，并请求给他一官半职。宋太祖说："他曾经诬害我的忠良之臣，现在办成了这件事，可以免掉他的死罪，但不能给他官职。"于是，命令将这个人还是交给郭进处理。郭进再次进言说："如果皇上让我失信于人，那我以后还怎么用人啊？"太祖听了，认为上下级之间也是应该守信的，就给那人赏了一个官职。

Long time ago, Duke Huan of country Qi intended to subdue the country Song after he became the leader of the central plains. He needs to hire a superior manager and his minister Guan Zhong recommended a man called Ning Qi. Another minister suggested Duke Huan to investigate this person before appoint him. But Duke Huan said that it was not necessary as he was recommended by Guan Zhong. It will affect my trust if I did the investigation and know some little problem of him. This is the original source of "employers do not suspect." As expected, Ning Qi made a great contribution in persuading country Song making a league with country Qi.

It happens that there is a similar case. In the beginning of the Song dynasty, Guo Jin's position was an inspector of Xishan district. An informant reported to the emperor that Guo Jin was in contact with Liu Jiyuan in secret and they may rebel in future. The emperor was furious after hearing this. He thought it was slander so he gave orders to arrest this person and let Guo Jin handle it. Guo Jin didn't punish the informant but told him that if he can capture any Liu Jiyuan's city or village, Guo Jin will give him an official position. After a period of time, near the end of the year, the informant came to Guo Jin and reported that he already persuaded all the people of a Liu Jiyuan's city surrender to Guo Jin.

Guo Jin reported this thing to the emperor and asked a position for the informant. The emperor said:" He used to frame my loyal minister, I can remit him from death but I can't give him anything." Guo Jin replied:"How can people trust me if your Majesty made my promise broken？" The emperor thought that superior and subordinate should be faithful to each other so he gave a position to the informant.

【点评】

故事给人的启发在于："用人不疑"是一种较为合理的人才使用观。在人才没有使用的时候，谨慎地考察是必要的。人才考察，强调德才兼备，兼顾其他方面，以便发现其优势和弱势，做好必要的预防和培养工作。在这个前提下，任用他，信任他，就能充分发挥人才的主观能动性。

The story inspired us that "employers do not suspect" is a reasonable conception in the use of talents. When personnel are not employed, a careful observation is necessary. Personnel investigation stressed that ability and political integrity are both important. Have consideration to other aspects so that some advantages and weaknesses will be found. It's good for making the necessary prevention and training work. In this premise, appointing and trusting the employee can inspire the initiative of talent.

陆 智(Wisdom)

画龙点睛
Huà Lóng Diǎn Jīng

【出处】《历代名画记·张僧繇》：张僧繇(yóu)于金陵安乐寺,画四龙于壁,不点睛。每曰"点之即飞去"。人以为诞(dàn),因点其一。须臾(yú),雷电破壁,一龙乘云上天,未点睛者皆在。

【释义】 画龙之后再点上眼睛。比喻在关键地方简明扼要地点明要旨,使内容生动传神。

【Definition】 "Hua Long Dian Jing"（Add the finishing touch）means highlighting the crucial point to make the works lively and vivid.

【造句】 文章的一个好题目,对作品常常有"画龙点睛"之妙,激发人们阅读的兴趣。

【Example】 Article with a good title like "Hua Long Dian Jing" can arouse the interests of readers.

【故事】

南北朝时期的梁朝,有位很出名的大画家名叫张僧繇,他绘画的技术很高超。当时的皇帝梁武帝信奉佛教,修建的很多寺庙,都让他去作画。

有一次,皇帝命令他在金陵安乐寺的墙壁上画龙。不一会儿,两条栩栩如生的龙就出现在墙壁上。这时皇帝发现这两条龙都没有眼睛,就问张僧繇这是为什么。

张僧繇回答说:"画上眼睛的话,它们就会飞走的。"围观的人都不相信,皇帝就下令要他画上眼睛。张僧繇被逼得没有办法,不得不给龙画上眼睛,但是他为了要让庙中留下一条龙,只肯为其中的一条龙"点睛"。

紧接着,奇怪的事情果然发生了。突然间,天空乌云密布,狂风四起,雷鸣电闪,在雷电之中,人们看见被"点睛"的那条龙震破墙壁凌空而起,张牙舞爪地腾云驾雾,飞向天空……

目睹此情此景,在场的人都惊得目瞪口呆,说不出一句话来。过了一会,云散天晴。再看看墙上,只剩下那条没有被点上眼睛的龙。

In the Liang dynasty of Northern and Southern Dynasties, there was a famous painter called Zhang Sengyou. He has excellent skill in painting. The emperor then who believed in Buddhism asked him to paint for a lot of temples.

Once, the emperor ordered him to draw dragons on the wall of An Le temple in Jin Ling. After a while, two dragons as vivid as life appeared on the wall. The emperor found that the dragons didn't have eyes. So he asked the painter for a reason.

Zhang Sengyou answered: "They will fly away if I draw the eyes." Nobody believed him. The emperor asked him to add the eyes. Under the pressure, the painter had to draw eyes for the dragon. But he would only add eyes for one dragon because he wants to keep one dragon in the temple.

Strange things happened when he finished. All of a sudden, the sky was clouded over, strong wind blew, lightning flashed and thunder rumbled. People saw the dragon with eyes broke the wall and flew up to the sky and then disappeared in clouds.

Seeing this, people present were all shocked and stunned. Sooner, clouds were gone and sun came out again. Only the dragon without eyes was left on the wall.

【点评】

张僧繇画龙的故事,只是一个传说,人们根据这个传说形成了

陆 智（Wisdom）

"画龙点睛"这个成语，比喻说话或写文章，在主要处用上关键性的、精辟的一两句话，来点明要旨，内容就更加生动有力了。因为张僧繇给龙"点"了眼睛，就发生了一个"质"的飞跃；而"质"的飞跃之所以出现，即在于张僧繇运用了创新的手法。这就是故事给人的启示。

The story of Zhang Sengyou is just a legend. The idiom "Hua Long Dian Jing" was from this story. It means using some crucial words in key point to clarify the main ideas when talking or writing can make the whole content more vivid and more powerful. Added with eyes, a qualitative leap happened. This story inspired us of being creative.

柒 忠

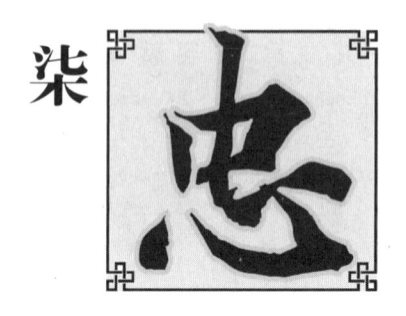

Loyalty

忠者,敬也,诚心尽力的意思。"忠"是中国传统伦理中的一个重要的观念和规范,是中华民族的伟大精神。就其社会内容而言,"忠"包含着政治社会伦理的广泛意义。孔子认为:忠表现在与人交往中的忠诚老实,即"己欲立而立人,己欲达而达人",意思是指自己想成功,首先使别人也能成功;自己想被人理解,首先要理解别人。

所谓"敬笃、敬事、敬人、笃实"是对"诚"的要求;"形于外必发于中"则要求人的言语行为必须出于本心,必须用认真的态度对待:心于意识,志于梦想,志于心守。就这个意义而言,"忠",是忠于自己的心志。

忠有"大忠"和"小忠"的区别,大忠于己,小忠于国。"忠己",就是忠于自己的意识和梦想,一个不忠于己的人,就谈

柒 忠（Loyalty）

不上忠于人、忠于家、忠于组织、忠于国。不少人认为："忠"国"是忠的最高表现，其实这只是忠的终极荣誉，忠"己"才是忠的终极体现，因为如果放弃忠己，则必定失去"忠"的灵魂，根本谈不上忠于国。再者，忠己需要勇气，也需要能力，更需要责任，甚至牺牲。本篇中所选的，就是这样一些故事。

    Loyalty is about respect, which means doing one's utmost for someone with sincerity. Loyalty is one of the essential notions and norms of the Chinese traditional ethics, which reflects the great spirit of the Chinese nation. In a large sense, loyalty is embedded with the notion of politics, social ethics in terms of its social content. Confucius the great philosopher believes that loyalty manifested in the intercourse with others when people are honest and faithful, namely, ? a humane person is one who helps others establish what he himself wishes to establish and to achieve what he himself wishes to achieve.

    To behave discreet, dedicate to one's occupation, respect for others and being upright are the requirements of loyalty. People's conducts are in accordance with their thoughts, which demand people to behave and speak form their own heart with an earnest attitude, that is to say, to know his own heart, to stick to his dreams and to keep a clear conscience. In that sense, loyalty is about observing to one's mind.

    Loyalty differs in its significance, and there are major loyalty and minor loyalty. People mainly loyal to his own heart, and then loyal to his country. To be true to oneself is to stick to his conscience and dreams. And people who are unfaithful to his own heart shall never meet the qualifications of being loyal to the others, his family and the community as well as his country. Many people believe that being loyal to one's country is the supreme expression of loyalty; however, in fact, it is merely the highest honor of loyalty. To be loyal to him himself is the supreme expression of loyalty. Because if a person gives up being true to himself, his spirit of loyalty will be deprived, not mention to be loyal to his own country. Furthermore, to be true to oneself requires courage, capability and responsibility, even sacrifice to some points. The stories collected in this chapter can well explain it.

比干死争

Bǐ Gān Sǐ Zhēng

【出处】 《史记·殷本纪》：比干强谏，尽其忠诚，纣王淫泆(yì)，遂以死争。

【释义】 商朝的比干，一生忠君爱国，因为向纣王强行进谏，却被剖心而死。

【Definition】 Bi Gan devoted all his life to the king and nation, but he was split on his heart just because of his advice to Emperor Zhou.

【造句】 比干死争，无愧于"亘古第一忠臣"的称号。

【Example】 Bi Gan deserved the title of the eternal first loyalists in this story.

【故事】

商朝初期，用"仁道"治理天下，国家非常兴盛。但在历经五百多年后，最后毁在纣王的手里，因为纣王听信妖言，荒淫无道，祸乱天下，非常残忍，结果众叛亲离。

纣王的叔父比干，在纣王身边做少师（丞相），见纣王过分荒淫、安逸，叹着气说："国君暴虐成这个样子，如果不去劝谏，就是不忠；因为怕死不敢说话，那就是不勇敢。国君有过失就应该去劝谏，如果做臣子的不用死去力争，那就是渎职，对不起天下的百姓。"

于是，比干就到纣王那里去强行进谏，对纣王说："不修先王的典法，却听信一个妖妇的话，您的国家大祸就不远了！"纣王生气地说："听说圣人的心上有七个窍。我想在你身上得到验证。"就下令剖开比干的胸膛，挖出他的心脏来和大臣们一起观看。

另一个贤明的大臣箕子，看到这个阵势，非常恐惧，于是假装疯癫去做奴隶。纣王就把他囚禁起来，受尽了屈辱和折磨。那些太师、少师官员们，为了避祸，就带着家人、财物，都逃奔到周国武王那里去了。于是，周武王顺应民意，率领诸侯起兵讨伐无道的纣王，纣王兵败被捉。武王下令割下纣王的头颅，悬挂在旗杆上示众，又把箕子从监狱里释放出来，还给比干建了坟墓作为后人瞻仰之用。

In early Shang Dynasty Empery Shang flourished under the rule of Benevolence policy. But Shang Dynasty came to a sudden downfall five hundred years later because the licentious and cruel Emperor Zhou caused national disorder.

Seeing the Emperor Zhou becomes more licentious and idler, Bi Gan who was Zhou's uncle and premier sighed angrily, "If I do not expostulate with the cruel emperor and leave him alone like that, I will be disloyal like a coward. If he fails to express disagreement with emperor's faults at the cost of his life, the vassal will feel guilty to people for his negligence of duty."

Then, Bi Gan forced his way to Emperor Zhou and said, "You followed the witch's fallacies rather than laws made by late emperors, the nation will fall into disaster soon." Emperor Zhou angrily replied, " I heard of seven holes in Saint's heart, so I want to verify it on you." So the Emperor Zhou ordered someone to split Bi Gan's chest and dig out his heart to other vassals.

At sight of this horrible event, another vassal named Ji Zi became frightened and pretended to be mentally insane slave. Ji Zi was then imprisoned by Emperor Zhou, totally insulted and tortured. To escape the disaster, many vassals of the government run away with their families and fled to Emperor Wu of Zhou Empire.

Therefore, Emperor Wu followed the public opinion, led all seigneurs to crusade against Emperor Zhou, and finally caught him alive. The head of Emperor Zhou was cut off and hung against the flagpole on wall. And then Emperor Wu freed Ji Zi out of prison and built a graveyard for Bi Gan in memory.

【点评】

比干因为强行劝谏纣王,最后被剖心而死。作为忠臣,比干为什么不怕死?因为他对百姓仁爱、对国家忠诚,一心只想解救天下百姓,所以能用牺牲自己生命的方式来表达心愿。由于他忠贞而有节操,为正义牺牲了生命,孔子评价说他是"杀身成仁",是仁人志士。

Bi Gan was killed by splitting heart only because he expostulated against the emperor. The reason why he did not fear death is his benevolence to people and loyalty to country. Due to his benevolence, moral integrity and sacrifice for just, Confucius praised him as a man of lofty ideals.

柒 忠(Loyalty)

张良复仇
Zhāng Liáng Fù Chóu

【出处】《史记·留侯列传》：张良狙(zǔ)击，为韩复仇，灭秦假手，从汉依刘。

【释义】 张良为报秦国灭韩之仇，刺杀秦始皇失败，投靠了汉王刘邦，最终如愿。

【Definition】 Zhang Liang wanted to revenge to Empery Qin because it destroyed Empery Han, but he failed to assassinate the Emperor Qin, so he seek refuge to Emperor Liu Bang of Han Dynasty and eventually succeeded.

【造句】 张良复仇，仇的对象是秦始皇，为的是重塑韩国在诸侯中的形象。

【Example】 In the story of Zhang Liang's revenge, the hatred objects are the emperor Qin but the point is to reshape the image of Empery Han among other Kings.

【故事】

战国时期，有秦、齐、楚、燕、韩、赵、魏七个国家，史称"战国七雄"。当初，这七个国家的实力、势力都相当，但最后是秦国统一了天下。其他六国中，最早被消灭的是韩国。张良作为韩国的臣民，一心想要为韩国复仇。

张良出生在韩国，他的祖先有五代人都是韩国的宰相，由此可知，张良对韩国的感情相当深厚。秦灭韩国的时候，他当时二十岁，家里有二三百个仆人，家境相当富有。可是，国家被秦灭了，国破家何在？张良为了报答深厚的国恩，一心复仇，连弟弟死了的丧事都没有办好，就在匆忙之中卖掉所有家产，全部用来收买刺杀秦始皇的刺客。

他到处打听有没有大力勇士，可以一击就除掉秦始皇的。后来花大价钱得到了一个大力士，并通过暗中调查，知道秦始皇在某天要经过"博浪沙"这个地方，于是在这里埋伏好，希望能击毙秦始皇。可是，秦始皇的车队都是四驾的车辇，分不清哪一辆是秦始皇的座驾，只看到车队最中间的那辆车最豪华，于是张良指挥大力士向该车击去。一百二十斤的大铁椎一下将乘车的人击毙倒地。张良趁乱逃离现场。

事后才知道，大力士只击中了秦始皇的副车。秦始皇为此大怒，查找凶手和主谋，于是张良便隐姓埋名在江苏下邳这个地方躲藏了很久。后来张良遇到刘邦，就一心辅佐他，直到灭了秦国，张良才离开刘邦，回到韩国，立韩成为王，他当宰相。

天有不测风云。后来，国王韩成被项羽所杀。张良又回到刘邦那里，协助刘邦消灭了项羽，被封为留侯。但张良是个懂得进退的人，并且对刘邦的为人很清楚：不久的将来，刘邦就会将那些有才干的文臣武将一个一个地除掉，于是找个借口，辞官学仙问道去了。

In the Warring State Period, Empery Qin united the whole nation at last though the Seven Powers were well-matched. As the official of Empery Han which was first defeated by Empery Qin, Zhang Liang all the time sought to revenge for his country.

Zhang Liang loved his country very much for his five-generation ancestors were premiers in Empery Han. The time when Empery Han was defeated Zhang Liang was only twenty-year old in a affluent family with about three hundred servants. To render his country, Zhang Liang planned to revenge against Empery Qin by selling all family property to hire assassinator even though he did not finish his brother's funeral arrangements.

With effort for a long time, Zhang Liang hired a strong assassinator at great expense and knew that Emperor Qin shihuang would get across the place named "Bolangsha". Zhang Liang prepared an ambush there and hoped to assassinate him, however, it was so difficult to recognize the chariot of Emperor Qin shihuang that he led the strong assassinator to hit the most luxurious chariot in the midst of fleet. After the strong assassinator killed everyone in the chariot, Zhang Liang escaped.

Zhang Liang later noticed that the assassinator did not hit the chariot of Emperor Qin shihuang. Emperor Qin shihuang was extremely angry and ordered to find out the chief instigator. After concealing his identity in Xiapi of Jiangsu for a long time, Zhang Liang met with Liu Bang and came back to Empery Han as the premier again since he helped Liu Bang defeat Empery Qin.

Unfortunately, because Emperor Han was killed by Xiang Yu, Zhang Liang went back to help Liu Bang again to defeat Xiang Yu. But Zhang Liang resigned soon after he was knighted because he knew that Liu Bang would soon kill him like other officials.

【点评】

在司马迁《史记》中，张良一亮相就显得光彩照人，不同凡响。但张良刺秦皇，远没有荆轲刺秦王来得有名，这是因为荆轲刺秦王，一再被史家与诗人所歌颂，早就妇孺皆知，所以深入人心。其实张良并不比荆轲逊色，甚至有过之而无不及。不过在事实上，无论荆轲刺秦王还是张良刺秦皇，其结果都是失败，这说明个人的力量是有限的，尤其是干大事，必须借助团队的力量。

In *Records of the Grand Historian* (*Shi Ji*), Zhang Liang was described as a sparkling and distinctive man. Though not so famous as Jing Ke who was praised for his brave assassination of Emperor Qin, Zhang Liang's bravery was by no means inferior to Jing Ke. In fact, they both failed, which indicates that one is limited and only teamwork can achieve something.

纪信代死

Jì Xìn Dài Sǐ

【出处】 纪信诳(kuáng)楚，假作汉王，易服代死，救主荥(xíng)阳。

【释义】 楚汉相争时，汉王被困荥阳，纪信化妆成汉王欺骗楚军，被识破后英勇献身。

【Definition】 Ji Xin disguised to be Emperor Han when the King Han was besieged by Empery Chu in Xing Yang so that the Emperor Han survived but Ji Xin was killed instead.

【造句】 纪信代死，忠臣事主，表现出来的是忠心、仁义、智慧和勇气。

【Example】 Ji Xin's death for the sake of the emperor represents loyalty, faithfulness, wisdom and courage.

【故事】

楚汉相争时期，汉王的将军纪信，与汉王刘邦一起镇守荥阳。楚霸王项羽，即将攻破荥阳城，楚王与汉王相争到了危急时刻，汉王无法突出重围。于是，纪信就向刘邦建议：用和汉王更换衣服穿的计谋来诈骗楚军，以便帮助汉王脱离险境。汉王同意了。纪信就穿着汉王的衣服，坐着汉王的车子，插着汉王的旗子，用两千名披甲持戈的女兵在前面开路，从东门出来并大声喊叫："城内粮尽，汉王投降！"

这话像炸弹爆炸一样，立即就在楚军中传开来，认为刘邦这时投降是理所当然的。四围的楚兵纷纷跑到东城门看热闹，因为这是千载难逢的机会。就在这个时候，荥阳的西城门被悄然打开，汉王刘邦穿

柒 忠 (Loyalty)

着纪信的衣服,和几十个护卫他的亲信们 冲了出去,骑着快马向西边飞奔逃离了险境。

东城门这边,半夜里围城和看热闹的楚兵看不清投降的汉军,等到近处才发现前面是一群女人,于是开始盘问并动手抓人。楚军看到赶过来的这辆车,确实是诸侯王的规格,以为里面坐的就是汉王刘邦,每个士兵都兴奋异常,一直押送着这辆车来到项羽的中军大帐。项羽没想到从刘邦的车里下来的竟然是纪信,就问纪信:"汉王不是投降吗,人呢?"纪信高声大笑:"我主汉王已经离开荥阳城了!"项羽大怒,下令用火烧死纪信。

后来刘邦得了天下,做了皇帝,是为汉高祖。为纪念纪信,在顺庆(今四川南充)为他建造了一座"忠佑庙"。汉高祖在诰词中说:"以忠殉国,代君任患,实开汉业。"

In war between Empery Chu and Han, General Ji Xin together with King Han (Liu Bang) guarded Xing Yang city. Just before the city was almost breached by Xiang Yu, Ji Xin suggested exchanging the clothes with King Han so as to help King Han escape, and King Han agreed. So Jin Xin put on King Han's clothes, drove King Han's chariot with King's flag and fought the way out with two thousands armed female soldiers. Jin Xin came out of the east gate of Xing Yang city and yelled, "Food supplies run out and King Han surrendered!"

At the news of King Han's surrender, Empery Chu's soldiers all run to east gate to witness King Han's surrender. Meanwhile, the west gate of Xing Yang city was open secretly; King Han put on Jin Xin's clothes and rode the horse fast out of the city together with a dozen of guards.

At the east gate it was chaos and the soldiers of Empery Chu finally realized that the King Han's soldiers were women and thought that King Han was in the chariot, and then they took the chariot to Xiang Yu's encampment. To his big surprise, Xiang Yu found it was Ji Xin instead of Liu Bang. Xiang Yu said angrily, "Where is Liu Bang?" Jin Xin replied in laughter, "King Han, my Lord, left Xing Yang already!" At last Ji Xin was burnt to death.

Later a temple named "Zhong You Temple" was built in memory of Jin Xin in Nanchong of Sichuan province since Liu Bang's conquer as the first emperor in Han Dynasty.

【点评】

在刘邦危难之际,纪信以他对刘邦的忠贞不二和亲密的感情,自愿代替刘邦来承受杀身之祸,这既是为国捐躯的忠的体现,也是仁义勇的品质表现。当时,纪信利用楚人容易上当受骗的弱点和深夜难辨真假的有利条件,出其不意地出现在敌人面前,给刘邦创造脱逃的机会,用的是智慧。在楚军团团围住、明知闯关必死的情境下,纪信毫不犹豫地坦然赴死,表现的是大无畏的英雄气概和耿耿忠心。

When Liu Bang was in great danger, Ji Xin, out of his loyalty and intimate feelings with Liu Bang, stood up for Liu Bang with no hesitation even it would cause him a disaster of being kill, which is not only the manifestation of the great sacrifice for loyalty, but also the presentation of benevolence, righteousness and courage. At that time, Ji Xin took advantage of the weakness of the Chu people, who are easily cheated and the favorable conditions of the dark night, appeared himself to the enemy unexpectedly, creating opportunity for Liu Bang to get away, which was great wisdom. When surrounded by the enemy troops and stood no chance for survival, Ji Xin went to his death bravely, which reflected his heroic spirit and loyalty.

朱云折槛
Zhū Yún Zhé Kǎn

【出处】《汉书·朱云传》：朱云借剑，请斩佞(nìng)臣，攀折殿槛，忠直无伦。

【释义】忠直无比的小小县令朱云，因为疾恶如仇，在朝堂上直言谏诤留下千古清名。

【Definition】Righteous Mr.Zhu hated evil people and criticized the official's faults on the court, because of which he left an eternal impression on people.

【造句】朱云折槛，是有关汉成帝时一个地方县令在朝堂上直言谏诤的典故。

【Example】Zhu Yun Zhe Kan is a story about a local magistrate who dared to bluntly criticize government's faults in the court at Han Dynasty.

【故事】

西汉时，有个人叫朱云，年少时就喜欢路见不平、拔刀相助。由于他身材高大，并且好勇善斗，对一般平民的疾苦，经常仗义执言，因此在社会上很有侠客的名气。在四十岁那年的一天，他突然感到过去的日子碌碌无为，后悔不已，决定人生重新开始。于是，他洗心易行，访求明师，发奋图强。经高人指点，朱云的德行已为大家所称颂，加上他很有义薄云天的侠义豪气，成为人们心中真正的高士。他坚守"国家兴亡、匹夫有责"的信念，天性嫉恶如仇，因此在官运方面一直受到权臣的压制。但他依然忠心耿耿，勤政爱民，深受百姓爱戴与赞许。

当时，朝廷有个奸臣叫张禹，身居高位，他欺上瞒下，善于谄媚。朱云知道有他这种人后，决心为国除害。于是他郑重地上书朝廷，希望能面见皇上，陈述国家社会安危的重大事情。当朝皇帝感到很意外，但还是接见了这个地方小官，并安排有朝廷重臣位列两旁。

朱云从容不迫地走进殿堂，慷慨激昂地对汉成帝说："当今朝廷有一位大臣，上不能辅佐主上，下不能为民众谋利益，却身居高位，牟取私利，贪得无厌，为非作歹。微臣愿借陛下的尚方宝剑，将这个奸臣斩首示众，以激励其他的官员为国家尽力。"

成帝惊讶地问："这个人是谁？"朱云说："安昌侯张禹！"这话一出口，满廷皆惊！众位大臣你看看我我看看你，有人暗中叫好的，也有人替朱云捏了一把冷汗的，汉成帝更是异常震惊。张禹则露出冷笑，一直注意着朱云的动静。

汉成帝当时大发脾气，喝道："你这个位卑小臣居然毁谤上官！辱骂皇帝的老师，罪死不赦！"即命左右推出去斩了。刀斧手奉命强推朱云下殿，朱云非常激愤——没想到众人交口称赞的英明皇上，却原来是非不分！他奋力抗争，但被强行推到了金銮殿外，他就死死抓住御殿栏槛不放，竟然把那栏槛折断了。当时，他大义凛然地高呼："我能跟龙逢、比干在地下相见，我很满足了！只是不知道陛下和朝廷的前途会如何？"

汉成帝听了这话，跌坐在龙椅上。这时，左将军辛庆忌被朱云忠烈的品质所感动，赶紧在地上连连叩头，留下了一片红红的血迹，恳求皇上收回成命。他不顾一切地大声说："皇上，朱云素来性情耿直，请陛下免他一死。他如果说得对，不能杀他；说得不对，也应该宽恕他，因

柒 忠(Loyalty)

为他忠于国家。假如您今天把朱县令杀了,您不就成为暴君了吗?不就同商纣一样了吗?"辛庆忌连哭带吼的劝谏,震醒了汉成帝,成帝转怒为喜,命左右将朱云放了。

后来,宫里准备修复被朱云折断的栏槛,却被汉成帝制止。因为这个折断的栏槛,可以时时提醒他自己不要受奸佞之臣的迷惑,同时也嘉勉像朱云这样忠直的谏臣。

In West Han Dynasty there was a man named Zhu Yun who acted like a swordsman ready to withdraw swords at the sight of injustice, especially helping the weak. At the age of forty, Zhu Yun decided to start a new life for he felt bored with his past unsuccessful days. He decided to reform thoroughly, studied hard and finally won respect and became the distinguished hermit for his nobleness and chivalrousness.

Zhu Yun stuck to the belief of "Every man shares a common responsibility for the fate of his country." In addition, he hated injustice and inequity as his enemy, because of which he was always repressed by other dignitaries, in contrast with respect from people.

At that time there was a treacherous official named Zhang Yu who was a flatterer disloyal to his emperor and people. Zhu Yun submitted a formal statement to the royal court and hoped to appeal to the emperor to his face even if he was only a county's governor.

Zhu Yun walked into the palace court at ease and declaimed: "There is a minister who cannot help our emperor and serve people but uses his high position to seek profits and break the law all the time. I appeal to you, your Majesty to use your sword to behead that treacherous official."

Emperor Cheng asked surprisingly: "Who is that?" Zhu Yun replied: "It is Zhang Yu." Immediately all officials in the palace court were surprised and Emperor Cheng also felt shocked. Only Zhang Yu stared at Zhu Yun with sneer.

Emperor Cheng reproached him with anger: "You dare to slander the superior official, my teacher! " So he ordered someone to behead Zhu Yun out of the court. Zhu Yun felt anger with such stupid emperor who cannot distinguish right from wrong, and he held the threshold of the palace court so tight as to break that threshold finally. Fearless of death, Zhu Yun yelled to the emperor: "I feel content with my death if compared with Long Feng and Bi Gan (who were all killed by emperors for strongly expressing disagreement with emperors. But I worry about the fate of my country."

Emperor Cheng was frightened to chair by Zhu's words. Moved by Zhu, General Xin Qingji quickly kneed down in front of Emperor Cheng and appealed to him to take back his words and free Zhu Yun from death. The angry emperor got awakened by the General's appeal, changed his mind and freed Zhu Yun.

Later Emperor Cheng ordered not to repair the broken threshold of the court because it reminded him not to be subject to the crafty sycophant but to encourage those loyal officials like Zhu Yun.

【点评】

朱云是一个地方县令，人微言轻，但他忠心耿耿，忧国忧民，发现朝廷里有张禹那样的奸臣，全然不顾生死，要求借尚方宝剑为民除害，结果招来杀身之祸。幸亏汉成帝并不糊涂，被劝谏后幡然醒悟，不但没有治他的罪，而且连被折断的栏槛也不再修复，以此作为借鉴，同时表彰这位忠直的大臣。这是难能可贵的。

Humble as he was from a local county, Zhu Yun was totally loyal to his country and emperor. His fearlessness of death in appeal to the emperor to kill the treacherous officials like Zhang Yu almost brought about his death. In short, Emperor Cheng deserved praise for he changed his mind after General Xin's plead for rectification and did not convict Zhu Yun at last.

柒 忠 (Loyalty)

敬德瘢痍
Jìng Dé Bān Yí

【出处】《旧唐书·尉迟恭列传》:敬德忠主,赠金固辞,人言其反,解衣示痍。

【释义】 尉迟(chí)恭一生忠诚事主、淡泊名利,深得唐太宗信赖和倚重。

【Definition】 Yuchi Gong won the trust and reliance of Emperor Tang Taizong for his loyalty and indifference to fame and wealth.

【造句】 敬德瘢痍,是为了证明自己对主上的忠诚,而不是为了表功。

【Example】 The story Jing De Ban Yi shows the loyalty to the Lord rather than showing off one's achievements.

【故事】

唐朝开国名将尉迟恭,青年时因为勇武在乡里就很出名。起初,他参加了刘武周领导的起义军,大败唐高祖李渊军队,俘虏了永安王李孝基和五名唐将。但后来,他被秦王李世民战败,经劝降,归附了唐朝。李世民就安排他担任右一府统军。

尉迟恭作战勇武,实战中不但善于避矛,还能夺取敌矛返刺。齐王李元吉也善于在马上使用长矛,听说尉迟恭也会这一招,很不以为然,就要与他比试。李世民问尉迟恭:"夺取长矛和避开长矛,哪种难些?"尉迟恭说:"夺取困难些。"于是命令他表演夺取李元吉手中的长矛。李元吉手执长矛,长驱骏马,一心想刺尉迟恭,但终究没有刺到他。而尉迟恭不一会儿工夫,就一连三次夺得李元吉手中的长矛。一向骁勇的李元吉虽然口里赞叹,心里却深深感到很大的耻辱。他和太子李建成为了共同对付李世民，就用重金去收买尉迟恭，准备为自己所用。没想到尉迟恭很坚决地拒绝了。他们发现这个办法行不通，决定用计铲除李世民的这个羽翼，就派人去行刺。尉迟恭果然是英雄，索性大开门户，若无其事地睡觉，刺客多次潜入他家厅堂，却终究不敢进他的卧室。李元吉和李建成实在没办法了，就在父皇李渊面前诬陷尉迟恭，使他被问罪下狱，想借父亲的手除掉尉迟恭。李世民知道后经多方周旋，他才免于被害。

后来秦王做了皇帝，就是唐太宗。因为尉迟恭对自己的忠心和作战勇武，太宗封他为鄂国公。渐渐地，有人就在太宗面前说尉迟恭的坏话了。一天，唐太宗问尉迟恭："有人常说你要造反，什么原因啊？"尉迟恭回答说："我能反吗？我跟从皇上您征讨四方，身经百战，能够幸存，实在是刀箭下逃生才活下来。现在天下安定了，又为什么要反呢？"说完就解去衣服抛在地上，露出身上枪箭伤疤，一处一处地指给皇帝看。

唐太宗是一个性情中人，看到他身上伤痕累累，感动得流下眼泪，抚摸着他的伤痕安慰说："穿上衣服吧，正是由于我不怀疑，才对你说这番话啊。"从这以后，更加信任尉迟恭了，还对他说："我想将女儿许配给你，怎么样？"尉迟恭叩头辞谢说："我的妻子虽然微贱，但与我同甘共苦好多年。我虽然才疏学浅，但听说古人富贵了不换妻子。"李世民只好作罢。

柒 忠 (Loyalty)

The co-founder of Tang Dynasty, Yuchi Gong, was very famous in his youth for his valor. At the beginning of war, Yuchi Gong joined the Rebellion led by Liu Wuzhou which defeated Li Yuan's army and captured one king and five generals of Tang army. But later defeated by King Li Shimin, Yuchi Gong yielded to Tang Dynasty as one General.

King Qi named Li Yuanji, however, wanted to compete against the valiant Yuchi Gong because he did not accept that Yuchi Gong could seize enemy's spear at horse and bayoneted back. So in the competition arranged by Li Shimin, Yuchi Gong easily seized the spear of Li Yuanji three times but Li Yuanji failed to bayonet him all along.

Seriously insulted by the loss, Li Yuanji and his brother Li Jiancheng schemed against Li Shimin by bribing Yuchi Gong. They were rejected undoubtedly and so decided to kill him through assassination. But the assassinator was too frightened to break into Yuchi's bedroom several times. Failing to assassinate Yuchi Gong, the two brothers decided to frame him up in face of their father king Li Yuan, but also failed due to the help of Li Shimin.

When Li Shimin was throned as Tang Taizong, Yuchi Gong was also honored as E Guogong. But someone still spoke ill of him in the presence of Tang Taizong. One day Tang Taizong asked him: "I've told that you wanted to revolt. Why?" Yuchi Gong answered: "How dare me? I followed you and survived so many battles, and how can I revolt at such peaceful dynasty?" He immediately put off his clothes and showed Tang Taizong his scared back.

Looking at scars on the back of Yuchi Gong, Tang Taizong was moved into tears, touched his back and comforted him: "Please take on your clothes. I have no doubt about your loyalty." With much trust in Yuchi Gong, Tang Taizong wanted Yuchi Gong to marry the princess, but Yuchi Gong declined and said: "Humble as my wife is, she's stayed with me through hardships so many years, and how can I betray myself to marry another girl?" Accordingly Tang Taizong did not mention that any more.

【点评】

尉迟恭作为唐初大将,从归附李世民后,始终对李世民忠心耿耿。他凭着高超的武艺,为唐太宗征战南北,驰骋疆场,赴汤蹈火,在所不辞,多次冒险救李世民于危难之中,立下不世之功。他为人纯朴忠厚,说话、做事毫无心机,在拒绝娶公主作妻子的事情上,更显示出高贵的品质。

Yuchi Gong has been always loyal to Li Shimin since his surrender and he has risked his life to rescue Li Shimin many times in battles. He is a man of sincerity, honesty and simplicity. He shows the noble quality for his decline to marry the princess.

柒 忠(Loyalty)

李绛善谏
Lǐ Jiàng Shàn Jiàn

【出处】《李相国谈事集》:李绛直谏,以尽忠忱,屡触帝怒,卒启君心。

【释义】 李绛对唐宪宗忠心耿耿,直言劝谏,虽然多次冒犯皇上,但最终开启了君心。

【Definition】 Li Jiang is loyal and respectful to Emperor Tang Xianzong with his blunt criticism. Although repeatedly offended the emperor, he eventually won the trust of the emperor.

【造句】 李绛善谏,最终开启了唐宪宗纳谏的心扉,也算是功德圆满了。

【Example】 Li Jiang is good at giving suggestions and eventually wins the trust of Emperor Tang Xianzong, which can be considered a perfect virtue to him.

【故事】

唐宪宗时期,李绛善于劝谏,皇帝常常因此很感动,曾经几次提拔他,官至宰相。为了肯定李绛的功劳,皇帝甚至说:"李卿所言,朕应该把它记下来绑在腰带上,天天作为警诫来反省自己。"

白居易一生为官,不好名利,实事求是,不阿谀奉承。有一天,白居易因为劝谏得罪了皇上,皇上要治他的罪。李绛就劝皇上说:"因为皇上能够容纳正直的人说话,所以一班臣子们才敢尽心劝谏。白居易劝谏的本意,是贡献他自己的忠忱。现在皇上如果因为这个就治他的罪,恐怕天下的人以后都要闭住嘴不敢讲话了。"皇上听了李绛这话,本来很难看的脸色转变过来了,就没有治白居易的罪。

李绛虽然善于进谏，但也有不给皇上面子、惹皇上不高兴的时候。一次，皇上曾责怪李绛太过分地指责他的不是，令他很难堪。李绛这时非常难过，流着眼泪说："我身居国家重要职位，如果只图保全自己性命而不敢直谏、不说真话，那是我辜负了陛下，对不起天下人啊！如果我为国为民不看圣上脸色说话，因此做出不顺从圣上的事，却被治罪，那是圣上辜负了做臣子的一片忠心啊。"皇上听了，很受感动，更加理解李绛的良苦用心。

Due to his positive suggestions to Tang Xianzong, Li Jiang had been promoted as the prime minister. The emperor praised Li Jiang by stating: "As the emperor I shall note down Li's words on my waistband to reflect on myself."

Another famous official and poet named Bai Juyi who sought truth never flattered for fame and wealth. One day when the emperor decided to punish Bai Juyi for his criticism, Li Jiang said to the emperor, "Because you are a man of tolerance and integrity, every official dares to offer suggestions. Bai Juyi intends to be loyal to you through his suggestion. If you punish him just for that this time, I'm afraid that no one dares to speak." At his words the pale-looking emperor changed his mind and did not punish Bai Juyi.

Occasionally Li Jiang angered the emperor to lose face for his blunt criticism. The emperor once blamed Li Jiang in that Li's criticism made him embarrassed. Li Jiang said sadly, "If I cannot speak the truth and criticize you for your mistakes, I will not deserve the position as top official and I will fail to live up to you and everyone." Moved by Li's words, the emperor understood his good intentions.

【点评】

李绛性子直爽，一生不与小人为伍。对大臣无原则地奉迎上意、

柒 忠 (Loyalty)

粉饰太平,就给予迎头痛击。他喜实厌虚,在朝敢于犯颜直谏。常言说:在什么位子上,就应该说自己应说的、做自己应做的,不能怕丢自己的位子和性命,否则就是不忠不义。李绛是宰相,虽然多次因劝谏而触犯皇上,但最后都能为皇上理解。这凭借的就是一颗爱国、爱天下百姓的忠诚之心。

    Li Jiang is a very upright and straightforward person, who never keeps company with the flunky. And he inclined to debunk and bash those minister of the royal court whoever is always brown-nosing or presents a false appearance of peace and prosperity. He favors truth while hates falsehood, and he would expostulate it straight even if it may infuriates the emperor. It is often said that people are supposed to say what needs saying and do what needs doing in compliance with their position and should not be afraid of getting fired or killed, otherwise, it would be recognized as disloyalty and un-righteousness. Li Xiang, served as the Imperial Chancellor, who repeatedly offended the emperor for his expostulations, but he could be understood by the emperor in the end. And it is by virtue of his loyalty and patriotism.

孟容制强

Mèng Róng Zhì Qiáng

【出处】《唐书·许孟容传》：孟容执昱(yù)，贷债令偿，不奉诏旨，抑制豪强。

【释义】 许孟容做首都行政长官时，约束豪强的不法行为，即使卫戍司令官也不放过。

【Definition】 When Xu Mengrong was the Chief Executive of capital city, he restricted the tyrannical constraints of wrongdoing, even to the garrison commander.

【造句】 孟容制强，展现出一个忠于职守、为民做主、疾恶如仇、敢于碰硬的好官形象。

【Example】 Meng Yung Zhi Qiang, shows the image of a good officer of dedication, full support to people, hatred for the evil people, and the courage to challenge authority.

【故事】

唐朝许孟容，他做首都长官的时候，修理了保护皇宫的神策军军官李昱。原来，李昱手下的军吏，凭借特权，仗势欺人，借老百姓的钱不还。李昱虽然是管这些人的，但他也不是好官，例如他向当地的富人借了八百万铜钱，三年来从不提还钱的事。老百姓因为借给他们钱，没有办法收回，于是就到衙门告状。

许孟容还没有到任以前就已经了解到：这些神策军吏我行我素，没有章纪，为非作歹。不畏权贵的孟容到任、掌握这些证据后，就把李昱抓了起来，收押在狱中，审查核实后，并要李昱立下契约，在规定的时间内偿还欠债，否则就按律处理。

柒 忠（Loyalty）

当时军队里的同僚感到非常害怕,虽然从来没有一个官吏敢查办他们,但现在这个许孟容不怕权势偏要查办他们,于是就集体向朝廷反映这件事。皇上听后,觉得禁卫军是自己的靠山,应该帮他们说话,就派了一位代表前往孟容的办事处,要他将李昱送回军队去。

但是,孟容不吃这一套,还态度坚决地说:"我不服从诏命有死罪,但我不能接受这个诏令,因为我治理京师、弹抑豪强,这与京师的安全息息相关。如果不能抑制豪强,又如何能使京城得到安宁呢?京城不安宁,皇上又如何治理整个国家呢?明确地说:如果李昱不还借的钱,我就不可能送他回军中。"

宪宗听后,认为他刚正、尽职,就同意了他的做法。从此,京师的豪强大为震惊,他们的行为明显有所收敛,整个社会风气明显好转。

The capital official Xu Mengrong detained Li Yu who was chief of imperial guards because Li Yu allowed his guards to bully the civilians through their advantages and Li Yu also never paid back eight million copper cash he borrowed from a local millionaire. Through verification in the case investigation, Xu Mengrong required that the detained Li should make a contract to pay back all that he owed by due date, or he will be charged again by law.

At news of arrestment of Li Yu, all army officials felt scared and then reported to the emperor. Considering that these army officials were his steady supporters, the emperor sent a representative to ask Xu Mengrong to send Li Yu back.

However, Xu refused the emperor's order this time by saying, "I know that I will face death if I do not follow the emperor's order, but I cannot accept it for the peace of the capital city will not be kept if I failed to run the city's security administration. And how will the emperor run this country if the capital city is disordered?"

The emperor thought Xu Mengrong was upright and disinterested and then took back his order. From then on those dignitaries in the capital restrained their behaviors and observed the law.

【点评】

许孟容刚直不阿,心地无私。他一心为老百姓着想,依法办事,不畏权势,即使皇上派人来要求放李昱,他仍然据理力争,绝不纵容豪强,很有大臣的风采,因此得到皇上的肯定。这个故事告诉我们:如果做了管理工作,或者有了一官半职,就应该为老百姓的利益着想,为老百姓办事。

Xu Mengrong is upright and disinterested for the sake of civilians. He acts in strict accordance with law and does not fear power at all, due to which he is praised by the emperor.

柒 忠 (Loyalty)

金藏剖心
Jīn Zàng Pōu Xīn

【出处】《后唐书·安金藏传》：金藏工籍，赤胆忠诚，皇嗣(sì)不反，剖心以明。

【释义】 安金藏以他低微的出身，对太子赤胆忠心，为证明太子清白，当众剖心。

【Definition】 Despite his humbleness, An Jinzang showed his loyalty to the prince by splitting his heart publicly for proving the innocence of prince.

【造句】 金藏剖心的故事说明：人活着，就要活得真诚，活得实在，活得有德行、有价值。

【Example】 The story of Jin Zang illustrates that a man should live in honesty, virtue and value.

【故事】

安金藏，本来是唐代中亚的安国胡人，精于音乐。由于他父亲安菩归附了唐朝，他因此成为负责宫廷祭祀乐舞的太常寺的乐工。武则天临朝称制，唐中宗立李旦为东宫太子。当时武则天对李姓宗室很有戒心，许多官员因为私下拜见李旦而获罪被处以极刑。安金藏等乐舞艺人由于职业的原因，才可以在李旦的左右侍奉。

当时，诬告之风盛行。不久，太子李旦被人诬告反叛。武后下令让当时有名的酷吏来俊臣查处这件事。来俊臣将安金藏抓来，对他施用酷刑逼供，安金藏大声喊道："来俊臣，我说皇嗣不反，你不相信！那么，就让我剖开心来，给你看看吧！我要用我的一颗红心，来证明皇嗣是不会造反的！"说着，突然拿过旁人的一把佩刀，刺向自己的腹部。顿时鲜血迸射，肠子流出来了，安金藏也晕倒在地。

武后听说这事，大为吃惊，命人将安金藏抬到宫中，请御医仔细诊治。也许是安金藏命不该绝，过了一宿，他竟然奇迹般苏醒过来。武后亲临探视，感叹地说："太子有冤，自己却不能辩白，而你却为他剖腹洗脱罪名，你能做到这个地步，说明你确实是个忠臣啊！"随即下诏终止案件审理，李旦因而幸免于难。

李旦即皇帝位后，为感激安金藏当初舍身相救之恩，将他提拔为右武卫中郎将。玄宗时期被封为代国公。后来，安金藏老病而卒，追赠为兵部尚书。

An Jinzang, a barbarian in Northern China, was good at music. He was the chief of musicians in Court of Imperial Sacrifices of Tang Dynasty because his father An Pu surrendered to Tang Dynasty. Under the rule of the female emperor Wu Zetian, many officials were sentenced for they paid private visits to Li Dan, the prince who was fully distrusted by emperor. Thanks to his musical profession, An Jinzang was free from imprisonment and could stay with the prince in palace.

But later the prince Li Dan was accused of revolt against the emperor by rumors. Wu Zetian sent Lai Junchen, a strict official and torturer, to investigate Li's case and arrested An Junzang under torture. An defied in the face of torture, "If you distrust me, let me split my heart to prove that my prince will not rebel." Then An Jinzang suddenly grabbed a knife and stabbed it into his own heart.

Greatly surprised by An Jinzang, the emperor Wu ordered the imperial doctor to cure him in palace. Miraculously An awoke the next morning. The emperor Wu came to see him and was deeply moved by his loyalty and soon ordered to cease this case to free Li Dan and An Jinzang.

Upon throne, Li Dan assigned An Jinzang as chief of imperial guards to appreciate him for loyalty.

【点评】

乐工安金藏,只是个小官,在太子李旦遇到诬告、被审讯时,他挺身而出。但他明白,任凭他一张嘴,即使再能说会道,酷吏来俊臣都不会放过他的。既然为人臣子,必当忠诚事主,实话实说,即使献出性命也在所不惜。于是,他用一般人做不到的方式方法,宁愿剖心,坚决不说假话,其壮烈行为令当时朝中士大夫为之赞叹不已、自愧不如。在生与死的严峻考验时刻,他的忠肝义胆,感动了武后,救下了李旦。

Humble as his position is, the musician An Jinzang showed his loyalty by splitting his own heart publicly at cost of his life in prison. His fearlessness of death and loyalty impressed Emperor Wu Zetian and also saved Li's life.

洪皓就鼎

Hóng Hào Jiù Dǐng

【出处】 《宋史·洪皓列传》：洪皓不降，愿就鼎镬(huò)，此真忠臣，光明磊落。

【释义】 洪皓奉命出使金国，面对强敌视死如归，表现出对大宋国的无限忠诚。

【Definition】 During his diplomatic mission to Empery Jin, Hong Hao was unafraid of threat and death, showing his infinite loyalty to Empery Song.

【造句】 洪皓就鼎，用现在的话来评价，颇有大无畏的革命英雄主义气概。

【Example】 Hong Hao Jiu Ding, in other words, can be evaluated by a spirit of indomitable revolutionary heroism.

【故事】

南宋的洪皓，奉宋高宗的使命，出使金国议和。但金国没有议和的意思。洪皓来到太原，被金人扣留近一年，到第二年转至云中（今山西大同），才见到金国的权臣完颜宗翰。完颜宗翰不但没有答应洪皓请归二帝的要求，还逼迫他到金廷操纵的伪齐刘豫政权去当官。

洪皓严词拒绝说："我不远万里，奉命出使金国，不能够奉迎两宫南归。我恨不得能把叛逆的刘豫给杀了！我决不会忍受这种屈辱来苟且偷安！如果要我屈从，我宁愿去死！"完颜宗翰顿时大怒，下令推出斩首。刀斧手将他架起来准备行刑。洪皓面不改色，从容而去。当时，金国的一位贵族见状，深受感动，不觉失声称赞说："这才是真正的忠臣啊！就用目光制止刀斧手暂缓行刑，并亲自跪下请求完颜宗翰免除洪皓一死。完颜宗翰就把他流放到遥远的冷山，直到绍兴十三年

柒 忠(Loyalty)

(1143)时,才让洪皓回到杭州。

早在洪皓做秀州司录这样的小官时,一次碰上大洪水,许多食物不能及时发放给老百姓,他就向郡守建议:将官库里的谷粮,直接发给受灾的百姓。当时秀州是粮食的转运站,粮食送到这里后再转送到一般小的城市,因为秀州地区正遭遇洪灾,所以他就向郡守提出这个建议。那郡守开始不敢担当,洪皓就恳切地说:"我愿意用自己的生命来换这十万人生命,恳请郡守将粮发放给这些坐以待毙的百姓。"太守因此深受感动,就这样救了十万人的命。老百姓对这件事刻骨铭心,大家把洪皓比喻跟佛一样救苦救难的人,称他为"洪佛子"。此后不久,秀州这里又遇到了盗贼洗劫,当盗贼抢到洪家的时候,知道他就是洪皓洪佛子,盗贼说:"不能抢洪佛子。"可见当时百姓是多么尊重他。

Hong Hao was assigned by the Emperor Gao Zong of South Song Dynasty to the peace negotiation with Empery Jin, in which he was refused and detained for one year. Hong Hao finally met the top official Wanyan Zonghan in Yunzhong (Datong city of Shanxi) one year after his detainment. In spite of Hong's request to set free the two captured emperors, Wanyan Zonghan forced Hong Hao to be an official in Liu Yu's regime, a puppet regime controlled by Empery Jin.

Hong Hao strongly refused and said, "I'm delegated here to take the two emperors back home, but I feel it a humiliation not to finish that assignment and I would rather kill that traitor Liu Yu. I'd rather die than surrender to you." Wanyan burst into anger and ordered Hong Hao to be beheaded. Impressed by Hong's indomitability in the face of death, an aristocrat stopped the executioner and kneed down to request Wanyan Zonghan to free Hong Hao. And then Hong Hao was sent into exile in an unknown mountain. Hong Hao did not get back to Hang Zhou until 1143 A.D.

Actually Hong Hao was praised and respected for his timely actions taken to distribute government foodstuff to civilians in Xiu Zhou city who suffered flood, though he was a small officer. Afterwards people called him "Buddhist Hong" because Hong Hao is a man of benevolence like a Buddha.

【点评】

洪皓受命出使金国。针对金国的无理要求,他义正词严,并痛斥叛徒;面对敌人的淫威,他大义凛然,宁死不屈;在流放的苦役生活环境中,他顽强地生存着,最终回到了祖国的怀抱——他凭的是一颗赤诚的爱国之心,忠贞可嘉。有道是"位卑未敢忘忧国",即使是年轻、做小官的时候,他一心想的是南宋治下的普通老百姓的祸福哀乐。所谓"食君之禄,忠君之事""食君之禄,担君之忧",在洪皓身上得到了生动的体现。

During the peace negotiation with Empery Jin, Hong Hao was insulted and detained but he showed a spirit of justice and indomitability in the face of threat and death. What helped him to survive the exile and get back to his home country is his patriotism. A small officer as he was, Hong Hao always thought about the civilians' difficulties.

岳母刺字
Yuè Mǔ Cì Zì

【出处】 《宋史·岳飞列传》：岳飞兵寡,善破众军,尽忠报国,盖世功勋。

【释义】 岳飞牢记母亲教诲,报效朝廷,一心抗金,善于用兵,立下不朽功勋。

【Definition】 Yue Fei beared his mother's instruction on his mind to serve the country as well as fight against Empery Jin, and he is good at commanding the troops and made a great contribution to his country.

【造句】 岳母刺字,刺的是"尽忠报国"而不是"精忠报国";"精忠报国"是当朝皇帝和皇后赠送岳飞一面旌(jīng)旗上的刺绣文字,"精忠"是当时朝廷的意志。

【Example】 The story Yue Mu Ci Zi means thorning the word "jin zhong bao guo"(loyal patriotic) instead of "jing zhong bao guo" (Decisive Battle).

【故事】

小岳飞家里很穷,母亲用树枝在沙地上教他写字,还鼓励他好好地锻炼身体。岳飞勤奋好学,在十几岁时就读《左氏春秋传》,对于忠贞报国的事情了如指掌。他不但知识渊博,还因臂力过人练就了一身好武艺,成为文武双全的人才。母亲谆谆地告诫他,一定要用这些本领好好地报效国家。

在岳飞小时候,金国就入侵中原,所以当时的国仇家恨都铭记在他心里,一心要报效国家。母亲为了鼓励儿子报效国家,就在他背上刺了"尽忠报国"四个大字。岳飞不敢忘记母亲的教诲,把这四个字当成终生遵奉的信条。每次作战时,岳飞都会想起这四个字。由于他勇猛善战,取得了很多战役的胜利,立了不少功劳,名声也传遍了大江南北。他因为精通武艺,又懂兵法,作战时比别人精明,常常能够以少胜多,屡立战功,多次受到朝廷的嘉奖。但每次面对朝廷的褒奖,他总是说:"这些功绩,都是将士们浴血奋战的结果,我哪里有什么?"所以手下的人非常效忠岳飞,战场上英勇奋战,杀得金兵闻风丧胆,被称为"岳家军"。

岳家军的士兵都严格遵守纪律,宁可自己忍受饥饿,也绝不打扰百姓。如果晚上借住在民家或商店,他们天一亮就起来,为主人打扫卫生、清洗餐具后才离去。岳家军的士气,让金兵闻风丧胆。金兵统帅发自内心地长叹道:"撼山易,撼岳家军难!"

可惜的是,在一次岳家军与金军的战役中,当岳家军追到距金兵大本营只有四十五里,眼看就要大功告成、收复江山失地的时候,皇帝赵构因怕岳飞打败金兵、接回原先被俘虏的皇帝,这样自己的王位就保不了,于是和奸臣秦桧密谋,连发十二道金牌命岳飞退兵还朝,并用"莫须有"的罪名杀害了岳飞。岳飞死时只有三十九岁。他一生谨记母亲的教诲,即使在死的那一刻,也没有忘记母亲"尽忠报国"的教训。

Yue Fei was taught by his mother to learn writing on sands in the poor family. As a teenager, Yue Fei was diligent enough to read out the book Zuoshi Chunqiu Zhuan, a Confucian historical biography and classic, through which he learned the commitment of "loyal patriotic". He was knowledgeable and good at fighting skills (martial arts).

The Empery Jin's invasion into Empery Song haunted Yue Fei since his childhood.

柒 忠 (Loyalty)

To encourage Yue Fei to serve his country, Yue's mother tattooed the characters "Jin Zhong Bao Guo" on his back. Yue Fei bore these characters as a creed on his mind to fight against invaders in every battle, due to which he achieved many victories.

Because he was good at martial arts and military strategy and tactics, Yue Fei defeated invaders many times and received awards accordingly. However, he owed all victories to his fellow soldiers for their bravery and sacrifices. The Jin army was frightened with extreme fear on hearing Yue Fei and his army, and so Yue's soldiers won the title of "Yue Jia Jun".

All soldiers of "Yue Jia Jun" were disciplined and would rather suffer starvation than disturb the local civilians for board and lodging. A chief of Jin army even felt it easy to break down Empery Song but impossible to defeat Yue Jia Jun.

Unfortunately Yue Fei was forced to retreat his army hastily by the twelve continual orders of Emperor Zhao Gou before he almost broke through the supreme headquarters of Jin army to win the final battle. Afterwards Yuc Fei was killed at age of thirty-nine by the schemes of the emperor and the traitor minister Qin Hui.

【点评】

历史上的伟人之所以伟大，在于他光明磊落的立身行事足以经受住反面的揭发，在于他的高尚情操足以感召世人，在于他的丰功伟绩足以使后人敬仰。岳飞"尽忠报国"的精神已成为中华民族爱国主义的一面旗帜。一代民族英雄岳飞的英雄气概，令中华后人万分景仰。

Every historical giant like Yue Fei is honored for his/her strength, great actions, nobleness, and gigantic contributions. Yue Fei has been always respected for his legacy in his spirit of "Jin Zhong Bao Guo", an image of Chinese patriotism.

捌 信

Integrity

信即诚实、守信。诚实,就是说老实话、办老实事,不弄虚作假,不自欺欺人,表里如一。守信就是讲信用、守诺言、不欺诈等。守信的人,不随便说话,不轻易表态,说了就一定做到,不恃才夸功;无信的人,则事事皆假,人所厌弃。

对个人来说,"诚实守信"既是一种道德品质和道德信念,也是每个公民的道德责任,更是一种崇高的人格力量。一个人,如果失去"信",就像车轮没有中心轴一样,是无法使车子行走的。

孔子认为,在社会生活中,"信"是一个人的立身之本,如果没有诚信,就失去了做人的基本条件。他把"信"列为对学生进行教育的"四大科目"(言、行、忠、信)和"五大规范"(恭、宽、信、敏、

捌 信 (Integrity)

惠)之一,强调要"言而有信",这样才能得到他人的相信并加以任用。这也是本篇中所选故事的要义所在。

对一个国家和政府来说,诚实守信是国格的体现。在国内,它是人民拥护、支持和赞成政府的一个重要的支撑;在国际上,它是显示国家地位和国家尊严的象征,是国家自立自强于世界民族之林的重要力量,也是良好国际形象和国际信誉的标志。所以,我国古代大教育家孔子在谈到统治者怎样才能得到老百姓的信任时,特别强调"民无信不立"。

当然,诚实守信是中华民族传统美德的一个重要规范,也是中国传统道德的一个重要内容。随着时代的不断发展和变化,诚实守信也不断体现出时代精神的新内涵。

Integrity is about honesty and trustworthiness. Honesty requires people to be honest when talking and acting, not to resort to deceit, nor deceive himself (as well as others) and keep his deeds accord with his words. And trustworthiness asks people to keep his words and not to commit fraud. People with integrity are cautious about his words and will not easily take a stand and, if he makes a promise, he will live up to his words but only boast his prowess. People without integrity, however, will be despised and isolated for all his promises are false.

personally, honesty and trustworthiness is not only a moral character and belief, but also a moral responsibility of every citizen as well as a lofty personality power. Man without integrity is like the wheel without central axis, which enables the car move around.

In Confucius's opinion, in the social life, integrity is the basis of man, and people without integrity will never be an upright person. He listed integrity as one of the Four Principles (Words, Deeds, Loyalty and Integrity) and Five Norms (Respect, Tolerance, Honesty, Diligence and Generosity), which are established for the education of students. And he emphasized that only by keeping his word can people earn other's trust and then show his ability. This is also the essence of the following selected stories.

Honesty and trustworthiness is the embodiment of national dignity to a country or government. In the country, it is an important pillar for the public to acclaim, support and approve their government; internationally, it is the symbol of national status and dignity, and the strength to stand proudly in the family of nations as well as the emblem of good international image and prestige. Thus, Confucius the ancient famous Chinese educator strongly emphasized that "the people have no faith do not stand" when talking about how to earn the trust of the masses as a ruler.

Honesty and trustworthiness, of course, is a norm of the traditional virtues of the Chinese nation and an important part of it as well. With the development of times, honesty and trustworthiness is increasingly reflecting the new connotations of spirit of the age.

以身作则
Yǐ Shēn Zuò Zé

【出处】 《韩非子·外储(chǔ)说左上》：心口如一，童叟无欺。人有善愿，天必佑之。

【释义】 为人处世，说话一定要算话，答应过别人的事情就要尽力而为。

【Definition】 While dealing with others, we should keep our promises.

【造句】 以身作则，即用自身的实际行动给人做出榜样，不虚假，不要花架子，有诺必践。

【Example】 "Yi Shen Zuo Ze" means setting an example by taking actions to keep promise, not pretending and not playing tricks.

【故事】

曾参是位列孔子七十二贤能的学生中的一个。他教育子女，用自己的行动作出榜样，同时也严格要求孩子。

一天，曾参的妻子要上街买东西。在一旁玩耍的儿子曾元，赶紧跑过来，扯着母亲的衣服，哭闹着也要去。因为儿子还小，曾参的妻子考虑带他去办事不方便，但又被儿子缠得实在没有办法，只好哄儿子说："好孩子，你听话，留在家里。等娘回来，娘把咱家的肥猪杀了，炖肉给你吃。"

曾元一听有肉吃，就眨巴着眼睛，认真地问："真的？"妈妈（曾妻）连忙点头说："当然是真的！"曾元高兴地大声喊道："太好了，有肉吃了！"蹦跳着到一边玩去了。

曾参妻子办完事回来，老远就听到从家里传来猪的凄惨叫声。她赶回家，看见曾参正拿绳子捆着家里的肥猪，旁边还放着一把杀猪刀。妻子大吃一惊，连忙上前拉住曾参，着急地问："你这是在干什么？要杀猪吗？"曾参说："是呀，你不是对儿子说：等你回来杀猪给他炖肉吃吗？"妻子说："你疯了！我那是被儿子缠得没办法，才故意哄他的，怎么能当真呢？"

曾参严肃地说："你是做母亲的，怎么能欺骗孩子呢？年少无知的孩子，智慧来自听从父母的训教，学习父母的样子。今天，你说话不算数，欺骗孩子，答应孩子的事不兑现，就是让孩子也学说假话骗人。还有，做母亲的欺骗孩子，孩子就觉得母亲的话不可信，以后再对他进行教育，他就很难相信母亲的话了。这样，你以后还怎么教导孩子做人、识礼呢？"

妻子听了曾参的话，觉得有理，十分赞同关于教育孩子信守诺言、培养孩子诚实品德的做法，于是和曾参一起把猪杀了，给儿子做了一顿丰盛的晚餐。

Zeng Shen was well-known as one of the 72 virtuous and competent students of Confucius. He educated his child by setting good examples for and being strict with him.

One day, his wife set off for the market, and his son Zeng Yuan, who was playing nearby, ran hastily towards her and grabbed at her clothes, crying for going with her. Considering that her son was too young and may cause her much trouble, yet she could not get away from it, so she comforted her son, "Good boy, listen to me, stay at home. when I come back, I will kill the pig and cook it for you."

On hearing that he will have pork for meal, Zeng Yuan blinked and asked seriously, "Really？" Her mother replied with nod, "Yes, of course！" Zeng Yuan exclaimed with excitement, "Great！ I will have meat！" And then he scampered off to play.

When the wife finished her shopping and went back home, she heard the pained animal's voice before she could see it. So she rushed to home, only to find that Zeng Shen was tying the pig with rope, a knife for killing pig laying nearby. She was astonished and hurriedly to take hold of his husband, asking anxiously, "what on earth are you doing? Kill the pig?" "Yeah, didn't you promise our son that you will kill the pig and cook a meal for him?" Zeng Shen replied. Then his wife exclaimed, "You are crazy! He kept asking me to take him to the shopping; I had no choice but to tell a lie. How can you take it seriously?"

"How can a mother deceive her own child? As for those young and ignorant children, they mainly obtain wisdom from instructions of parents and act like them. Now, you break your words, deceive your child and refuse to fulfill your promise, all your deeds are telling the child to cheat others. And if a mother deceives his child, the child will no longer believe his mother, and what makes thing worse, it would be difficult for the mother to instruct the child after that. Then how can you teach the child to be a noble man with an awareness of Ritual?" Zeng Shen said gravely.

His wife thought it did make sense after hearing his words, and she quiet agreed with him to educate the child about keeping one's promise and cultivating the character of honesty. So she helped Zeng Shen kill the pig and made a good dinner for her son.

【点评】

父母是孩子的第一任老师，一言一行，都影响着孩子的成长。要想让孩子有诚信品质，父母必须做到言而有信。如果父母言而无信，那么，孩子以后还会有谁值得他信任？慢慢地，欺诈和谎言可能会占据孩子纯洁的心灵。所以，做个说话算数的家长，对孩子良好品德的培养有着积极的作用。这就是曾参"以身作则"给我们的启示。

Parents are the first teacher of their children. Every word and deed of them has a great impact on the growth of the children. Parents must earnestly keep their promises if they expect their child to be honest. Otherwise, who else they can trust with? And even worse, deception and lie will occupy their pure mind. Therefore, parents who never break their promises will exert a positive influence on cultivating good virtue of their children.

季札挂剑

Jì Zhá Guà Jiàn

【出处】《史记·吴太伯世家》：延陵季子，不负初心，徐君已死，挂剑坟(fén)林。

【释义】季札做人非常诚信，哪怕只是心里的一个念头，都要落实在行动上。

【Definition】 Ji Zha was a person of integrity and would carry out what he promised to others.

【造句】季札挂剑的故事耐人寻味，影响深远，对我们理解孔子"人而无信，不知其可也"的圣训，很有启发意义。

【Example】 The story of Ji Zha is thought-provoking because it enlightens people on understanding Confucius's idea –If a man dose not keep his word, he will lose trust of others.

【故事】

春秋时期的季札，是吴国国君的公子。一次，他出使鲁国时经过徐国，顺便去拜会徐君。徐君一见到季札，就被他的气质、涵养所打动，内心感到非常的亲切。徐君默视着季札端庄、得体的仪容与着装，突然，被他腰间的那把祥光闪动的佩剑深深地吸引住了。

古时候，剑是一种装饰，也代表着一种礼仪。无论是士臣还是将相，身上通常都会佩戴着一把宝剑。季札的这柄剑的构思精湛，造型温厚，几颗宝石镶嵌其中，典丽而又不失庄重，因此很有气魄。只有像季札这样气质的人，才配得上这把剑。徐君虽然心里喜欢，却不好意思说出来，只是目光不住地朝它观望。季札看在眼里，内心暗暗想道：我还有出使上等国的任务，为了完成出使的使命，我暂时还无法将这柄

捌 信 (Integrity)

剑送他。等我办完事情之后回来,一定将这把佩剑送给徐君。"岂料世事无常。等到季札返回徐国的时候,徐君已经过世了。季札来到徐君的墓旁,内心有说不出的悲戚与感伤。他望着苍凉的天空,将那把剑挂在徐君墓旁的一棵树上,心中默默地祝祷:"徐君您虽然已经走了,但我内心那曾经有过的许诺却常在。希望您的在天之灵,在遥望这棵树的时候,能感受到我送您这把剑,向你道别的复杂心情。"他静穆地对着墓碑躬身而拜,然后离去。

季札的随从非常疑惑地问他:"徐君已过世了,您将这把剑悬在这里,又有什么用呢?"季札说:"徐君很喜欢这把剑,虽然他已经离开了人世,但我内心对他曾经有过承诺,我心想回来之后,一定要将剑送给他。君子讲求的是诚信与道义。我不能因为徐君的过世,而背弃作为人应有的信与义,违背原来的初衷。"

  Ji Zha of the Spring and Autumn Period was the prince of the State of Wu. Once, he passed the State of Xu when he went to the State of Lu for a diplomatic mission, so he decided to pay a visit to the King of Xu. Upon their meeting, the King was deeply touched by Ji Zha's elegant temperament and self-restraint. While the King was appreciating Ji Zha's demure and decent appearance and dress, he was suddenly attracted by the shining sword Ji Zha wore on his waist.

  In ancient times, sword was both a decoration and an etiquette. Man of figure like scholar, general and minister usually all wore a sword. The sword of Ji Zha with exquisite design and plain appearance and several gems inlaid looked both elegant and beautiful but not gorgeous. Only man like Ji Zha deserved to wear such a sword. Although the King liked it very much, he felt embarrassed to say so but kept watching the sword. Ji Zha noticed it and thought to himself: I was on my diplomatic mission to the State of Lu, so I couldn't present this sword to him. However, when I finished my mission, I will present it to the King.

However, things changed constantly. When Ji Zha returned to Xu after the mission, the King had already died. Ji Zha went to the tomb of the King, sad and doleful. Looking at the sky, he hung the sword on a tree near the tomb, praying silently in mind: Although you have passed away, the promised I made to myself before never change. I wish you can feel my mixed feeling to present this sword and bid farewell to you when you look to the tree. After that, he bowed to the tombstone solemnly and left.

One attendant asked with confusion, "The King has already died, so what's the point for you to hang this sword here?" "The King liked the sword very much and I have promised in mind to send it to him after the mission. A gentlemen should never break his promise. Though the King passed away, I can not violate the principle of integrity and faith and break my promise." Ji Zha replied.

【点评】

古代圣贤教诲我们，高迈的志节，往往表现在内心之中。就像季札，他并没有因为徐君的过世，而违背做人应有的诚信，何况他的允诺只是生发在内心的一闪念之中。这个故事耐人寻味。季札这种"信"到极点的行为，凸显出他高尚的信义品质。

The ancient sages taught us that one's moral integrity often find expressions in his mind. Ji Zha never violate the basic principle of integrity because the King of Xu has died, let alone the promise was only made in his mind. This story is quiet thought-provoking. The behavior of Ji Zha keeping his promise highlights his lofty character of integrity and faith.

捌 信(Integrity)

季布一诺
Jì Bù Yī Nuò

【出处】 《史记·季布栾布列传》：得黄金百斤，不如得季布一诺。

【释义】 季布的人品很好，他说话、做事特别讲信用，从不食言。

【Definition】 Ji Bu was a good person, credible for his words and behavior.

【造句】 成语"一诺千金"源于"季布一诺"的故事。

【Example】 The Chinese phrase "Yi Nuo Qian Jin" (A promise is worth a thousand onces of gold) derives from the story of "Ji Bu Yi Nuo".

【故事】

秦朝末年，楚地有个人叫季布，性情耿直，为人侠义、好助。生平对人家请求他的事情，只要是他答应过的，无论有多大困难，都一定设法办到，因此受到大家的赞扬。

楚汉相争的时候，季布是项羽的部下，曾几次为项羽出谋划策，都使刘邦的军队吃了败仗。刘邦当了皇帝后，一想起季布帮过项羽这些事，就又气又恨，于是下令通缉季布。在这种情况下，那些敬慕季布人品的人，都在暗中帮助他。易了容的季布逃亡到山东，在一个姓朱的员外家里做苦力。朱员外知道他就是季布，不但收留了他，还找机会特意到洛阳去找刘邦的老朋友汝阴侯夏侯婴为他说情。在夏侯婴的劝说下，刘邦不但取消了通缉令，还封季布做了郎中，不久又改任河东太守。

有一个季布的同乡人叫曹邱生，专爱结交有权势的官员。他听说季布已经做了大官，就去见季布。季布本来看不起他这种作派，听说曹邱生要来，就绷着个脸，准备数落他一番，要他下不了台。谁知曹邱生一进厅堂，不管季布的脸色多么阴沉，说话多么难听，他对着季布又是作揖又是佩服的，只和季布拉家常叙旧，并吹捧季布说："我听到楚地到处流传着'得黄金千两，不如得季布一诺'这样的话，您知道自己为什么能有这样好的名声传扬吗？因为我们是同乡，我就到处宣扬你的好名声。今天我来拜访您，您还不愿意见到我，不知是什么缘故啊？"

季布听了曹邱生的这番话，高兴起来，留他一住就是几个月，当作贵客招待，临走时，还送他一份厚礼。后来，曹邱生果然替季布到处宣扬，季布的名声也就越来越大。

In the late years of the Qin Dynasty, there was a man of Chu named Ji Bu who was well-known for his integrity, gallantry and kindness. Once he made a promise to others, he would managed to keep it no matter how hard it was, thus earning people's praises.

While the Chu and the Han was fight with each other, Ji Bu, then a subordinate of Xiang Yu (leader of the Chu), offered many advice and suggestions to Xiang Yu, which delivered a heavy blow to the army of Liu Bang (leader of the Han). After Liu Bang became the emperor of the Han Dynasty, he felt both angry and detestable at the thought of Ji Bu's past behaviors of helping Xiang Yu, so he gave an order to arrest Ji Bu. Under this circumstance, many people who admired Ji Bu's personality offered secretly help to him. Ji Bu fled to Shandong through disguise and worked as a cooly for a rich man whose surname was Zhu. The rich man knew his real identity, but he still accepted Ji Bu to work for him. What's more, the rich man also sought opportunities and went to Luoyang specially to call on Xia Houying (Marquis Ruyin) pleading for mercy for Ji Bu. At his old friend Xia Houying's persuasion, Liu Bang not only canceled the order, but appointed him as Langzhong, and later changed to another post as Governor of Hedong.

There was a fellow countryman named Cao Qiusheng who enjoyed associating with those influential officials. He heard that Ji Bu was a high-ranking official and de-

捌 信 (Integrity)

sired to call on Ji Bu. Having always despised such a fawning behavior, Ji Bu decided to meet him coldly and scold his behavior to put him on the spot when he heard Cao Qiusheng was about to see him. However, after entering into hall, he bowed to Ji Bu with admiration and just talked about the old days, keeping flatter Ji Bu, "I heard a saying that 'A promise from Ji Bu is worth more than a thousand catties of gold' in the area of Chu. How can you enjoy such a reputation in Chu? Since we are both from Chu, so I have done much to spread your fame everywhere. Now I come to visit you, yet you seem to be unwilling to see me. Why is this?"

Ji Bu was very glad after hearing this. So he invited Cao Qiusheng to stay for several months as his respected guest, giving him with many gifts when he left. Later, Cao Qiusheng indeed helped to spread Ji Bu's fame, and Ji Bu became even more famous than before.

【点评】

季布当初是项羽的部下，帮助项羽攻打刘邦，这本来是很自然的事情。由于季布的帮助，刘邦多次身陷险境，所以刘邦战胜项羽后，就悬赏捉拿季布，并下令对胆敢窝藏季布的要灭三族。即使这样，凭着季布诚信为人的品质，还是有人保护季布，并且还联合其他力量共同对付拥有至高无上皇权的刘邦。由此可见，诚信的季布在他人心目中的崇高声誉和威望。

At first Ji Bu was a subordinate of Xiang Yu, so it was quiet natural for him to assist Xiang Yu to fight against Liu Bang. Because of Ji Bu's help, Liu Bang was trapped in danger on several occasions. That's why he would offer a reward to arrest Ji Bu upon defeating Xiang Yu, and even threatened anyone who dared to shelter Ji Bu with the destruction of three classes of their relatives. Even so, because of his character of integrity, there were still someone coming to his rescue and allying with others to go against the powerful emperor. From this, we can know the lofty fame and prestige of Ji Bu in others' mind.

孺子可教
Rú Zǐ Kě Jiào

【出处】《史记·留侯世家》：父以足受，笑而去。良殊大惊，随目之。父去里所，复返，曰：孺子可教矣。

【释义】 张良年轻的时候，因为好心对待了一个奇怪的老人，而得到这个老人的教诲、指点，最终成为一个很有出息的人。

【Definition】 At Zhang Liang's yong age, because of his kind treatment with a strange old man he got this wise man's teaching and guidance and finally became a promising person.

【造句】 孺子可教的典故说明：年轻人要善于把握受教育的机会，才可以增长有用的本领。

【Example】 The allusion Ru Zi Ke Jiao illustrates that young people should catch the opportunity for education to develop useful skills.

【故事】

张良行刺秦始皇失败后，逃亡到下邳过隐匿生活。有一天，张良来到下邳附近的圯水桥上散步，遇到一个穿粗布衣裳的老人。老人等张良走到面前，故意把一只鞋子掉到桥下，然后对张良说："喂！小伙子！帮我把鞋子捡上来！"

张良很惊讶，本来不想理他，但看到老人年纪很大，于是下桥去把鞋捡了上来，还恭敬地跪着，替老人穿上。可是老人伸脚穿好鞋后，没说什么，然后笑着，转身就走了。

张良更加吃惊了，盯着老人的背影若有所思。那老人走了约一里路

捌 信 (Integrity)

后,返身回来对张良说:"你小子不错,值得我指教。五天后的早上,到桥上来见我。"张良连忙答应。

第五天早上,张良赶到桥上,只见那老人已先到了。老人生气地对张良说:"跟老人约会却迟到,你怎么回事啊?再过五天,早些来见我!"

五天后的凌晨,公鸡一打鸣,张良就出发赶到桥上。不料那老人又先到了,老人说:"你又迟到了!五天后再来见我!"

又过了五天,张良半夜摸黑来到桥上。过了一会,那老人也来了,见了张良,高兴地说:"小伙子,你这样才对嘛!"老人说着,拿出一本书给张良,并交代说:"你要下苦功钻研这部书,领悟透了,以后就可以做帝王的老师,十年后有大成就。十三年后,小子你将再见到我,济北谷城山下的黄石公就是我了。"张良对老人表示感谢后,老人扬长而去。

第二天早晨,张良翻看那本书,竟然是《太公兵法》。张良觉得这一经历很奇特,于是就用心研读这本书,果然很有成效,终于成为一个深明韬略、文武兼备、足智多谋的人。后来作为汉高祖刘邦的重要谋士,为刘邦建立汉朝立下了汗马功劳。

After the assassination of the First Emperor of Qin failed, Zhang Liang fled to Xiapi and lived there secretly. One day, he was walking on Yishui Bridge near Xiapi and came across a old man in rough homespun. When Zhang Liang walked in front of the old man, the old man dropped deliberately one of his shoes under the bridge, and said to Zhang Liang, "Hey, boy! Go down and get back my shoe!"

Zhang Liang was astonished, intending to ignore it. But he still went down the bridge to fetch the shoe because of the man's old age. Besides, he even knelt down to put the shoe on for the old man. The old man, however, just stood up and then left with a smile.

Zhang Liang was more surprised, watching the back of the old man as if deep in thought. After going nearly one mile, the old man turned back. "Your are worth teaching, boy, " he said, "meet me five days later at dawn." Zhang Liang agreed immediately.

At dawn five days later, Zhang Liang hurried to the bridge, only to find that the old man had already arrived. The old man said angrily, "what do you mean to let a old man wait for a young man? Come earlier five days later." Five days later, Zhang Liang came at the first crow of rooster, only to find again that the old man was already there. Likewise, he was asked to come earlier five days later.

Five days later, Zhang Liang set out in midnight and waited at the bridge in darkness. After a while, the old man also came. "That's right! " the old man said gladly and handed a book to Zhang Liang, "read this book carefully and you could become the teacher of the emperor. Ten years later, you will achieve a great success. Thirteen years later you will once more see me: a yellow stone at the foot of Mount Gucheng north of the River Ji." Zhang Liang expressed his gratitude and then the old man left, never appearing again.

Next morning, Zhang Liang looked at the book and found it was master *Lü Wang's Art of War*. Feeling amazing about this experience, Zhang Liang pored over this book and finally became a resourceful and ingenious person skillful in both politics and military. Later, Zhang Liang, served as counselor of Emperor Gaozu of the Han Dynasty, made great contributions in the founding of the Han Dynasty.

【点评】

张良在圯水桥上遇到一个奇怪的老人。这时的张良,不再是当年血气方刚的莽撞青年了,面对老人的过分且无礼要求,他不但为老人捡来鞋子,还对老人礼遇有加、谦卑有度。结果,他受到老人的赏识与指点,成为后来运筹帷幄、决胜千里的张子房。这个故事告诉年轻人:做

捌 信 (Integrity)

人行事，要诚信，受得住考验；有爱心，能尊老敬贤，并虚心求教；像张良一样，才能学到真正的本领，为以后的成就打下良好基础。

Zhang Liang came across a strange old man at Yishui bridge. Since he was no longer impulsive like before, facing with the old man's excessive and impolite demand, he not only went down to fetch the shoe, but treated the old man with respect and humility. As a result, he obtained the appreciation and guidance from the old man and later became well-known as a resourceful strategist. This story tells us that we should be honest and withstand test in our lives; we should respect the old and the wise, and always be willing to take advice; we should act like Zhang Liang of this story so that we can learn the true knowledge, thus lying the basis of future achievements.

郭伋亭候

Guō Jí Tíng Hòu

【出处】《后汉书·郭伋传》：郭伋归早，止于野亭，候期乃入，不欺童龄。

【释义】 郭伋和一帮小孩有再次见面的约定，因为自己的时间提前了，就在半道上停留下来住了一宿，第二天再如期赴约与小朋友相见。

【Definition】 Guo Ji and a group of kids had agreed to meet again one day, but he arranged his time ahead, so he just stayed halfway down for the night and scheduled to meet with the children the next day.

【造句】 为人处世，要像郭伋亭候那样：童叟无欺，有言必行，诚信到极点。

【Example】 Dealing with others, a man like Guo Ji should be fair to them and keep words no matter young or old.

【故事】

郭伋，是西汉武帝时大侠郭解的孙子。他从小就立志高远，要为百姓谋福利，后来官至太中大夫。他为官清廉，为人讲信义，很有治世的本领，特别受当时百姓的爱戴。

到东汉光武帝即皇位的时候，社会还未安定，盗贼土匪四处作乱。武帝常听闻郭伋的名声，就多次委派他到渔阳、颍川等治安问题严重的州郡做太守，治乱除暴，安抚百姓，政绩卓著，皇帝称他为"贤能太守"。

过了些年头，郭伋被调往做并州牧。早在王莽时期，郭伋就被征召做过并州牧，前任并州牧的时候，郭伋勤政爱民，常常微服私访，解决民生疾苦，整顿吏治，扫除流寇，平定许多冤狱大案，所以百姓在心中一直感念郭汲的恩义。这次得知郭汲又到并州做官，老老少少夹道欢迎。郭汲心里也感到很欣慰：做官能做到这份上，才不枉在这世上活了一场！于是，更加小心谨慎，所到之处，常常问民疾苦，虚心求教。

转眼到了中秋八月，按例又要到各地州县巡查吏治情况。郭汲就带着几名随从，一路骑马赶往西河郡美稷县。行至县城郊外，突然远远望见有一群小孩嬉戏而来，及至近旁，小孩列队相迎，稽首跪拜。郭汲下马还礼问道："小朋友，不必多礼，快快请起，你们从哪里来？在这里干什么呀？"一个稍大的孩子回答道："我们听说郭爷爷今日来美稷，都很欢喜，特来这里恭候！"郭汲心下感叹不已，于是在众小孩的簇拥下进了县城。

过了一段时间，郭汲要离开县城外出公干。刚到城门口，没想到众孩童又来相送，一直送到了城郊外，郭汲就对孩童说道："大家早点回家吧！我很快还会回来的。"为首的小孩问："郭爷爷，您哪一天回来呀？我们还要来接您！"郭汲内心感动，就计算了一下，把回来的日子告诉了孩子们，并与众孩童约定了那一天在郊外相会，不见不散。

不曾想很快便将事情办完，归来时比预计的时间提前了一天，郭汲惦记着与小孩的约定，便决定与随行人员暂不入城，在郊外寻得一个小亭，歇息过夜。那时正值深秋，昼夜温差较大，郭汲便叫随从捡拾柴火取暖抗寒，围坐着烤火，随从人员显得有些不解地问："老爷，天气寒冷，还是早点回去吧，万一感染风寒可就麻烦了！"郭汲郑重地告诫道："君子言出必行，一诺千金。我与孩子们有约定，不可以言而无信。"于是，等到了第二天，才进城来。当天，那些孩子们果然都在路上欢迎郭汲的归来。

Guo Ji was grandson of Guo Jie, a famous gallant citizen of the western Han Dynasty. He resolved to be a great man to benefit the public since childhood and later served as Taizhong Dafu. As an upright and honest official, he performed his duties extremely well, thus enjoying much respect and support of the public.

When Emperor Guangwu of the eastern Han Dynasty came to the throne, the society was still unstable with bandits and robbers keeping emerging everywhere. Emperor Guangwu heard fame of Guo ji and often appointed him as prefecture of places with serious security problem like Yuyang, Yingchuan and other places. In these places, he pacified the public by cracking down the evil and maintaining social stability and made remarkable achievements, thus being praised by the emperor as "capable prefecture".

Several years later, Guo Ji was transferred to Bingzhou as prefectural governor. As early as the reign of Wang Mang, he had been appointed as prefectural governor of Bingzhou. At that time, he was diligent in governance and loved his people. He often visited the public with civil dressing to address hardships of the people, rectify administration of local officials, wipe out roving bandits and solve many cases of wrongly, falsely and unjustly repudiated. Hence the people all remembered him with gratitude. Knowing that he would take office in Bingzhou again, the local people, young and old, all lined the street to welcome his arrival. Guo ji also felt glad about this, thinking that an official could be welcomed like this had lived a worthy life. Thereafter, he carried out his duty more prudently, solved difficulties of the people in places he visited, and was always willing to take advice from others.

Soon the Mid-Autumn Festival which fell to the August was coming and it was time for him to inspect prefectures and counties of Bingzhou. So he rode a horse and went to Meiji county, Xihe prefecture with several attendants. When approaching the suburb of Meiji county, he saw from a distance a group of kids who were coming toward them while playing. After getting close, all kids lined up and knelt to welcome. Guo Ji got down from the horse and asked, "kids, don't do this, get up quickly. Where are you come from? And what are you doing here?" A older kid replied, "we heard that grandpa Guo would come to Meiji and were all happy about it. So we come here to welcome." Guo Ji felt pleased and entered the county together with these kids.

After a period of time, Guo Ji was about to go out the county for business. When he reached the gate of the county, these kids came again to see him off until the suburb.

Guo Ji said to the kids, "all come back early! I will be back soon." A kid asked, "So grandpa Guo, which day it is? We will come to welcome you again." Moved by this, Guo Ji counted for a second and told them the date. Besides, he also agreed with the kids to meet here on that day.

However, Guo Ji finished his duties the day before the expected date. Bearing the promise made to those kids in mind, he decided not to go to the county right away and found a pavilion in the suburb for the night. Since it was then the late autumn, temperature between day and night was large. Guo Ji had to asked his attendants to gather some firewood and sat around the fire to get warm. One attendant asked with puzzle, "My lord, it is cold outside. Let's go into the county in case you may catch a cold." Guo Ji instructed seriously, " A gentleman never eat his words. I have made a promise with these kids. I must keep my promise." Therefore, they stayed at the pavilion and entered the county the next day. And the kids waited at their way as expected welcoming the arrival of Guo Ji.

【点评】

做人要讲信用。郭汲不失信于儿童，树立了很好的榜样。成人要为儿童作出好的表率，即使是对小孩子说话也要算数，做到言行一致。"守信"与"诚实"往往结伴而行，是人与人之间正常交往、秩序稳定的重要保障。对个人来说，诚实守信作为一种道德品质和道德信念，可以养成一种崇高的人格力量，因此，需要好好修炼。

A man should keep his word. Guo Ji didn't break his promise made to the kids, thus setting a good example. Adults should act like this for children and ensure that they practice what they preach. "Keeping promise" is usually go along with "being honest", which is an important guarantee for normal relations among people and order and stability. Personally, as a moral character and a moral belief, honest and integrity can be developed into a lofty personality power. Therefore, we need to to cultivate it.

魏征妩媚

Wèi Zhēng Wǔ Mèi

【出处】《新唐书·魏征传》：魏征妩媚，不肯面从，责上失信，应对从容。

【释义】 魏征对太宗皇帝的不足，总是当面批评，且不留情面，但皇帝感到他很可爱。

【Definition】 Wei Zheng always criticised Emperor Tang Taizong for his shortness without mercy, but the Emperor felt he was adorable.

【造句】 魏征妩媚，是唐太宗对魏征敢于犯颜直谏的品质的一种评价。

【Example】 The story "Wei Zheng Wu Mei", is an good evaluation of Emperor for his boldness to criticize the monarch.

【故事】

魏征在太宗皇帝朝中做官，曾经责问皇上对百姓们失信的事情。每逢劝谏皇上不肯听从时，他就对皇上提出的要求也不答应。唐太宗说："你答应了我之后，再来劝谏，又有什么关系呢？"魏征说："从前舜帝警诫他人：不要在表面上服从。现在做臣子的倘若心里明知不是，但是口里却勉强答应皇上，这就是表面上的服从了，哪里是自愿服从上级的初意呢？"太宗皇帝就笑着说："别人说魏征做人疏慢，可是我看他的态度，觉得越来越妩媚可爱了。"

魏征由于能够犯颜直谏，即使太宗在大发脾气的时候，也敢当面廷争，从不退让，所以，唐太宗有时对他也会产生敬畏之心。有一次，唐太宗想要去秦岭山中打猎取乐，行装都准备好了，但却迟迟未能成行。后来，魏征问到此事，太宗笑着说："当初确有这个想法，但你

捌 信（Integrity）

知道后肯定又要直言进谏，所以就取消了这次活动。"还有一次，唐太宗得到了一只上好的鹞鹰，把它放在自己的肩膀上，很是得意。在他远远地看见魏征向他走来时，就赶紧把鸟藏在袖中。魏征故意奏事很久，致使鹞鹰闷死在袖中。

魏征担任尚书左丞时，有人告他私自提拔亲戚做官。唐太宗立即派人调查此事，结果查无证据，纯属诬告。但唐太宗还是对魏征说："今后要远避嫌疑，不要再惹出这样的麻烦。"魏征当即面奏说："我听说君臣之间，相互协助，义同一体。如果不讲秉公办事，只讲远避嫌疑，那么国家兴亡，或未可知。"并趁机请求太宗要使自己做良臣而不要做忠臣。太宗就问忠臣和良臣有何区别？魏征答道："使自己身获美名，使君主成为明君，子孙相继，福禄无疆，是为良臣；使自己身受杀戮，使君主沦为暴君，家国沦丧，空有其名，是为忠臣。这样比较而言，二者相差很远。"魏征这样巧妙地提醒，唐太宗听后大笑，后点头称是。

一天，太宗从外边回来，往寝宫边走边说："气死我了！我一定杀了这个乡巴佬！"长孙皇后问生谁的气，太宗气愤地说："还不是那个魏征！他天天在朝廷上当面指责我的不是，今天还当面顶撞我，气死我了！"长孙皇后听到后，马上换上朝服，走到太宗面前说："恭喜皇上，贺喜皇上！只有明主出现，臣子才敢直谏。"太宗听后，怒气就顿消。

正是由于魏征这样正直的大臣和长孙皇后的贤明，才有唐朝时期的盛世，这一时期政治开明，经济发达，社会安定，称为"贞观之治"。

During the reign of Emperor Taizong of the Tang Dynasty, he once criticized the emperor for breaking his promise made to the people. When it came to that the emperor refused to accept the suggestion, he would refuse to agree about requirement the Emperor raised. Then Emperor Taizong would said, "Why don't you agree with me first and then put forward your suggestion?" Wei Zheng replied, "The Emperor Shun once warned us: do not submit to others only superficially. As your loyal officer, if I agree with you against my own will, that's a superficially submission. It is not the original meaning for an officer voluntarily submitting to his superior." Emperor Taizong laughed, "people all say that Wei Zheng is arrogant. In my view, however, he is becoming more adorable than before."

Wei Zheng dared to speak against the emperor's opinion and would never make a concession even when the Emperor Taizong lost temper. Therefore, Emperor Taizong sometimes respected Wei Zheng and would concede to his suggestion. Once, Emperor Taizong would like to go hunting for fun in Qinling Mountain, yet he didn't go for a long time despite that all things needed were prepared. Later, when Wei Zheng asked about this, Emperor Taizong smiled, "I did intend to go, but I knew you would speak against it after knowing this. So I canceled the hunting." There was another thing. Emperor Taizong got a good sparrow hawk and put it happily on his shudder. When he saw Wei Zheng was coming toward him, he hurried to hide the hawk in his sleeve. And Wei Zheng, who already knew about this, discussed with him for a long time on purpose, causing the hawk being suffocated in sleeve.

When Wei Zheng served as a deputy head of the executive bureau of the government, he was accused of nepotism by someone. Emperor had his officer investigate, only to find no evidence proving the accusation. But Emperor Taizong still rebuked Wei Zheng, "you should keep yourself free from such a suspicion, and never cause same troubles again." Wei Zheng responded immediately, "I heard that a ruler and his ministers should assist each other like a unity. If we only focus on how to free from suspicions instead of performing duties with justice, then the country's future remains unknown." After this, he further seized the opportunity to be allowed to make himself an excellent minister instead of a loyal minister. Then Emperor Taizong asked about the difference. He replied, "an excellent minister refers to one who enjoy good fame and assist the ruler to be a responsible and ambitious emperor with prosperous posterity and endless happiness, while a loyal minister refers to one who get himself killed and reduce the ruler to be a cruel and incapable emperor with declining country and hollow reputation. In comparison, these two kinds of minsters differ considerably." Hearing Wei Zheng's subtly caution, Emperor Taizong burst into laughter and nodded in agreement.

One day, Emperor Taizong walked to the imperial harem angrily from outside, "Damn it! Dame it! I am gonna kill this bumpkin!" Empress Zhangsun asked who he was mad at, and Emperor Taizong replied wrathfully, "who else could be but Wei Zheng! He always criticize my mistakes without mercy at court. And today, he even speak against me." Hearing this, Empress Zhangsun changed into her court dress right away and walked to Emperor Taizong, "Congratulations, my Majesty! Minister dare to speak against only when the ruler is wise and kind." Emperor Taizong's anger was thus dispelled.

It is owing to upright ministers like Weizheng and sagacious wife like Empress Zhangsun that the Tang Dynasty could enjoy such a prosperity. During the reign of Emperor Taizong, the politics was democratic, economy prosperous and society stable, thus was later called as "Zhen Guan Zhi Zhi".

【点评】

魏征是唐代大政治家、思想家和史学家。他辅佐唐太宗十七年，以性格刚直、才识超卓、敢于犯颜直谏而闻名。魏征进谏实话实说、注重效果，唐太宗因此对魏征言听计从，并尊他是雕琢"美玉"的良工、矫正己过的"人镜"。世人则把魏征誉为"一代名相""千秋金鉴"。从魏征的进谏活动和主要表现看，他作为中国古代最负盛名的杰出的谏官代表，忠心辅国，犯颜直谏，获此殊荣，名实相符，当之无愧。

Wei Zheng was a famous politician, thinker and historian of the Tang Dynasty. He served Emperor Taizong for seventeen years and was well-known for his upright character, brilliant ability and daring to advise frankly against the ruler. Whiling giving a advice, Wei Zheng always talked bluntly and emphasized on practical result. Hence, Emperor Taizong often followed his advice, praising him a skilled worker carving "fine jade" and "a mirror" correcting one's misbehavior. The later generations regard him as "a distinguished chancellor" and "a mirror though the ages". Considering his major behaviors, Wei Zheng, as one of the most eminent representative of remonstrating officials, did live up to these praises.

宋璟责说

Sòng Jǐng Zé Yuè

【出处】《天宝遗事》:宋璟拒诬(wū),许友偕(xié)死,张说实言,魏免弃市。

【释义】 宋璟办案严查诬告,责成证人张说讲实话,使得御史大夫魏元忠幸免于难。

【Definition】 In the investigation of a false accusation, Song Jing ordered the witness to tell the truth and finally helped the royal officer Wei Yuanzhong out of a death penalty.

【造句】 刚正不阿、不畏权贵、疾恶如仇、道义高尚,是"宋璟责说"故事的人物形象。

【Example】 Integrity, straightforwardness, justice and nobleness are completely reflected by Song Jing in the story "Song Jing Ze Yue".

【故事】

武则天时代,为了打击异己,大用酷吏,大臣们都胆战心惊。有一次,武则天的宠臣张易之诬告御史大夫魏元忠有谋反言论,并拉上张说作假证明。

在这之前,张易之私下里许诺张说:做了这个见证,就给他一个肥缺的官差干干。张说惧怕他的权势,就答应了,但要违心诬蔑魏元忠也感到心里不安。

在朝堂对质的时候,张说非常惶恐。担任监察御史的宋璟就对他说:"一个人的名誉和道义,是很重要的。不可以违背道义去陷害正直的人,以此希图自己苟且免于损害。要坚持正义,如果因此有了什么不测,我

捌 信（Integrity）

就向皇帝求情来救你，倘若救你不成，我就陪你一起死。"张说听了这一番话，内心有所感触，就醒悟了，当场就把真实情况对大家说了，御史大夫魏元忠因此得以免死获救。武则天对宋璟这样刚正的官员十分欣赏，不久升任他为御史中丞，相当于现在的检察总长。

During the reign of Empress Wu Zetian, many brutal officials were appointed to crack down those dissidents, many officials thus being nervous and afraid. Once, Zhang Yizhi, a minion of Empress Wu Zetian, trumped up a charge of conspiratorial speech against Grandee Secretary Wei Yuanzhong and asked Zhang Yue to make a false testimony.

Actually, Zhang Yizhi promised Zhang Yue secretly that he would offer him a nice job after making the false testimony. Being afraid of Zhang Yizhi's power, Zhang Yue had to agree in spite of his uneasiness to set up Wei Yuanzhong against his own will.

When checking testimony in court, Zhang Yue was terrified. So Song Jing, then served as Supervisory Censor, said to Zhang Yue, "Reputation and integrity are of great importance in our lives. We can not violate the principle of integrity to frame upright person just to keep ourselves free from persecution. If you get into trouble because you uphold justice, I will plead with the Empress to save you; if I fail to make it, I will die with you."

After hearing this, Zhang Yue realized his mistake and brought the truth out entirely on the spot. And Wei Yuanzhong was thus relived from death. The Empress Wu Zetian quiet appreciated upright officials like Song Jing, and soon promoted him to Yushi Zhongcheng, which was equal to the chief Procurator now.

【点评】

宋璟为人刚正，讲道义。他做官很是正直无私，从来都毫不含糊，因此很有名气。张易之打算通过诬告、治罪来修理御史大夫魏元忠,为坐实魏元忠的罪名,就请张说出庭作伪证,并许以"好差事"。但在宋璟面前,张说的良心最终获得了复苏,实话实说,既揭露了张易之的阴险奸诈的小人嘴脸,又还了魏元忠的清白、保住了他的性命。这戏剧性变化的结果,关键在于刚正不阿的宋璟对张说的一番"道义监察"和坦诚承诺。

Song Jing was a man of integrity and valued mortality and justice. He was famous for uprightness and selflessness in performing duties. Zhang Yizhi wanted to frame Wei Yuanzhong and, to affirm his accusation, asked Zhang Yue to make a false testimony with "a good job" as a promise. However, Zhang Yue realized his mistake after hearing the words of Song Jing and told the truth, thus not only disclosing the sinister trick of Zhang Yizhi, but eliminating Wei Yuanzhong's accusation and saving his life. Such a dramatic result mainly owe to Song Jing's moral enlightenment and sincere promise made to Zhang Yue.

捌 信(Integrity)

曹彬激诚
Cáo Bīn Jī Chéng

【出处】《宋史·曹彬列传》:曹彬守诚,称疾保民,江南城下,不杀一人。

【释义】 曹彬奉命攻取金陵,设法激起了官兵的爱心,兑现了"不杀一人"的诺言。

【Definition】 After the conquest of Jinling, Cao Bin provoked the solders' mercy and promised not to kill a person in that town.

【造句】 曹彬激诚的故事说明:曹彬做事是很讲究策略的,有大家风范。

【Example】 The story of Cao Bin illustrates that he was strategic in his demeanor.

【故事】

北宋开宝七年(公元974年),名将曹彬奉命去讨伐金陵(今江苏南京市)的南唐李煜。在这危急时刻,李煜派他的大臣徐铉拿着国书到宋,请求宋朝暂缓攻打,没有如愿。宋朝在对李煜的长期围困中,曹彬有意放缓了进攻的节奏,希望李煜能够降服。曹彬还派人告诉李煜说:"事情已经到了这个地步,我可怜的是全城百姓。如果你能归降,这才是上策。"这之前,太祖皇帝曾对曹彬说:"城池攻下的时候,千万不可杀戮平民百姓。"于是,就在即将攻克金陵的时候,曹彬忽然称病不管事。于是众将领们都来看望病情,希望能早日康复。曹彬趁机说:"我的病不是打针吃药能治好的,只有你们大家共同表态,发誓在城攻下的时候,不滥杀一人,那我的病就自然好了。"

众将领都答应,并发了誓。到第二天,曹彬就说他的病好了;再过一天，金陵城被攻陷。到了金陵攻克的时候，兵士们的刀上果然没有沾着一点血迹，城中十分安定，百姓如同平常一样。李煜与他的大臣们来到军营请罪，曹彬安慰他，还用贵宾礼接待他。

In the seventh year of Kaibao of the northern Song Dynasty (974 B.C.), famous general Cao Bin received an order to attack Li Yu of the southern Tang Dynasty in Jinling (now Nanjing, Jiangsu province). At this critical moment, Li Yu sent his official Xu Xuan to Song with a state credentials, pleading in vain for the suspension of attack. During the long-term besiegement of Li Yu, Cao Bin slowed down its pace deliberately of its attack, hoping that Li Yu would surrender. He even sent people to inform Li Yu, "At this stage, what I sympathize with is the people in this city. The best thing you can do is to surrender."

Before his departure, Emperor Taizu of the northern Song Dynasty told Cao Bin, "upon the occupy of Jinling, you are not allowed to slaughter the common people." So when Jinling was about to be taken, Cao Bin refused to take charge of the army on account of disease. And other generals all went to visit him and wish him a speedy recovery. Cao Bin seized the chance and said, "My disease can not be cured by medicine. It will recover naturally as soon as all of you promise not to kill any innocent people after occupy of Jinling."

These generals all agreed and made their promises. Next day, Cao Bin said that his regained his health; another day later, the city of Jinling was taken and weapons of all soldiers had no blood stained with at all. The whole city was peaceful and all people lived as usual. Li Yu and his ministers came to the barracks asking for forgiveness. Cao Bin welcomed him as a honorable guest and comforted him.

【点评】

曹彬生性仁义、谦敬、和气、厚道，严于律己，诚信为本，有诺必践，谨

捌 信（Integrity）

慎行事，忠于职守，勤政廉明。正是这些秉性，使得曹彬在攻陷金陵的时候，不杀一人，传为千秋佳话。就当时的情形来看，他信守太祖告诫他时所说的话肯定没有问题，但关键在于他手下的官兵能否也如同他一样地落实太祖的指令？于是，他设计留下缓冲、妥善安排的余地。凭他为人处世的良好声誉和在官兵中的绝对威望，众官兵知道他的心思后，都很忠诚地发誓承诺。结果，既落实了太祖的指示意见，又遵守了对李煜的承诺与保证。

Cao Bin was benevolent, humble, polite and honest in nature. He set strict demands on himself, upheld integrity in performing duties and earnestly kept his promise. Because of these characters, he did not slaughter a single person while occupying Jinling, which was praised through the ages. At that moment, he could keep the words Emperor Taizu of the northern Song Dynasty told him, but it mainly depended on whether his subordinates could abide by the order? To this end, he thought of a method to reassure implementation of the order. With a good reputation in dealing with others and absolute authority in the army, all generals and soldiers promised to strictly abide by the order. As a result, he not only practiced the words of Emperor Taizu of the northern Song Dynasty, but kept his promise with Li Yu.

杨荣谏征

Yáng Róng Jiàn Zhēng

【出处】《明史·艺文志》：杨荣警敏，止调民兵，示天下信，成祖罢征。

【释义】 机警敏捷的杨荣，建言明成祖以诚信昭(zhāo)示天下，不再征用江西地方民兵服役。

【Definition】 As a smart person, Yang Rong suggested Ming Cheng Emperor treat all folks with good faith and not exploit Jiangxi people in military service.

【造句】 杨荣谏征的结果，皇帝采纳了他的意见，决定以诚信昭示天下。

【Example】 The result of "Yang Rong Jian Zheng" was that the emperor adopted his suggestion and decided to treat all folks with good faith.

【故事】

明朝有个大臣叫杨荣。在明成祖皇帝时期，与杨荣一同在文渊阁里当差的，共有七个大臣。这七大臣中，杨荣最年轻，同时也是最机警、最敏达的一个。

一天，有个报告送到朝廷，说是宁夏城给敌人围住了。皇帝就把这个消息的奏章给杨荣看。杨荣看后，分析说："宁夏城是很坚固的。况且那地方的人，个个都很勇敢，能够应付战事。从时间上看，这个奏章现在传到这里已有十多天了，照此推算起来，这时候宁夏城的围困，恐怕已经解决了。"

皇上听后，将信将疑，就说这事明日再议。果不其然，到了这一天的半夜，有个新奏章呈了上来，报告说宁夏城已经解围了。皇帝对

捌 信（Integrity）

杨荣的准确判断大加赞赏，就更加信任他了。

后来，明成祖下诏出征阿鲁台。为解决军粮的运输问题，有朝臣建议：调用建文帝时所征集的江西民兵和运丁夫。杨荣当即对此表明了自己的立场："皇上已经答应了这些人，恢复他们的职业，让他们休养生息。如果现在又征调他们去打仗，这就是朝廷对天下老百姓不守信用了。"皇帝觉得杨荣说的在理，就接受了他的意见，不再征用。

There was a high-ranking official named Yang Rong in the Ming Dynasty. During the day of Emperor Chengzu of the Ming Dynasty, seven officials served together in the Imperial Library, of which Yang Rong was the youngest and also the most vigilant and smart.

One day, a report was sent to the court, telling that the city of Ningxia was besieged by enemies. The Emperor showed the report to Yang Rong for advice. After watching it, Yang Rong replied, " The city of Ningxia boasts both strong city walls and courageous soldiers, which should enable it to defeat the enemy. Besides, ten days have passed before the report reached here. Hence, I am afraid that the problem has already been solved."

The Emperor was not convinced after hearing his words and decided to discuss it next day. Just as expected, a new report proving the correctness of Yang Rong's analysis reached at midnight. The emperor expressed much appreciation about it and trusted Yang Rong more.

Later, Emperor Chengzu of the Ming Dynasty issued an imperial edict to conquer Alutai, a leader of then Tartar. To address the problem of transporting army provisions, one official suggested to requisition those militiamen and porters in Jiangxi collected at the reign of Emperor Jianwen. Yang Rong immediately expressed his dissent, "Your Majesty has promised to let them resume their jobs and live in peace. Now you Majesty call up them to engage in the war, then you will break your promise before all people."

Holding what he said was right, the Emperor accepted the advice not to call up these people.

【点评】

杨荣秉性警敏通达，谋而能断，老成持重，尤其擅长谋划边防事务，他对被围的宁夏城的形势分析得出的结论就是一个典型的范例，因此深得明成祖器重。他向皇帝进言，阻止征用江西民兵征战，是从昭示天下百姓以诚信的角度，作出的树皇帝威信、为国家立威的战略思考，不仅使民众免遭苦楚，也有利于发展农业生产。

Yang Rong was observant, experienced and prudent. He was especially skillful in handling affairs concerning border defense, which can be seen from his correct analysis based on the situation of the besieged Ningxia. Thus Emperor Chengzu of the Ming Dynasty thought highly of him. Starting from the point of integrity, he advised to the Emperor not to call up those militiamen in Jiangxi, thus maintaining prestige and majesty for the emperor. Besides, it could not only relive the people from sufferings, but promote the development of agriculture.

捌 信(Integrity)

宋濂借书
Sòng Lián Jiè Shū

【出处】《送东阳马生序》:余幼时即嗜(shì)学。家贫,无从致书以观,每假借于藏书之家,手自笔录,计日以还。

【释义】 家境贫苦的宋濂从小就非常好学,因无钱买书,就经常借人家书读,终成大家。

【Definition】 Song Lian, from a poor family, was eager to learn since childhood, though poor not to afford books, he often borrowed books from others and finally became a great person.

【造句】 宋濂借书的故事提醒青年学子:应该学习宋濂精神,勤于苦学,甘于淡泊,严于律己,尊师重教,专心致志,必然学有所成。

【Example】 Young readers can infer from "Song Lian Jie Shu" that we should learn Song Lian's spirit, be diligent and willing to stay indifferent, be self-disciplined, respect teachers, and be dedicated to become successful.

【故事】

宋濂是明代的大学问家。小时候就非常好学,由于家里贫穷,无钱买书,因此常常向有书的人借书看,并自己抄录,按预定的日期归还。即使天气寒冷的时候,砚台上的墨水都冻成冰了,手指冻僵了,伸屈很不方便,但抄录从不懈怠。抄录完了,就赶紧把书送还过去,一点也不敢超过预定的日期。

宋濂就是这样一个勤奋好学、守时守信的孩子。一年冬天的某一天,他向一位富人借了一本厚厚的书。富人限他十日内归还书本。于是,宋濂每天从早读到晚,终于在第十天冒着大雪把书送了回去。富人因为他不顾寒冷而守时的表现很感动,就答应他以后可以随时来借书。这样,有书的人都愿意把书借给宋濂,宋濂也因此能够读到大量的书。

宋濂成年后,更加仰慕圣贤的学说,却又担心不能与学识渊博的老师和名人交游,就跑到百里之外,向那些有道德有学问的前辈求教。前辈的道德高、名望大,学生挤满了老师的房间,老师的言辞和态度从来都严厉。宋濂站着陪侍在前辈的左右,提出疑难,询问道理,低身侧耳向老师请教;有时遭到老师的训斥,表情更为恭敬,礼节更为周到,默默受教;等到老师高兴时,又继续质疑问难:于是得到不少教益,终于成为一个大学问家,与高启、刘基并称为"明初诗文三大家",被明太祖称为"开国文臣之首"。

Song Lian was a great scholar in the Ming Dynasty. He was fond of learning since childhood. Without money to buy books due to the poor family, he had to borrow from others and transcribed the book while reading, returning them on time. Although the inkstone was crusted with ice and fingers were hard to stretch because of the frigid weather, he still never slackened off the transcription. Upon transcription, he would rush to return the book, not daring to exceed the appointed day at all.

Song Lian was diligent in studying and punctual and trustworthy in life. One day in winter, he borrowed a thick book from a rich man, agreeing to return it in ten days. Hence, Song Lian read the book from dawn to night and finally finished reading at the tenth day braving the heavy snow. Touched by his punctuality despite of the cold weather, the rich man agreed that he could borrow books at any time. Thus many people with book would like to lend him book, and Song Lian was able to read piles of books.

After coming of age, Song Lian admired all the more doctrines of the sages. Worrying that he could not make exchanges with those knowledgeable masters and celebrities, he once walked a hundred li to learn from an eminent local scholar. Since the scholar was famous in both morality and fame, his room was filled with students, with whom he was always strict. Song Lian stood by the scholar, bowing to him respectfully to raise questions and inquire reasons; once being reproved, he became even more deferential and obedient; when the scholar was happy again, he continued to asked questions and reasons. Hence, Song Lian learned a lot and finally became a great scholar, enjoying the title of "three master of poems and prose in the early Ming Dynasty" with Gao Qi and Liu Ji. Emperor Gaozu of the Ming Dynasty even praised him as the "leader of civilian official in the founding of the Ming Dynasty".

【点评】

从宋濂的读书经历，可以看出他遵守诺言、勤奋学习、诚心求师、严于律己、不断克服困难的品质。他深知"严师出高徒"的道理，所以非常尊重自己的师长，在老师面前，毕恭毕敬，诚心向学。功夫不负有心人，最终得到了真传，成为明代的大学士。不过，在现实教育活动中，我们主张师生之间相互尊重，民主平等，共同交流，有利于教学相长。

From these experiences of learning, we know that Song Lian was faithful in promise, diligent in studying, sincere in seeking instructions, strict with himself and constantly surmounted difficulties. Being Keenly aware of the truth that "capable students are trained by strict teachers", Song Lian learned from his teachers with respect and deference. Thus he eventually learned genuine knowledge and became an eminent scholar of the Ming Dynasty. At present, however, we advocate that teacher and student should exchange with each other with respect and equality so that both can benefit from the teaching.

玖 廉

Honesty

人有高行谓之"廉",具体内涵包括廉直、廉明、廉能、廉静、廉洁和廉平。一言以蔽之:不外乎气节清高,品行峻洁,而无利蔽之私。

大学之道,在明明德,在亲民,在止于至善。凡洁身自好的人,都会通过"格物、致知、诚意、正心"来"修身",通过"修身"来"齐家、治国、平天下"。

修身,必要潜心道德修养,恪守道德规范,以此作为立身处世的根本。而"廉洁"正是修身养性的重要一环。个人的行为廉与不廉,取决于道德素养的高低。有道德的人往往廉洁,不廉洁的人必不道德。正如孟子所说:如果存在"可以拿取,也可以不拿取"的情形,拿取了就有损廉洁。因此,对自己的思想意识和道德品质进行主动、自觉的锻炼和修正,按照社会道德标准的要求,

玖 廉 (Honesty)

不断消除、克制自己内心的各种非道德的欲望，十分必要。廉洁，作为一种重要的社会道德，恰好是"修"的对象。廉洁是一种操守，是自爱、自重与自我约束，或者说是一种行为准则。这种行为准则不仅体现在现实的制度与法律约束中，还体现在千百年来中华文化中最看重的道德层面，即清廉、正气、明辨是非。我们应多关注那些用高尚品格感动别人的人，从而激发廉洁修身的向往与追求。本篇中的故事主人公，都是这样的典型代表与鲜活教材。

As a high quality of noble man, "Lian" is meant to be honesty, integrity, incorruptibility, purity or sense of honor. A man of honesty and integrity is absolutely pure and lofty and well-conducted. A man of honesty and integrity will support his own family and serve his own country by cultivating his moral character, which means studying essence of things and keeping integrity.

To cultivate one's moral character is required to devote himself to moral cultivation and moral regulation all life. Honesty or incorruptibility, a critical way to moral cultivation will determine one's moral quality. There is a sharp contrast between a honesty man and a man of dishonesty and corruptibility. It is necessary that a man should follow social moral standard, get rid of amoral temptation, and actively cultivate his own moral sense.

Meanwhile honesty or incorruptibility can be enhanced by moral cultivation. Honesty or incorruptibility is a code of conduct to regulate man's behavior. In Chinese traditional culture this code of conduct has been reflected by a moral sense of honesty and uprightness, a moral sense of distinguishing between truth and falsehood.

子罕却玉
Zǐ Hǎn Què Yù

【出处】《春秋左氏传》：子罕守廉，却玉有道，使富而归，不贪为宝。

【释义】 子罕本性没有贪欲，并以这种清心寡欲的品质为"宝"，不接受别人送的玉。

【Definition】 Zi Han was a person of no greed and he regarded the quality of ascetic as a "treasure", indeed, he never accepted others' gift of jade.

【造句】 子罕却玉的故事告诉我们：培养自己高尚廉洁的品质，才是世界上最宝贵的东西。

【Example】 The story of "Zi Han Que Yu" illustrates that the most precious thing in the world is to become noble and disinterested.

【故事】

春秋时期，宋国有个贤臣叫乐喜（字子罕），担任司城官职，主管一国的建筑工程、制造车服器械和监督手工业制造。一天，有个农民耕地的时候，从地里挖出一块玉来，就恭敬地把玉送去给司城官，可是子罕却不愿收下。送玉的农夫说："我请做玉器的师傅鉴定了，说是件宝物，才敢贡献给您的啊。请收下吧！"

子罕说："我把不贪心作为宝，你把宝玉作为宝。如果你把玉给了我，而我又收下了你这块玉，那我们就都失去了自己的'宝'了，还不如我们各人留着各自的宝物好嘛！"

那人听后跪下磕头，说："我是个小老百姓，藏着这么贵重的宝物回家，实在不安全；把玉石送给您，我就能在回家的路上免遭杀身之祸。"

于是，子罕就把这个人安置在自己的住处，并派专家替他雕琢、加工这块玉，直到这块宝玉卖出去，得了许多钱。那个送玉的农夫就拿着卖玉的钱，高高兴兴地回到了家。

这件事被宋国那些道德高尚的人知道后，都说：子罕不是没有宝贝，只是他的宝贝，和一般人的宝贝不同啊。

In ChunQiu period, there was a virtuous minister named Zi Han. He was in charge of the construction industry, manufacturing and handicraft industry of country Song. One day, a farmer dug out a jade while ploughing. He took it respectfully to Zi Han. But Zi Han refused to accept it. The farmer said: "The jade was proven to be a real treasure. I dare not to give it to you if it's not. Please take it."

Zi Han replied: "I'm not a greedy person and I regard 'no greed' as my treasure. Jade is your treasure. If you give it to me and I accept it then both of us lose our treasure. It is not as good as we just keep our own treasure."

The farmer kneed down and said: "I'm only an ordinary man; it's really not safe for me carrying such a valuable jade home. If you accept it, I can avoid being killed on my way back." Then Zi Han arranged a place for him to stay and asked a master to carve this jade and turned it into an art. The jade was sold at a good price and all the money were given to the farmer. Finally he went home happily with the money.

When other noble people of country Song heard about this story, they said that Zi Han does not lack treasure, but his treasure is different from the ordinary.

【点评】

宋国那个献玉的人认为：人世间最珍贵的是玉，所以把美玉献给子罕；子罕却认为人世间最珍贵的是廉洁。这叫"人各有其宝"，也就是"人各有其志",这是不同的人生价值观的反映。璞玉是宝贵的,但不贪图宝贵的璞玉才更是难能可贵的。我们赞美子罕洁身自好、不贪钱财的品质,同时也期待现实生活中为官的人都有子罕这样"不贪"的品德。

The farmer thought jade is the most valuable treasure so he offered it to Zi Han. But for Zi Han, honesty is the most precious thing. Different people have different aspirations. It´s the reflection of different views of life values. Jade is valuable, but being not greedy is more rare and precious. We praise the good qualities of Zi Han and hope the officials in real life can have the morality of honesty.

杨震拒金
Yáng Zhèn Jù Jīn

【出处】《资治通鉴》:(杨震)四迁荆州刺史、东莱太守。当之郡,道经昌邑(yì),故所举荆州秀才王密为昌邑令,夜怀金十斤以遗震。震曰:故人知君,君不知故人,何也?密曰:天黑,无人知晓。震曰:天知,地知,我知,子知。何谓无知者?

【释义】杨震拒绝学生感恩戴德的馈(kuì)赠,并要求学生做清正、廉洁、务实、为民的好官。

【Definition】Yang Zhen refused the gifts of his students who wanted to show their gratitude and instead asked his students, as officials, to be honest, uncorrupted, and pragmatic to serve people.

【造句】在当今社会上,有些人当了官,就利用手中的权力干尽坏事,最终无法立足于社会。这与杨震拒金的言行相比,其境界实在是天壤(rǎng)之别。

【Example】In today's society, some officers abuse their rights to do all sorts of evil and ultimately found no place in society, which is a sharp contrast with Yang Zhen.

【故事】

东汉的杨震为官公正廉洁,不牟私利。他任荆州刺史时发现王密的才华出众,就向朝廷举荐王密做昌邑的县令。后来杨震调任东莱太守,途经王密任职地界时,王密亲赴郊外迎接恩师。

晚上,王密前去拜会杨震,两人聊得非常高兴,不知不觉已是深夜。王密准备起身告辞,突然他从怀中捧出一袋金子,放在桌上,说道:"恩师难得光临,我准备了一点小礼,感谢栽培之恩。"杨震说:"以前因为我了解你的真才实学,所以推荐你,希望你做一个廉洁奉公的好官，为老百姓做好事。可你现在这样做，岂不是违背了我的初衷和对你的厚望？你对我最好的回报，就是为国效力、为百姓做主，而不是送我什么东西。"

王密听了很是感动，但还是诚恳地说："这三更半夜的，不会有人知道的，请收下吧！"杨震立刻变得非常严肃，严厉地说："你这是什么话？天知，地知，我知，你知！你怎么可以说没有人知道呢？再说，以为别人不知道就宽容自己，难道就不讲良心了吗？这可是很要不得的啊！绝对不能这样！"王密见恩师真的动了气，只得连连认错，赶忙收起金子，惭愧地告辞。

Yang Zhen was an honest official of Jing Zhou in East Han dynasty. Wang Mi was a talented person. So Yang suggested him to the government to be the county magistrate of Chang Yi. When Yang Zhen passed by Chang Yi years later, Wang Mi welcomed him passionately.

In the night, Wang Mi and Yang Zhen had a long chat. When it was late and Yang Zhen was about to leave, Wang Mi took out a bag of gold to him as the appreciation for his help. Yang Zhen said: "The reason I recommended you is your talent. I hope you to be an honest official and do good things for the people. What you're doing now is against my original intention and expectations. The best way to pay me back is do your best for the country and for the people, not giving me anything."

Wang Mi was touched by the words. But he still said with pure-heartedness: "It's so late now; no one would know that you took the money. Please accept it." Yang Zhen suddenly became very angry and answered strictly: "What are you talking about? You know, I know and the God knows. How can you say no one would know? What's more, it's so dishonest to tolerant yourself when nobody would know. You can not do like this absolutely!" Wang Mi had to acknowledge his fault as he saw his respectful teacher was really furious. Wang Mi took back the gold and left ashamedly.

【点评】

无论学习还是生活,无论为官还是做人,都不能因为别人不知道就放纵自己,要时刻坚持自己为人处世的底线。以诚对己,以诚待人,慎微慎独,时刻记住"要想人不知,除非己莫为"的告诫,时刻记住"天知,地知,你知,我知"的教诲,决不能因为别人不知道就宽容和放纵自己。特别是为官者,更应该自省、自警、自戒,像杨震一样,做清正廉明的好官。

No matter in study or in life, we can't indulge ourselves if nobody knows. Be honest to others and also yourself. Just remember and old saying: "If you want to keep it as a secret then don't do it." Behave yourself all the time and being an honest official like Yang Zhen did.

刘宠钱清
Liú Chǒng Qián Qīng

【出处】《后汉书·刘宠传》：刘宠别任，仅受一钱，出境之后，投于深渊(yuān)。

【释义】汉朝刘宠是一个清正廉明的好官，他离任会稽(kuài jī)太守、与当地老百姓作别接受赠礼时，留下了千古佳话。

【Definition】 Liu Chong was an honest and clean officer at Han Dynasty and on his retirement at Kuaiji, Liu Chong made a famous speech when receiving many gifts from the local people.

【造句】因为"刘宠钱清"而形成、流传的"一钱太守"的美名，至今为人们所乐道。

【Example】 "One-coin chief" named after Liu Chong has been still loved by the people in Kuaiji.

【故事】

东汉时，刘宠在绍兴做太守。他勤政爱民，改革不良的政治体制，把地方所有烦琐苛刻的制度都废除了，同时严禁部属扰民等不法行为和地方所有非法的事，整个绍兴的秩序井然，社会风气得到了很好的改善，老百姓安居乐业。

由于在地方政绩卓著，朝廷调他进京做官。到他离任的时候，老百姓非常舍不得，有几个老年人代表郡里向刘宠表达大家对他的感激、敬重之情，于是每人奉上百钱相赠，并且说："自从您到我们这里来做官以后，境内都没有盗贼了，连狗在夜里都不叫了。大家看不到县里的差人了，老百姓也不因为官司连累了。现在您就要去京城做官，我们特地来

玖 廉(Honesty)

送行。"

对如此盛情,刘太守再三推辞不受,但见几位老人长跪不起,只好象征性地分别从中拿了一个钱币留作纪念,总算接受了老百姓的人情。但在他行至西小江、就要出境的时候,刘宠把这些钱币扔到江中,以此表示还给绍兴。

未料想,奇迹的一幕发生了:原本浑浊的江水,立刻变得清澈起来。

为了纪念这位勤政清廉、为民造福的太守,当地人就称这个地名为"钱清",称这段江为"钱清江"。

Liu Chong was the prefecture chief of Shao Xing in East Han dynasty. He was diligent in politics and took good care of the local people. He reformed the bad political system there and abolished all the harsh terms. He also strictly prohibited officials disturb the citizens and other illegal things. Under his management, Shao Xing was in a good order and the ethos was improved greatly. People were living a happy life.

As he did a good job in Shao Xing, the government transferred him to another position in the capital. The local people hated to part with Liu Chong when he was about to leave. Some old people representing the whole citizens gave Liu Chong hundreds of money due to appreciation and respect. They said: "Since Your Excellency came here and did many good works for us, our lives changed a lot. No more thieves and dog's barking at night. Bad people were gone and we won't be implicated in any official business. Now you're leaving, we came here to see you off."

Liu Chong refused this great kindness repeatedly. But seeing the old men kneeing down at the ground, Liu Chong decided to take only one coin from those old men. When he came to the West River and near the border, he threw the coin into the river to show that he paid the money back to Shao Xing.

However, a miracle happened. The muddy water suddenly became very clean. To memorize this good and kind chief, local people named this place as "money clean" and named this river as "money clean" river.

【点评】

清廉爱民的刘宠,是中国历史上一位鼎鼎有名的清官,千百年来受到人们的称颂和敬仰。正如故事中所说的:自刘宠投钱后,投钱地段的江水更加清澈。为纪念这位老百姓敬爱的太守,人们除更了换地名、江名外,还建祠纪念他,称"一钱太守庙";在临江又建一亭,取名"清水亭"。由此可见他"为官正,来钱清"的高尚品质。

Liu Chong is a very famous honest and upright official in Chinese history. He was praised and admired by people for hundreds years. As the story said, the water became cleaner after Liu Chong threw the coin in. Apart from changing the names of the place and the local river, people also build a temple called "one-coin chief" and a pavilion named "clean water" to memorize him. These all show us the noble qualities of Liu Chong.

玖 廉(Honesty)

孔明洁身
Kǒng Míng Jié Shēn

【出处】《三国志·孔明传》：诸葛孔明，盖世清贞，鞠躬尽瘁，不别治生。

【释义】诸葛亮一生以忠诚、坚贞、清白、简朴的美好品德立世、传人。

【Definition】 Zhuge Liang is famous for his loyalty, constancy, innocence, and simplicity, setting a good example to us.

【造句】孔明洁身自爱，他留下的风范遗教，长久地化导着对他怀念至深的人民。

【Example】 The good quality and demeanor teachings left by Kong Ming have instructed people all the time.

【故事】

三国时期，蜀汉有一个贤能的宰相，叫诸葛亮。刘备驾崩，他的儿子继承帝位，是为后主，封诸葛亮为"武乡侯"，后来又让他兼任益州的主政官。这样，大大小小的政务都由诸葛亮来决断。

由于他日夜操劳，后主就给他很多赏赐，但诸葛亮都婉言谢绝。为表明自己对朝廷忠诚不二的志节，以及始终处在臣子位置的态度，诸葛亮对后主恳切地说："我家在成都，有八百株桑树，四十五顷薄田。家人靠这些来生活，已经是绰绰有余。至于我带兵打仗、在外随身的衣食用品，靠着朝廷的俸禄就足够了。因此，我并不需要另外去筹措营生的产业，不需要为家里添加任何财产。希望有一天当我过世的时候，全家上下都不会留下任何多余的衣食财物，不然的话，我就辜负了朝廷的深恩和陛下对我的厚爱。"

诸葛亮过世后，人们悼唁时发现他的家里，果然就如他所说的那样俭省朴实，清贫如洗。

In the three kingdoms period, there was a virtuous prime minister of country Shu called Zhuge liang. The king was Liu Bei and after Liu Bei died, his son inherited the throne. The young king conferred Zhuge liang as Marquis Wu Hou and appointed him as the political chief of Yi Zhou. Zhuge liang was in charge of all the political businesses.

The king awarded him a lot for his hard work. But Zhuge liang refused them all. He was very loyal to the royal and regarded himself as an official. Once Zhuge liang said to the young king: "My hometown is in Chen Du and I have 800 mulberries and 45 hectares of farmland. My family can live a good life with these sources. As for me, my salary is enough to support my daily life. My family and I don't need any extra money. I hope when I died, there would be no redundant properties in my home otherwise I will let the royal and the king down."

Later when Zhuge liang died, people found out that his home was really as simple as he said.

【点评】

诸葛亮身为辅国重臣，得到主上的倚重，手握重权，但他从不居功自傲，特别注重洁身自好。纵观他的一生，在先主刘备去世之后，身为一国的军辅，总理一国之政，大权在握而又不失礼度，堪为国家柱石。他事奉凡庸而又年幼的后主，始终兢兢业业，恪守为臣的本分，尤其他对后主所表白的一番心声，至今读来，仍令人对他的忠贞事主、廉洁奉公感怀万千。

Zhuge liang was the most powerful minister and the king thought highly of him. But Zhuge liang never claimed credits for himself or became arrogant. After Liu Bei died, he supported and helped the young but mediocre king with political affairs. He once wrote an article to clarify his pure heart to the king. The words in it touch us deeply even now.

玖 廉(Honesty)

傅昭静廉
Fù Zhāo Jìng Lián

【出处】《梁书·傅昭传》：傅昭廉德，布衣粝(lì)食，不纳荐鱼，委之门侧。

【释义】傅昭为官不结党营私、不贪腐，生活简朴，为人耿(gěng)介，德高望重。

【Definition】 Fu Zhao never formed a clique with other officials and never corrupted, actually, he lived in a simple life and was upright and highly respected by people.

【造句】傅昭静廉的美好品质，是贪官污吏的一面镜子。

【Example】 The good quality of Fu Zhao is a mirror to warn all corrupt officials.

【故事】

南北朝时期，梁朝的傅昭在朝为官，他一生靠谨慎和清廉立足。南齐萧昭业继帝位时，旧时的臣僚纷纷争权求宠，只有傅昭不参与其中。后来，萧昭业仅当了六个月皇帝便被废，傅昭由于没有卷入这场政治斗争而免祸。

明帝萧鸾登上帝位后，任命傅昭为中书通事舍人。这个官职联络上下，左右逢源，权势很大，可他仍然保持清廉的品性，家中陈设简陋，粗茶淡饭，甚至连必备的烛盘用具都没有添置。明帝听说后，感慨不已，特意赐给他漆盒、烛盘等用品，并敕书赞扬说："您有古人的风范，特赐古人之物。"不久后，提升他为尚书左丞。

后来，傅昭调任临海。临海郡中有一种蜜岩，经济价值很高，以前历任太守都把这里作为宝地，借以谋利。他到任后，一改旧制，废除禁令，开放

— 271 —

蜜岩，让老百姓共享其利，受到群众拥戴。一些下属官员知道他生活俭朴，时常送些粮菜布帛给他，他都一一谢绝。

一天，有人送他一尾活鱼。这就让他为难了：送来的礼肯定不能收受，但这是一条活鱼，让来人再拿回去，说不定半路上就会死掉。既然不能收受这条鱼，但又不能拒绝别人的一番好意，更不愿这条鱼好生生地死于非命，他就让管家用回礼的方式收下，等送鱼人走了后，再把那条活鱼放回到河水之中。

Fu Zhao was an official of Liang dynasty. He was famous of being prudent and honest. When another king succeeded the throne, the old bureaucrats were all apple-polishing the king. Only Fu Zhao didn't. However, the king was replaced only half a year later. So luckily Fu Zhao wasn't involved in the political conflict.

When Xiao Luan became the king, he appointed Fu Zhao a position which was very powerful. But Fu Zhao still kept a honest and upright character. His house was very simple without any luxuries. It even lacks home basic things. The king heard this and was touched by him. So the king awarded some appliances to him and praised him: "You have the characters of ancient saints." Soon, Fu Zhao was promoted.

Later, Fu Zhao was transferred to a prefecture called Lin Hai. There was a kind of rock called honey rock which has great economic value. The former chiefs took the rock as great treasure and earned lots of money from it. But Fu Zhao reformed the old system and opened the exploitation of the rock. People were shared with the benefits. Many villagers often gave Fu Zhao some food and cloths due to respect. But he never accepted.

Once, a person gave him a live fish, he was intended to refuse but if he did the fish would die. So he took it temperately and when the giver left, he put the fish back into a river.

玖 廉 (Honesty)

【点评】

傅昭作为正人君子,洁身自好,很注重细节。生活中,他时时处处都能够保持警醒,小心处理每一件小事,免至早晚因一些处理不周的小细节而贬损自身原有的好不容易积累起来的良好声望。君子生活在人世间,做的是他们可以做的那些合法正直的事情,不搞邪门歪道,并且总是以谦恭好礼、守法合矩的态度自处,从不放纵自己的欲望。傅昭就是这样的人。

Fu Zhao is really an honest person. He kept prudent all the time and took care of every little thing in life to keep his good reputation. Noble people would only do the things that are good, right and legal. They know how to behave themselves and never indulge their desires. Fu Zhao is one of those noble men.

甄彬赎苎

Zhēn Bīn Shú Zhù

【注音】 zhēn bīn shú zhù

【出处】《谈薮》：甄彬赎苎，得五两金，送还寺库，朝野同钦。

【释义】 贫困的甄彬将隐藏在苎麻里的五两金子送还当铺的行为，受到朝野的一致高度敬重。

【Definition】 Poor Zhen Bin returned the five ounces of gold that was lost in the hemp to the pawnshop manager; he was unanimously respected by the government and the public for this act.

【造句】 甄彬赎苎是一个廉人的廉洁故事，传递的是不贪、不沾、不染的正能量。

【Example】 The honest and clean quality reflected in the story of Zhen Bin showed the positive energy-spirit of no greed, no stick, no stained.

【故事】

南北朝时，梁国有个人叫甄彬。他品质高尚、才能出众。在他还贫困的时候，一次，他用一束苎麻到寺观的钱库作抵押换了一些钱用。在赎回苎麻后，他发现在麻里有用一条手巾包着的五两金子。甄彬就把这些金子送还寺观的钱库里去。

管理钱库的和尚非常吃惊地说："近来是有人用金子抵押换钱。因为匆忙，我没有记清放到什么地方了。您得到后，还能送还，这恐怕是从古到今都没有的事情。"和尚特意将一半金子给他作为酬谢，两个人你推我辞地往复了多次，甄彬最终还是坚决不肯接受。

梁武帝在做平民的时候，就知道有这件事，到他做了皇帝，就派甄彬到郫县去做县令。将要去上任之前，甄彬去向武帝辞行，同时去辞行的

玖 廉 (Honesty)

共有五位官员。武帝对其他四人都警告、劝诫他们要廉洁谨慎，梁武帝对甄彬只说："你从前就有还金子的美名，不需要再嘱咐这些话了。"因为这个缘故，甄彬的名誉、德行更突出了。

Zhen Bin was a noble and talented man of Liang dynasty. Once when he was very poor, he pledged a bunch of ramie for some money in a temple. And when he redeemed the ramie, he found a bag of gold in it. So he took the gold back to the temple.

The monk in charge of money was really surprised, he said: "Recently some people came to pledged gold for money. I might be too busy that left some to the place I don't remember. It's impossible for a man to give it back." The monk insisted to give some gold to Zhen Bin as thanks. But he refused it with a firm resolution.

The king then knew this story when he was not a king. After he got the throne, he appointed Zhen Bin as the chief of Pi prefecture. Zhen Bin alone with other four officials went to say goodbye to the king before setting out. The king advised the other four officials to be honest and prudent. But he said to Zhen Bin: "I know you have the good reputation already, so you don't need my advice at all." Due to the words of king, Zhen Bin's fame and virtue became more outstanding.

【点评】

做人廉洁谨慎，就能赢得别人的信任与尊重。廉洁做人，即坚守自己的做人底线，做到不贪、不沾、不染。不贪，就是不存任何私欲贪心杂念；不沾，就是摒弃一切不良习惯；不染，就是具有莲花一样的品格，出淤泥而不染。谨慎做人，即凡事谨小慎微，才能可堪任用。甄彬就是这样的一个正人君子，所以受到皇帝的器重。

One man can be trusted and respected by others if he is honest and prudent. There are three points of being a noble man: The first is being not greedy for anything. The second is abandoning all the bad habits. The last is keeping you not influenced by other bad people. Zhen Bin was such a noble man and that´s why he can be trusted by the king.

老虎引路
Lǎo Hǔ Yǐn Lù

【出处】 《居士传》偈曰：异相奇人卓不群，忍饥挨饿志出尘。猛虎驮经寻静处，天女送食著宏文。

【释义】 卓尔不凡的李长者，一生专注研习《华严经》，并多有建树，赢得了支助。

【Definition】 Mr. Li, a distinguished man, dedicated his life to studying *Flower Adornment Sutra*, gained many achievements, and won the support.

【造句】 老虎引路的传说表明：当一个人真诚为"法"而奉献一切时，可能得到意想不到的帮助。

【Example】 Li's story indicates that a man can receive the unexpected help when he is fully committed to learning the doctrine.

【故事】

李通玄，世称李长者，是唐代的大学者。他一生不爱名利，最喜欢的就是以研习《华严经》为终生事业。有一次，他离开现在住的地方，想找个地方专心地为《华严经》作注。在路上遇到了一只老虎，而这只老虎仿佛就是在那里等候他一样，对他非常的驯服。

李长者毫无惧怕的感觉，走上前去抚着老虎的背说："我打算写一本解释《华严经》的书，你是不是能够为我选一个可以适合写书的地方？"说完后，他把装经书的袋子放在老虎的背上，自己骑上了这只家猫一样的老虎，随他任意地走开。

老虎温顺地动身了。走了约二三十里路的时候，这一人一虎来到了神

玖 廉(Honesty)

福山(现在的山西寿阳县内),山下有一个土龛。老虎就依着龛蹲下来。李长者会意,就跨下虎背,卸下经书袋。直到李长者进了土龛,老虎才转身慢慢地走了。

本来,这山中没有水。未料想当晚,狂风暴雨滚滚而来,吹倒了土龛前面的一棵大松树。连根拨起的松树下面,涌出一泓清泉,泉水十分甘美。到了晚上,井口中吐出来一束白光,李长者就用它来照明写书。更神奇的是,还有两个不知从哪里来的青年女子,白天为李长者做打水、烧香、研墨、摆纸这些家务活,等到该吃饭时,她们就做好饭菜放在李长者面前,等到李长者吃后,她们收拾好东西又不见了。李长者也从来不问她们的来处与去处。

李长者就这样生活着,一住就是十一年。也就是这十一年,他的《华严经释论》终于完成、面世了。

Li Tongxuan was famous scholar of Tang dynasty. He didn't like fame or money. Studying a book called *Hua Yan Jing* was his life-time career. Once he left the place he was living and wanted to find a quiet one to focus on study. Li Tongxuan met a tiger on the way but the tiger was very docile. It was just like waiting for him.

Li Tongxuan was not afraid of the tiger at all. He got closer, stroked its back and said:"I'm planning to write a book as the explanation of *Hua Yan Jing*. Can you find a good place for me?" Then he sit on the tiger's back like it was a cat. The tiger walked in a gentle way. After a 20 miles walk, they reached a shrine under a mountain. The tiger stopped and crouched at there. Li Tongxuan knew this is the place. The tiger went away when he enter the shrine.

Actually there was no water in the mountain, but in the night, a big storm came and pulled out a big tree in front of the shrine. Suddenly a clean and sweet fountain showed up. A bunch of white light shined on the shrine so that Li can write at night. What´s more, two young women of nowhere came to him. They did all the houseworks and cook for him. Every time they will disappear after Li finished dinner. Li never asked who are they or where are they from.

Li Tongxuan lived here for 11 years and finally he finished his book *Shi Lun*, the explanation of *Hua Yan Jing*.

【点评】

李长者是一个值得敬重的修行人。故事中有些不可思议的神秘情节,说明李长者的内证境界与外境感应所达到的高度。有人认为,道德高尚的人能感应万物生灵。李长者不仅能与动物、天人相感应,而且能与自然相感应,山中无水,风雷帮忙,树下就涌出泉水来。反观现在的一些学人,被周围的环境弄得烦恼连连,心浮气躁,难成正果,值得反思。

Li Tongxuan is an honorable stylite. The mystery plots in this story show the unification of his inner world and the outside environment. Some people think that noble people can feel the spirit of all the creatures. Li Tongxuan was helped by nature because he was focused on one thing. Some scholars now are impatient and easy being disturbed by the outside. They should learn from Li Tongxuan.

玖 廉(Honesty)

裴度还带
Péi Dù Hái Dài

【出处】《芝田录》:裴度遇妇,遗带未知,收待明日,妇至还之。

【释义】 裴度还是普通老百姓的时候,因为拾宝不昧(mèi)而使自己避免了一场有性命之忧的大灾难,传为佳话。

【Definition】 Before his post in the govenment, Pei Du picked up treasure and returned it to the loser so that he avoided a disaster.

【造句】 裴度还带,是许多人都知道的颇具神秘的传奇色彩的故事。

【Example】 The story Peidu Huan Dai still remains mysterious up to now.

【故事】

唐朝的裴度,在他还没有发迹前,父母就已双亡,且家境贫寒,尽管文武全才、道德品质高尚,怎奈时运不济,遭遇不顺,年已三十,屡试功名不如意,只得白日在洛阳白马寺觅得三斋,晚上在城南山神庙中安歇。某日,他在白马寺遇见一位道人。这个道人为裴度相面,断定他命该横死。裴度对这种话根本没当一回事。

一天,他去香山寺游玩,看见大雄宝殿内,一个年轻女子在佛前礼拜,拜完匆匆离去。裴度在殿内瞻望了一周,回头忽然看见殿内栏杆上有一个花包袱。他再看看寺内也没有其他人,心想这包袱应该是刚才那位香客遗忘的,只是不知包内究竟是什么东西?就打开一看,发现有玉带一条、犀带两条,都是稀世之宝,非常值钱。

他料定失主会回来寻找,就坐下来等候,许久,果然看见那拜佛的年轻女子慌张走来,像寻找什么东西。裴度起身问她找寻何物?那女子哭泣说道："小女子韩琼英，父亲为官廉洁，因得罪国舅被诬入狱，我和母亲辛苦筹资准备营救父亲。幸得朝廷采访使李邦彦相助，赠送玉带一条、犀带两条，准备托权贵疏通说情，以赎父罪。由于我当时心神不宁，礼佛后匆忙离开，丢失了财宝，恐怕我父的罪名从此再难洗脱，一家人也没什么希望了。"

裴度听了，就将捡到的那个包袱拿出，问是这个么？那女子看了，点头称是。裴度就毫不犹豫地还给了她。她接过一看，宝物丝毫不错，眼里含泪，心中非常感激，就拿了一条犀带给裴度作谢礼。裴度哪里肯受，提醒她赶紧回去办事，自己则赶回山神庙去。就在他来到庙前，还没有进去的时候，山神庙轰然倒塌，裴度得以逃脱厄运。

过了些时候，偶然又遇到以前说他犯横死相的道士。道士仔细看了看他，很惊奇地说："你的相貌和从前大不同了！不但死相已经完全祛除，而且前程远大，不可限量啊！一定是积了极大的阴德，才有这样的转变。"裴度心里明白道士所指的"阴德"，从此心善更坚，善行更多。后来果然出将入相，官至丞相，封晋国公，德披寰宇，威服四夷。

Before Pei Du became famous, he was a very poor man and his parents were dead. He failed in all the imperial exams though he was noble and talented. He had to live in a waste temple. Once a Taoist priest saw him and judged that Pei Du would die in an accident. Pei Du didn't take it seriously.

One day, he went to Xiang Shan temple for a visit and saw a lady left in a hurry after worshiping the Buddha. Pei Du looked around in the hall and saw a bag in the handrail. He thought it might belong to the lady. Pei Du opened the bag and found three jade belts in it. The belts are really treasures and worth a lot of money.

He knew that the lady would come back for it so he sit there and waited for a long

玖 廉 (Honesty)

time. Then he saw the young lady came in worriedly and looked for something. Pei Du asked her what she was looking for. The lady said with tears:" My name is Han Qiong Ying. My father was an honest official but was framed into jail by a powerful minister. One of my father's friends gave me three jade belts. I can give them to someone with great powers who can save my father from prison. I was obsessed and left my bag here. I'm afraid that it's hopeless to save my father."

Pei Du took out the bag and asked:" Is this bag yours? " She nodded and said yes. Then he gave it to her without any hesitation. The lady was so touched when she saw her belts. The lady wanted to gave Pei Du a belt as appreciation. Pei Du refused firmly. He hastened her to do the business. Then Pei Du went back to the temple he lived. But before he entering it, the temple suddenly collapsed. Pei Du was saved fortunately.

After some days, Pei Du met the Taoist priest again. The priest looked at him carefully and said surprisingly:"You are so different from what you used to be. No worry about death, you will have a great and bright future. You must did something good that resulted this change." Pei Du knew what the good thing is. So he did more good things in daily life. Later, he became the prime minister and was famous for his virtue all over the country.

【点评】

君子与小人的区分，有时候只在贪之一念。尤其在穷困潦倒或者只有"天知地知"的时候，仍然不生贪念的人，才是真正的君子。裴度就是这样的一个人，可见他的心量广大。由于心量广大，所以福德同样广大。说故事的人让一个神秘道士对裴度命运做了神秘的解释，客观上宣扬了人的命运本来就是由自己主宰的思想。

The difference between noble men and villains is that noble men won't be greedy especially when they are poor. Pei Du is such a noble man. The Taoist priest made a mystery explanation for his fate. But it also shows that a person's destiny is controlled by himself.

清官包拯
Qīng Guān Bāo Zhěng

【出处】《宋史·包拯传》：宋有包拯，公正诉讼，替民申冤，立朝刚毅，贵戚宦官为之敛手，闻者皆惮之。

【释义】 包拯为官廉洁公正，在依法处理诉讼方面，以刚直不阿、不避权贵闻名于世。

【Definition】 The great official Bao Zheng is clean and disinterested, and he is famous for his uprightness and fearlessness of dignitaries.

【造句】 清官包拯在严明执法、依法断案方面，给人们留下了非常深刻的印象。

【Example】 Upright official Bao Zheng was very strict in law enforcement, and left a deep impression to all people.

【故事】

宋朝的包拯，是历史上特别有名的清官，为官公正。那时判案的惯例是：来打官司的百姓只能在衙门外击鼓喊冤，等衙门里的公差转递给办案的官员，案子才升堂审理。这样一来，就有些公差们常找借口向告状人要钱；如果不给钱，就扣着状子不送。他们这一刁难，穷苦的百姓就遭殃了：拿不出钱，告状无门，有冤无处诉。

所有这些，都被新上任的开封知府包拯知道了，他命令衙门办公的时候大门都开着，让告状的百姓直接上公堂、当面向他诉说是非曲直，当堂论断。从此以后，穷苦百姓告状有门了，不再为无处申冤发愁了，因此对包拯十分信任，都愿意找他断案。

他做开封知府不仅执法严明，而且处处以身作则，从不为自己牟私利。对皇亲国戚、官宦权贵的不法行为，一律绳之以法。一次，他的舅舅犯了罪,照样依法论处。从这以后,他的亲戚朋友再没有人敢依仗他的权势,为非作歹了。

Bao Zheng of Song dynasty is a very famous upright judge. The habit of judging a case then is that the accuser should hit a drum out the court first and then officials will deliver your case to the judge. However, some officials would ask accusers for money otherwise they won't deliver the case to judge. It's so injustice for the poor people.

Bao Zheng changed this bad habit. He asked officials should open the gate o the court to let the accusers into directly and he can judge the case right after the accuser's statement. From then, poor people trusted Bao Zheng very much. They all came to him for justice.

As a judge, Bao Zheng was really serious. He would punish the people with crimes even if the people are his own relatives. Once he punished his uncle without mercy. From then on, none of his friends or relatives dares to rely on his power to do bad things.

【点评】

大力平反冤狱,是包拯生前与死后深为百姓所赞扬和称颂的主要话题。包拯一生为官清正,铁面无私,不避权贵,刚直不阿,不徇私情,执法如山。老百姓都非常尊敬和爱戴他,称他为"包青天"。包拯在当时和后世都享有盛名,特别在他死后,作为清官的典型形象,被不同体裁的文艺作品大肆渲染,使之带有传奇色彩,并赢得了世界声誉。

Spreading justice was the best contribution of Bao Zheng. He was honest and people all liked him. He has great reputation no matter when he was alive or dead. The stories of him were praised by the entire world.

杨罗出俸

Yáng Luó Chū Fèng

【出处】《桃林罗氏族谱》：杨氏年耄(mào)，种苎园中，纺绩不懈，散俸惠穷。

【释义】 杨万里的夫人一生勤俭持家，勤劳不息，将儿子供养自己的生活费用分给那些穷苦的人家。

【Definition】 Yang Wanli's wife lived a thrifty life, hard-working and persistent, and she distributed all the money from his son to those poor people.

【造句】 杨罗出俸的故事，展现了一个不让须眉的巾帼形象，令人敬仰。

【Example】 The story "Yang Luo Chu Feng" shows the image of a great heroine deserving our respect.

【故事】

南宋时，诗人杨万里的妻子罗氏，生性清正、勤俭。杨万里在京城里做官，他的儿子做了元帅，可是罗氏的家里，仍然是泥土堆的阶沿，像农户一样简陋的屋子。但她住着，自得其乐。

在天气很寒冷的时候，每当天刚亮，罗氏就起来了，到厨房里亲自做饭菜，安排男女佣人们吃了，然后才派他们去做事。就这样，她忙碌了一辈子，在她八十多岁高龄时，还在菜园里种苎麻，亲自纺织，不肯懈怠。

后来，她儿子杨东山到广东去做官，把一个月的薪俸送给母亲用。罗氏说："我福份很薄，得到了这种薪俸，会惹出毛病来的，我得把它都分散了。"于是，就把这些薪俸尽数分给了那些穷苦人家。而她平常在家穿的服饰，却没有一件是华丽的。

她总共生了四个儿子、三个女儿,都是吃着自己的奶水养大的。好心的奶妈担心她奶水不够,想帮她分忧、喂养孩子,她却说:"饥饿人家的孩子,来哺养我自己的孩子,这种事情是我不忍心做的。"

A woman named Luo was the wife of the poet Yang Wanli. She was very hard-working and thrifty. Yang Wanli was an official in capital and his son was an marshal. But Luo still lived happily in an very poor house.

When it's very cold, Luo got up very early. She made breakfast herself for the servants and arranged things for them after they had the food. She was busy through her whole life. Even when she was 80 years old, she still planted ramie herself.

Later, her son was transferred to Guang Dong. He gave her a month's salary. Luo said: "I don't need so much. It's not good to keep it. I will give it to the poor."

Luo had four sons and three daughters. They all grew up with Luo's milk. The wet nurse worried that her milk was not enough and wanted to help her. But Luo said: "How can I leave other people's children hungry to feed my children?"

【点评】

人有"廉"的品性,往往气节清高,品行高洁。罗氏品行高尚,教子有方。杨东山是一位清官,被宋宁宗称赞为"廉吏第一人",显然与母亲对他的教育分不开。罗氏身教言传,无非让儿子知道:治家与施政同理,当官的更要懂得官民平等,善待百姓,体恤下情。罗氏的一生,言行一致,表里如一,真诚做人,说到做到。

Luo is noble and kind. Her son was also regarded as a famous honest official. It absolutely owed to Luo's good education. She taught her children to be kind to other people and be honest as a noble man.

拾 耻

Shame

有"知耻"感,是人洁身自好的根本所在。羞恶之心,人皆有之,这是人的一种良心美德。古人说:"耻之于人大矣""人不可以无耻"。无耻即是无良。品行无良的人,是人所不齿的。一个人如果没有"良心",他的存在还有什么意义呢?

近代思想家康有为说:"孔子论士,贵行己有耻;论治,贵有耻且格。人之有所不为,皆赖有耻心;如无耻心,则无事不可为矣。风俗之美,在养民知耻。耻者,治教之大端。"由此可见,在古人和近代人的眼中,都把"知耻"作为衡量遵守社会道德、评判有识之士、为善之人的一个基本准则。

耻,"是人区别于动物的一种文明意识,也是社会正常运转的预警机制。耻德作为否定性价值基础上的内在精神活动和

拾 耻 (Shame)

道德约束力量，既是"一切社会关系总和"的人的基本情感构成，也是类存在物的人的本质体现和推己及人的意志超越，是人与动物鲜明的旗帜分野，是人成为"人"的道德底线，更是人类社会在奔涌的历史长河中弦不断、流不息的动力源泉"。本篇所选的故事，就是对这一判断的最好诠释。

It is crucial for man of moral integrity to possess the sense of shame, which is a fine virtue shared by all. The ancients once said, "A sense of shame is of great importance to man." and "A man must have a sense of shame." Having no sense of shame means unscrupulous conduct, and a man like that will be despised. If so, what's the point for a man to exist?

Kang Youwei, a modern thinker, once said, "when mentioning the virtue, Confucius emphasized that one should conduct himself with sense of shame; when mentioning state governance, he emphasized that one should conduct himself with sense of shame and self-restraint. People with sense of shame leave something undone; only people without sense of shame will do everything. The beauty of customs lies in enabling the people to foster the sense of shame. Shame is an important part of education." This shows that both the ancients and the modern people regard sense of shame as a basic principle in evaluating social morality and judging a man of insight and a man of kindness.

Sense of shame is an awareness of civilization that distinguishes human beings from animals and also an early warning mechanism that ensuring smooth functioning of society. The virtue of shame is a kind of an inner spiritual activity and a moral restraint force which is based on negative values. It is not only basic emotional component of human beings that is the sum of all social relations, but reflection of the nature of human beings and transcendence of the will of putting yourself in the place of another. Besides, it is an obvious distinction between human beings and animals, a moral bottom line that human beings can be themselves and even is source of inexhaustible force driving human society forward in the long course of history. The following stories selected here can well explain it.

卧薪尝胆
Wò Xīn Cháng Dǎn

【出处】《史记·越王勾践世家》：越王勾践反国，乃苦身焦思，置胆于坐，坐卧即仰胆，饮食亦尝胆也。

【释义】 人躺在柴薪上，吃饭、睡觉都尝一尝苦胆，形容人刻苦自励、发奋图强。

【Definition】 A man tasted the gall bladder, lying on firewood to eat and sleep——means that a man is diligent, self-encouraged and determined.

【造句】 勾践卧薪尝胆、励精图治、最终雪耻灭吴的故事，一直在流传。

【Example】 The story still spreads that Gou Jian endured the hardships and made great efforts to defeat Empery Wu.

【故事】

吴、越两国素来不和。公元前496年，吴王阖闾派兵攻打越国，但被越国打败，阖闾身受重伤而亡。两年后阖闾的儿子夫差率领兵马在会稽打败越国，越王勾践被俘押送到吴国，从此开始了做奴隶的生活。因此，勾践忍辱负重，伺候吴王三年后，夫差才对他消除戒心，并把他送回越国。

其实，勾践始终没有忘记这个耻辱、放弃报仇。回到越国后，他表面上还是服从吴王，但暗中训练精兵，强政励治，等待时机反击吴国。艰苦能锻炼意志，安逸反而会消磨意志。勾践害怕自己会贪图眼前的安逸、消磨报仇雪耻的意志，他便为自己设置了艰苦的生活环境。他睡觉的

拾 耻 (Shame)

床铺不用被褥，只铺些柴草（古时叫薪）作褥子用；又在屋里挂了一只苦胆，他不时地尝尝苦胆的味道。这样做，为的就是不忘过去的耻辱。勾践为鼓励民众的斗志，他和王后与老百姓一起劳动生产，通过同心协力，用了十年工夫，越国强大起来。最后找到一个时机，灭亡了吴国，洗净了当时在会稽地方的羞耻。

The State of Wu and the State of Yue was always on bad terms. In 496 B.C., King Helǔ raised a army to attack Yue, but was defeated and later died from serious injury in the war. Two years later, Fuchai, son of the King Helǔ, led an army defeating Yue at Kuaiji county. As a result, King Goujian was sent to Wu as a captive, living as a slave there. King Goujian endured all humiliations to serve the King Fuchai and, three years later, eventually succeeded in eliminating King Fuchai's vigilance and was sent back to Yue.

Actually, Goujian never forgot the humiliations endured in Wu and decided to take revenge. After coming back, he still remained submissive to King Fuchai superficially, yet secretly spared no effort to train soldiers, strengthen governance and enrich the country, waiting for the right time to counterattack Wu. Hardships could build up a strong will, yet coziness could only lead to a weak one. Being afraid that he may indulge in current leisure and wear off his strong will to take revenge, he set up a hard living environment for himself. He slept on a bed laying with brushwood instead of bedclothes; he even hung a gall in his room, tasting constantly to remind him not to forget the disgraces suffered at Wu.

To encourage the morale of his people, he and his wife worked together with the people. After ten years of concerted efforts, Yue grew strong gradually. In the end, he seized an opportunity and defeated Wu, wiping out the disgrace of Kuaiji country.

【点评】

知耻而后勇。越王勾践为了使自己不忘记以前所受的耻辱,激励自己的斗志,以图将来报仇雪恨,回国后卧薪尝胆,最终东山再起,一举灭吴,诠释了"生于忧患,死于安乐"的真谛。卧薪尝胆的故事所表现的勾践的超人意志,或许更具有人类意义。

Being aware of the disgrace and then be brave. In order to remind himself not to forget the disgraces suffered before and encourage himself to move forward, King Goujian slept on brushwood and tasted the gall, finally rising from failure and destroying the Kingdom of Wu. It well illustrates the meaning of "one survives in worries and perishes in ease and comfort." The strong will that Goujian reflected in the story of sleeping on the brushwood and tasting the gall is of great importance to us.

拾 耻 (Shame)

夷齐采薇
Yí Qí Cǎi Wēi

【出处】《史记·伯夷叔齐列传》：武王已平殷乱，天下宗周，而伯夷、叔齐耻之，义不食周粟(sù)，隐于首阳山，采薇而食之。

【释义】 伯夷、叔齐不赞同西周取代殷商的"以暴易暴"的做法，认为留在朝中、吃周朝的粟米是一种耻辱，就隐居在首阳山，靠采食薇草度日。

【Definition】 Masters Bo Yi and Shu Qi disagreed with West Zhou Dynasty on replacing Yin Shang´s practice of violence against violence and they also regarded their employment in West Zhou Dynasty as a insult, therefore, they lived in recluse in Mountain Shouyang by eating black swallow wort.

【造句】 因不满现实，而仿效夷齐采薇的生活方式，现在已经不提倡了。

【Example】 The lifestyle like "Yi Qi Cai Wei" to show discontent against reality is not suggested any longer.

【故事】

商朝末年，有两个兄弟隐士，哥哥名叫伯夷，弟弟名叫叔齐。他们都是商王朝属下孤竹国的君主的儿子。孤竹君在位的时候，想传位给小儿子叔齐。后来孤竹君死了，叔齐不肯即位，认为兄为长，应该由哥哥伯夷即位做君主。但伯夷遵守父亲的遗命，坚决不接受，就悄悄地出走隐居起来。叔齐见哥哥避走，他也逃到外面隐居去了。孤竹国的人没办法，只好拥立孤竹君的另一个儿子当国君。

过了一段时期，伯夷、叔齐得知西伯侯姬昌（文王）的兴起，听说文王很敬爱老人，于是不约而同地去投奔他。但他们到了那里，文王已经死了；文王的儿子武王继位，并说奉了文王的遗命去讨伐商纣。伯夷、叔齐两兄弟见武王刚死了父亲，还没有安葬，就起兵去打仗，认为这不是做儿子应有的道理，况且他攻伐的又是商王，这不是忠臣的样子。于是跪在马前，扣住武王的马，进行劝阻。武王不听，还要处死他们。姜太公见这兄弟俩很有义气，就求情把他们放了。

武王灭了商朝，建立了周朝，天下百姓也都归附。但伯夷、叔齐却认为武王的行为不正，不但不肯留在周朝，并且立志不吃周朝的东西，兄弟俩就到首阳山去隐居，摘些野菜充饥。

未料想，有人讽刺他们说："既然不吃周朝的东西，就连野菜也别吃啊，因为野菜也是周朝土地上长的东西。"于是，他兄弟俩就不再吃野菜，最后饿死在首阳山中。

At the end of Shang Dynasty, there were two brothers, the elder named Bo Yi, and the younger Shu Qi, both of them were hermits. They are the sons of the monarch of Guzhu State that affiliated to the Shang Dynasty. During the reign of the King of Guzhu, the King already wanted to pass the throne to his younger son. Then the King was dead, but Shu Qi refused to ascend the throne because he thought his brother was much suitable for being a King. While Bo Yi followed his father's last order and firmly refused to take the throne, so he ran away secretly and lived in solitude. Knowing his brother left home to get out of the enthronement, thereupon he shirked his responsibility and lived a cloistered life. The people of Guzhu had no choice but to crown another son of the former King as the new King.

After a period of time, Bo Yi and Shu Qi heard about the rise of the Marquis of Xibo Ji Chang(also named the King Wen), who respects and loves the elders, so both of them go to the marquis for shelter simultaneously. But when they got there, the King Wen passed away. And his on King Wu took the throne, who determined to crusade against King Zhou of the Shang Dynasty so as to achieve the unfulfilled wish of the former King.

The two brothers, Bo Yi and Shu Qi, thought that King Wu violated the filial piety for he prepared the expedition before finishing the funeral of his father, besides; he was attacking King Zhou, which violated the principle of being a loyal minster, so both of them kneed down before the cart of King Wu to persuade him not to attack King Zhou. But the King would not listen and decide to execute them. Jiang Taigong, the imperial master, thought the two brothers were rather loyal, so implored the King to spare their life.

Later King Wu overthrew the rule of Shang Dynasty and built the Zhou Dynasty with all the people submitted to his authority. Bo Yi and Shu Qi, however, believed that the King Wu's accession to the throne was rather unrighteous. So they not only refused to stay in the country, but also determined to feed on nothing of the country, and they fled to Mountain Shouyang to lead a cloistered life, lived on berries and wild herbs.

But unexpectedly, someone pointed out sarcastically, "Since you don't live on the food of the country, you'd better spare the wild herbs, because it also belongs to the country." Consequently, the two brothers didn't eat the wild herbs any more, and at last starved to death in the mountain.

【点评】

武王伐纣,历来被看作是以仁伐暴、正义战胜邪恶的历史壮举,周武王也被后世视为圣明君主的楷模。但在伯夷、叔齐眼里,却完全不是那么回事。伯夷、叔齐之所以隐于首阳山,就是反抗不仁义的行为。值得注意的是,隐逸之士是中国古代社会的一个特殊群体。伯夷、叔齐可以说是中国隐逸传统的起点。这个故事,使人感受到这二位上古"隐逸"之士为仁义而献身,具有丰富的"不降其志,不辱其身"的精神内涵。

The crusade against King Zhou of Shang by King Wu of Zhou has long been considered the historical feat of the triumph of good over evil as well as the model of sage King. But in the eyes of Bo Yi and Shu Qi, things were very different. The reason why Bo Qi lived in solitude in Mountain Shouyang was that he wanted to resist against the unrighteous behavior of the King. It should be noted that the hermits are a special group of the ancient society. Bo Yi and Shu Qi are the pioneer of the Chinese tradition of hermit. This story not only depicted that the two ancient hermits gave their life for righteousness, but also embedded the spiritual content of never demoralize the spirit of a man of honor and never insult the body of a man of honor.

节姑赴火
Jié Gū Fù Huǒ

【出处】《德育故事·中国古代二十四耻》：梁有节姑，其室失火。兄子被焚，生存不可。

【释义】 在火烧房屋的天灾面前，面对别人家孩子处在危难之际，节姑以大义为重，在"生"与"义"不可兼得时，舍生而取义。

【Definition】 In the fire accident, Jie Gu bravely rushed into the burning house to rescue other kids at the cost of her own life.

【造句】"节姑赴火"故事中所蕴含的舍生取义，值得人们沉思。

【Example】 Jie Gu's story reflects a philosophy of giving up one's life for greater justice.

【故事】

周朝时的梁国，有一个名叫节姑的妇女。有一天，她住的房屋失了火。她哥哥的儿子和自己的儿子，都在着火的房子里，但节姑首先想到的，是要救出他哥哥的儿子。

她赶紧冲进迷茫的浓烟中，还真的救了一个小孩。出来定睛一看，哪里晓得抱出来的偏偏是自己的儿子。于是决定再次投入火中，去救哥哥的儿子。但那时的火势，已经很大了，是不能够再进去的。节姑执意要进去救人，被邻舍人家的人竭力阻止着。节姑冷静地说："我哥的儿子在火屋里不知生死，我还有什么面目见我兄弟和大家呢！我想，如果把自己的儿子再丢到火里去，那就丧失了做母亲的资格。现在我哥的儿子还在大火中，我宁愿被火烧死也要去救他，否则，我活在世上也没有意思了。"

于是，再次跳进大火之中，结果，就再也没能够活着出来。

In the State of Liang during the Zhou Dynasty, there was a woman named Jie Gu. One day, the house she lived in caught on fire, and her child, together with her brother's child was trapped in the burning house. But her instant thought was save his brother's child from the burning house first.

She immediately rushed into the thick smoke, and did rescue a child from the fire. While she took a closer look and realized with horror that the child was her own child, not the one she wanted. So she determined to throw herself into the fire again to save her brother's child.

While at that moment, the fire was already fierce and large, and it was impossible to save the child. Jie Gu, However, insisted on saving the child, though her neighbors tried to hold her back, and she said calmly, "I don't know whether my brother's child is still alive or not, I am ashamed to face my brother! And I wonder, if I throw my child into the fire, I would be unqualified for motherhood. Since my brother's child is still trapped in the burning house, I'd rather risk my life to save him; otherwise, I have nothing to live for.

Henceforth, she plunged into the fire and never came back.

【点评】

节姑本来要先救哥哥的儿子，但在仓卒和浓烟中，却救了自己的儿子。这或许是现场目睹情景的人感到她愧对兄长的原因所在。事实已经这样，这使她无论如何也不能原谅自己的过错，因此感到非常的惭愧和可耻，于是纵身大火之中救人，最终身葬火海。像节姑这样品德高尚，足以使那些平时只顾自己孩子却不顾他人孩子的人感到羞愧。

Jie Gu meant to save her brother's child, but unexpectedly, through haste and the interfering smoke, she saved her own child instead. May be that was the very reason that people on the spot thought she was ashamed to face her brother. Since that was what it was; she cannot in any way forgive her own fault, so she felt very shamed and guilty, and plunged into the burning house to save the child, eventually buried in flames. People like Jie Gu who are woman of high moral character are enough to make those people who only care for their own children rather than others' feel ashamed.

胡妻耻见
Hú Qī Chǐ Jiàn

【出处】《中国古代二十四耻》：鲁秋胡妇，出外采桑(sāng)。耻夫淫泆(yín yì)，投河而亡。

【释义】 秋胡的妻子发现自己丈夫不孝、不义，认为与他相见是一种耻辱。

【Definition】 Being aware of her husband's impiety and disloyalty, Qiu Hu felt it a shame to meet him again.

【造句】 胡妻耻见的故事，教育意义深刻，它告诉我们：作为一个人，必须有修养、知廉耻、洁身自好，品行端正，才能为他人所尊重。

【Example】 Qiu Hu's story tells us that a man, in order to win respect, should be quite cultivated, have a sense of honor and virtue.

【故事】

周朝的时候，鲁国有一个叫秋胡的男人，娶了妻子才五天，就被派到陈国做官去了。秋胡这离家一去，就是五年。五年后回家探亲，在路上看见一个采桑的妇人，心里很欢喜，就下了车，拿了金子去引诱她。可是那采桑的妇人不理睬他。秋胡感到很无趣，就继续赶路回家。秋胡到了家里，捧了金子献给他的母亲，又叫来他的妻子。他一见妻子，就傻了眼——原来就是回家路上被他调戏过的采桑妇人。秋胡觉得很惭愧，感到无地自容。

秋胡的妻子毫不客气地当面训斥他，说："好你个秋胡！因为喜欢外面

拾 耻（Shame）

的女子，给她金子。这是忘记自己母亲的教导了！忘记了母亲的教诲，就是不孝；好贪女色，动了淫心，就污秽了自己的品行，污秽了品行，就是不义！你已经没有了孝和义。我实在羞来见你！"说完话，就去投河自尽了。

During the Zhou Dynasty, there was a man in the State of Lu named Qiu Hu, who had just married a wife for five days, then assigned to be an official in other states. And he left his home for nearly five years.

Five years later, he came home to visit his family. On his trip home, he encountered with a woman who was picking mulberry, and glad–hearted, he got of the cart and lured the woman with gold coins. While the mulberry‑picking woman just ignored him, which made Qiu Hu rather bored and tired, so he continued his journey to his home.

When he came to his house, he gave the gold coins to his mother respectfully and called in his wife. Unexpectedly, he felt dizzy at the sight of his wife, who was the very mulberry‑picking woman he just had flirted with. Qiu Hu felt quite shamed and embarrassed, wishing him could sink through the ground for shame.

His wife reproved him to his face, and said sharply, "How dare you! As you liked the woman outside, so you lured her with your gold coins. You forgot what your mother has taught you! And forget your mother's teaching is equivalent to the disobedient to your mother; you lusted after women and the sexual lust hoodwinked your mind is a smear to your character and morality, which is unrighteous! Since you have lost the sense of filial piety and integrity, I really just felt ashamed to live with you！" After finished her words, she jumped into river and killed herself.

【点评】

秋胡的妻子，只是一个采桑的农家妇女，针对丈夫的胡作非为的一番训斥，多么义正词严、光明磊落！在中国传统节操方面，女性比男人更注重耻德的修养,并将"知耻"列在传统的"八德"之首。秋胡的妻子,认为自己丈夫不孝不义玷污了自己的品行,就羞于同他一起生活,最后投河自尽,成为贞洁的典范。而秋胡,从一个知书达理的人变为不孝、不义、荒淫的无耻之徒,被人唾骂。

The wife of Qiu Hu was just a mulberry- picking farmwife, while she rebuked his husband sharply for his misbehaviors. She, rather frank and forthright, speaks sternly out of a sense of justice. In terms of the Chinese traditional moral principles, women attach more importance to the self-cultivation of Shame Morality than men, and they listed the "Shame" as the first norm of the traditional "Eight Norms of Moralities". Qiu Hu's wife, who thought his husband's misbehaviors tarnished her own personality, so she felt ashamed to live with him, then plunged a suicide. And she set a good example of being chaste and undefiled. Qiu Hu, however, an educated and reasonable man has reduced to be an unfilial, unrighteous, dissolute and shameless person, cursed by people forever.

拾 耻 (Shame)

负荆请罪
Fù Jīng Qǐng Zuì

【出处】 《史记·廉颇蔺相如列传》：廉颇闻之，肉袒(tǎn)负荆，因宾客至蔺相如门谢罪。

【释义】 背上荆条请求责罚，表示真诚地认罪赔礼。

【Definition】 Putting on twigs of vitex on one's back to ask for punishment means a genuine apology to others.

【造句】 这事本来你就不对，你昨天的做法太过分了，应该去向他负荆请罪。

【Example】 It is your fault to overdo yesterday, so you are supposed to apologize to him with twigs of vitex on your back.

【故事】

战国时，廉颇是赵国的大将军。蔺相如因为在渑池会盟活动中立了大功，被赵王封为上卿，职位比廉颇还高。廉颇因此很不服气，他对别人说："我廉颇攻无不克，战无不胜，立下许多大功。他蔺相如有什么能耐？就靠一张嘴，反而爬到我头上去了。我碰见他，就要给他个下不了台！"这话传到了蔺相如耳朵里，他就请病假不上朝，免得跟廉颇见面。

有一天，蔺相如坐车出去，远远看见廉颇骑着高头大马过来了，他赶紧叫车夫把车往回赶。蔺相如手下的人就看不顺眼了，说："主人，您怕廉颇像老鼠见了猫似的，为什么要怕他呢！"蔺相如对他们说："请大家想一想，廉将军和秦王比，谁厉害？"他们说："当然秦王厉害！"蔺相如就说："秦王我都不怕，会怕廉将军吗？你们知不知道：秦王为什么不敢进攻我们赵国？就因为武有廉颇、文有我蔺相如啊。如果我俩闹不和，就会削弱赵国的力量，秦国必然乘机来攻打我们。我所以避着廉将军，是为我们赵国着想啊！"

蔺相如的话传到了廉颇的耳朵里。廉颇静下心来想了想，觉得自己为了争一口气，就不顾国家的利益，真不应该！于是，他脱下战袍，背上荆条，上蔺相如的家门去请罪。蔺相如见廉颇来了，连忙出来热情地迎接，并与他进行了诚恳、友好的交流。从此以后，他们成为生死与共的好朋友，同心协力保卫赵国。

During the Warring States Period there is senior general named Lian Po, who was then the commander-in-chief of the Zhao army. Lin Xiangru, who achieved a great merit in the banquet of Mian Pond, was conferred to be the premier by the King, a position above general Lian Po. Thus Lian Po was quite recalcitrant, and compliant, "There is no battle I cannot win and no fortress I cannot storm, and I have accomplished many praiseworthy achievements. Lin Xiangru, what true skill does he have? Yet he should climb right to the top of the tree just through talking! I am determined to humiliate this upstart in public as soon as I meet him." after Lin Xiangru heard about this, he just pretended to be ill and didn't go to the court for a few days so as to avoid meeting Lian Po.

One day, Lin Xiangru was on an outing by chariot, from far away he saw Lian Po riding a tall horse coming towards him, so he quickly ordered his driver to turn around to avoid a confrontation with Lian Po. While the fellows were unpleasant and confused, "My lord, why are you fear general Lian like a mouse fear a cat？" And Lin Xiangru replied, "Please just think about it this: who is more powerful, the King of Qin or gen-

拾 耻（Shame）

eral Lian? "Of course it's the King." They answered. "I fear for nobody even though the King of Qin, how then would I fear general Lian? Do you know the reason why the Qin country dares not invade us? It is because general Lian and I are guarding our country. If we can't get along with each other, or even conflict with each other, which weakens the national strength of Zhao, and Qin will definitely take the chance to invade. So I avoid the confrontation with Lian Po with the consideration of the whole country."

When these words were conveyed to Lian Po, he calmed down to think about it, and thought that he was not supposed to fight for his fame and benefits while disregarding the King and the people. Thus with a bramble stick tied on his naked back, he went to Lin Xiangru's house to humbly apologize. When Lin Xiangru knew that Lian Po came for apologizing, he instantly ran out to welcome him warmly, and communicate with him honestly and friendly. Henceforth, the two became close friends, defending the country of Zhao together.

【点评】

"将相和"是一个传颂千古的名人佳话。故事告诉我们：人世间没有无缘无故的恨，也没有无缘无故的爱；爱恨之情是可以转化的，人与人之间的感情是可以培育的。在现实生活中，我们对一个人的看法或评价，不可以有先入为主的成见；认识一个人，要看清他的本性和全部，而不是他的表面或某些言行的表现。

General Reconciled with Chief Minister is a celebrity story that has been read through all ages. The story tells us that there is no hatred or love for no reason in this world; the affections of love and hatred can be converted, and the emotions among people can be developed. In real life, we should hold no pre-conceptions when judging a man; and to get to know a man, we should see the true nature of a heart rather than the surface behaviors or actions.

管宁善化
Guǎn Níng Shàn Huà

【出处】《三国志·管宁传》:管宁割席,以愧希荣。牵牛代牧,备汲息争。

【释义】 管宁用"割席断义"的方式使朋友华歆明白追逐名利是可耻的,并以宁愿人负我而我决不负人和想他人之所想的实际行动来感化、教化那些品德低下的人。

【Definition】 The way of Ge Xi Duan Yi (unwillingness to take seat next to a friend) was used by Guan Nin to assure his friend Hua Yin that any deliberate pursuit of fame and profit was a shame and the best way to educate those people of low morality was the deep consideration of others.

【造句】 管宁善化,令许多人自愧不如。

【Example】 The story of Guan Nin Shan Hua makes many people feel ashamed.

【故事】

管宁是三国时期的人,他从小做事认真专注,从不分心。他有个朋友叫华歆。一次,他俩坐在一张席子上读书,管宁十分认真,专心地阅读,华歆却不那么用心。

忽然门外的大街上人声嘈杂,议论纷纷,说是一个有名的大官经过这里。华歆再也坐不住了,心想:出去看看,也许可以多交一个朋友。于是,放下书本看热闹去了。管宁对华歆这种三心二意的读书态度很不满,就拿出刀子割断了坐在身下的席子,表示自己决不和华歆一样,要和这种人绝交,并且对华歆说:"你不是我的朋友了!"华歆听了,觉得十分惭愧。

一天,有邻居家的一头牛,在田里乱跑,损坏了稻田里的庄稼,管宁

拾 耻 (Shame)

设法控制住牛后,就牵着牛到清凉的地方放牧,并且还替邻居家看守着。牛主人知道后非常地羞愧,好像受到严厉的惩罚一样。

在管宁做官的乡里,只有一口井,汲水的人为了抢先,经常很早起来排着长队,后来的人有的还恃强抢先,因此经常发生争斗。管宁就买了许多汲水的器具,早晨比那些汲水的人起得都早,在大家都还没有到来之前就盛满了水,放在井旁边等着他们取走。于是,抢先汲水的人都深受感动,感觉很惭愧,就责问自己。就这样,当地的社会风气逐步变好了。

During the late Eastern Han Dynasty, there was a scholar named Guan Ning, who was earnest, devoted and diligent. One day, he was sitting on one xi (seat) with his friend Hua Xin, studying together. Guan Ning was in dead earnest, reading attentively, while Hua Xin was careless and showed no interest in reading.

When there were noises from sedan carriages going past the house, it was said a famous official passing the street. Hua Xin, curious, could hardly sit still, so he sat up and rushed out to see what was going on outside with the thought of making a new friend. Guan Ning was frustrated about Hua Xin who read with half a heart, so Guan Ning cut the xi as a sign of contempt against him, saying, "You are no longer my friend." When Hua Xing heard this, he felt quite ashamed.

On another occasion, a buffalo of his neighbor was running wild in the cropland and ruined the crop, Guan Ning managed to controlled the buffalo, led it to a cooling shelter for grazing and watched it over for his neighbor. When the owner of the buffalo knew it, he was rather abashed as if being punished severely.

In the countryside where Guan Ning secured an official position, there was only one well. And the villagers would get up very early to line up so as to fetch water pre-emptively, later some bullies jumped the queue and get the start of others, which consequently initiated fights among the villagers. So Guan Ning bought many buckets used for holding the well water and got up earlier than anyone else to fill the bucket with water before anyone came to the well, and left those water buckets to the villagers around the well. Henceforth, people who used to jump the queue were deeply moved and shamed, and rebuked themselves for their bullying. Thus the local social atmosphere was getting better gradually.

【点评】

管宁是管仲之后,一生不慕名利,是一个有高尚德行的人。管宁割席、牵牛代牧和备汲息争的行为,历来是人所称颂的厚德载物的品质表现。尤其是他用割席来提醒华歆,让华歆知道追逐名利与金钱的心理和行为是可耻的。在管宁的影响下,华歆始终很注重廉洁自奉。

Guan Ning, a man with noble character, was descendant of Guan Zhong, who was indifferent to fame and wealth. His deeds of cutting the xi, grazing the neighbor's buffalo and preparing the bucket for the villagers have always been considered as the embodiment of self-discipline and social commitment, which was praised by people all the time. Especially, he reminded Hua Xin that the pursuit of fame and money was shameful through cutting the xi. Under the influence of Guan Ning, Hua Xin kept clean and lived a simple life.

拾 耻 (Shame)

朱冲送牛
Zhū Chōng Sòng Niú

【出处】《待人宽厚的朱冲》：晋有朱冲，偿犊高风，送刍无恨，化及羌戎。

【释义】 朱冲人品好，不记仇，能容人，有智慧，善于以德服人。

【Definition】 At Jin Dynasty Zhu Chong, a person of good character and tolerance, was a intelligent man.

【造句】 朱冲送牛的故事说明：为人要低调、谦虚，与人相处要宽容，才能广结善缘。

【Example】 The story about Zhu Chong implies that it is a man of modesty and tolerance who can win good reputation among people.

【故事】

晋朝时候，有个人叫朱冲。他从小就很喜欢读书，待人宽厚，特别有智慧，但由于家境贫寒，没钱上学读书，只好在家种地、放牛过生活。

有一天，邻舍人家走失了一头小牛，却把朱冲家的小牛认去了。没有想到的是，后来，在树林中找到了邻居家那一头走失的小牛。于是，邻舍人家觉得自己的举动太冲动了，感到很惭愧，就把朱冲的小牛送还回来。朱冲并没有责怪对方，反而向对方一再表示歉意和谢意。

村里另有一个人，心眼很坏，平时喜欢占便宜，三番五次地把牛放到朱冲家的地里吃庄稼。朱冲看到后，不但没有发脾气，反而在收工时带一些草料回来，连同那吃庄稼的牛，一起送给主人家，并说："你们家里牛多草少，我可以给你们提供一些方便。"那家人听了，又羞愧又感激，从

— 305 —

此再不让牛去糟蹋别人的庄稼了。

朱冲待人厚道,赢得了乡邻的一片赞扬。

In the Jin Dynasty (265–420), there was an intelligent man, called Zhu Chong, who was well known for being tolerant and generous towards others. He was fond of reading from childhood, but because his poor family couldn't afford it, he had no choice but do farm work and raise cattle for a living.

One day, a calf of his neighbor has strayed, and his only calf was mistakenly claimed by the neighbor. Unexpectedly, later the missing calf was found in the woods, so the neighbor felt ashamed and guilty of his impulsive behavior, and returned back the calf to Zhu Chong. Zhu Chong, however, didn't blame the neighbor for that thing; instead, he expressed his apologies and gratitude.

There was a vicious guy in Zhu Chong's village who always liked to take advantage of others, and he repeatedly grazed his cattle in Zhu's cropland. When Zhu Chong knew that, he was not angry about it at all; on the contrary, he brought some forage grasses with him after having finished his work and gave back the buffalo together with the forage to the owner, and said, "Since there are too little forage grasses for so many livestock. I am ready to give you a hand to raise your cattle." When that guy heard this, he felt both guilty and grateful about it, and no longer grazed the cattle in others' croplands to ruin the crops any more.

The kindness of Zhu Chong was such that all fellow villagers complimented a lot.

【点评】

现实生活中,如果遇到自己吃亏的事,或遇到别人有意无意地损害了自己利益的时候,是横眉竖眼地与对方争吵,还是宽以待人、仁厚为本?在这个时候,才可以真切地看到一个人的修养。朱冲礼让恶邻,以德服人,使身边一些恬不知耻的人受到很大的触动,并由此转变为知礼义廉耻

拾 耻(Shame)

_{de rén   duì gǎi shàn dāng dì shè huì de bù liáng fēng qì   qǐ dào shì fàn zuò yòng   shòu rén zūn zhòng}
的人，对改善当地社会的不良风气起到示范作用，受人尊重。

In real life, when you suffer a loss, or catch someone hurt your benefits intentionally or unintentionally, will you quarrel with him with a fierce look, or just forgive him and treat it liberally? When it comes to this, people truly show their cultivation. Zhu Chong was courteous to his horrible neighbor and convinced him by kindness and generosity, which influenced those who have no shame and changed into men with sense of propriety, justice, honesty and honor. And Zhu Chong was respectable for his exemplary role in improving the social morality.

崔卢仕训
Cuī Lú Shì Xùn

【出处】 《旧唐书·列传》：崔母卢氏，训子官箴。轻裘（qiú）肥马，内愧于心。

【释义】 崔玄晖（wěi）的母亲卢氏告诫即将赴任的儿子：为官应廉洁奉公，简朴生活。

【Definition】 Before his assignment to a new post, the mother of Cui Xuanwei warned him that he should live a simple life, uncorrupted and disinterested.

【造句】 崔卢仕训的故事，为后世母亲们提供了生动的教育孩子的好教材。

【Example】 The story about Cui Lu is a vivid lesson for all mothers to teach their children.

【故事】

唐朝时候，有一个人叫崔玄晖。他的母亲卢氏，有贤良的操守。崔玄晖考取功名后，就要出去做官了。临行前，母亲卢氏训诫儿子说："我常常听到这样一种说法：有在外做官的，人家说他穷得不能够生活，这就是好的消息。如果听说的是积蓄的资财很充足、穿轻柔的裘衣、骑肥壮的马，这就是不好的消息。假如他用做官所得的俸禄来奉养双亲，那是可以的；如果不是这样，而是用别人送的东西来供养父母，那就同强盗们没有什么区别了。这种人，就算没有明显的过失，但在他自己心里，也应该是觉得惭愧、可耻的。儿啊，这种说法很有道理。你做了官，一定要廉洁不贪，忠诚做人做事，一心为公，不能有任何令人感到羞耻的行为。不这样的话，在社会上做人就没有立足的资本了。相

拾 耻 (Shame)

信你会好好地记着妈妈的话。"

于是,崔玄晖一生为官,始终恪着守母亲的教训,赢得了很好的名声。

In the Tang Dynasty, there was an official named Cui Xuanwei, whose mother was virtuous and righteous. When Cui Xuewei obtained the scholarly honor and official rank, he was ready to go to his post. And before he left home for his assignment, his mother admonished him and said,

"I usually heard a saying that as for those people who are non-native official, it would be good news if he was believed to be too poor to make both ends meet; and if he was believed that he accumulated abundant wealth, dressed in fur coat and rode fat horses, which would be a bad news. And it is okay if he supports his parents by using his official salary; if it is not, or supports his parents by using the gifts given by others, which is no different than robbery. Such persons should feel ashamed and guilty even though he didn't have any administrative demerits. My son, this saying does make senses. When you become an official, you ought to be honest and clean in performing your official duties and don't conduct any shameful behaviors. Otherwise, you will lose the capital to gain a place in society. And I believe that you will keep my words in your mind."

【点评】

现实生活中,一般做官的人,会通过一些非正当手段敛财、聚物,并以此来奉养家里的亲人。至于这些财物是怎样获得的,他家里人是从来都不问的,并心安理得地享用着。这是社会道德丧失、没有廉操、不知羞耻的表现。为人父母,要使子女成人成才,必当重视对子女的言传身教。崔氏教导儿子的一席话,明白并且深刻、肯切,不仅体现了崔玄晖

mǔ qīn gāo shàng de dé xíng cāo shǒu　yě zhǎn shì chū tā fù yǒu yuǎn jiàn zhuó shí de nèi cái
母亲高尚的德行操守，也展示出她富有远见卓识的内才。

In reality, people who are governmental officials would accumulate wealth by unfair means so as to support their families. With regard to the methods of obtaining the property, their families are not concerned and, they feel at ease and justified instead, which indicates the declining of social morality and integrity and the absence of sense of shame. And parents are supposed to instruct their children by their words and deeds in order to bring up their children into civilized person. The admonition of Chui Xuanwei's mother is clear, impressive and earnest, which not only embody the virtue and personal integrity of her, but also her capability of farsightedness.

拾 耻（Shame）

唾面自干
Tuò Miàn Zì Gān

【出处】《新唐书·娄师德传》：其弟守代州，辞之官，教之耐事。弟曰：人有唾面，絜(jié)之乃已。师德曰：未也。絜之，是违其怒，正使自干耳。

【释义】 别人往自己脸上吐唾沫，不擦掉而让它自干。

【Definition】 If someone spits on your face, do not wipe it but leave it alone.

【造句】 现实生活中，遇事是否采取"唾面自干"这种逆来顺受的策略，要具体问题具体分析。

【Example】 In reality whether we take the strategy of Tuo Mian Zi Gan—resigning ourselves to adversity or not depends on different situations.

【故事】

唐朝有个以仁厚宽恕、恭勤不息、闻名于世的宰相，叫娄师德。朝廷任命娄师德的弟弟做代州刺史。临走的时候对弟弟叮嘱一番，娄师德说："我的才能不算高，但做到了宰相。现在你呢，又去做职位很高的地方官。我们是光宗耀祖了，可是你要知道，有多少人因为嫉妒而记恨我们。你在外地为官，千万别闯出祸来。"

他弟弟赶紧恭敬地发誓、保证说一定不闯祸。娄师德便问他怎样才不闯祸。他弟弟说："从今以后，即使有人把口水吐到我脸上，我也不还嘴，把口水擦去就是了，还要以此来自勉。您就绝对放心吧。"

娄师德说："这恰恰是我最担心的。你想一想：人家对你吐口水，就是对你发怒，羞辱你了。如果你把人家的口水擦了，说明你不满。因为不满而擦掉，这会使人家更加发怒。我告诉你：如果人家吐你一脸的口水，你别管，慢慢地它就会干掉的。这没有什么感到可耻的，记住了吗？"他弟弟认真地点点头。

In the Tang Dynasty, there was a prime minister of the loyal court named Lou Shide, who was famous for his kindness and generosity as well as diligence.

As the loyal court appointed his brother to be the prefectural governor of Daizhou, so Lou Shide exhorted his brother attentively before his brother proceeded to his post, and said, "Although I don't possess the remarkable capability, I still attained the post of prime minster. And now you are assigned to be a senior official of local government, we did bring honor to our ancestors. But you know, there are people have grudges against us out of envy. So don't make any trouble when you exercise your administrative power."

His brother swore quickly with great respect, and promised that he would keep himself out of trouble. Then Lou Shide questioned him that how would he do that, his brother replied, "From now on, I will never talk back or show any anger even if someone spits on my face, and I will just wipe it out and get myself cheered. And you can count on me."

Lou Shide said, "That's what I was afraid of. Just think about it a little, when someone spits on you, he is angry with you and intends to humiliate you. If you wipe the spit off, which means you are not convinced, and the spitter will fly into a fury. Let me tell you this, if someone spits on you face, just leave it alone, and it will get dried slowly. And you are not supposed to feel ashamed, remember?" His brother nodded in all seriousness.

【点评】

娄师德是个出将入相的能人，他最大的特点就是能忍。这个故事说

拾 耻 (Shame)

明两点:一是官场的明争暗斗使人害怕,不可以轻视。因为,娄师德没当宰相之前,只是个文人,但他投笔从戎后,曾东征契丹,西打吐蕃,是一个很有气节、保家卫国的人;后来到中央任职,竟然变成另一个人——遇事谨慎、逆来顺受、处处退让——足以说明官场尔虞我诈的那种激烈程度。二是即使投笔从戎过,毕竟还是儒生,儒生注重文静、温情;而儒家讲的那种温和,是促使娄师德性格上稍显懦弱的根源。

Lou Shide is an able man who can be the General for the expedition and the Prime Minister in the court. This story illustrates that: Firstly, the fierce bureaucratic infighting is frightening, which cannot be taken lightly. Before Lou Shide took the post of prime minister, he was just a scholar. But then he renounced the pen for the sword, joined the army to conquer the Qidan in the East and resisted the army of Tufan in the West, so he was integral and patriotic, later he held a post in the royal court, and became a different person, who were cautious and resigned himself to adversity, which also indicated that the intensity of the fierce bureaucratic infighting; secondly, even though he has given up civilian pursuits to join the army, he was still a Confucian scholar, who emphasized gentle and quiet as well as tenderness. Moreover, it is that moderation that made Lou Shide weak in character.

弄巧成拙

Nòng Qiǎo Chéng Zhuō

【出处】《拙轩颂》:弄巧成拙,为蛇画足。

【释义】本想卖弄聪明、做得好些,结果做了蠢事,甚至把事情弄得不可收拾。

【Definition】 Something done through clever means turns out to be stupid and even out of control.

【造句】如果老师仍然按自己的喜好选书逼学生读,那只会弄巧反拙,让学生更反感。

【Example】 If a teacher forces his students to read his favorite books, he will make it worse and students will get really disgusted.

【故事】

北宋时期,有个大画家叫孙知微,擅长人物画。一次,他受成都寿宁寺的委托,画一幅《九曜星君》图。他用心将图画好,人物栩栩如生,衣带飘飘,宛然仙姿,只剩下着色的最后一道工序。正好这时,有朋友请他去饮酒。他就放下笔,将画仔细看了好一会,觉得还算满意,便对徒弟们说:"这幅画的线条我已全部画好。只剩下着色,你们须小心些,不要粗心大意出差错。我去朋友家有事,回来时,希望你们着好色。"

孙知微走后,徒弟们围住画,反复观看老师用笔的技巧和总体构图的高妙,互相交流心得。其中有一个叫童仁益的徒弟,平时喜欢卖弄小聪明,做些哗众取宠的事,只有他一个人装模作样地一言不发。有人问他:"你为什么不说话,莫非这幅画有什么缺欠?"童仁益故作高深地说:"水曜星君身边的童子神态很传神,只是他手中的水晶瓶好像少了点东西。"众弟子说:"没发现少什么呀。"童仁益说:"老师每次画瓶子,总要在瓶中画一枝鲜花,可这次却没有。也许是急于出门,来不及画,我们还是画好了再着色吧。"童仁益说着,用心在瓶口画了一枝艳丽欲滴的红莲花。

孙知微回来后,发现画中童子手里的瓶子生出一朵莲花,哭笑不得地说:"这是谁干的蠢事?若仅仅是画蛇添足倒还罢了,这简直是弄巧成拙嘛。童子手中的瓶子,是水曜星君用来降服水怪的镇妖瓶,你们给添上莲花,把宝瓶变成了普通的花瓶,岂不是天大的笑话!"说着,把画撕了个粉碎。众弟子看着童仁益,默默低头不语。

In the Northern Song Dynasty, there was a famous painter named Sun Zhiwei, who was good at figure painting. One day, he was commissioned to draw a picture of the Nine Gods of Stars by the Shouning Temple of Chengdu. He attentively painted the picture, and the figures of the painting are both vivid and lively with clothes flowing gently, bearing the carriage of celestial. And coloration is the final stage of this work. Just then, he was invited by his friends to go drinking, so he put down the brush and looked his painting over carefully, which was rather satisfactory. So he told his apprentices, "As the lines of this painting have been drawn well, what I need is get it colored, so I will leave it to you. You have to be careful with it and don't make any careless mistakes. When I came back, you are supposed to have colored the painting."

After Sun Zhiwei was gone, his apprentices crowded around the painting and looked it over again and again to grasp the methods and techniques of drawing as well as the ingenious composition, and shared their views with each other. One of those apprentices named Tong Renyi, who usually liked to show his smartness and do something sensational, pretended to be silent and speculating. Then someone asked, "Why are you so quiet? Is it possibly that this painting have some defects?" Tong Renyi replied with a profound look, "The appearance of the boy next to the God of Shui

Yaoxing was rather expressive while the crystal bottle in his hand turns to be imperfect." And the others argued, "There are nothing left out in the painting." "Every time our master draws a bottle, he always draws a flower in the bottle, but this time he didn't. Maybe he was so hurry to keep his appointment that he just cannot draw it timely. We'd better draw the flower before getting the painting colored." Tong Renyi said, and painted a flamboyant red lotus at the bottle mouth carefully.

When Sun Zhiwei came back and found that a lotus was added to the bottle in the boy's hand, he thought it both funny and annoying and asked, "Who did this stupid thing? Painting the lily, I can get over with it; but what you painted turns out to be a clumsy sleight of hand. The bottle in the boy's hand is used for vanquishing the water monster. You painted a lotus in the bottle, which turning the divine bottle to be a common vase. What a joke!" Then he tore the painting into pieces. All the apprentices looked at Tong Renyi, who lowered his head in silence.

【点评】

自作聪明，想表现自己、出风头，结果反而坏事，把情况弄得更糟。这个故事告诉我们：凡事要深思熟虑，千万不要自作聪明、自以为是地出馊主意，否则，到头来成事不足、败事有余，反成为别人笑柄。聪明、理智的人，要慎记这一点。

Those who try to be smart and show off will always turn to be foolish and even make things worse. This story tells us that we are supposed to give careful consideration to everything and never try to be smart and smugly offering dotty advices. Otherwise, we will be unable to accomplish anything but liable to spoil everything, which will become the laughingstock of others. And those who are real smart and rational have to keep this in his mind.

后　记

　　为弘扬中华传统文化,在九江学院和学校公共外交研究中心的大力支持下,《国学经典故事传播与留学生华文素养提升的叙事研究》课题组编写了这本《中华经典故事精选通俗读本》(以下简称《故事读本》)。试图用我们的视角和眼光审视中华传统文化,弘扬体现中国民族特质和风貌的民族文化,传播具有鲜明民族特色、历史悠久、内涵博大精深的中华传统文化,以期促进高校跨文化公共外交活动,拓展高校留学生教育内涵,提升留学生华文教育品味,提高留学生的培养质量。

　　编写《故事读本》的具体分工如下:陈梦然拟定《故事读本》框架,撰写、校审全部书稿;石于瀚、黄安平共同负责对"读本故事体例"中的"条目""释义""造句"的中文内容的英文翻译,石于瀚还负责对"双语"文本的全部内容校审;蒋潇、唐自辉协助编写文献检索与信息筛选工作,以及部分校对工作。在编写中,我们力求获得这样一种效果:选材精当,主题鲜明,内容集中,体例科学,形式活泼,经济实用,简明通俗,便于传播。

　　编写《故事读本》所用的史料,主要来自"二十四史",同时还参考了中国传统文化网和上海古籍出版社出版的一些文献资料,以及近年来在这一领域中的一些学者的研究成果;《故事读本》所用图片,通过网页搜索、遴选获得。由于条件限制,我们没能够获得与此相关的专家学者的有效联系方式,谨此,对原著作者一并表示感谢!同时也请有关人员在获此信息后与编者和出版社及时联系。

在编写过程中，九江学院副校长兼公共外交研究中心主任杨耀防教授、九江学院国际交流学院院长兼公共外交研究中心副主任夏修龙教授、九江学院国际交流学院洪萍教授，对本书的编写工作给予了高度关注和热心的指导，杨耀防教授还对全书稿作了统审。此外，九江学院2010级、2011级、2013级留学生教学班和孔子学院"奖学金班"的一批在校生，为编写本书的调研工作给予了积极的配合；尤其是课题组所在单位九江学院的党政领导对这项工作给予了充分肯定和大力支持。因此，向所有为本书编写工作表示关注、提供帮助的领导、专家、学者和同学们，致以真挚的谢意！

因为水平有限和时间限制，本书编写工作中难免存在这样那样的不足甚至错误，恳请广大同仁、读者给予批评、指正。

2016年4月16日